Nine to Five

Falling for the boss!

Acclaim for Jessica Steele, Susan Napier and Lindsay Armstrong

"Ms Steele pens a touching love story with vivid characterisations, gripping scenes and powerful conflict."
—*Romantic Times*

"Susan Napier is a whiz at stirring up both breathtaking sensuality and emotional tension that keeps readers hooked till the boiling point."
—*Romantic Times*

"Lindsay Armstrong imbues a storyline with strong characterisation and snappy dialogue."
—*Romantic Times*

Jessica Steele lives in a friendly Worcestershire village with her super husband, Peter. They are owned by a gorgeous Staffordshire bull terrier called Florence, who is boisterous and manic, but also adorable. It was Peter who first prompted Jessica to try writing, and after the first rejection, encouraged her to keep on trying. Luckily, with the exception of Uruguay, she has so far managed to research inside all the countries in which she has set her books, travelling to places as far apart as Siberia and Egypt. Her thanks go to Peter for his help and encouragement.

Susan Napier was born on St Valentine's Day, so it's not surprising she has developed an enduring love of romantic stories. She started her writing career as a journalist in Auckland, New Zealand, trying her hand at romantic fiction only after she had married her handsome boss! Numerous books later she still lives with her most enduring hero, two future heroes—her sons!—two cats and a computer. When she's not writing she likes to read and cook, often simultaneously!

Lindsay Armstrong was born in South Africa but now lives in Australia with her New Zealand-born husband and their five children. They have lived in nearly every state of Australia and tried their hand at some unusual, for them, occupations, such as farming and horse-training—all grist to the mill for a writer! Lindsay started writing romances when their youngest child began school and she was left feeling at a loose end. She is still doing it and loving it.

Nine to Five

Jessica Steele
Susan Napier
Lindsay Armstrong

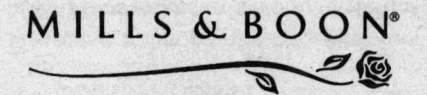

MILLS & BOON®

DID YOU PURCHASE THIS BOOK WITHOUT A COVER?
If you did, you should be aware it is **stolen property** as it was reported *unsold and destroyed* by a retailer. Neither the author nor the publisher has received any payment for this book.

All the characters in this book have no existence outside the imagination of the author, and have no relation whatsoever to anyone bearing the same name or names. They are not even distantly inspired by any individual known or unknown to the author, and all the incidents are pure invention.

All Rights Reserved including the right of reproduction in whole or in part in any form. This edition is published by arrangement with Harlequin Enterprises II B.V. The text of this publication or any part thereof may not be reproduced or transmitted in any form or by any means, electronic or mechanical, including photocopying, recording, storage in an information retrieval system, or otherwise, without the written permission of the publisher.

This book is sold subject to the condition that it shall not, by way of trade or otherwise, be lent, resold, hired out or otherwise circulated without the prior consent of the publisher in any form of binding or cover other than that in which it is published and without a similar condition including this condition being imposed on the subsequent purchaser.

MILLS & BOON and MILLS & BOON with the Rose Device are registered trademarks of the publisher.
Harlequin Mills & Boon Limited,
Eton House, 18-24 Paradise Road, Richmond, Surrey, TW9 1SR

NINE TO FIVE
© 1998 by Harlequin Books SA

Without Love, Savage Courtship and A Dangerous Lover were first published in separate, single volumes by Mills & Boon Limited.
Without Love in 1988, Savage Courtship in 1994
and A Dangerous Lover in 1992.

Without Love © Jessica Steele 1988
Savage Courtship © Susan Napier 1994
A Dangerous Lover © Lindsay Armstrong 1992

ISBN 0 263 80795 9

05-9802

Printed and bound in Great Britain
by Caledonian Book Manufacturing Ltd, Glasgow

WITHOUT LOVE
by
JESSICA STEELE

CHAPTER ONE

THAT Monday started in much the same way as any other Monday. For Kassia Finn, it ended very differently.

She was an early riser, and had time to check her appearance before she left her small ground-floor flat for her job at Mulholland Incorporated. Her eyes travelled from the tobacco-brown two-piece, which fitted her slender figure neatly, up to her face. She was used to the delicate complexion that went along with her red hair, but she was not used to the unenthusiastic light in her green eyes which spoke of her not being particularly interested in whether she presented herself at Mulholland Incorporated or not.

Kassia supposed she must thank that something in her, in her upbringing, that made her lock up her flat and make for her car in order to carry out her obligations. For, since she had accepted the job as secretary to Mr Harrison, the head of the contracts department, two months ago, she had to accept that she was obliged to stick with the job until she gave in her notice.

But how could she give in her notice? She couldn't, she realised. Not while Mr Harrison was still away sick. Mr Harrison had kept a fatherly eye on her, and she had taken to him from the first. Even though she had known him for only a short while, she felt that it would be like stabbing him in the back to resign the moment he was no longer able to cope because of his nervous breakdown.

Her thoughts were still on Mr Harrison when she parked her car and walked towards the Mulholland building. She had joined the firm at the tail-end of months of preparation work in connection with a giant engineering contract they were after. She rather guessed that Mr Harrison's breakdown had been coming on for some time, although it wasn't until the tender they had submitted was safely in the post that he allowed himself to succumb to his illness.

They had worked late every night of that preceding week, she recalled, as she entered the most modern of buildings and took the stairs up to her office. She had thought Mr Harrison had looked tired, but she had considered that perfectly understandable. She had been feeling a shade drained herself, and couldn't wait to be rid of the wretched tender which had seemed to dominate her first six weeks at Mulholland's.

It had been a very satisfactory feeling, though, when early on that Friday afternoon she had taken her work through for Mr Harrison to give the final once-over.

'As neat a piece of work as ever I've seen,' he had said, shelving some other correspondence he'd been dealing with to flip through the work she had handed him. Kassia remembered thinking as she looked at his tired eyes that he must be extremely relieved to be on the last lap of the long and exhausting task in hand. Yet even then he had shown what a considerate man he was, for he had looked up to recall, 'You're spending this weekend with your parents, aren't you, Kassia?'

'That's right,' she agreed. 'I'm making for Herefordshire straight after I leave here tonight.'

A feeling of guilt smote her when, back at her desk after that weekend, she had heard about his nervous breakdown. Only then did she realise that, instead of snatching the opportunity when he had said, 'You've worked like a Trojan all this week—why not get off now?' she should have insisted on staying around to help him with the final check on the Comberton tender.

But she hadn't done anything of the sort. 'Are you sure?' she'd asked, half-heartedly, her mind already on the pleased surprise on her parents' faces when she arrived a couple of hours sooner than expected.

'Certainly I'm sure,' he had smiled, and in case she was going to make some other protest—which she didn't think she was—he had teased, 'I'm quite capable of seeing that everything catches tonight's post.'

That had been over two weeks ago, Kassia reflected as she entered her office and stowed away her shoulder bag. Since then she had done her best to hold the fort and try to keep Mr Harrison's desk clear so that he did not have too much of a backlog to catch up on when he returned, but she had to admit that she was discovering little stimulation in the work that she did.

She was wondering if the guilt she had felt for going off and leaving Mr Harrison to cope on his own had anything to do with her reluctance to look for another job before he returned when Tony Rawlings looked in on his way to his own office.

'Light of my life,' he breathed semi-lecherously.

'No!' Kassia told him, answering his invitation before he voiced it. Tony was in charge of one of the other departments, but had been instructed to oversee Mr Harrison's department during his absence. Kassia had made the mistake of accepting a date with Tony when she had first started work at Mulholland's. That one date had been sufficient to tell her that she did not want another one.

'How can you be so heartless?' he protested dramatically, but he had to grin when she replied smartly,

'With you, it takes no effort.'

'In that case, I shall be but a phone call away should anything come in today which you can't handle,' he told her, and left her as the phone on her desk rang, and she went to answer it.

That phone call was the start of her day going in a direction which she had never contemplated.

'Mulholland,' a deep-timbred voice introduced himself as soon as she had told him who she was. 'Come to my office.'

The instrument went dead, and for a startled second or two, Kassia just stared at the phone in her hand. Then suddenly daylight started to trickle in. In the short time in which she had worked for Mulholland's she had never so much as clapped her eyes on its chairman, Lyon Mulholland. True, word had it that he had been spending some time at the offices of Insull Engineering—a newly acquired outfit—though why he wanted another company when he was on the board of countless firms already was beyond her. But—and she guessed that she had Tony Rawlings to thank for it—Mr Mulholland must have heard how she was coping in keeping the department afloat during Mr Harrison's absence. It had to be that, she decided.

Still fairly astounded that a man as busy as Lyon Mulholland should take time out of his early morning to give one of his minions a pat on the back, Kassia none the less could not help but feel pleased with herself as she stepped out of the lift at the top floor. Asking directions as she went, for she had never before visited the chairman's office, she eventually found herself in his secretary's office.

Kassia had never met Heather Stanley before either, but that lady was as efficient as she looked. For without waiting to ask her who she was, she had flicked a switch on the intercom. 'Miss Kassia Finn is here, Mr Mulholland,' she said.

'Send her in,' replied the deep voice she remembered.

Kassia smiled at Miss Stanley as she made her way towards the other door in the room. Miss Stanley did not smile back, but Kassia didn't notice. She was still recovering from realising that the great Lyon Mulholland was about to congratulate her in person!

She noticed that *he* was not smiling, though. In fact, she noticed several things at once as she crossed into his office. First of all she took in a large light and airy room with plush carpeting, a couple of large and deep settees, a smattering of matching easy chairs, and behind them an enormous desk. She noted too, as she recognised a man who had been pointed out to her as one of the directors, a Mr Cedric Lennard, that Lyon Mulholland was not alone. Both men were standing, but it was something of a surprise to realise that she was going to receive the firm's thanks in duplicate!

Lyon Mulholland was something of a surprise, too. When she had heard on the grapevine that he was a dyed-in-the-wool bachelor, she had imagined he must be quite ancient and crusty with it. But the tall, dark-haired man who broke off his conversation with Cedric Lennard as she went in was not ancient, but somewhere in his late thirties! Though, as he frowned darkly at her, Kassia had to consider that fifty per cent of her pre-estimate of him seemed to be accurate—for he certainly gave every appearance of being crusty.

Aware that appearances could be very deceptive, she hauled up her slipped smile and murmured, just as if she didn't know what was coming, 'I'm Kassia Finn. You wanted to see me?'

For a moment, when her smile was not returned by either man and she was not invited to take a seat, Kassia wondered if she had got it wrong. But, of course, she realised, both these top executives were much too busy, despite the luxurious furnishings in the room, to have time to sit taking their ease. Her smile disappeared as she wondered why on earth then they were wasting their precious time in praising a mere underling anyway.

'Mr Lennard tells me that you had quite a lot to do with the Comberton tender in its latter stages,' Lyon Mulholland commented when, after giving her a full scrutiny, he pinned her with an all-seeing, grey-eyed look.

'I've only been with the firm for two months,' she thought she should mention. 'And Mr Harrison did all the donkey work on the tender. But——' she strove to sound modest when, diverted at his peculiar way of praising her for keeping the office ticking over, she added, 'I did spend six weeks working on the project.'

'You worked closely with Mr Harrison on the tender right up to the very end?' Lyon Mulholland questioned.

'Right up until the very last,' Kassia agreed, her pleasure at this interview slightly dimmed as she remembered again that last day of working with Mr Harrison. Fair enough, she had no experience of anyone suffering from a nervous breakdown, but she should perhaps have noticed that it was not just tiredness that he had been suffering from.

But Lyon Mulholland was going on. 'So you would remember typing out the tender before mailing it?'

Who could forget it? Kassia felt she had typed her fingers to the bone in drawing up the tender. But she refrained from mentioning the hours of overtime she had worked, adjusting and re-adjusting the tender until Mr Harrison was confident that it was exactly right, and she confined her reply to, 'Yes. It all came together on the Friday before Mr Harrison went sick the next day.'

'You can remember that Friday clearly, Miss Finn?' Lyon Mulholland asked crisply.

To Kassia's mind, he was taking a trip around the houses before he got down to congratulating her. But a feeling of guilt again attacked her—perhaps she could have been more of a help to Mr Harrison? Aware that she was becoming a little more side-tracked, she made the effort to sound very confident as she asserted, 'Oh, yes, I can remember that Friday in detail.'

'Then you'll also remember that on that same day you typed a reply to an enquiry from Camberham Engineering?'

Kassia's brow wrinkled. She well remembered the letter which Lyon Mulholland referred to, just as she remembered that, despite his illness, Mr Harrison had not lost his sense of humour. Camberham's were their arch rivals, but that hadn't stopped them from courteously writing in for details of some work which

Mulholland's themselves were putting out to tender. Clearly could she remember the way in which Mr Harrison pushed his weariness aside for a few moments when, looking oddly innocent, he had requested that, if she had time, could she get together enough inconsequential literature on the matter to keep Camberham's contract department busy for a while. He had then proceeded to dicate the most courteous of replies to be sent with the enclosures. But what, she couldn't help wondering, had that letter to do with any of why she had been called up to the upper realms of the building?

'You *do* remember that letter, Miss Finn?' Lyon Mulholland pressed impatiently, when it seemed he believed he had waited long enough for a reply.

'Well—yes,' she answered, his short, impatient tone giving the lie to any idea that he felt she deserved a pat on the back for anything! 'But it was a courteous letter,' she said quickly as, in some confusion, she harnessed the flicker of temper his tone had caused. Then she felt a fresh gnawing of guilt when she realised that she must have been summoned to the top floor not to be congratulated, but to be taken to task for not seeing how ill Mr Harrison was.

'We know that the letter was courteous,' Mr Lennard, who had been silent all this time, chipped in.

Kassia moved her glance to the near-retiring-age director. 'You're saying that you've been to my office and checked the file copy?' she questioned, starting to feel more flickerings of annoyance. If they had wanted to see a copy of that letter, why couldn't they have just asked her for it?

'We had no need to do anything of the kind.' Lyon Mulholland took charge of the interview and, turning to the desk behind him, he took up the top piece of paper that lay on one particular pile. 'Have you seen this before?' he enquired, handing it to her.

Kassia had no need to do more than cast a quick eye over the sheet of notepaper that bore the Mulholland letterhead. 'This is the letter I typed to Camberham's,' she said as she passed the letter back to him.

'And these,' Lyon Mulholland said, referring to the pile of paper which had lain beneath the letter he dropped back on top, 'are the enclosures that went with it.'

'How . . . Why . . .' Surprised, Kassia took a grip on herself. 'But—how did they get here?' she asked, and as she realised that only Camberham's could have returned them, so her sense of humour began to surface. 'Did Camberham's see through Mr Harrison's courteous letter and take exception to being bombarded with our literature?' she asked, a curve starting to appear on the corners of her beautifully shaped mouth.

'This is no laughing matter,' Mr Lennard interrupted sourly, sending her smile fleeing before it could take a hold.

Kassia had no wish to be rude to the frosty-looking director, but it took something of an effort. She was twenty-two now, she reminded herself sternly, and she had far more control now than in her growing years when her fiery temper had seen her explode at the smallest provocation.

'My apologies,' she muttered, and saw that she was being frowned on by both men.

Lyon Mulholland, as if he was growing impatient with the two of them, told her bluntly, 'Camberham's did not take exception to either the letter or the enclosures, for the simple reason, Miss Finn, that they received neither!'

Kassia blinked, and then stared at the letter and enclosures which must have been returned from somewhere. 'I don't understand,' she had to confess when she could make no sense of what he had just said. 'I typed that covering letter on the same day that I . . .'

'Typed a covering letter to send with the tender which was supposed to go to Comberton's,' Lyon Mulholland chopped her off, when that was not what she had been going to add at all. But what she had been going to add suddenly deserted her completely. Because all at once, the brain-power which she had wanted a moment earlier was there. Oh, no! she thought. But even as she was fearing the worst, the chairman of Mulholland's confirmed it by saying, 'The contracts manager at Comberton's was at something of a loss to know why we should be sending him correspondence meant for the contracts department of Camberham's until he realised what must have happened.'

From a brain that had a minute before stood in neutral, Kassia's brain was suddenly in overdrive. And as all the implications sunk in, her throat went dry, and she was incapable of speech. What Lyon Mulholland made of her stricken silence, though, she was shortly to find out when, his expression as cold as the tone he was using on her, he left her in no doubt as to what had happened, and its ramifications.

'It became as clear to him, as it has become clear to me,' he grated, 'that the tender—the figures which Mr Harrison would have gone to endless pains to guard from our competitors—was sent to Camberham's, while Comberton's received the correspondence meant for Camberham's.'

Kassia opened her mouth and tried to speak, but she was so shaken to realise that the two lots of correspondence had been sent out in the wrong envelopes that she had to swallow first. And then all she could do was to say a faint, 'Comberton's have obviously let you have the wrongly addressed mail back, but—but—er—have Camberham's done the same?'

'It's irrelevant!' Lyon Mulholland looked down on her from his lofty height. 'Since all tenders had until nine this morning to be in, they've had ample time in which to adjust their own bid. You knew, of course,' he fired, 'that for every contract we bid, Camberham's do the same?'

She hadn't in actual fact worked it out that far. But honesty was an innate part of her. So when she did work it out, it was obvious that, since she was aware that Camberham's were their rivals, it therefore naturally followed that she must subconsciously have been aware that Camberham's would tender for the same contracts.

'Of course,' she replied, her voice, she had to own, a shade cooler than it had been.

'Then I can only suppose,' he said icily, his chin jutting aggressively at her admission, 'that either you were grossly negligent in your duties . . .'

'Negligent!' Kassia shot in to exclaim, not ready to take that from him or anyone after the hours she had slaved for the company.

'Negligent was the word I used.' Lyon Mulholland showed no sign of backing down. 'Either you were grossly negligent when you put the material in the wrong envelopes, or you were being deliberately criminally incompetent.'

'I beg your . . .' Kassia began, but as the full import of what he had just said sank in, she erupted, her hold on her temper gone, 'How *dare* you!'

'I dare because, either accidentally or by design, this

company, through you, may have lost a very worthwhile contract to our biggest rivals,' he grated, his aggression out in force to meet her fury. Though Kassia did not stay merely furious, but went white with rage when, not content with his efforts to mangle her pride thus far, he further questioned her honesty by daring to challenge, 'Well—are you being paid by Camberham's as well as by me?'

It was just *too* much! Leaving aside the fact that she had naïvely presented herself in front of this odious man anticipating something in the line of compliments for her devotion to duty, this was just too much!

'Neither!' she hissed between gritted teeth. 'I'm being paid by neither of you! I'm . . .'

'You catch on fast!' Lyon Mulholland sliced in before she could have the pleasure of telling him that she had just resigned. And he did nothing for her seething fury when, ignoring the angry sparks that were flashing in her green eyes, he pipped her at the post to add bluntly, 'You're dismissed!'

She had never been dismissed from a job in her life! Nor had she ever felt so incensed in her life! Indeed, so incensed was she at that moment that it became a very near thing that she didn't give way entirely and attempt to give Lyon Mulholland a stinging slap. Even as she observed the dangerous gleam that came to his eyes, for all the world as though her almost undeniable inclination had been telegraphed to him, Kassia was sorely tempted. It was not fear of any reprisal she might evoke which stopped her from relieving her feelings this way, but more that she suddenly acquired some semblance of hard fought-for control.

Grimly she hung on to that small control and, while she still had it, stormed to the door. At the door, however, she found that it was just beyond her to leave meekly without another word. She had the door open, with Heather Stanley and anyone else around in earshot when she turned. 'Stuff your job!' she yelled at Lyon Mulholland, and, taking what satisfaction she could from that, she turned again and slammed out.

It was Tuesday morning before Kassia had simmered down to begin to regret her three parting words. They were hardly dignified. And by Wednesday morning, with the whole scene still very much on her mind, she had thought of at least a dozen more cutting and far more ladylike parting shots than 'Stuff your job!'

By Thursday, although her pride was still bruised that anyone could dismiss her from her job, she was on the way to telling herself that she didn't care anyway. But oh, how she wished she had got in first. To think she had been comtemplating leaving in the first place! So much for her loyalty to Mr Harrison. So much for any idea that she had to stay and hold the fort for Mr Harrison in his absence. So much for any laughable notion that she might be anything approaching indispensable while Mr Harrison was off sick. It hadn't taken Lyon Mullholland a minute to dispense with her services!

Kassia spent most of Friday cringing every time she thought of her stupidity in imagining that a man as busy as Lyon Mulholland was reputed to be should take time out to congratulate a mere secretary for coping in her boss's absence.

She spent the weekend licking her wounds and realising that the only reason Lyon Mulholland had sent for her was so that he could gauge for himself the extent of her involvement with Camberham's. He had wanted to interview personally the person whom he suspected might be some sort of industrial spy.

To Kassia's mind the idea of her being an industrial spy was so ludicrous that she had to laugh. Though she soon sobered as she remembered the straight-from-the-shoulder way in which he had demanded, 'Well—are you being paid by Camberham's as well as by me?'

Detestable creature, she fumed, and blamed him entirely for the fact that she'd been too heated to tell him that it hadn't been she who'd put the post 'to bed' on that particular day. Quite obviously he would never dream of slipping anything inside an envelope once he'd signed it, but handed everything back to his down-trodden secretary to fold and seal for him.

Kassia thrust aside a mental picture of an anything but down-trodden-looking Heather Stanley, and again told herself that she didn't care anyway. Naturally she couldn't help but feel regret that the contract for the tender which she and Mr Harrison had worked so hard on must have gone to some other company. But, since she hadn't been planning to make a career with Mulholland's, she couldn't see any good reason to state at this stage that she was not the one responsible for the Mulholland tender going astray. And apart from anything else, she felt guilty enough about not noticing how close Mr Harrison was to cracking up, without putting a bad mark in for him for when he was well enough to return to work.

When Monday arrived she felt she had got herself sufficiently together to start looking for another job. Her qualifications were excellent, and she had no trouble whatsoever in establishing an interview for the first job she applied for.

The interview went well, she thought, and she was fully prepared for the question, when it came, 'And for what reason did you leave your last employer?' Though she had no intention of saying that the chairman of the company, no less, had dismissed her.

'I left my employer previous to Mulholland Incorporated in the hope of finding work that would make use of all my office skills,' she smiled. 'But within a month at Mulholland's I knew I hadn't made the right move. I gave it another month, just to be sure,' she added, and saw from Mr Arley's corresponding smile that this met with his approval.

From there the interview ball went backwards and forwards, with Kassia revealing that she had left her Herefordshire home shortly after her twenty-first birthday to work in London, and learning more of her expected duties should her present job interview prove successful. The smile on Mr Arley's face as he mentioned that he was obliged to see two other people who had been called for interview before he could write any job-offer letter told Kassia that the job was hers.

The interview was almost over when he suddenly said, 'Oh—references! You've no objection if I get in touch with your previous employers . . . ?'

In total Kassia had had three jobs since she had completed her secretarial training, and she knew full well that two of those three employers would give her a reference that was little short of outstanding. 'I've no objection at all,' she smiled promptly. 'Although, since I was at Mulholland's for such a very brief space of time, they probably won't even remember me.'

'I very much doubt that,' Mr Arley said gallantly, 'but perhaps it would be better if I contacted the employers who've known you for longer.'

Kassia came away from the interview certain of two things. One, that Mr Arley would not be contacting Mulholland Incorporated. The other, that she had found herself a new job.

A week later she realised that her confidence that she would shortly start work again was a shade premature. For she received a letter from Mr Arley stating that she had not been successful in her interview. By that afternoon she had recovered from being slightly shaken, to perceive that the job must have gone to someone better qualified than herself.

That evening she checked the paper, and wrote after another job. Subsequently, she was called for interview. Again she felt she had waltzed through the interview, but when, after another week of waiting, a letter from the firm in question arrived, Kassia was again shaken to read that she had failed that interview too.

Up until then she had not viewed getting herself another job with any great urgency, but it was going on for a month now since she had been employed, and the rent had to be found from somewhere. Not that she was desperate yet, for she had some small savings and, if the worst came to the worst, her super parents would always bail her out, though she was extremely reluctant to ask them for money.

Her thoughts stayed on her parents for some minutes. They were devoted to each other, and were parents any offspring would be proud of. She had told them she no longer worked at Mulholland's, but had given them a somewhat different version of the truth.

When Kassia came away from her third job interview, she was cautiously optimistic. This time, though, she did not just sit back and wait to hear, but, on seeing an advert for another job which looked interesting, wrote applying for the job. A few days later she was telephoned and asked to attend for interview at Heritage Controls the following Tuesday.

It was on the Monday preceding that Tuesday, though, that she received a letter in answer to the job interview which she had been cautiously optimistic about.

'I don't believe it!' she gasped out loud. For, incredibly, when that job too had seemed to be hers for the accepting, she had again been advised that she had not been successful!

Aware, without conceit, that her secretarial skills were first-class, Kassia just couldn't understand her wretched luck. It was just as though there was some conspiracy, she thought. As though someone was conspiring to make it impossible for her to ever work in London again. As though . . . Oh, my hat! Abruptly her thoughts changed tack and were suddenly steaming along. A minute later she had paused to check the much smaller print on the headed paper of the letter she had just received.

The answer to why she had not been offered this particular job was suddenly blatantly plain! Because there, among a string of other directors, one name in particular loomed large in the tiny print.. Lyon Mulholland!

It took her but another minute to collect the two other letters she had received telling her that she had not got the job. It took her less than seconds to discover that one Lyon Mulholland was on the board of both firms.

The swine, she fumed, as she realised then that the people who had interviewed her must—because of this connection with Mulholland's—have contacted that company for a reference for her after all! Either that or Lyon Mulholland must have sent a directive round to each and every company with which he was in any way associated, and advised them that on no account must they take one Miss Kassia Finn on to their payroll.

Kassia spent the rest of that day being fairly incredulous that of all the companies in London she should have applied to not one but three firms which had some connection with Mulholland's!

Mutinying against her ill-fortune, she was just deciding to have an early night so as to be fresh for her fourth job interview tomorrow when a sudden dreadful thought struck. What if Lyon Mulholland was associated with Heritage Controls too!

Don't be ridiculous, she told herself. It was stretching the arm of coincidence a bit much as it was to discover that he was on the board of those other three companies; no way, surely, could he be on a fourth. She shrugged the idea away, and went and got ready for bed. But she found, though, that the idea, once born, was proving too stubborn to be entirely shrugged away.

It was eleven o'clock when Kassia knew she was not going to get a wink of sleep that night. What she needed, she fumed as she started to get cross not only with herself, but with Lyon Mulholland also, was to see a list of the directors at Heritage Controls.

Ten minutes later and still wide awake, she was lying in bed and wondering how on earth, at that time of night, she was going to find out the information she required. Suddenly, however, she knew just exactly how.

On two occasions when she and Mr Harrison had

been working late, he had given her Lyon Mulholland's home number and had asked her to ring him at his home. On each of those occasions she had spoken with his housekeeper, and had put the call through to Mr Harrison while the housekeeper had gone to find her master.

Lyon Mulholland's phone number, although ex-directory, was, Kassia recalled as she got out of bed, an easy one to remember. After the way Lyon Mulholland had treated her, and was still treating her, she could not see so much as half a good reason not to use it.

Guessing that his housekeeper would be off duty by now, Kassia hoped as she dialled that Lyon Mulholland had gone to bed, and that the phone was a mile away from him. To her disgust it rang out for only a very short while before being answered, and he sounded as alert and as wide awake as ever when he answered, 'Mulholland.'

'Kassia Finn,' she said tartly. 'You may remember me.'

'What do you want?' he asked bluntly, and Kassia knew that, since the contract he had lost was so vast, it would be a long time before he forgot the woman he thought responsible for losing it for him.

'I've a job interview at Heritage Controls in the morning,' she began. But before she could get around to asking him if he was anything to do with the firm, Lyon Mulholland had confirmed that he was every bit as quick on the uptake as she had thought, and again he had pipped her at the post.

'I shouldn't bother going,' he told her coldly, and hung up, leaving her talking to the air.

CHAPTER TWO

WHEN Kassia awoke the next morning she discovered she had an untapped depth of obstinacy in her which she had never before known about. From Lyon Mulholland's comment last night, she had realised that Heritage Controls must be yet another pie in which he had a finger. And yet she found that there was something in her which insisted that she should still keep her appointed interview.

Much good did it do her, though. For when, dressed smartly in her Sunday best, she presented herself at the reception desk of Heritage Controls, she was politely informed that this time she wasn't even going to make it as far as the interview.

'Mr Neville asked me to pass on his apologies,' the receptionist told her, 'but the vacancy has been filled internally.'

'I hope Mr Neville soon gets better,' Kassia was angry enough to return.

'I'm sorry?' the receptionist queried as Kassia turned away.

Regretting that she had vented some of her anger on the receptionist, who was, after all, only doing her job, Kassia half turned back. 'My remark was intended to convey that, since his illness has left him so weak that he didn't have the energy to pick up the phone to ring me, I hope he soon regains his strength. But it's not your fault that somebody got to him before I did this morning, so I'm sorry I . . .'

Kassia had made to move away from the desk when, just then, two men rounded the staircase. Immediately she recognised one of the men, and saw red. Forgetting all about the receptionist, who stared after her, she went swiftly and planted herself straight in the path of Lyon Mulholland.

She was a couple of inches above average height herself, but even so, the man she considered the most hateful man she had ever had the misfortune to meet still managed to look loftily down at her. And that infuriated her even more, particularly when, despite it being perfectly plain that he—or more likely his secretary—had told Mr Neville not even to interview her that morning, Lyon Mulholland looked not a bit put out that she was blocking his way. Unhurriedly his eyes took in her trim shape and sparking green eyes. From her eyes his glance went to her mouth, beautiful still, even though mutiny could be read there.

'You swine!' Kassia hissed. 'You did this! You . . .'

She did not get any further. She was aware that he had signalled to someone over her shoulder, and the next thing she knew was that, on his instruction to 'Remove this woman' a muscular security guard appeared from nowhere, took hold of her arms, and removed her from Lyon Mulholland's path.

Positively enraged by such action, Kassia then discovered that when he and his companion went striding towards the exit, the security guard had no intention of letting her chase after him. Which, since she was too blisteringly angry to stay bottled up, left her with only one option.

'*You cretinous oaf!*' she shrieked at his departing back. 'You may think you're God Almighty, but you want to get your facts straight before you . . .'

Her words ran out as Lyon Mulholland and the man with him went through the door and outside into the street. Suddenly, with no one to hear her but a goggle-eyed receptionist and a muscle-bound security guard, Kassia came to and realised that she had been yelling like a fishwife!

Oh, lord, she inwardly groaned as through the plate glass she saw the man she loathed drive off in a sumptuous limousine, where was her self-control? It was all Lyon Mulholland's fault, of course; he somehow seemed to have this knack of stripping every bit of dignity from her.

'You can let go of me now,' she told the security guard quietly, and maybe it was his astonishment at the change in her from a yelling shrew to a dignified and controlled young woman, she couldn't have said, but suddenly she was set free. Looking neither to left nor to right, Kassia went from the building of Heritage Controls, and returned to her flat to lick more wounds inflicted by Lyon Mulholland.

She spent the rest of the day with her emotions divided between the humiliation she still felt, and anger with the man who had been the prime cause of her humiliation. No doubt his visit to Heritage Controls had been arranged ages in advance, but why did it have to be on the very day that she was there? Perhaps he hadn't left it to Heather Stanley to ring Mr Neville to tell him that on no account must he engage her. All he would need to do, Kassia fumed, would be to step into Mr Neville's office while he was in the building. He probably passed Mr Neville's door, so he wouldn't even have to go out of his way all that much.

By evening she was for the most part over the embarrassment of being physically restrained. But when she thought again of how that lordly swine had put the block on her interview at Heritage Controls, she had to do some restraining herself. For, quite without warning, she experienced an almost uncontrollable urge to telephone Lyon Mulholland again—this time to give him a piece of her mind. Good heavens! she thought, and she felt quite startled. She was behaving like some nutcase!

At that point Kassia took herself off to bed and away from where her hand might, of its own volition, creep towards the telephone. She didn't know what it was about him, but it seemed to her that, when it came to anything to do with Lyon Mulholland, she needed all the control she could muster.

By morning she was on a much more even keel. Her need to have a job was gathering more urgency as time went by, so she no longer thought of applying for jobs singly, but was ready to apply for anything remotely secretarial by the dozen.

She was aware that Insull Engineering was the firm which Mulholland's had recently acquired, but, perhaps as a gesture of defiance, when she saw that they were advertising for an audio-typist, she wrote applying for the job. She posted that application along with two other job applications.

To her surprise, Insull Engineering were the first firm to reply, and, for another surprise, they asked her to attend for interview the following morning.

Intrigued, though certain she would not be offered the job, Kassia discovered that she was contrary enough to attend for interview when she had no intention of accepting the job anyway.

At least she thought she had no intention of acccepting it, but when Mrs Tibberton, the lady interviewing her, smiled and said, 'You're over-qualified for the job, as you must know, but if you'd like to work with us, then we'd like to engage you,' Kassia was too shaken to tell her that she did not want the job.

'Are you sure?' she enquired.

'I couldn't be more sure,' Mrs Tibberton replied, looking puzzled and as though she thought the question was an odd one. 'Why do you ask?'

Kassia thought she might as well confess now. Quite clearly word had not yet reached Insull Engineering that one Kassia Finn was black-listed by Mulholland's, but it was only a matter of time before Mrs Tibberton withdrew her job offer.

'I did tell you that I worked for Mulholland Incorporated for a couple of months. I'm sure I mentioned it in my letter of application,' she went on, only to have Mrs Tibberton interrupt with another smile as she agreed,

'Yes, you did. Which is why I rang the personnel director at Mulholland's before I invited you for interview.' Pleasantly, she added, 'My goodness—you must have made your mark in the short time you were there! The personnel director had it from the topmost authority that should his department be contacted in relation to a reference for a Miss Kassia Finn, only the highest reference should be given.'

'Highest reference . . . Topmost authority . . .' Kassia gasped. 'You're sure—that you heard correctly?'

'My hearing, as it happens, is particularly good,' Mrs Tibberton told her. 'Now, can you start tomorrow? I believe you said you weren't working at the moment.'

Bemused, Kassia came away from Insull

Engineering vaguely aware that she had accepted the audio-typist's job, and that she would be starting work the following morning.

She was still fairly incredulous when she arrived back at her flat. Without digging too deeply into her memory, she could recall quite clearly the way in which she had reviled Lyon Mulholland. She had told him he was a swine and had *shrieked* after him that he was a cretinous oaf, and whatever else he hadn't heard, he must have heard that! Yet, for some reason, he had countermanded what must have been his previous instructions—that she must on no account be employed by any firm with which he was connected! Further, he must have stated that she *could* be employed under the Mulholland canopy and that, should anyone else be thinking of offering her a job, his personnel department must furnish none but the highest reference!

Kassia was eating her evening meal when the answer to the 'why' which had buzzed around in her head off and on since she had come away from her interview became obvious. Somehow, Lyon Mulholland must have discovered that she was definitely not in the pay of their rivals, Camberham's. It had to be that, she felt sure. Because there was no way otherwise that he would have countermanded his previous instructions about her reference.

Had the fact that she was now looking for another job confirmed for him that she was not working for Camberham's? she wondered as she cleared away her dinner things. Did he somehow have a spy-line at Camberham's himself, and had he discovered that they had never heard of her? Just *how* had he found out?

It was going on for nine that evening when, not too bothered whether she started work at Insull Engineering in the morning or not, Kassia thought of a very good way of finding the answer to the question that tantalised her. She had his phone number, hadn't she?

Having dialled Lyon Mulholland's number while the impulse was about her, she half expected that this time it would be his housekeeper who answered. But she was getting to know the deep-timbred voice quite well. And she would have known who he was without the 'Mulholland' with which he answered the phone. Why, though, she should suddenly start to feel all fluttery inside was beyond her.

'Good evening, Mr Mulholland,' she said firmly, coolly, as she called herself ridiculous and made efforts to control her fluttery feelings. 'It's Kassia Finn here.' She did not doubt that he knew full well who she was, but the moment or two of silence before he answered was quite unnerving. And when he did answer, she was not at all thrilled by what he said.

'I've missed hearing from you,' he drawled.

'There's no need to be sarcastic,' she fired, remembering that the last time he had heard from her she had been yelling that he was a cretinous oaf. Silence from the other end neither denied nor confirmed that he was being sarcastic, but it forced her on. 'I went for an interview at Insull Engineering today,' she told him, and when that brought forth no response, she demanded 'Are you still there?'

'Riveted,' he replied with another helping of sarcasm, which made Kassia wish she had not phoned him. Though since he hadn't yet put down the phone on her, it gave further fuel to her conviction that he knew she was not some Mata Hari from Camberham's.

'You owe me a hearing,' she pressed on, following her line of thought.

'I'm listening,' he replied, stumping her.

'Well—actually—I more—wanted to find out than . . .' Suddenly she realised she had to take a grip of the conversation. 'What made you change your mind about me?' she stopped stammering to ask forthrightly. She was left gaping at his reply.

'You suggested I should get my facts straight.' She hadn't thought he'd heard that bit! But he was going on. 'With you all too plainly without an employer—and that included the people I'd thought you could well have been working for—I, in the interests of fair play, checked back to source.'

'You contacted Camberham's?' she asked faintly.

'I contacted Gordon Harrison,' he replied. 'I went to see him.'

'You contacted . . . You went . . . You didn't upset him?' Kassia gasped in a rush, having telephoned Mrs Harrison early on in Mr Harrison's illness and discovered from her that he was not well enough to see visitors.

'Have faith, Miss Finn,' Lyon Mulholland drawled, and went on to relieve her mind somewhat by telling her, 'As far as I'm aware he doesn't even know that that tender never reached its intended destination. Although he seemed to be coping with his indisposition, I judged that he has enough stress to cope with without my adding to it.'

'But if you didn't so much as mention the tender, how did you . . .' Suddenly she halted, as loath as ever to say anything that would put the blame squarely on Mr Harrison's tired shoulders.

'How did I find out that he, and not you, might be the one responsible for the mail going out that Friday?' Lyon Mulholland took up, and when she failed to answer, he told her crisply, 'I didn't, and there's still a whisper of doubt in my mind.'

'Why, then . . .'

'But Gordon Harrison revealed one or two things during my visit, which gave credence to my having *not* got my facts straight,' he cut through what she was saying.

'Oh . . .?' Kassia murmured warily.

'Oh, indeed, Miss Finn,' he muttered. 'During the course of my relating one or two minor office matters, I also mentioned that you were no longer with us.'

'You told him that you'd dismissed me?' Kassia chipped in with some degree of frost.

'No,' he denied. 'I didn't think it politic to tell him anything that might in any small way be detrimental to the recovery he's making. I learned enough, however, to put a doubt in my mind when he spoke of his regret that you had left the company.'

'He—er—gave me a good reference?'

'Little short of glowing,' said Lyon Mulholland crisply. 'According to him, you had uncomplainingly put in hours of overtime in that week leading up to him going off sick.'

'So did he.'

'You had worked so tirelessly, he told me,' he continued as if she had not spoken, 'that, knowing you were going away for the weekend, he waited only until you had handed over the completed typed project you were on to give you the rest of that Friday off.'

'Ah . . .' Kassia breathed. 'So you—er—came to

the conclusion that there must be a seventy-five-per-cent chance that Mr Harrison, and not I, was the one to put the post inside its various envelopes that night?'

'Did he?'

'Didn't he say?' Kassia countered.

'By that time he was showing signs of strain. It seemed better that I should leave and not stay to ask questions which—if I stirred some memory cog—might give him nightmares later.'

Kassia opened her mouth in surprise that a man as hard-headed as she knew Lyon Mulholland to be should have shown such consideration towards his contracts manager. Quickly, though, she overcame her surpise, realising that if she did not want him to go back to the question of who had got the post ready that Friday, she had better get him off the subject.

'Well, anyway,' she said hurriedly, 'since I didn't hesitate to ring you before—about that job at Heritage Controls—I thought it was only fair that I should ring you now that, thanks to you, I've got this job at Insull Engineering if . . .'

His drawled 'Don't mention it' cut off the 'if I want it' which she was just about to add. Oddly, though, when she knew that he had said all he was going to say, and that he had just terminated their conversation, Kassia experienced the most reluctant feeling to put down the phone. Indeed, she still had the receiver against her ear when, just as though he was reluctant to end the call too, she heard his voice again. 'Er—don't forget to give me a ring when you get promotion,' he murmured, and then, quietly, his receiver was put down.

Kassia came away from the phone a little unsure quite how she was feeling. Dazed, perhaps, didn't quite explain it. Though maybe, since she was more used to Lyon Mulholland stirring her to anger than lulling her into feeling at peace with her world, it was hardly any wonder that she should feel something akin to being dazed.

Whatever that feeling was, it lasted for a good many hours, and followed her through into the next day. For she discovered that she had started work at Insull Engineering without being aware that she had made any conscious decision to begin a career as an audio-typist.

She adapted to her new surroundings quite easily, but she found that the work in no way stretched her capabilities. Which was perhaps why, during her first few days of working at Insull Engineering, she found she was doing her job on 'automatic pilot'—which gave her plenty of free time for her thoughts to wander. But, since she already knew a lot of people, and was meeting many more in her new job, it was strange, to say the least, that her thoughts should stray so often to one person in particular—Lyon Mulholland.

His parting shot, 'Don't forget to give me a ring when you get promotion', had been liberally laced with sarcasm, of course. But quite obviously he wasn't as hard-headed as she had thought him. Not that he had given a tinker's cuss about her feelings when he had bluntly told her 'You're dismissed', but he had shown a high degree of sensitivity towards Mr Harrison's mental welfare when he had set about getting his 'facts straight'.

Kassia returned to her flat that night aware that Lyon Mulholland still held some doubts about her. She herself doubted, since it was unlikely that their paths would cross again, that he would ever know the truth.

During that week she received replies to the other jobs she had applied for, but she burned her bridges by telephoning to say that she was now suited. By the end of her first week, though, she had faced the fact that she would soon be driven up the wall if she had to be an audio-typist for much longer. It was a dull sort of job, she decided.

In fact, life itself was pretty dull just now. Her closest friend, Emma, had recently started going steady, and while Kassia couldn't have been more pleased that things were going so swimmingly for Emma, these days she hardly ever saw her. It hadn't taken the wolves at Insull Engineering very long to check out the new face in the typing pool, but although she was between boyfriends at the moment, Kassia had turned down all invitations. Somehow any man under thirty seemed, all at once, to be most immature.

When another dull week followed, Kassia decided that it was time to pay a visit to her old home in Herefordshire. Her parents were the dearest couple, and even though they appeared to not need a third Kassia knew herself loved by them, and was always sure of a welcome.

'We've been looking out for you!' Paula Finn beamed as she and her husband Robert came out on to the drive of their small detached house to greet their only child on Friday evening.

'I've come straight from the office,' said Kassia as she hugged her parents in turn. 'And no,' she grinned to her father, 'I haven't been speeding.'

'Much!' he grunted, and the three of them went inside to catch up on each other's news.

Though since they spoke with each other on the

phone an average of once a week, there was very little Kassia had to add to what she had already told them. Her mother, however, was not beyond referring back to a telephone conversation of some weeks ago, and it was over the supper table that she began, 'We haven't seen you since you lost your job at Mulholland Incorporated; what on earth happened there?'

'I told you, Mum. I'm sure I did,' Kassia hedged. It was one thing to not want to worry her parents and to cover her fury and her hurt pride with a very dressed-down-version of the truth over the telephone, but it was quite another, she found, to hide the pride-wounding truth by lying to her parents in the flesh.

'You said there was no work for you when Mr Harrison was taken ill with a nervous breakdown.' Her mother, for Kassia's sins, had a faultless memory. 'But in your father's opinion, Mr Harrison going off on sick-leave seemed more like a very good idea for keeping you on. I mean,' she went on, 'surely someone has to run the department, and you're so efficient in your work . . .'

Kassia jumped in to take advantage of her mother's remark and try to turn the conversation. 'You've worn rose-coloured glasses about my brilliance as a secretary ever since you bumped into Mr Evans in Hereford,' Kassia mentioned the first employer she'd ever had, 'and he sang my praises. I told you at the time that the only reason he thought I was so good was because my successor turned out to be so dim.'

'Such modesty!' Robert Finn teased.

'Oh—you!' Kassia grinned at him. Her grin soon fell away, though, when she discovered that her mother was not to be fobbed off.

'Are you now saying that Mulholland Incorporated —let you go—because you were inefficient?' Paula Finn asked, and even though she looked as if she would not believe anything of the kind, she looked sufficiently agitated for Kassia to know that she was going to have to come near to telling her the whole truth.

'No, I'm not saying that,' she denied, and added carefully, 'I didn't want to worry you at the time, but the chairman of Mulholland's, Lyon Mulholland, and I—well, we had a bit of a spat, and . . .'

'You had a—spat? With the chairman of the company?' Paula Finn asked in shocked tones.

'Kassia never did do things by halves, as I remember,' Robert Finn put in, and was, for once, ignored by his wife as she asked her daughter,

'You didn't lose your temper?' And as Kassia reluctantly nodded, 'You *did* lose your temper?' she amended.

'Only a little bit,' Kassia replied, with first-hand knowledge of the patience her mother had exercised in getting her to learn some self-control.

'How much is a little bit?' Paula Finn asked, a shade fearfully.

'I told him to—stuff his job,' Kassia owned.

'*Kassia!*' exclaimed her mother.

'That's what you call losing your temper only a little bit?' her father queried, looking every bit as though, but for his wife's shocked tones, he might burst out laughing at any moment.

'Well,' Kassia said defensively, 'he had just told me that I was dismissed, so I . . .'

'He *dismissed* you!'

Kassia started to give a brief outline as to why

Lyon Mulholland had dismissed her, but her mother paid scant heed. It was one thing, Kassia discovered, for her to be saucy to the man who ultimately paid her salary, but quite another for him to dare to dismiss the daughter of Paula Finn. Straight away her mother was on her side, showing that she had something of a temper herself as she demanded to know who Lyon Mulholland thought he was. Which was fine by Kassia, who thought she could happily listen to her mother's comments on what a dreadful man Lyon Mulholland must be. But suddenly, and most strangely, she found she could not! Indeed, all at once she was overcome by an almighty urge to defend him!

'Oh, he's not such a monster, Mum,' she found she was interrupting her flow to state.

'He's not . . .'

'Not really,' Kassia replied, and discovered that she was going on defending him, and even pointing out his good points, as she told her parents, 'He carries such a lot of responsibility, but he must have the welfare of his long-serving members of staff at heart, because he personally went to see Mr Harrison when he could just as easily have sent him a basket of fruit or something. Anyway,' she went rapidly on in case either one of her parents thought to ask how she knew that Lyon Mulholland had been to see Mr Harrison, 'when I applied for the job at Insull Engineering Mr Mulholland himself ensured that I was given the highest of references.'

'He did?' both her parents asked at once.

Kassia felt a little pink about the cheeks without quite knowing why, as she explained, 'Mulholland Incorporated recently bought out Insull Engineering.'

In bed that night she felt much calmer than she had been, and she could only wonder why she had suddenly felt so flustered when she had been defending Lyon Mulholland!

It was good to wake up in her old home, and even if she knew she did not want to return there for more than a weekend or perhaps a week or two, Kassia gave herself up to enjoying Saturday and a good deal of Sunday with her parents.

Whether her mother and father had discussed her, her job, or Lyon Mulholland she had no way of knowing, but none of Friday night's topic came up for discussion for the remainder of her stay. What did dominate the conversation was the approaching advent of Paula and Robert Finn's silver wedding anniversary in a few months' time.

'How many guests have you got coming?'

'Don't ask!' her father exclaimed with a fond look at the guiding light in his life, his wife.

'It keeps going up all the time,' Paula said, and sounded so clearly just a shade worried that her husband immediately declared,

'I could save you all this anxiety, love.'

'How?' they both wanted to know.

'Cancel the shindig,' he said promptly, 'and let's celebrate by blowing what we would have spent in feeding the masses on a second honeymoon somewhere in foreign climes.'

'Robert Finn,' declared Paula, 'is it any wonder that I quite—like you?'

'Come here and say that,' he growled. Kassia grinned and left them to it while she drove over to the next village to see her grandparents, who'd had a big wedding anniversary themselves last year—their fiftieth.

She remembered her parents, and the weekend the three of them had just shared, with much pleasure as she drove to work on Monday morning. By Friday, though, she was back to thinking that life was particularly dull at the moment.

She toyed with giving in her notice when the next Monday rolled around and, within an hour of being at Insull Engineering, she had renewed her opinion that an audio-typist's lot was not a happy one. But the week dragged on until, on leaden feet, Friday had arrived—and Kassia had still not resigned.

She awoke the following Monday and viewed the approaching boring week without pleasure. She was fully decided by the time she reached her desk that she would give in her notice that morning. Another month while she worked out her notice was the maximum she could take.

Before she could go and seek out Mrs Tibberton to acquaint her with her decision, however, she was called to see Mr Denham. Kassia had been at Insull Engineering for long enough to know that Mr Denham was in charge of office administration, but as she left her desk to answer his summons, she had no idea why he had asked to see her.

Within a very short time, though, she knew there was no need for her to give in her notice.

'As you may know,' Mr Denham began as soon as she was seated opposite him, 'Mulholland Incorporated are now our parent company.'

'Yes,' Kassia nodded, 'I knew that.'

'We were taken over by them some months ago,' he continued, 'but it has taken until now for the modernisation of offices and equipment to get under way.'

'Oh, yes?' Kassia murmured, showing interest,

but not sure yet where the conversation was going.

'Yes, indeed,' Mr Denham smiled. 'Much to my delight, we are now ready to put the plans for bringing Insull's up to date into operation.' His pleasure at the prospect caused him to digress a little, but Kassia kept up with him and, if she had got it right, it seemed that soon the typing pool would be a thing of the past. Word processors, computers and the like were here to stay! 'You won't mind leaving the audio-typist section, Miss Finn?' he asked.

At that stage Kassia was uncertain if this was not just his polite way of telling her that she was being made redundant. But since she had been going to give her notice in anyway, she remained as polite as he, replying, 'No, I won't mind at all.'

'I didn't think you would,' he smiled. 'Mr Mulholland himself speaks very favourably of your secretarial skills, which leads me to think you're wasted doing the work you've been doing since you joined us.' For a moment Kassia thought that Lyon Mulholland had personally spoken favourably of her to Mr Denham, and the blood started to course through her veins. She quickly realised, though, that Mr Denham must be referring to the fact that Lyon Mulholland had stated that only the highest reference should be given for her. 'Which is why,' Mr Denham was going on, 'with your agreement, naturally, I wish to transfer you from your present department.'

'You want me to transfer?' Kassia queried slowly, with due regard for the 'from the frying pan and into the fire' syndrome. 'To which department?' she asked.

'My secretary will be moving up to supervise a lot

of the changing over,' he replied. 'Which means that I shall be without a secretary myself. Of course, she'll be on hand to help you too with your new job. But . . .'

'You want me to be your new secretary?' Kassia asked, rather startled.

'Yes,' he said with a smile, but his smile started to fade when she did not immediately jump at the chance. 'What's the matter, Miss Finn,' he enquired, 'don't you want promotion?'

Quite suddenly, Kassia wasn't thinking of Mr Denham. Her thoughts had winged back to that telephone call she had made to Lyon Mulholland about a month ago. His sarcasm had been rife, but he had definitely drawled, 'Don't forget to give me a ring when you get promotion.' Kassia blinked, and discovered that she was still in Mr Denham's office and that, clearly, he was waiting for her reply. All at once, she was smiling.

'Oh, yes, Mr Denham,' she beamed, 'I should very much like promotion.'

CHAPTER THREE

KASSIA, with Mr Denham's ex-secretary's assistance, began her new duties immediately, although her first immediate impulse—to ring Lyon Mulholland to tell him of her promotion—seemed less and less of a good idea the longer she thought about it.

Over the next few days she found that the work she did for Mr Denham was varied, interesting and, if not totally stimulating, was far from being boring. Thoughts of Lyon Mulholland, and of telephoning him, refused to disappear, though.

It was crazy, she told herself. It was stupid, ridiculous. She knew it was all three, and yet, as idiotic as she knew it to be, she found she was having the utmost difficulty in putting the idea of ringing him completely away from her.

Wednesday evening in particular saw her alternately checking the clock and stifling the insane urge to dial his number. He'd think she'd gone barmy, she counselled herself, but she was glad when bedtime arrived so that she could hide under the covers and know that it was too late to make that call.

With the arrival of Thursday, Kassia was ready to break out into a cold sweat at the thought of how near she had come to telephoning him last night. By evening, however, she again started to be possessed by the feeling that to ring Lyon Mulholland wouldn't be so very terrible after all. She could match him for sarcasm any day, she considered, as she visualised herself telling him airily that, rather than have him die of suspense, she thought she should ring to tell him that promotion had come her way.

Had she not had to pass the telephone en route to bed, she reckoned she might well have completed Thursday without dialling that number which now seemed to be burned into her brain. But she did have to walk by the telephone, and suddenly, almost without a conscious thought, she found she had picked up the receiver and dialled those well-remembered digits.

At any second she might have given in to the impulse to slam down the receiver. But suddenly the ringing tone had stopped, the receiver at the other end was picked up, and a voice she would know anywhere answered, 'Mulholland.'

Suddenly, Kassia went numb. She forgot completely about some vague intention to replace her own receiver, just as she forgot completely about the sarcasm she had intended to use.

'Hello,' she said faintly. And when she thought he could not have heard, for he made no reply, she went on, 'It's me, Kassia,' and, feeling herself growing hot at the fool which she was making of herself, she found some vocal strength from somewhere to say sharply, 'It's Kassia Finn!'

'Whatever it is I've done, I'm sure I'm sorry,' he responded good-humouredly in response to the aggression in her voice, and at that good humour, Kassia felt light-hearted all at once.

'I got promoted,' she said swiftly.

'I'm—pleased for you,' Lyon Mulholland replied, but by then she was on the lookout for sarcasm which might or might not have been there.

'You asked me not to forget to tell you. I didn't want you to think I had a bad memory,' she added quickly, and hung up.

She went to bed that night feeling at odds with the world and wishing she had not telephoned him. She awoke the next morning and got ready for work feeling the biggest idiot of all time and knowing that she had been unwise in the extreme. She arrived home that evening and didn't know how she felt when she read the card attached to the superb bouquet of flowers which had been delivered to her door. 'Congratulations,' the card read. It was signed, 'L.M'.

Kassia knew only one L.M., and she took the beautiful bouquet inside her flat, her mind busy as she found a couple of vases and arranged the flowers to advantage. Was this another instance of Lyon Mulholland being sarcastic? She rather thought it was. And yet, as she munched her way through her evening meal, it seemed to her only polite that she should, in some way or another, thank him for the floral tribute.

I'll write to him, she thought, and she took out paper and pen intending to scribble off a cool but polite thank-you note. An hour and many screwed up pieces of paper later, she was still striving to find just the right cool and polite-sounding thank-you line.

In the end, she gave up. I'll ring him, she thought, but then had to stop to give serious consideration to this penchant she seemed to have for wanting to ring him at the smallest excuse. Hardly the smallest excuse, prompted the voice of pride. There had been sound reasons for her making each of her previous calls. In the event Kassia took herself off to bed without either writing to state her thanks or telephoning to offer them verbally. She well remembered what an idiot she had felt in the cold light of day this morning. She would, she decided, leave it until the cold light of *tomorrow* morning to decide what to do.

The first things she noticed when she came in with her Saturday morning shopping the next day were the two vases of flowers which she had arranged the previous evening.

'Bother it!' she exclaimed out loud, more in annoyance with herself at the dithery person she suddenly seemed to be than anything else, and she put down her shopping and went over to the phone.

She was angry enough with herself not to have anything rehearsed when, having dialled, she waited for that remembered 'Mulholland' to hit her ears. She then discovered she did not need to spout anything rehearsed, for it was not Lyon Mulholland who answered the phone.

'Hello,' said a mature-sounding female voice shortly after the ringing tone had stopped.

'Oh—er—hello,' Kassia collected herself to reply. 'My name's Kassia Finn—er—is Mr Mulholland there, by any chance?'

'I'm afraid not. Is there any message I can . . .'

'No, no. It's all right,' Kassia said quickly, and as the familiar feeling of having made a fool of herself yet again overcame her, she said a rapid, 'Goodbye,' and replaced the receiver, telling herself she would never, ever ring that wretched number again.

By mid-afternoon she had no earthly idea why she had allowed herself to become so het up over that telephone call. By early evening she was scorning every one of her actions. It was plain for anyone to see, she ruminated, that, beautiful though Lyon Mulholland's bouquet had been, there was no need for her to thank him for it!

With her equilibrium satisfactorily restored, she had just turned her attention to what she was going to cook for her dinner when a knock came to her flat door. She went to answer it, and promptly her hard-found equilibrium was shattered.

'I was passing,' drawled Lyon Mulholland casually, his grey eyes holding her startled gaze. 'I thought I might as well call in person to collect the message which you declined to leave with Mrs Wilson.'

'I—er—come in,' Kassia discovered she had bidden as she made giant efforts to get herself back together again. 'Mrs Wilson?' she queried, in the hope of having a few more seconds in which to get herself more of a piece.

Lyon Mulholland was inside her small sitting-room, the door closed behind him, when, flicking a glance around the neat and tidy room, he replied, 'Mrs Wilson's my housekeeper. I've been in town working for most of the day, but she told me of your call when I rang her a short while ago.'

'Oh . . .' Kassia murmured, and felt more of an idiot than ever when she said weakly, 'It wasn't anything important—my phone call, I mean.' She motioned in the general direction of the two vases of flowers and, having down-graded them as not important, wanted the floor to open up and swallow her when she was forced to add, 'I just wanted to say "Thank you" for the bouquet you sent.'

'My pleasure,' he murmured, but his eyes were

not on his gift, but on her. Abruptly he turned, and his hand had gone down to the door-handle when Kassia came alive to the fact that she did not want him to go.

'Can I get you a cup of coffee—or something?' she blurted. Oh, lord, she thought when, slowly, he turned to face her. He was so tall, so sophisticated, so—so—everything, while she was acting—and feeling—like some gauche sixteen-year-old. 'I mean,' she floundered on when he didn't answer, 'you did say you rang your housekeeper only a short while ago, so—if you've only just left the office, I thought . . .'

She was heartily grateful to him that he stopped her from rattling on any further when, with a charm she had not known he possessed, he said pleasantly, 'A cup of coffee is the best suggestion I've heard all day.' He smiled then, and so did Kassia.

'Take a seat,' she told him, 'I won't be a minute.'

In her kitchen she made more strides in getting herself together. Although since it wasn't every day that she entertained anyone such as Lyon Mulholland to a cup of coffee in her flat, it was no wonder that she should feel all shaky inside.

She was outwardly calm, however, when she joined him in the sitting-room with two cups of coffee, milk jug and sugar bowl on a tray. 'Have you been working all day?' she enquired as she handed him his coffee and placed the milk and sugar within his reach.

'I frequently do,' he answered.

'But it's Saturday!' she exclaimed, and added quickly before he could beat her to it, 'I don't suppose you could have created an empire like

Mulholland Incorporated by working a five-day week.'

It appeared that he hadn't been about to tell her anything of the kind, apart from acknowledging, 'Provided one doesn't forget how to play, hard work never hurt anyone,' for he went on, 'Have you had your evening meal yet?'

'Er—no,' she admitted, but suddenly she was wary.

'Then how about having dinner with me?' he asked.

'I . . .' she said, while her thoughts went off at a tangent. Lyon Mulholland lived in Surrey, she was sure he did. Which made his 'I was passing' a nonsense, because he wouldn't have to pass anywhere near her flat to get from his office to his home. 'Provided one doesn't forget how to play . . .' he had only just said. Had being reminded of her by his housekeeper given him an idea for a way to while away a few 'play' hours? Had he been encouraged by her offer of coffee? Had she been too forward? Had . . .

'You appear to be having some difficulty in coming to a decision.' Lyon Mulholland cut in lightly to her heavy thoughts.

But Kassia had worked herself up into quite a state. She felt most let down that he could well be thinking that, for the price of a dinner, she might be anybody's. And whether he thought her gauche, or whether he didn't—and although he had not so much as held her hand—the words would not stay down, and she just had to say, 'I don't want an affair.'

Watching him, she saw him blink as though her bald statement was the last thing he had expected to hear. But, having made the statement, Kassia would not retract it. To her relief, though, his reply, when it came, held humour and not anger, and she was inordinately pleased to discover that she'd had no need to feel let down, when he said easily, 'Forgive me, Kassia, but I have no recollection of asking you for one.'

'Oh,' she said.

'All that was in my mind when I suggested you had dinner with me was that, if you're at the same loose end as me tonight, since we both have to eat, we might just as well eat together.'

'Oh,' she said again, and as she read nothing save good humour in his suddenly twinkling grey eyes, her mouth parted to reveal her splendid teeth, and with a beautiful smile she told him happily, 'That's all right, then.' She stood up. 'If you'll excuse me,' she murmured as she tried to control the singing in her heart, 'it won't take me more than five minutes to throw on something more presentable than these jeans.'

Without apparent haste she sauntered to her bedroom. But once her bedroom door was closed, she acted like a mad thing. Inside the next ten minutes she had stripped to her skin and, working from fresh underwear out, her jeans were exchanged for a pair of black velvet trousers, her T-shirt discarded for a black silk blouse, and her feet were now adorned by a pair of black patent leather pumps.

The high colour she observed in her cheeks when she did have a moment to look in the mirror had nothing to do with excitement, she determined, but came solely from her mad rush round so as not to keep Lyon Mulholland waiting over-long for his dinner.

Kassia fastened a necklace around her throat, applied powder and lipstick, and pulled a comb through her red hair. She could have done with another half-hour in which to get her hair and everything else looking 'just right', but Lyon Mulholland did not seem to think she needed so much as another minute. He rose from his chair as she walked into the sitting-room and, ignoring that she was five or six minutes over the time she had said she would be, he looked appreciatively down at her. 'Perfect,' he said, and while, slightly mesmerised, Kassia looked up at him, he added matter-of-factly, 'But then you have a head start on most women to begin with, don't you, Kassia.'

'Er—if you say so, Mr Mulholland,' she answered, rather witlessly, she had to own.

'Make it Lyon,' he commented, and taking a hold of her elbow, he added, 'Let's feed,' and escorted her out of her flat.

The restaurant to which he took her was one which she had heard of as being famed for the quality of its cuisine. She witnessed, though, that her escort was plainly a favoured visitor to the establishment when, although there appeared not to be a free table available, he had no problem in being found a table for two.

'This is an unexpected surprise,' Kassia told him as, seated in a discreet alcove with him, she experienced an unexpected moment of shyness and felt the need to say something.

'A pleasant one, I hope,' he remarked as a waiter arrived to hand them both a menu.

Unhurriedly Kassia opened hers and, taking a glance at the bill of fare, said, laughing, 'It beats the cauliflower cheese I was going to have.' But on raising her eyes to Lyon Mulholland she found that he appeared busier studying her than he was studying the menu. He smiled at her, though, revealing white, even teeth, and as his glance went from her, Kassia knew, without comprehending why it should be so, that she had never been happier in her life.

'So,' Lyon said, as their first course arrived and Kassia waded into the *moules marinières* which she had ordered, 'tell me about Kassia Finn.'

'There's not a lot to tell,' she replied, and added with a mischievous grin, 'Save that she's not an industrial spy. Or,' she said quickly when she observed that the eyes that were fixed on the mischief in hers were unsmiling, 'do you still have your doubts about me?'

'I could be dining with you to find out what kind of espionage you've been up to at Insull Engineering,' he said, 'but I'm not.'

'In other words,' Kassia cottoned on, 'what you're really saying is that if you still held the least little doubt about me, we wouldn't be here dining together, the way we are now.'

'That's about it,' he agreed, and suddenly she saw things a lot more clearly.

'Those flowers, the flowers you sent—were they a—sort of apology for all you thought, all you said . . .' She broke off and, not giving him time to answer, she was asking as the thought came . . . 'You haven't been to see Mr Harrison again! You haven't asked him if he . . .' Again she broke off, but this time because she was afraid she might be putting her foot in it where Mr Harrison was concerned.

'What a loyal creature you are,' Lyon Mulholland observed evenly, and when he could see that she was not going to utter another word about her ex-boss, he went on to tell her, 'As a matter of fact I have been to see Gordon Harrison again, but not to ask him anything about his last day in the office. I went to see him,' he continued, still in that same even tone, 'because his wife had been in touch with the office to say that he was having anxiety problems about his job no longer being there for him to come back to when he's well again.'

'You went to reassure him?' she questioned, liking Lyon Mulholland the more she knew him, because even though he must be sure by now that it was Mr Harrison who had mixed the post up—costing his firm hundreds of thousand of pounds—he had still gone to see him.

'Since it appeared that he'd heard from some source or other that his department had been disbanded, I thought it only right that he should hear it direct from me that his department is only on 'hold' until he returns.'

'His section's work is being done elsewhere?' Kassia guessed.

'It wasn't on that Tony Rawlings should oversee Gordon Harrison's section as well as his own for too long a time,' he replied.

'How was Mr Harrison when you saw him?' she asked as she realised that other staff under Mr Harrison's supervision had probably been sent to work with whoever was responsible for the Mulholland Incorporated work or had been redeployed elsewhere.

'These things take time,' Lyon replied, and they both fell silent as their waiter came and cleared away their first course.

But Kassia still had a further question to ask, and

although she felt it must still be a sore point with the chairman of Mulholland Incorporated, she felt she must ask it.

Their second course had been served, though, before she could voice the question. 'Mr Harrison—you—er—you didn't tell him that Mulholland's—er, you—didn't get the Comberton contract?'

'I did not,' Lyon replied.

'I'm—glad,' Kassia said slowly, liking her host more and more as the meal progressed. 'It wouldn't do any good for him to learn just yet that all the hard work which he put in on that tender had been for nothing.'

'Leaving aside that it was he who fluffed it at the very last, what makes you think his hard work was all for nothing?' the man across from her queried urbanely.

Kassia wasn't quite with him. Perhaps, though, she mused, the figures that were now on file might be useful at some future date should some similar tender be invited. 'Perhaps some of the work might come in useful,' she answered reflectively, and added sincerely, 'I never said how sorry I was that you didn't get the Comberton contract, but . . .'

'Who told you we didn't get it?' he interrupted her smoothly.

Her head jerked back, and as she stared at him, she could not miss seeing a warm look of amusement in his expression at her perplexity. 'But—you couldn't have got it!' she protested.

'Why?' he wanted to know.

'Why? Because . . .' her voice trailed away as she sent her thoughts flying back. 'That Monday . . .' she said. 'That Monday when Comberton's sent you back the mail that had been put into the wrong envelope—that was the Monday when all tenders had to be in. Even supposing that by then Camberham's hadn't underbid us, it had gone past the nine o'clock deadline by the time you knew what had happened . . .' her voice faded completely as Lyon started to move his head from side to side.

'Not so,' he told her.

'Not so?' she queried. 'But . . .'

'As you know,' Lyon cut her off pleasantly, 'Comberton's instructed all bidders to mark their envelopes clearly denoting that a tender was inside. But, fortunately for us, they had the idea of having the tenders unpackaged and waiting in alphabetically ordered files ready for nine o'clock that Monday. To that end, trusted staff were asked to go in on the Saturday before that Monday to . . .'

'To unseal all the envelopes?' Kassia took up on a gasp.

Lyon nodded, and went on, 'The mistake we made was spotted at once and reported to a supervisor, who in turn reported it upwards until it got to the ears of someone who, realising that a genuine mistake had been made, tipped me off.' Kassia was still gasping when he added, 'We earned our corn that weekend, Heather Stanley and I.'

'You called your secretary in?' Kassia asked open-mouthed, and made what turned out to be an accurate guess when she questioned, 'You raided the files in my office and Heather Stanley spent the rest of her weekend typing out a fresh tender?'

'With adjustments,' Lyon confirmed.

'Adjustments?' Kassia queried. 'But there was nothing wrong with those figures! Mr Harrison and I checked and double-checked and . . .'

'As the figures stood there was nothing wrong with them,' he agreed. 'But in view of Camberham's having had a look at our figures, I thought I'd better take a look and pare whatever I could down to the bone.'

'Which you did—over that weekend.'

'And which Heather Stanley substituted for the figures which you had typed,' he went on. 'From there things were easy. Our messenger was on Comberton's doorstep with that tender well before nine o'clock on Monday morning,' he informed her, and added, 'Having handed in our re-vamped tender, he was handed the envelope with the contents which were meant for Camberham's.'

It was on the tip of her tongue to say 'And as soon as you had that envelope in your hands, you sent for me', but the natural follow-on from that was for her to remember how he had bluntly sacked her, and how she, equally bluntly, had told him to stuff his job.

'I'm staggered,' she confessed instead, somehow not wanting to be reminded of the unpleasantness that had gone on between them. Then she was asking quickly, 'So the tender you—we submitted was in on time and stood the same chance as every other firm who put in a bid.'

'Oh, yes,' he said lightly.

'And—Mulholland Incorporated—actually got it?' she enquired, her green eyes wide on his.

'Oh, yes,' he said in the same light tone, for all the world as though, having left the competition standing, he had been fully confident that they deserved to win it. At which Kassia burst out laughing, and Lyon, as if enjoying hearing her laugh, smiled.

Kassia did her best to come down from what was fast becoming a permanent state of elation, when the waiter came again to attend at their table. 'I'll have the raspberry pavlova, I think,' she told him sunnily, and had to acknowledge that since she had drunk only one glass of wine, the way she was feeling inside must have quite a lot to do with the man she was dining with.

'To get back to my original request,' Lyon said when the most delicious-looking raspberry pavlova had been set before her, 'tell me about Kassia Finn.'

'As has been said before,' she told him, as she sampled a piece of meringue, 'there's not a lot to tell.'

'You live alone?' he queried.

'My flat would be a bit cramped for two,' Kassia told him, and thought she had adequately answered his question. When he looked at her, however, and seemed as though he was waiting to hear more, she found she was going on to tell him, 'I'm twenty-two . . .' she broke off when he nodded, and she realised from his nod that he already knew her age. Which must mean, she concluded, that he had taken a very thorough look at the application form she had completed when applying for the job as Mr Harrison's secretary. 'I came to London a little over a year ago,' she continued after a moment or two spent in racking her brains for something to tell him which wasn't on that application form.

'Where did you live before?' Lyon enquired.

'A small village near Hereford,' she replied, and since he was showing this much interest, 'I lived with my parents up until then, and . . .'

'Your parents—they didn't mind you leaving home?'

Kassia shook her head, and would have told him that her parents shared so much 'togetherness' that her leaving hadn't upset them as much perhaps as it might had she been a daughter on whom they doted to the exclusion of all else. But, because she feared he might think her parents had no regard for her at all, when she was happily aware that she was much loved by them, she confined her reply to, 'I think all parents must expect their offspring to leave home at some time.'

'I expect so,' he conceded, and before Kassia could do some questioning of her own and ask him how old he had been when he had left home, he was saying, 'You've lived in London for over a year now—is it all you hoped it would be?'

'I was a bit lonely at first,' she said cheerfully, 'but life soon bucked up when I began making friends.'

'You have one—friend—in particular?' he queried.

Kassia supposed Emma was a particular friend. Up until the time Emma had started going steady the two of them had gone almost everywhere together. 'My one particular friend has just defected,' she grinned, 'so I'm . . .'

'You've got guts, I'll say that for you,' Lyon murmured warmly, and while her eyes shot to his as she did a double-take at his comment, he showed how much at cross-purposes they were and how he had mistaken her grin for pluck by remarking, 'If the end of your love affair hurts, you're not going to let anyone know it, are y . . .'

'I haven't been having a love affair!' Kassia exclaimed, as she wondered what on earth she had said which had given him that idea.

'You haven't?'

'No, I've not,' she told him indignantly; but for all her indignation she was not at all sure that he believed her when he said,

'As I recall from that last Friday we saw Gordon Harrison at the office, he sent you off early because you were going away for the weekend with . . .'

'I went on my own!' Kassia interrupted him. 'As a matter of fact, I went to Herefordshire that weekend.'

'To your parents,' Lyon documented, and he was at his most charming when he apologised, 'I seem to be forever begging your forgiveness, Kassia. I thought I knew what made women tick, and then some, but you,' he went on to charm her some more, 'seem to be very different from any other woman I've known.

'Don't let it throw you,' Kassia dared, and, suddenly realising how they had started to get their wires crossed, she said, 'I suppose some of the blame is mine. The particular friend I spoke of who has just defected is my girl-friend, Emma, who's just defected to the ranks of the "going steady". Naturally she wants to spend as much time as she can with the man she has fallen in love with.'

'Naturally, too,' Lyon took up, 'when you made a point of telling me you didn't want an affair, I assumed that you must have just come to the painful finish of one.'

'Why should you "naturally assume" anything of the kind?' asked Kassia, looking for some insight into the way his mind worked.

'Well,' he shrugged with a grin, 'it just couldn't be, after the terrific way I've acted towards you, that you simply didn't fancy me. So it had to be that you didn't want another involvement so close after the last one.' She had started to grin too at his sauce, when suddenly he went very still. 'That . . .' he said slowly, as though something had only just come to him, 'That,' he repeated, his grin gone as solemnly he fixed his gaze on her green eyes, 'or you, Kassia, are a virgin!'

Slightly shaken at his perception, she dropped her eyes to her now empty pudding plate. Desperately she searched for something trite, for something witty, for any sort of smart comment, but as she again raised her eyes to his, nothing at all had come to her. And then the sudden gentleness which she observed in Lyon Mulholland's eyes so startled her that she had less chance than ever of gathering her scattered wits.

'You are,' he said softly, his eyes never leaving hers, 'aren't you?'

'Er . . .' she demurred, as she tried to get over a sudden hammering in her heart, before, folding competely, she admitted huskily, 'Guilty as charged.'

Shortly after that Lyon took her home. Leaving his car, he went with her through the outer door of the house which had been converted into flats. Taking her door-key from her hand, he inserted it into the lock, turned it and stood back, and unexpectedly, Kassia, who had romped through her teens without ever knowing a moment's shyness, suddenly, and for the second time that evening, was swamped by it.

'W-would you like to come in for a coffee?' she asked.

'Better not,' he replied, and while she was ready to imagine that he might be touched with the same emotional vulnerability that she was experiencing, he showed he was more concerned with getting back to his home when he added, 'It's quite a run to Kingswood.'

Kingswood, she rather thought, must be the name of his home. 'Goodnight, then,' she said sedately as he pushed her door open.

'Goodnight, sweet Kassia,' he said gently and, bending to her, he placed the briefest of kisses on her upturned cheek—then he was gone.

Kassia spent the following day reliving again and

again every moment of the time she had spent with Lyon Mulholland. She took herself off for a walk with him very much in her mind. She returned from her walk—and he was still there in her head. She went to bed that night knowing that there was something just a tiny bit special about the man who had invited her to use his first name.

She went to the office on Monday and tried to settle down to her work, but if she was able to cope with the routine of her day, then when she went home that night, she had to own that she felt anything but settled inside.

By Wednesday evening of that week Kassia acknowledged that her nerves were starting to play her up. Time and again she had told herself that Lyon Mulholland's taking her out to dinner was a 'one-off', and that he would not come calling again. Yet that did not stop her from listening with a quickening heartbeat every time she heard the outer door open. Her heartbeats would even out when, proving that it was not Lyon arriving unannounced, the ensuing footsteps would cross to the stairs and go up to one of the flats above.

When her phone rang on Thursday, she jumped like a scalded cat, and although Lyon had never phoned her at her flat, she had to take several deep and steadying breaths before, afraid he might ring off before she got to it, she made a lunge for the phone.

'Hello,' she said breathlessly into the mouthpiece.

'What in the name of rice pudding's the matter with you?' her mother asked.

'Not a thing,' Kassia answered, and tried her best to sound enthusiastic when over the next five minutes her mother told her that the party to celebrate her twenty-fifth wedding anniversary was off, and that she and Kassia's father were going on a package tour of China instead.

When Friday evening came around Kassia definitely knew what she had been telling herself since Monday that she knew—that she would not be seeing Lyon Mulholland again. It was a sad fact of life, she sighed as she sat staring into space, but a true one, that Lyon Mulholland *must* have been just passing by her flat last Saturday as he had said. It had been impulse, and nothing more, which had made him call—impulse which had made him ask if she had eaten yet.

Why then did she still nurse this feeling that his visit, his calling like that, must be something more than impulse? Apart from that lightest of kisses to her cheek, he had acted quite unemotionally.

Fed up with herself, she had to wonder—was she so used to the men she had so far dated not leaving her alone until she had agreed to a second date that she couldn't take it when she met a man who showed no further interest? Not that you could call her outing with Lyon a proper date, she thought. It wasn't as though it was pre-arranged, or anything like that, was it?

Kassia took herself off to bed when the terrible and pride-wounding thought struck her that Lyon Mulholland had only thought to take her out from some feeling that perhaps he owed her some small treat after the despicable way he had previously prevented her from getting the jobs she had applied for.

Loath to spend any more time in her flat waiting for footsteps which weren't going to be his, or answering the phone to a voice which was not his,

Kassia spent Saturday morning window-shopping and making the occasional purchase.

She returned to her flat about midday, and having put her purchases away, she was in the middle of boiling herself an egg when her phone started to ring.

In defiance to a suddenly fast-beating heart which didn't know when it was licked, she ambled to the phone as if to defy it to stop ringing. 'Hello,' she said, on picking up the instrument. She almost had heart-failure as she recognised the voice that answered, and which referred to the time it had taken her to pick up the receiver.

'Did I catch you at an inconvenient moment?' Lyon asked.

'I was boiling an egg,' she replied, and could have groaned at her idiocy.

'The timing of which can be most crucial,' replied Lyon, leaving her to guess whether or not he was being sarcastic. 'Most remiss of me,' he went on, 'but I somehow find that I'm again at a loose end tonight.'

Kassia was ready to wholeheartedly forgive him endless quantities of sarcasm. He had to be asking her for a date. He just had to be! It therefore seemed only most natural to want to meet him half-way.

'You want to take me out to dinner?' she suggested.

'I want to give you dinner,' he replied, and asked, 'You do have a car, Kassia?'

'You want me to meet you somewhere?' she questioned, and very nearly fainted when he answered,

'I'd like to give you dinner at Kingswood. Pop your nightshirt into a bag and come and spend the night here.'

'Th-the night?' she stammered.

'I promise I've no designs on your virtue,' Lyon coaxed, and Kassia knew, as his charm covered her, that he was smiling.

CHAPTER FOUR

LYON had needed to say little to persuade Kassia that to have dinner with him in his home was something which she would enjoy above all else. Nor did he stay on the phone very long. After giving her concise details of how she should get to Kingswood, he hung up.

A moment after he had rung off, Kassia went to pieces. Normally she was quite controlled and in charge of herself. But that, she realised as she began to wonder agitatedly what she was going to wear, had been before she had met Lyon Mulholland. Since she had met him, her whole world seemed to have gone slightly crazy.

In her bedroom, she went to her wardrobe and sorted through every item of clothing hanging there. Nothing she possessed seemed even remotely suitable, she thought with a churning stomach, and she wondered desperately if she had time to go out and buy something new. Only for that to lead her on to another distracted thought—time!

What time was she supposed to arrive? Lyon hadn't said. Yet she did not want to arrive too early, nor did she want him to fault her manners if she arrived late.

When she found that she was dwelling on the risk of ringing his home in the hope of his housekeeper answering the phone, so that she could ask her what time dinner was, Kassia sank down on the bed and

took herself in hand. She had been invited for dinner
—she would arrive at seven. Because of the drive
back from Surrey, and Lyon clearly not wanting her
to have that sort of a drive after they had eaten, she
had been asked to stay the night. She would no
doubt see him again, briefly, tomorrow morning,
possibly at breakfast, when she would thank him
nicely for his hospitality and then drive back to her
flat.

Having sorted all that out in her head, Kassia
found she had ample time in which to fret about
what she was going to wear. Last Saturday the
choice had been relatively easy. Lyon had been
waiting to take her to dinner and she had not wanted
to keep him too long. This Saturday, he wasn't
waiting—well, not in the other room he wasn't—nor
was he expecting her for hours.

But in any case the two Saturdays did not
compare. While there had been only seven days in
between, last Saturday she had not known that she
was in love with Lyon; this Saturday . . .

Kassia's mouth fell open in shock as that last
thought began to penetrate. A minute or so later she
was wondering why the realisation that she loved
him should be such a shaker, because it had been
staring her in the face all this week!

Uncertain if she wanted to laugh or cry that the
mystery of being in love had been revealed to her,
she sat for a long time with one thought chasing after
another.

Half-past six that evening saw Kassia driving
nearer and nearer to the man who held her heart.
Where her love for Lyon would lead her she had no
idea, but having been engulfed by her discovery, she
had surfaced to realise that she was on her own in

this one.

It was a few minutes before seven when, following his directions to the letter, she turned into the drive which led up to the elegant three-storeyed stone building that was Kingswood, Lyon Mulholland's home. It was a minute before seven when she stopped her car, got out, bent back in again as she retrieved her overnight bag, and then went up to the stout wood door.

A porcelain bell with a metal surround was built into the stone doorframe. Kassia swallowed hard, and extended a finger to the porcelain, pressed, and waited.

The door was opened by a short woman who looked at her, looked at the overnight bag in her hand, then smiled. 'You'll be Miss Finn, I expect,' she said cheerfully.

'And you're Mrs Wilson,' Kassia guessed. 'I think we've spoken on the phone.'

'That we have,' Mrs Wilson replied, and taking Kassia's bag from her, 'If you'd like to follow me, Miss Finn, I'll show you to your room.'

Kassia crossed the threshold of Kingswood, and after pausing only to secure the stout door after her, she followed Mrs Wilson along a wide black and white chequered hall, and up a wide staircase.

Burning to know where Lyon was, Kassia only just refrained from putting the question to the housekeeper. And she had been shown to a tastefully furnished bedroom before that lady gave her a clue to what she wanted to know.

'Mr Mulholland has gone for a walk, but he'll be back well before dinner, I dare say,' Mrs Wilson informed her as she placed Kassia's overnight bag down. Kassia was trying not to feel hurt that, knowing she was expected, Lyon had taken himself off for a walk, when the housekeeper cast an experienced eye around the room, pointed out the adjoining bathroom, and added, 'Now I think you should have everything you'll need, but if there's something I've forgotten, please tell me.'

'I'm sure I shan't have to trouble you,' Kassia told her, and the housekeeper was on her way from the room when she thought to ask, 'Oh, what time is dinner, by the way?'

'It's eight o'clock,' Mrs Wilson told her, 'but if you'd like some refreshment . . .'

'Oh—no, thank you, Mrs Wilson,' Kassia cut in, certain that the housekeeper had enough to do with only an hour to go before dinner.

But no sooner had the housekeeper departed than Kassia was attacked by nerves about how she would act when she saw Lyon again. If she ever saw him again, she thought as she passed through a glum moment. How *could* he go for a walk? Why shouldn't he go for a walk? came a counter-argument. He didn't know that she was in love with him and how she ached for a sight of him. Nor must he know.

Undoing her bag, Kassia shook out the dress she would shortly put on, and hung it on a hanger. She had taken a bath before leaving her flat, but, deciding that the small amount of make-up she wore needed renewing, she went into the bathroom and proceeded to wash and change.

At a quarter to eight she was dressed in a red silky-feel dress which, although full-skirted, fell in soft folds about her hips and long legs. Checking her appearance, Kassia couldn't fail to see the anxiety in the large green eyes that looked back at her from the mirror. Her pale complexion which went with her red hair seemed to be more translucent than ever, she thought. But when, nerves biting, she started looking for plus points, she conceded that she had made the right choice with her dress. Somehow there was something very feminine about it.

As ready as she would ever be, she turned from the mirror, suddenly all mixed up inside. Her longing to see Lyon again was almost painful, and yet, at one and the same time, she felt too nervous to leave her room.

By dint of giving herself a lecture which ran something along the lines that if she felt like that she should never have left the security of her flat, Kassia paused only to push a handkerchief into the hidden pocket of her dress, and went swiftly to the door.

Assuming a confidence she was far from feeling, she made a serene shape of her features and went lightly along the landing. She was on her way down the wide staircase when one of the oil paintings on the high wall caught her attention. She halted her step and was absorbed in taking in the aristocratic bearing of the grey-eyed man who stared back at her when she suddenly felt as though someone was likewise absorbed in looking at her.

Her head jerked round to her right, her eyes going to just beyond the head of the stairs where, on the curve of the landing, looking as though he had forgotten that he had invited her there and thus seeing her in his home had arrested him, stood Lyon.

Kassia's heart set up a painful beating. Once her pride would have made her think that if he had forgotten he had invited her that she could easily jolly well leave. But she was so hungry for some time with him that pride did not stand a chance.

Not in that direction at any rate, but it was pride alone that made her the first to speak, as airily she enquired of him, 'Enjoy your walk?'

'Sorry I wasn't here to greet you,' he apologised pleasantly, leaving the spot where he had been standing and starting down the stairs towards her.

'That's all right,' she replied, in the manner, she hoped, of one who hadn't even noticed that he was not there. 'Mrs Wilson has looked after me very well.' Her heart started to thunder as he came and stood but one stair-tread from her, and swiftly she looked again to the portrait. 'This gentleman just has to be one of your ancestors,' she commented, surprising herself at how remarkably even her voice had sounded in the circumstances.

'Why do you say that?' Lyon enquired, his good-humoured glance resting on her and not on the portrait, she saw when she flicked him a look.

'Apart from his eyes being almost identical to yours,' she replied, cursing herself for revealing that she had taken note of Lyon's eyes, 'he's got that same look of superior arrogance that you wear.'

Hoping to have retrieved some of the situation with that last comment, she took her eyes off him and, lest her unwary tongue again betrayed her, she continued her way down the stairs, her heart hammering as Lyon fell into step with her.

'Who was he, by the way?' she asked when at the bottom of the stairs she halted, not knowing in which direction the dining-room lay.

'My great-grandfather,' he told her, and caused her heart to hammer even more when he placed a hand beneath her elbow. 'Would you like something to drink before we eat?' he enquired, as he escorted her along the hall.

'I don't think so, thanks,' she replied, fully aware from the way her knees wanted to buckle just from his touch that she needed to keep a tight rein on all her senses.

'You found Kingswood without any difficulty?' he asked as he led her into a large dining-room.

'Your directions were spot-on,' she answered, and for the first time ever she knew the sickness which jealousy could bring as she wondered whether his directions were so exact because he was used to inviting females to join him at Kingswood for dinner.

There was room enough in the dining-room to seat a score or more guests, but as she got on top of her jealousy, Kassia was glad that the dining-table had been left unextended. With just the two of them at dinner, she would have hated it had they had to sit a mile away from each other. This way, their dinner seemed much more intimate.

All such thinking ceased temporarily when Mrs Wilson came in with a soup tureen, and bustled out again. Then Lyon was pulling out a chair for Kassia, and no sooner was he seated than he was ladling soup into a dish and passing it over to her.

'So,' she took the bull by the horns when nerves again started to get to her, 'how come you were at a loose end again this Saturday night?'

'I was just going to ask you that,' he drawled, and Kassia wondered if she should have hemmed and hawed some before she had accepted his invitation.

'I got in first,' she managed to grin. But she had the greatest difficulty in keeping a semblance of that grin in place when he replied to her original question,

'I start a tour of our holdings in Australasia on

Monday, and didn't expect to have any free time if I was to clear up all outstanding business before I leave.'

'But you've managed it,' Kassia said, and could have groaned at her inane remark. Of course he'd managed it, or she wouldn't be sitting here dining with him now!

'So how come *you're* free tonight?' he asked smoothly. 'With your looks I shouldn't have thought you had a moment to call your own.'

Kassia shrugged, and tried to appear unaffected by his compliment to her looks. 'True,' she said mock-demurely. 'But one tries to be selective.' And because what she had said sounded so much like a compliment to him—that she had selected *him* to spend her evening with—she just could not help bursting out laughing. When, his sense of humour on the same wavelength as hers, Lyon joined in her laughter, she looked at him and wondered why it had taken her so long to realise that she was in love with him.

She fell deeper and deeper in love with him as the meal progressed. She loved everything about him. The way his eyes crinkled at the corners when he laughed. His courtesy to Mrs Wilson each time she came in. She loved the way he drew her out to talk, and listened intently as if he was really interested in what she said.

By the time they had eaten their way through a superb meal, if Lyon had learned more about her, Kassia in turn had learned sufficient about him to know that they had a lot of likes and dislikes in common.

'Shall we take our coffee in the drawing-room?' he consulted her when she declared she could not eat another crumb.

She nodded, and, folding her napkin neatly on to her side-plate, she was ready to leave the table as he came round to her. 'That's the best meal I've eaten since . . .'

'Last Saturday?' Lyon suggested as he took hold of her hands and standing looking down at her, pulled her to her feet.

'Er . . .' Kassia hesitated, not wanting him to think she hadn't been out for a meal with anyone since she had dined with him last Saturday. But her knees were ready to buckle again and she felt tingly all over from the touch of his hands holding hers, and then suddenly she thought she saw some of the warmth leave his expression, so she prevaricated no longer. 'You could just be right,' she told him.

The drawing-room was as large and as gracious as the dining-room. Kassia, at Lyon's bidding, took a seat on a couch while Mrs Wilson came in with a tray of coffee, and enquired, 'If there's nothing else . . . ?'

'That was a splendid meal, Mrs Wilson,' Lyon thanked her as he took the tray. He then told her that if they did want anything else they would get it themselves, and bade his housekeeper goodnight. Kassia added her 'goodnight' too, and Lyon set the tray he was holding down on a table near to where she was sitting. 'Are you going to pour?' he enquired with some charm, having left her with very little option.

'Naturally,' she murmured, but only when he had moved away was she able to pour out two cups of coffee without slopping it into the saucers.

Had he come and sat close, or even next to her on the couch, she might have thought that perhaps he had a spot of seduction in mind. She would have been disappointed had he been that obvious, but she didn't know what she felt when, seduction not in his mind apparently, he chose to pull up an easy chair and place it just across from the coffee table.

'Have you always lived in this house?' she asked him as she placed his coffee near him.

'Kingswood has been in the family for years,' he replied, and left it there.

But Kassia did not want to leave it there. She'd had a lovely dinner, with the only dinner companion she wanted, and although it seemed to her that they had talked all through the meal, she had not learned nearly enough about him.

'Do you have any brothers or sisters?' she asked, taking a sip of her coffee.

'I've two sisters,' he told her abruptly, and at his clipped tone, suddenly every instinct was at work in Kassia to give her the dreadful impression that he would not thank her for another intrusive question into anything so personal as his family.

Which, when she would have willingly answered every personal question he asked about her family—had he been minded to want to know—caught Kassia on a raw spot. But because she was easily able to recall how they had laughed and chatted freely over dinner, she wondered if she was being a shade sensitive. She must be imagining it! Besides, she loved him, and she needed to know more, much more about him.

She paused to take a few more sips from her coffee cup, then she felt she just had to tell him, 'I'm sorry you no longer have your parents. It must . . .'

'As it happens,' Lyon chopped her off shortly, 'both my mother and my father are in extremely good health.'

'Oh . . .' she gasped, almost crushed to a pulp by his short tone while doing all she could not to show it. 'I just thought . . . With you saying that this house had been in the family for years, and since your parents aren't around, I assumed . . .'

'You assumed too much, it seems,' Lyon said icily. 'I don't wish . . .'

What he wished or did not wish, Kassia was not staying to find out. Nobody spoke to her like that, and that *included* him! Hurt to her very soul that he could intimate she had assumed too much from a mere dinner date, she was rapidly on her feet, and on her way to the door.

'*No!*' Lyon's voice rang out as he came after her. He caught her just as she had the door open. He pushed it to and held tightly on to her upper arms so that she could neither open the door again, nor do anything else.

'Let go of me!' she exploded, aware that she was out of control and needing to be alone to get herself back together again.

'Stay! Be still!' Lyon urged, his cold tone gone as she struggled to get free and he fought to hold her.

'Go to hell!' she snapped, aiming a wild kick at his shin, which missed.

'Very probably, I shall,' he replied, 'but I didn't mean to hurt you. I . . .'

'You—*hurt* me!' she scoffed, and even as tears of hurt sparkled in her eyes, she was yelling, 'Don't think anything you do could bother me in the slight . . .'

'Shut up, Kass, do,' Lyon cut through her hurt anger, and when her jaw dropped briefly before she looked ready to give forth again, his glance left her shining green eyes, and he effectively shut her up in the only way left open to him.

Kassia continued to struggle for about five seconds after his mouth had claimed hers—then her resistance gave out. This different sort of emotion he was charging in her was something over which she had no control and which, as he continued to kiss her, she had no wish to control. The bunched hands with which she had been attacking him suddenly flattened out, and with a moan she used her hands to hang on to him.

When Lyon broke his kiss and looked into her eyes she was as silent as he had earlier wanted her to be. What he read in her eyes, she neither knew nor cared. All that she knew was that she had never known such rapture as she experienced being held in his arms, and that she wanted him to go on kissing her, and never to stop.

She saw his eyes go to her trembling, parted lips, and suddenly the pressure of his arms about her increased and, as if one kiss was not enough for him either, he pulled her yet closer up to him so that their bodies seemed to merge as one and—he kissed her.

Time stood still for Kassia as she wound her arms up and around his neck. Her fingers splayed over his shoulders as she pressed herself to him and gave her ardent lips into his keeping.

'Dear Kassia,' he breathed as he pulled back to look down into her enraptured face, and Kassia was again lost to everything but him.

How they came to be on the couch from which in another lifetime she had rushed in pain, she did not know. Nor did she care. She was on that couch with Lyon and that was all that mattered. His caresses were making her whole body sing, and she wanted him with the whole of her being.

His mouth was over hers when, on fire for him, she felt the gentle touch of his hand caress down the side of her throat and inside the neck of her dress. More rapture was hers when Lyon moved her bra strap aside, and caressed the bare silk of her shoulder.

'Oh, Lyon,' she moaned his name, when he let go his dominance of her mouth. She adjusted her position on the couch to get nearer to him, and had an impulse to tell him she loved him. But the moment went when, with one hand still caressing her shoulder, his mouth again claimed hers.

She made a convulsive movement when that caressing hand invaded the cup of her bra, and Kassia was in a mindless world of longing when his warm, masculine hand covered the swollen globe of her breast.

She was not sure that she did not cry out his name again when, her bodice somehow undone, her bra somehow undone, Lyon traced kisses on both her uncovered breasts, sending her into ecstasies of wanting when his gentle mouth saluted the pink crown of each breast in turn.

A moment of shyness caused her to clutch tightly at him when he took his mouth away from her breasts and drew his head back. 'You're beautiful,' he murmured as his eyes rested on the rose-coloured hardened peaks his arousal of her had created.

Kassia coped with her shyness by leaning forward to kiss him. And having hidden her face from him, she promptly forgot all about shyness as Lyon, accepting from the initiative of her kiss that she was in agreement with whatever happened from then on, took over.

Deepening the kiss which she had begun, he took

her to new heights. Soon they were lying with each other, their legs intertwined, as they kissed some more.

When Lyon moved to half lie over her, Kassia was in a no man's land of wanting. She felt his hand caress beneath the skirt of her dress, and grabbed hard on to him when she felt his warm touch on her thigh.

'Lyon!' she gasped his name when his hand came to her briefs. Before, when she had cried out his name, it had been because of the wanting, the needing, the emotion he had evoked in her. But this time she was suddenly not sure if it was from nerves, shyness, the passion of the moment, or what it was that had caused her to cry out his name.

But Lyon knew. Perhaps there had been something a fraction different in the way she had called out his name. But he looked up—and in looking at her flushed face he just seemed to know that the high colour on her translucent skin came not from the ardour of their lovemaking alone. And while Kassia was in a state of utter bewilderment to know what was happening, Lyon had suddenly sprung up from the couch and standing with his back to her, was grating harshly, 'Put yourself straight, and get to bed, Kassia.'

'Bed . . . !' she echoed blankly.

'Get to your room!' he cut in toughly.

'But I . . .' she stayed to argue with his rigid back.

'For God's sake!' he snarled. 'Do I have to spell it out for you?'

Kassia had an abundance of pride. She was never more glad that the floodgates of pride found that moment to open wide. Without being able to comprehend why Lyon had gone so abruptly from wanting her as desperately as she wanted him to now be scorning her with a large helping of his superior arrogance, she bolted from the couch. Dearly did she wish for some sizzling cutting-down-to-size comment with which to leave the room. But she was in such a state of shock that nothing that might sound in any way as arrogant as he would came to her. Clutching the fastenings of her clothes to her as she went, Kassia fled.

Her initial reaction on reaching her room was to want to toss her belongings into her bag and to get out of there. Two things stopped her. She had never run away from anything in her life, and her feelings against Lyon were starting to become rather violent. She knew she could not trust herself not to send him flying backwards down the stairs should she chance to meet him on the way up as she was going down. Once before he had left her with very little dignity. Pride demanded that she heaped no more indignity on herself by having a physical, pugilistic set-to with him on the stairs.

Kassia did not sleep well that night, but as the hours of darkness ticked away she realised exactly why Lyon had acted the way he had. No doubt he had cut his teeth on women who knew how they should respond to each move he made. Her responses, quite clearly, must have been on the naïve side. Even though—nothing wrong with her memory—Kassia thought her responses had erred on the side of eagerness rather than the reverse, she realised that her gauche response must have put him off.

She dozed off to sleep again wondering if she had been *too* eager, and awoke to find Mrs Wilson in her room with a cup of tea. 'I . . . ' Kassia gasped.

'Good morning, Miss Finn,' the housekeeper greeted her cheerfully.

'You shouldn't have,' protested Kassia as she sat up and the housekeeper placed the tea on the bedside table.

'Mr Mulholland's having a working breakfast in his study,' Mrs Wilson volunteered, and asked, 'Is there anything special you would like for your breakfast, Miss Finn?'

'Oh, I don't eat breakfast,' she lied, and even though Mrs Wilson did not look as though she approved of this modern no-breakfast idea, Kassia had no intention of eating another morsel at Lyon Mulholland's table.

She drank the tea the housekeeper had brought, then hurried to get bathed and dressed. Quite plainly Lyon must be sorely regretting this morning that time which could have been better spent in his study had last night been spent in furthering her love-making education.

No doubt he'd got a diploma in it himself, with honours, she sniffed. But if he was so busy that he had to have a working breakfast, then she was darn sure she was not going to interrupt him by knocking on his study door to wish him goodbye.

Her pride was in an uproar when it came to her that Lyon could not want to see her again anyway. Somehow, if he wanted to see her, he'd have found time to have a breakfast cup of coffee with her at least!

Never was she more glad that she had told the housekeeper she did not take breakfast when, taking up her overnight bag, Kassia sailed from her room and sailed down the staircase. Her footsteps rang out as she sailed over the black and white chequered hall floor, but she carried on, and sailed straight out to her car.

As sometimes happened, it took her a moment or two to locate her car keys in the bottom of her shoulder bag, but having run them to earth she opened up the boot, tossed in her overnight bag and went to the driver's door. She had her back to the house as she unlocked the door and, now that she was on the point of leaving, she battled to keep her emotions under control.

She had just turned the key in the door-lock, though, when a voice from behind her made every one of her emotions go haywire.

'You're leaving without saying goodbye?' Lyon queried, his deep-timbred voice making her legs go like jelly.

'Goodbye,' she said stonily without turning round, and would have opened her car door and got inside, but Lyon, speaking her name, stopped her.

'Kass,' he said, the shortened version of her name making her backbone wilt. 'Kassia,' he said after a second or two of seeming to be stuck to know how to go on, 'once before, I wronged you. When I believed you were either criminally or incompetently responsible for that tender going astray, I wronged you.'

'So?' she queried coldly, determined—despite Lyon seeking her out—that she was never again going to show him her weaker side.

'So,' he said, and from the nearness of his voice she knew he had taken a step closer to her, 'I don't want you to leave my home without knowing that I didn't want to—hurt—you last night when I . . .'

'Hurt!' she scoffed proudly, just as though she hadn't lost one wink of sleep last night.

'Hush,' he said softly, and he was close enough to

take hold of her by her upper arms. 'Perhaps,' he said, as he turned her round to face him, 'there was a better way of going about it, but I wanted you so badly last night, Kass, that I had to take some sharp action or—be lost.'

Slowly, she raised her head. Pink came to her cheeks as she made herself look into the eyes of the man who had last night caressed her naked breasts. 'I'm not sure—that I understand,' she told him hesitatingly.

'What happened between us was not supposed to have happened,' he said, looking into her bewildered eyes.

'Because—you didn't think you fancied me—that way.'

'You know better than that,' he said with a trace of a smile, but as her heart warmed and she began to love him more, that trace fell away. 'Let's say,' he continued, 'that it wasn't in my mind when I invited you to dine with me here that I should afterwards seduce you. I'd given you my word that I'd no designs on your virtue, yet there I was, caught unawares. Suddenly you were in my arms, and I confess that when you reacted the way you did I forgot everything—even your innocence.'

'Oh . . .' said Kassia, which must have spoken volumes, because he replied,

'Exactly. It was almost too late when I did remember it. Your voice sounded strained when you called my name and, looking at you, I just knew you weren't ready for the commitment you were about to make.'

Dearly did Kassia want to tell him that she had been ready for that commitment, if a little shy about it. But, in the cold light of day, the words would not come.

So, dumbly, she looked at him, and Lyon went on, 'All I could think of then was how I had wronged you once, and that by bringing you into my home and seducing you I was going to wrong you again. I had to make you go to your room, to your own bed, my dear,' he ended, 'because had you not gone when you did, I feared I would take you to mine.'

For long moments after Lyon had finished speaking, Kassia just stood and stared at him. All of a sudden she no longer knew then whether she had or had not been ready for the commitment she had been about to make last night. What she did know, though, was that for him to have bothered to have explained what he just had must mean that he liked her a little—mustn't it?

Promptly, her day was sunshine-filled, and that sunshine was in her voice when, referring to the way he had only just let her know his fear that he might have taken her to his bed, '*Now* he tells me!' she exclaimed, and as Lyon witnessed the happy smile that was all at once upon her face, just as if he could not stop himself, he hauled her into his arms.

His embrace lasted about a minute, and Kassia could have stayed in his arms for ever. But all too soon he was putting her away from him.

'Get out of here,' he growled with mock severity.

Kassia grinned again and got into her car. She started the engine and wound the window down. ''Bye—thanks for the dinner,' she said cheekily to cover the pain of parting.

Before she could move off, though, Lyon had stooped down to the open window and, laying a kiss on her cheek, he whispered, ''Bye, love.'

Over the next week Kassia dwelt many times on

Lyon's warm sounding ''Bye, love.' That word 'love' had sounded so natural, and yet she was sure he wasn't the kind of man who used endearments easily.

Since each day started with thoughts of Lyon, it was not surprising to her that she had thought over every word, look and nuance that had passed between them endless times. She had realised early on in that first week of Lyon being away that he was a much more complex man than she had at first understood. But she thought that she was beginning to understand him. He was a man with a very high regard for what was right and what was wrong, as was evidenced by the way he had heeded her hint that he might have got his facts wrong over that tender, and had taken the trouble to investigate further. That same high regard for right and wrong had again been in evidence when, suddenly aware that he was seducing a guest in his home—a virgin guest in his home—he had found the strength of will to call a halt to their passionate lovemaking.

Lyon was still very much to the forefront of Kassia's mind when, in the midle of his second week away, she received a picture postcard from him.

Excited and happy to be remembered by him, she pored over the card. With more excitement and a thrill of wonder, she was soon able to deduce that Lyon had not waited until he had reached his destination before writing to her. For, before he had got that far, but while in an airport transit lounge, he had penned, 'Have dinner with me when I get back,' and he had signed it, 'Lyon'.

For all that he was many thousands of miles away, suddenly Kassia's world was brighter. He had been thinking of her on his journey to Australasia. As she held his postcard up against her heart, her expression grew dreamy. Lyon wanted them to dine together when he got back!

Her hopes high, the only cloud on Kassia's horizon just then was the fact that she had no idea how long he intended to be away. She wished with all her heart that it would not be *too* long.

CHAPTER FIVE

COUNTLESS were the times in the days that followed when Kassia wished she had asked Lyon how long he would be away. Countless, too, were the times she was to tell herself that she must not read too much into the endearment which Lyon had used when he had said goodbye. Nor, she told herself time and time again, must she make too much of the fact that he hadn't waited to get to his destination before sending her a card asking for a date when he got back.

The fact that she had not received another communication from him since that one and only card seemed to bear out that she should not read reams into his verbal ''Bye, love' and his written, 'Have dinner with me when I get back'. Yet, somehow, all her senses seemed to call out loudly that she was not imagining it when she felt that Lyon had some—regard—for her.

Kassia felt she coped quite well with waiting for Lyon to return during the week. Her job at Insull Engineering was starting to become more interesting, and from Monday to Friday she was able to become absorbed in it to some minor degree.

The weekends were terrible, though. Never had she known such loneliness. Even so, she turned down several invitations out, and when she could quite well have motored down to Herefordshire each and every weekend—and have been warmly welcomed—she did not go. For it was not loneliness for other people's company that ailed her. Quite simply, Kassia, in love with Lyon, was suffering from a loneliness of spirit.

Which was probably why, when Lyon had been away for four weeks, she got into her car one Saturday and took herself off for a drive around Surrey. When she found herself in the area of his home, she tried to ease some of her loneliness of spirit by driving nearer until, at the gates of Kingswood, she halted her car. Looking up the drive, her eyes found the spot where her car had stood when Lyon had stooped down and had laid his lips to her cheek, and had whispered ''Bye, love'.

Kassia sat there for only a few minutes, then, not wanting Mrs Wilson or any of Lyon's staff to catch sight of her and wonder what she was doing, she set her car in motion, and motored back to London.

It was a Saturday again, and six weeks since Lyon had gone away when she once more felt a compulsion to take a drive around Surrey. With difficulty, she resisted it, but when she awoke on Sunday morning, the compulsion was there with stronger force, and just refused to go away.

Although determined that she would go nowhere near to Kingswood, Kassia finally had to give in to that compulsion, and a little after half-past nine, she left her flat.

Her determination not to go anywhere near to Lyon's home, however, was weakened when traffic on a section of road she was travelling on was diverted because of road-works up ahead. The diversion took her within a couple of miles of Kingswood.

She could suddenly see no harm in driving past

his home—but she wouldn't even stay a minute this time, she promised. Her foot seemed to come off the accelerator without her knowledge, however, the moment she came with a hundred yards of his driveway. And when, dawdling to a near crawl, she glanced up the drive to Kingswood, suddenly her foot went on the brake. Because there, spotted and recognised, was a car in which she had once been driven.

A familiar churning made itself felt in her insides when she saw Lyon's car and she agitated to know if he had lent his car to someone or if his car was on his drive because—he was home!

Oh, crumbs, she thought, and for a nerve-torn couple of minutes she didn't know what to do. It came to her then that what she could not do, and in fact seemed incapable of doing, was to drive on to—just wait—for Lyon to telephone to say that he was back and how about that dinner.

Her hands were shaking as, automatically, she took the keys out of the ignition, and stepped from her car. Her clothes seemed to be sticking to her back as she walked up the drive. In fact, she was in such a state that she never afterwards knew why she had opted to walk up the drive when the more obvious thing to do would have been to have driven up to the front door.

Once she had reached the front door Kassia was at a loss to know what to do next. But, since she couldn't stand there dithering all day, she pressed the well-remembered porcelain button and, hoping that the housekeeper remembered her equally well, she prepared to ask Mrs Wilson if she had found an ear-ring she thought she had mislaid while staying there. From there, she decided, she would make some casual enquiry about Lyon, and she would either learn that he had just got back, or might be put out of her agony if Mrs Wilson told her when he was expected to return.

Kassia's plan to say anything to the housekeeper backfired when a firm masculine tread coming to the other side of the door warned that it was not Mrs Wilson who was going to answer the door. And in fact, when the door was pulled back, and she stood face to face with the man she had so ached to see, Kassia could not think of a thing to say.

The fact that Lyon appeared to be similarly dumbstruck to see her so unexpectedly passed her by for the moment. But, as his expression started to change, at the same time Kassia remembered something he had said which might amuse him to have bounced back.

'I was just passing, and . . .' she began lightly, but her voice quickly faded when she saw that his face, far from being amused, had become a chiselled mask of hostility! 'Y-you've just—got in,' she faltered, forced to go on when from his expression alone she knew she had made a most dreadful mistake in pressing that doorbell. 'You're j-jet-lagg . . .'

'I've had over a week in which to recover from my travels,' Lyon cut in harshly, brutally severing her desperate searches for excuses for his cold behaviour.

'You've b-been back in England for a week?' she enquired, nowhere near ready to believe what he was saying.

'Nine days, to be exact,' he replied shortly, aloofly.

Forced to believe, to accept, that he had been back for over a week and had not been remotely interested in contacting her, Kassia was left with a tremendous fight on her hands. He was making no move to invite her to cross his threshold, and indeed, he was showing such a lack of interest in her that what she needed more than anything just then was a face-saving way out of the situation which she herself had created.

But although nothing in the way of a face-saver presented itself, she had the way out she wanted when Mrs Wilson bustled into the hallway and, smiling a surprised greeting, hurriedly told her employer, 'There's a phone call from New Zealand —he's holding on . . .'

'I won't keep you,' Kassia said abruptly. 'Goodbye,' she added, and she meant it.

It took a lot of will-power, when she turned from Lyon, for her not to race down the drive to her car. But even though she knew he had gone to take his long-distance phone call and would not be watching her, Kassia was too proud to scurry away from anyone. Her world might have just collapsed about her but, as she kept up a strolling pace as though she was taking full pleasure from the trees that lined the drive, she was determined that she was the only one who would know about it.

She was in something of a daze as she drove back to her flat, although the self-recriminations had already begun. When she closed her flat door to the outside world, she was drowning in a sea of embarrassment caused by her actions.

How could she have called at Lyon's home? How could she have so misread the situation? How could she have let herself imagine, for so much as a moment, that Lyon had even the most minuscule amount of feeling for her? How could she have spent all last week mooning about him and wondering when he was coming back when—all the time—he was back in England? How could she have got hope and reality so dreadfully mixed up?

Did everyone who fell in love react in the way she had and get hope and reality so terribly muddled? For it was for sure that her hope that he cared for her in some small way was poles apart from the reality of it all. She needed no more proof than his cold, harsh attitude today to know that, in reality, he didn't care a damn for her.

Kassia was glad to see Monday morning arrive. She had barely slept, and she got up at first light glad to have something constructive to do, if it was only to get ready to go to work. She had thought long and hard about whether she was going to stay on at Insull Engineering. At first she had been all for resigning. But on thinking about it more deeply she'd realised that her chances of bumping into Lyon Mulholland at his subsidiary firm were about nil. Also, she was getting on well at Insull's and, using all the objectivity at her command, she could not see any reason why she should give it up.

She owned as she left her flat to go to work that Monday that she felt a shade belligerent. But, she reflected as she sat down at her desk, she felt better able to cope feeling as she did now than yesterday when she had felt as if everything she held dear had risen up and kicked her in the teeth.

'Good morning, Kassia.' Shaun Ottway, a junior executive who never took no for an answer, stopped by her desk to greet her. 'How did the weekend go without me?'

Were all young men of his age so sure of themselves? she wondered. 'Morning, Shaun,' she replied, and, telling him the truth, though drumming up a grin so that he would never know it, added, 'The weekend was tough, but I survived.'

She survived for the whole of that week, too, and by Friday, if she was still nursing a few mental bruises, then a quiet sort of anger had come along to help her out a little. All right, so perhaps she had taken too much on herself to imagine that Lyon Mulholland had some feeling for her but, dammit, prior to his going away he *had* been friendly! Jealousy threatened at that point, but she pushed it away. She had quite enough to handle without going into the realms of wondering if he had met some woman while he was away who had made any other female friend pale into insignificance.

Another weekend dragged past, with Kassia being glad when Monday arrived. 'You should have come to that party with me on Saturday,' Shaun Ottway told her when he made a detour to her desk while on some errand or other.

'I'll bet it made my Saturday night look dull,' she quipped, while hoping to convey that she had flown to Paris in her private jet.

'There's always next Saturday?' he said.

'I'll check my diary,' she told him—such banter helped her get through the day.

'That's what you said last Monday,' he complained, and when Friday arrived and he again asked her out, he received the same answer he had received the previous Friday.

Kassia let herself into her flat that night not wondering why she could not bring herself to accept any of Shaun's invitations. A few minutes spent each day in idle chat was one thing, but a whole evening of his brash chat would drive her insane.

Besides, there was only one man with whom she wanted to spend an evening, and he just didn't want to know. For the umpteenth time she got out the postcard which Lyon had sent her. 'Have dinner with me when I get back,' he had written.

'Huh!' she scorned; she'd get thin if she waited for him to take her out to dinner! But, for all her sarcastic thoughts, when Kassia went to throw away his card, she found, as she had found last night, and the night before, that she could not do it. She returned the card to the drawer of her bedside table.

When she went to work the following Monday she thought she had just about started to get herself together. Aware, though, that the ache in her heart was going to take longer to heal, she dealt with Shaun Ottway's Monday morning overtures, but half an hour afterwards she found out that she was nowhere near as back together as she had thought she was.

Mr Denham, his expression serious, had called her into his office. But, when she had her pencil poised, to her incredulity she learned that he had not called her in so that she could take down his dictation.

'I've just had a call from head office,' he opened, and while she kept her expression impassive at the knowledge that he had just finished speaking with someone at Mulholland Incorporated, he went on to positively astound her, by saying, 'I'm sorry, Kassia, but reluctantly, I shall have to let you go.'

Shaken to the core and quite unable to believe that Lyon could be capable of such vindictiveness—for the order to dismiss her must have come from him—Kassia, without a word, was on her feet.

'You don't have to go straight away!' Mr Denham

exclaimed, looking a trifle startled himself. 'Mr Harrison won't be there himself until tomorrow, so . . .'

'Mr Harrison . . . ?' The only Mr Harrison she knew was her old boss back at . . .

'Perhaps I've said it all wrongly,' Mr Denham smiled. 'Take a seat, Kassia,' he urged, 'while I explain.'

A few minutes later Kassia was doing her best to mask the growing agitation she felt at all he had told her. Apparently the staff recruitment officer at Mulholland Incorporated had rung to say that Mr Harrison was going to try to return to work on a part-time basis. But, as he was not yet fully fit, someone at Mulholland's had had the bright idea that it would be less of a strain on him if he worked back with his old secretary.

Kassia was instantly a mass of nerves. She might see Lyon again! Her agitation persisted even while she was silently counter-arguing that until he had sent for her and had dismissed her, she had never bumped into him before. Which augured that there was every chance that she would not see him—especially when it went without saying that he would never send for her again.

'But—what if I don't want to go?' she protested, and, remembering he had said that he was reluctant to let her go, she went on quickly, 'Can't you tell them at Mulhollands that it isn't convenient for me to . . .'

'I wish I could,' Mr Denham said, looking pleased at her obvious disinclination to leave his service, 'but it seems I have no say in the matter.' And while Kassia was getting ready to protest again, he added, 'Apparently Mr Harrison's need is far greater than mine.'

He could have said nothing that was more guaranteed to settle the matter where Kassia was concerned. She had never forgotten the guilt she had nursed that she had missed seeing how close Mr Harrison had been to cracking up. It now seemed she was being given a chance to make up for her past omissions. It was pretty near certain that neither she nor Lyon Mulholland were going to clap eyes on each other while she was working there anyway, so what was she worried about?

She had to give her attention to Mr Denham then, because he was going on to tell her that to begin with, Mr Harrison was only going to come into the office on Tuesdays and Thursdays. Mulholland Incorporated had requested that she report at her old desk on Tuesday, which meant she had a little less than a full day at Insull Engineering in which to leave everything ready for someone to take over from her.

She went home that night not a little exhausted and, despite all the inner arguments she had used, still very much in conflict about returning to Mulholland's in the morning.

Unable to sleep when she got to bed, Kassia lay awake thinking how at one time she would have given odds *against* her going back, or being allowed to go back, to Mulholland's. When she again started to relive the way in which Lyon had dismissed her, however, she just had to wonder—did he know that she was going back? She recalled how he had once put a bar on her working for any company with which he was associated. She recalled too how he had, handsomely, removed that bar once he had checked his facts about that fateful Friday afternoon.

And she realised that, since her personal file at Mulholland's now bore the endorsement 'highest reference', no one would think to query her transfer to Mulholland Incorporated with the chairman of that company. Which all boiled down to the fact that she could safely assume that he did not know she was going back.

Kassia dressed with great care the next morning, and within minutes of walking through the portals of Mulholland Incorporated, it felt as though she had never been away.

'How could you leave without a word?' reproached Tony Rawlings, coming up to her just as she was about to enter her old office.

'As it was only temporary, I didn't think you'd mind,' she replied.

'I'll forgive you everything if you'll come out with me tomorrow evening.'

'You're washing your hair tonight?' she quipped.

'I'll cancel it if you can make it tonight,' he responded straight away.

'Wash your hair, Tony,' she laughed, and ducked inside her old, familiar office.

'Kassia, my dear,' Gordon Harrison, already in harness, greeted her warmly when, dropping her bag on the desk she would use, she continued on through to his office to welcome him back. 'So good of you to agree to return. They tell me you were getting on very well at Insull's, too.'

'How are you?' she enquired, thrusting out a hand to shake the one he offered.

'I'll let you know at the end of the day,' he said.

Remembering her previous omissions, Kassia kept her eye on Mr Harrison whenever she could without being observed. 'Well,' she asked him when it was time to go home, 'how did it go?'

'I think,' he said slowly, 'that I'm going to be all right.'

Kassia beamed her pleasure at him, and said goodnight, to drive home and to wish that she too was going to be all right. At the back of her mind when she had got up that morning had been some half-thought hope that to return to Mulholland Incorporated might bring about a start of a more settled feeling within her. But it had not done so.

If anything, she was more all over the place than ever. For, she had discovered, it was all very well to decide logically—and numerically, too—that all the odds were against her and Lyon bumping into each other, but that did not stop her from being on the alert for a sight of him. Nor did it stop her heart from skipping a beat when she caught a glimpse of anyone looking even remotely like him.

Kassia again fought to get herself somewhere near together, and to that end she gave herself something of a lecture. Sternly she pointed out to the person who had given her heart where it was not wanted that she might as well stop getting churned up at the thought of expecting to see him around every bend because, for all she knew, he could well have gone abroad again. On that spirit-dulling thought, she went to bed.

She got out of her bed on Wednesday in a very sombre frame of mind. She drove to Mulholland Incorporated without enthusiasm and contemplated going down to Herefordshire at the weekend. The only trouble with that, though, was that, while she could deceive her parents that she was as happy as a lark over the telephone, she wasn't all that sure she could keep up a bright façade all over the weekend.

On the basis that her discerning parents should know only happiness in this time of their approaching silver wedding anniversary, she made the decision to stay in London at the weekend. Her mother, in particular, was getting most excited about the forthcoming tour of China, and Kassia didn't want worry over her to mar this happy time for her parents.

The one thing wrong with being a secretary to a part-time boss, Kassia discovered early on that day, was that, until she got into the swing of things again, she was not fully occupied.

With too much time on her hands in which to think, she took herself off to lunch and resolved that, since Tony Rawlings had been nominated the one to keep an eye on Mr Harrison's department when he'd gone off sick, she would go and see if Tony had anything she could do.

In actual fact, she did not have to go looking very far. For as she approached the Mulholland building on her way back from lunch, she saw Tony reach the entrance to the building from the opposite direction. He had seen her and, not one to miss any sort of any opportunity, he had halted and was waiting for her.

'You're the very person I wanted to see,' she got in first as she drew level.

'My luck must be improving,' he said, and held the plate-glass door open for her to go through.

Kassia took one step inside the building—and stopped dead. Because on stepping over the threshold of Mulholland Incorporated, she saw none other than the chairman of the company!

How she managed to retain some control she never knew, for living proof that Lyon was not away overseas as she had thought he might be was suddenly there. As though to defy any instruction her brain had issued that she must not so constantly be on the lookout for him wherever there was a vague possibility of seeing him, her eyes had immediately focused in on him.

He was standing to the right of the door and, partly concealed by a tall, decorative pot plant, he was in conversation with another man. But Lyon had seen her, and she knew he had. Their eyes met for the briefest moment of time. But it was then that Kassia drew on all her reserves of pride. With a tilt of her chin, aloofly, she looked through him.

Drained by the experience the moment she was past him, she had only just realised that Tony was too busy looking at her to have seen Lyon when, striking while the iron was hot, Tony did not trouble to lower his voice. 'You've changed your mind, you will come out with me tonight?' he questioned warmly.

A date with Tony was the last thing on her mind just then, but since one certain person must never be allowed to think that he might be the only pebble on the beach, 'In truth, Tony,' she prepared to lie, 'I just can't hold out against your charm any longer.'

They were in the lift, and out of earshot of anyone but their two selves when Kassia, remembering her one and only other date with Tony, wondered what in the name of stupid pride she had let herself in for now.

Encouraged, Tony walked with her to her office door after they had left the lift. 'I'll call for you at eight, Kassia,' he told her, and sounded in the best of spirits.

She went into her office to realise that she had forgotten all about her real reason for wanting to see Tony—to request that he furnish her with some work. Though the fact that she had forgotten was not so astonishing to her.

Instead of going to see him, she spent the next five minutes in the familiar exercise of trying to get herself back together again. But the expression which Lyon had worn when he had seen her was still in her mind. He hadn't appeared surprised to see her there, she recalled, and she had to wonder if he had known she had been called in to help ease Mr Harrison back into business life.

She ceased wondering when she faced the realisation that Lyon had looked more immune to seeing her there than surprised. But, hurt at having to accept that he was entirely unaffected by her one way or the other, she started to grow angry.

The phone on her desk began to ring for attention just as she became glad that Lyon must have read pretty much the same message—that she was immune to him—in her own aloof look. Heart-soothing pride filled her as she picked up the phone, fuming—who the devil did he think he was anyway?

But no sooner had she got the phone to her ear than a well-remembered voice roared, 'Get up here!' and then bang, his phone went down.

Kassia looked at the phone in her hand in amazement. She had just wondered who the devil Lyon Mulholland thought he was anyway. From the furious sound of him, it seemed she would soon be finding out!

CHAPTER SIX

MAKING her way up to the top floor of the Mulholland building, Kassia did not make the same mistake she had on the first occasion she had gone that way. She was still stunned, but she had a clear memory of Lyon's furious 'Get up here!' so she had no doubts that for whatever reason he wanted to see her, it was not so that he could congratulate her on a job well done.

She tried to keep weakening thoughts about again seeing him at bay as she stepped out of the lift on the top floor, but she had to take several deep and steadying breaths before she could open the door to Heather Stanley's office.

His secretary was as efficient-looking as she had been the last time she had seen her, Kassia observed as she went in. 'Mr Mulholland wishes to see me,' she told the unsmiling woman when she looked up from what she was doing.

With a small inclination of her head in her direction, Heather Stanley flicked a switch on her intercom. 'Miss Finn is here,' she said.

'Thank you,' came Lyon's firm tones—and that was all.

With the butterflies in her insides doing cartwheels, Kassia did not wait for Heather Stanley to deign to tell her to go through. She had taken no more than two steps towards the door of Lyon's office, though, when with some urgency the secretary found her voice.

'You can't go in yet!' she exclaimed, and added more slowly, 'Mr Mulholland didn't say for you to go in. Will you take a seat, please?'

Kassia almost apologised for reading Lyon's 'Thank you,' as 'Send her in', but Heather Stanley's attitude was starting to niggle her. But, because there were certain politenesses that were ingrained in her, she did as she was bidden and took the chair indicated and sat down to wait.

Five minutes ticked by, and seemed like an hour, with not a sign of the intercom again breaking into life. I mustn't get cross, I mustn't get get cross, Kassia adjured herself when another five minutes went by and still Lyon had not asked for her to go in.

He's a very busy man, she repeated, silently and frequently. And really, since she hadn't got all that much to do, she could as easily waste her time sitting up here, as she could sitting at her own desk. But when another five minutes had passed and she was still where she had been sitting for the past fifteen minutes, mutiny set in.

She hadn't asked to come back to work at Mulholland Incorporated in the first place, she rebelled, and from her point of view, she decided she had two options. Either she went back to her own office to wait—when she could well experience the humilation of being called back up to the top floor, only to have to wait again—or she could . . .

'Does Mr Mulholland have anyone with him?' she asked Heather Stanley abruptly.

Kassia guessed her abrupt tone as much as anything was responsible for Lyon's secretary giving her a forthright answer. She was definitely startled, at any rate, when she snapped coldly, 'No, he hasn't, as a matter of fact. But . . .'

Kassia didn't wait to hear any more. Fleet of foot, she was off her chair and was making for Lyon's door. She had the door open and was through it before Heather Stanley knew she had moved.

Lyon Mulholland was seated behind his desk as Kassia rocketed in. But as her glance shot to him and she saw that he looked tired and as if he was overworking, some of her mutiny faded. Her gaze fell to his desk, where she observed that he must have worked hard, because his desk was clear. Which meant, she realised a second later as her ire began to rise again, that she had been left cooling her heels out there for no good purpose!

'You wanted to see me?' she challenged sharply, as he got to his feet.

For answer he walked round his desk and, going over to where Heather Stanley stood in the doorway, he ushered his secretary to the other side of it, and closed the door. Kassia guessed then that, since he wanted no third party overhearing what he had to say, he must be intending to haul her over the coals regarding a personal matter. The natural sequence of thought from there was for her to remember how, not so long ago down in the reception area, she had treated him to a helping of his own aloof arrogance when she had looked through him. All too apparently, she realised, no one treated Lyon Mulholland like that and got away with it.

'Yes, I wanted to see you,' he grunted sourly, coming back from the door to stand surveying her coldly. The fact that he wasn't asking her to sit down told Kassia she was in for something short, sharp, and to the point. Which was why, after a moment while he seemed to pause to select his words, she was thoroughly amazed that, not taking her to task for her lofty manner at all, he should suddenly say jerkily, 'You *do* know Rawlings' reputation?'

Blankly, Kassia stared at him. '*Tony* Rawlings?' she questioned faintly, and was further struck dumb, though not for long, when, revealing that he had been tuned into her conversation with Tony as they'd passed him in the lobby, Lyon grated,

'He's taking you out tonight, I believe.'

'Good grief!' Kassia erupted as what Lyon had said sank in. 'I've just waited fifteen minutes to hear *this*?'

'Somebody has to put you wise,' he snarled, plainly not liking her tone any more than she was liking his.

'Two dinners with you doesn't entitle you to take on the role of Solomon,' Kassia hurled back, and saw from the sudden jut of his chin that he wasn't taking kindly to her answering him back.

'From what I've heard, Rawlings will want more than dinner!' he barked.

'As you did!' Kassia accused, uncaring that she was being unfair. 'You think he's got the same big seduction scene planned that you put into action once dinner was over?'

'You bitch!' Lyon called her grimly. 'You know perfectly well that seduction wasn't in my plans for that evening! Just as anyone less naïve than you would know, without having to be drawn a picture,' he went on furiously, 'that seduction damn well *is* in Rawlings' plans when he takes you out this evening!'

'Aren't I the lucky lady?' Kassia threw at him, thanking him neither for the 'bitch' label, nor for the fact that he obviously thought she had just come down in the last shower.

'You won't be if you keep your date tonight,' he retorted sharply. 'Already he's been divorced twice —what he's not looking for is a third wife.'

That Tony Rawlings, still in his early thirties, had been married and divorced twice was news to Kassia, but she had no intention of revealing that fact. Hurriedly, she made full use of the information that Tony was not looking for a third wife.

'Super!' she snapped tartly. 'Since I'm not on the lookout for a husband either, we can both have a good time without worrying about any matrimonial complica——'

'I'm just not getting through, am I?' Lyon cut in thunderously, and, wasting no more time, he laid it on the line when he blazed, '*His* idea of a good time will be to try and get you into bed.' Ignoring the furious sparks flashing in her green eyes that he could talk to her so, even if it was unbeknown to him that she loved him so much that she was just not interested in any other man, Lyon went roaring on, 'Given half the chance, he'll rob you of your virginity, and . . .'

But Kassia had had enough. 'Given half the chance, I might let him take me to his bed!' she exploded, and went storming towards the door to fling furiously over her shoulder, 'A lot can happen in two months, Lyon Mulholland—who says I've still got my virginity?'

She had been so beside herself in her fury that she was barely aware of what she was saying. But she had only just got the door open when she received the shock of her life. Because, so fast that she didn't immediately comprehend what was happening, Lyon had come after her. And suddenly, the door she was about to surge through was slammed hard to and, as suddenly, Lyon had her slammed up against it.

Shaken to her foundations, she shot him a startled look, and she had to suck in a panicky breath. For Lyon's face was devoid of all colour, and the expression he wore could only be described as demoniacal!

'*What,*' he said tautly, his voice ominously quiet, 'did you say?'

His hands were gripping her shoulders like a vice, and Kassia had never felt so threatened. But she had more spirit than to go down without a fight. And, when she knew exactly how long it was since that evening when he had called at her flat and had taken her out to dinner, she found her voice to tell him defiantly, 'The memory is somewhat sketchy, but it must be all of two months since you discovered that I'd never had a lover. A lot can happen in two months,' she defied him further, just as she defied him to hurt her when the pressure of his hands on her shoulders increased and made her want to cry out. 'Tonight——' her tongue refused to be still '——won't be the first time I've been out with Tony Rawlings.'

Had there been any suspicion lurking in her head that, once Lyon had got fed up with her determination not to be browbeaten, he would open the door and push her through it, she soon found out her mistake. For, with a roar that all but rattled the pictures on the walls, instead of pushing her out from his office, Lyon unceremoniously hauled her up against him! At the same time his head came down and, in a lightning move, before she could evade him, his mouth had fastened on hers in a punishing kiss.

Suddenly too, she was pressed up against the door by his body, all chance for her to get free eliminated. But that did not stop her from trying. She did not want to be kissed by him, she fumed furiously, when with her feet and hands she struggled, kicked and pummelled.

But Lyon would not let her go. Impervious to her outraged blows, brutally his mouth continued to assault hers, his lips forcing hers apart.

'Take your hands off me!' she hissed, when his mouth left hers to seek the warm hollows of her throat.

Feeling him move from her a fraction, Kassia did not delay to give a violent push to let some more daylight between their two bodies. But her action seemed only to spur Lyon to more anger, for in the next instant his body came violently up against hers and again she felt the wood panelling of the door against her back, and his mouth was once more over hers.

'You swine!' she reviled him when she had the chance. But his mouth was back over hers and she knew she was weakening.

Where before she had thought, I don't want to be kissed by him, suddenly two more words were added, and now that thought had changed to, I don't want to be kissed by him *like this*.

'Don't—Lyon,' she pleaded when he broke his kiss and stared down into her wide, wounded green eyes.

'Oh, God!' escaped him on a groan, and he was so close she felt the shudder that rocked his body. Whether that shudder came from self-revulsion, or revulsion for her, she knew not, but though the assault of his kisses did not let up, the next time that his lips claimed hers his mouth was gentle and not in any way bruising. And, despite him being every bit the swine which she had just called him, his were the only arms she wanted to be in, and suddenly what little resistance she had left disappeared completely.

Slowly her arms crept up and around his shoulders. She felt a spasm take him as he felt her compliance, and all at once as he gently eased his body from her, Kassia was on the receiving end of the most tender and the most beautiful kiss she had ever known.

She was quite captivated when that kiss ended. Speechlessly she looked up into the grey eyes of the man who but a minute before had bruised her lips with his fiercely furious kisses, but who had just knocked her sideways by showing that he had so great a tenderness in him.

She was in a state of breathtaken wonder when Lyon, his mouth still close to hers, whispered, 'You haven't been with any man, have you, Kass?'

'No,' she told him huskily, and she was so transported by him, by his wonderful tenderness, that she fully accepted that for a man such as Lyon she might lie down and let him walk all over her.

But that was before he gave her a fresh shock. She had been confused for some time about how any of this had begun. Even the question he had just asked had not truly impinged on her consciousness. But when his reply to her huskily answered 'No', was a shout of triumph, she began to come out of her entranced state.

When, to reveal that he had not for so much as a split second forgotten what it was all about, Lyon, his voice no longer a whisper, exclaimed victoriously,

'I knew it!' Kassia was suddenly no longer spellbound. And as for letting him walk all over her then—she'd die sooner!

Shaken to the core that she had allowed herself to *respond*, when the whole object of the exercise had been his intent to discover whether or not she had been telling the truth, she found her temper immediately at flash-point.

At once she was a mass of totally enraged womanhood. What Lyon was expecting, she neither knew nor cared. But as red-hot rage encompassed her at being picked up and brutally let down again, she launched her right hand.

The sound as it landed was the most satisfying sound she had ever heard. Whether Lyon staggered back a step from the violence of the blow, or whether he stepped back shaken that she could pack such a punch, Kassia was not waiting around to find out.

Possessed with the strength of ten in her fury, she pulled the door back so fiercely that it juddered on its hinges. Back in her own office, Kassia's first instinct was to grab up her bag and, as she could vaguely remember doing once before, storm out of Mulholland Incorporated with the intention of never coming back. But as her hand reached down for her bag and she dipped inside for her car keys, she saw the physical evidence of her inner uproar. Her hands, along with the rest of her, were shaking so much that she'd be a menace on the roads.

A ragged, nerve-torn breath left her, and she sat down at her desk to try to get herself together enough to decide what to do. Before she could decide, though—and she faced the fact that she was not just then in any condition to make firm decisions—her thoughts winged back to the top floor.

Swiftly she brought her memory away from Lyon Mulholland and her rapid departure from his office, to remember how she was so enraged that she could *not* remember so much as walking back through Heather Stanley's office. Nor, for that matter, could she remember whether she had taken the lift down to her own floor, or if she had used the stairs.

Which all endorsed her realisation that, since Lyon Mulholland had rendered her incapable of knowing where she was or what she was doing, in the interests of road safety she had better stay where she was for a while.

Half an hour later, with the help of a cup of tea made with the assistance of Mr Harrison's personal kettle, Kassia had ceased outwardly shaking. She had cooled down a great deal too, and was in the middle of contemplating going home to her flat when the sound of someone coming in through her office door made her jerk her head up.

Oh, lord, she thought, as her defensive aggression retreated when she saw that her visitor was not Lyon Mulholland. She had not in fact thought Lyon would stop by her office anyway, but to look up and see Tony Rawlings, the man at the root of that terrible scene, reminded her that she was supposed to be going out with him that night.

'Oh, I'm glad you popped in,' she began, on her way to getting herself out of that date by inventing a desperate attack of migraine which was going to send her home at any moment now.

'Sad news, Kassia,' Tony said, donning an unhappy air. 'I'm afraid I can't make our date tonight.'

It was the brightest piece of news she'd had all day, but even so, she was feeling so much at rock-bottom that she found it hard to feel cheered.

'Wouldn't you know it?' she got in quickly, as she sensed an invitation for some other time on its way. 'My only free evening for weeks, and you remember that you've promised to take your Aunty Flo out.'

'For you, I'd let Aunty Flo—if I'd got one—stay at home,' Tony told her with some feeling. 'And I don't have another date, if that's what you're thinking,' he went on—as if she cared! 'I've come to you straight from our chairman's office,' he said, making Kassia, figuratively speaking, sit up.

'Oh . . . ?' she queried, trying to show only the right amount of interest.

'There's a bit of a flap on, apparently,' Tony told her and, hardly able to stop preening himself, added 'Mr Mulholland, in person, has asked me to work late tonight.'

Kassia left the offices of Mulholland Incorporated having declined Tony's suggestion that, providing that it wasn't midnight, he would call in and see her on his way home after he'd finished work that night.

By the time Kassia reached her flat enough time had elapsed, since her initial determination that once she left the Mulholland Incorporated building she was never going back, for her to rethink that decision.

There were hours to go before morning, though, when she had to make that final decision. And, since she had stayed in her office long enough for Lyon Mulholland to have had a message relayed to her that her services were no longer required, she supposed that if she wanted to go to work tomorrow her job was still open for her.

After a long-drawn-out evening of one thought chasing after another, she went to bed with no sure answer to what she was going to do.

She lay awake for hours and wondered at the fairness in Lyon that had seen him not sacking her when she'd lashed out at him with her hand, and yet the nerve of him in thinking—no doubt in view of his past unfairness to her when he *had* dismissed her—that he should warn her of Tony Rawlings' reputation.

Suddenly, though, she could not quite understand why Lyon should go out of his way to warn her about Tony. For that to have been the reason he had sent for her would have to mean that Lyon at least liked her a little. Her heart gave an involuntary flutter at that thought, but it steadied to a dull throb when she thought of how she had called at his home that time. If that was the way Lyon greeted someone he liked a little, then she wouldn't want to be around when he greeted someone whom he *dis*liked!

All of which left her back with her original thought. Lyon Mulholland had taken the greatest exception to the way she had as good as snubbed him in the reception area of his own office building. He had not at all liked being served with a helping of his own lofty arrogance, and had been out to show her who was who—as was evidenced by the way he'd made her wait in Heather Stanley's office to see him.

Kassia reckoned that if she hadn't gone charging in to see him then, she might have been kept waiting until five o'clock! Silently she called him a few unpleasant names, but it did not make her feel any better.

The rat, he'd needed a way to get back at her! He'd found that way in lecturing her about Tony Rawlings, and when she'd flared up, he'd taken more revenge by kissing her so insultingly. Then, realising he could not subdue her that way, he'd used other tactics. He'd kissed her, oh, so tenderly . . .

Kassia brought herself up short as she realised that she'd drifted off to be thrilled again by just the memory of Lyon's tenderness. Startled to find that she had been on the way to believing that Lyon's tenderness, his tender kiss, had been genuine, she soon made short work of any such idea.

She fell asleep knowing that Lyon did not give a button whether she was still a virgin or however many men she had been to bed with. The only reason he had set about getting the truth from her was because something in her rubbed him up the wrong way. And whatever that something was, it had needled him sufficiently for him to make quite sure that her date wouldn't be free that night.

Kassia was up early the following morning, but things looked very little different from the way they had looked the previous evening. After long moments spent in thought, she went and had her bath—and got dressed in her business clothes.

'Good morning, Mr Harrison,' she replied cheerfully to his greeting when she went through into his office. He would never know that, but for her last-minute guilt at the thought of letting him down in this time of him being eased back into harness, he might well be without her as his secretary.

She was in her own office when, a few minutes later, the door opened and, setting her heart pounding, Lyon Mulholland walked through. He neither looked at her nor spoke to her, though, but went striding on to see Mr Harrison.

Since this was the first time she had known him to call at Gordon Harrison's office, Kassia felt certain she knew the reason for his visit. She discounted the possibility that he was there to enquire how things were going with her part-time boss. Instead, she was sure that, since there appeared to be a certain protocol in these matters, and since Mr Harrison had not been in business yesterday, Lyon was there to instruct him to dismiss her.

But, she realised, there must have been an element of doubt in her mind. For had she been so certain, she would have been on her way well before Lyon came out from seeing him, but she was still there when the door opened and he came out.

Her heart started beating nineteen to the dozen, but bearing in mind the way in which Lyon had passed her desk without a word or a look, she didn't see how he could be offended if she did likewise. She was still pretending to be thoroughly absorbed in the business communication in her hand when, Lyon having passed near by her desk, she heard the door into the corridor close after him.

'Come in, Kassia, please,' Mr Harrison called. Kassia went, and felt she hated Lyon that he should give Mr Harrison the stress of having to dismiss her. But he did not dismiss her. 'Do you remember where I put that Abernathy file on Tuesday?' he asked.

Kassia had a lonely time of it over the weekend. Her hate for Lyon Mulholland had not lasted above a minute, and she had never spent so wretched a Saturday and Sunday. The only thing that made her go to the office on Monday was the thought that she would at least have something to keep her occupied if she went to work. Whereas if she gave up her job before she had found another, she didn't know just how she was going to fill her day.

Thoughts of the lonely evening she had before her, with her thoughts going the same wearisome round, almost saw her give in to Tony Rawlings' renewed efforts to get her to go out with him.

'Is your engagement book really so full?' he pressed when, remembering the one and only time she had gone out with him before, Kassia had realised that a lonely evening on her own was preferable to having to fight him off when he took her home.

'Some weeks are like that,' she murmured, and to get away from him, she found a suddenly urgent errand she should be doing.

Monday evening was every bit as gloomy as she had anticipated. Kassia gave herself a pep-talk over breakfast the following morning, and she took herself off to work determined, since thinking about Lyon so constantly only made her feel worse, that she was not going to think about him any more.

Which proved difficult when barely had she got seated at her desk than Lyon marched in through the outer door and went striding past her to Mr Harrison's office, and closed the communicating door. At that point Kassia left her desk and took herself off to the cloakroom until she was sure his visit to Mr Harrison was done. From the trembling that had over-taken her at the non-speaking, non-glancing contact with Lyon, she realised that she was never going to get over him if he chose to call and see how Mr Harrison was faring every Tuesday and Thursday.

Kassia finished her day at Mulholland Incorporated, and went home to spend another depressing evening where she gave more serious thought to giving in her notice. She awoke on

Wednesday still unsure what to do. She went to work wondering at this love she had for Lyon Mulholland because, prior to falling in love with him, she had been much more decisive.

She was at her desk and had just made up her mind that—hang love—she was going to be more positive, when her phone rang.

'Shaun Ottway,' her caller introduced himself. 'Remember me?' And while Kassia put a face to the name and recollected him from Insull Engineering, he added, 'I've missed seeing you around the place.' He paused as if expecting her to comment, 'Likewise', and when she did not, he asked 'How about coming out with me?'

In view of her non-comment a moment since, Kassia was about to refuse with some gentle prevarication. She then remembered how, only seconds ago, she had decided to be more positive. 'Why not?' she heard herself say, when she had been certain she had been about to give him a blunt 'No'.

'Great!' he exclaimed and, not giving her the chance to back out of it, asked enthusiastically, 'How about tonight?'

Grief, Kassia thought, but since she had committed herself, and since she had nothing planned for that evening other than the possibility of another evening of desolation on her own, she told him, 'I'd like that.'

Of course you'll like it, she repeated positively to herself throughout the rest of that day, but there was a part of her which knew, positively, that she wouldn't.

Shaun had suggested that he take her somewhere for dinner, and as Kassia started to get ready that evening, she just could not help but remember the last time she'd had a dinner date. Having given scant thought to what she would wear tonight, she was tucking the hem of her white silk blouse into the waist of the full, flared, almost ankle-length black skirt when she recalled the panic she had been in about what to wear to dine at Kingswood with Lyon.

She had drifted off into a moist-eyed reverie of that time at Kingswood when Shaun Ottway arrived. 'You're as lovely as I remembered,' he said gallantly as she opened her door to him.

'Thank you,' she accepted his compliment, and went with him to the low-slung sports car parked at the kerbside.

'Out of deference to you, and for fear you might not want to come out with me again if your hair gets blown about, I've put the hard top on,' Shaun told her.

'Thank you,' said Kassia again, and promptly took time out to give herself a short talking-to. It wasn't Shaun's fault that he wasn't Lyon Mulholland, and, since she had accepted Shaun's invitation out, if nothing else she owed him the courtesy of more conversation than a murmured repetitious 'Thank you' for the rest of the evening. 'Have you had this car very long?' she asked, and discovered that since his MGB roadster was his pride and joy she could not have started the conversational ball rolling with a better subject.

That was not her only discovery of the evening, for she found that Shaun Ottway improved on acquaintance. He kept up an amusing flow of chatter over dinner, and given that occasionally she had to drag her attention back to him, she realised that he was nowhere near as brash as she had once thought him. She had started to learn, too, that

Shaun had a responsible side to him.

'I enjoyed that,' she told him when, having left the restaurant, she was seated beside him as he drove out of the parking area.

'Does that mean you'll come out with me ag . . .'

Shaun did not get the chance to finish his question. Because just then someone else making for the same car park exit, and at speed, suddenly appeared out of nowhere and cut him up.

'*Idiot!*' Shaun yelled, as he swerved and stood on his brakes. The MGB came to an abrupt standstill, but the 'idiot' who had very nearly caused an accident had gone careering blithely on his way. 'Strewth, Kassia, that was a close call!' Shaun remarked as on a relieved breath he turned to her.

But Kassia did not answer. The hard top had saved her from maybe being flung out of the car, but it was the hard top on which she had hit her head. She was out cold!

CHAPTER SEVEN

'LYON!' Crying out the name of the man she loved, Kassia awoke from a deep sleep. But Lyon was not there. Within a very few seconds someone was there, though.

Alerted by her cry, a nurse was soon making her way through the curtains which screened the bed from the rest of the ward. 'How's the head?' she enquired, flicking her professional gaze over Kassia and automatically fastening her fingertips on to the pulse that beat in her patient's wrist.

'Fine,' Kassia answered, feeling strangely unsurprised to find that she was in hospital, and putting that down to some vague awareness of someone shining a light into her eyes at some time during the night. 'How did I get here?' she asked what seemed a very natural question as the nurse let go of her wrist.

'Your boyfriend—in something of a panic—drove you to Casualty after the accident,' the nurse replied.

'Boyfriend?' Kassia queried, her heart beginning a familiar rapid staccato beat when her first thought was that Lyon had brought her to the hospital. Her brow wrinkled, however, when the lightning thought followed that she could not see Lyon Mulholland ever being in something of a panic—especially about her.

'You—don't remember your boyfriend?' the

nurse asked.

Feeling a trifle bewildered, she heard the casual-sounding question—which didn't quite tie up with the sharp, searching look in the nurse's eyes—but, as Kassia began to wonder what was wrong with her, she felt too confused to answer.

'You remember Mr Ottway?' the nurse reframed her question, her casual tone gone as she looked intently at the pale-faced young woman in the bed.

'Ah!' exclaimed Kassia, feeling tremendously relieved to have something slot into place. 'I was out with Shaun Ottway, wasn't I?'

'Giving me a fright like that!' the nurse teased her with a smile. 'I thought you'd lost more than just your immediate memory of the matters leading up to the event!' She then went on to clear some of Kassia's confusion by telling her as much as she knew of the accident.

'So—I banged my head, and when I wouldn't wake up, Shaun drove me here?' Kassia documented when she had finished, having recalled that she had gone out to dinner with Shaun Ottway, but having no memory of leaving the restaurant.

'That's about the size of it,' the nurse agreed. 'Luckily your boyfriend still had his car in low gear and wasn't driving at all fast, or things might have been very different.'

'Shaun's all right?' Kassia asked, realising she had been a bit remiss in not asking after his welfare when he had been in such a panic about her.

'Not a scratch on him,' the nurse replied.

Kassia dozed off to sleep again as soon as the nurse went about her other duties. But an hour later she was fully awake and her head was much clearer, and questions were queueing up on her tongue to be asked.

'Your boyfriend's just rung to see how you are,' the nurse told her cheerfully when she came around the screens to take another look at her.

'L . . .' Kassia broke off, and had to wonder how clear she thought her head was that Lyon should be synonymous in her head with the word 'boyfriend'. 'You mean Shaun?' she asked.

'Just how many do you have?' the nurse ribbed her, but she let up to tell her, 'Yes, it was Shaun. He wanted to know how you were, and asked me to give you his love.'

'Thank you,' Kassia murmured, and asked, 'How am I? I mean, I feel all right, can I go home?'

'Not until the doctor's seen you,' the nurse replied. 'And he'll most likely want you here for twenty-four hours' observation.'

'Oh!' Kassia said, crestfallen. 'Does that mean I can't go home until this evening?'

'We'll wait until the doctor comes,' the nurse smoothly dodged the question, and while keeping her eye on her she allowed her to go to the bathroom to take a bath, and saw her back into bed again.

It was still early when Kassia ate some breakfast and then settled down to try and doze once more while she waited for the doctor to arrive. But her brain was too active and, remembering that it was Thursday, she also remembered that Mr Harrison would be in business today.

She had her eyes closed, and had just begun to worry if she should try to get a message to him that—the doctor permitting—she would be late in that morning, when she heard the sound of male footsteps. The footsteps neared her bed, then halted. Kassia kept her eyes closed for a few seconds more as she built up all she had to show the doctor how bright and alert she was so that he would let her home.

Then she opened her eyes, and, as her eyes grew wider, she had to make great efforts not to let her jaw drop. For the grim-faced, tall, dark-haired man who stood looking down at her was not the doctor, but was none other than the man whose name had involuntarily broken from her when she had awakened that morning.

'You look awful!' he rapped without preamble as soon as he saw that she was awake.

'Good morning to you, too!' she flared, and as a sudden fractured sob took her, purely reaction, she was sure, she didn't know whether to laugh or cry.

As if he had gleaned that she could be near to tears, though, some of the aggression had suddenly gone from Lyon's tone as he asked, 'How are you feeling?'

In truth Kassia was starting to feel as awful as he had said she looked. But that was because she had just become overwhelmingly aware of her hospital-issue nightshirt, her tousled hair, and the fact that her normally pale face was without a scrap of make-up. She found it an uphill slog to be able to tell him airily, 'Never better.'

'Huh!' he grunted, clearly not believing it for a second. 'Anything in particular you need?' he then enquired.

'I shan't be in here that long,' she told him with more hope than actual knowledge.

'Who says?' he asked, with a trace of his old aggression.

'I'm going home as soon as the doctor's been to see me!' Kassia told him, belligerent in the face of his returning aggression.

'Home! To your parents' home in Herefordshire, you mean?' he queried sharply.

A feeling of weakness washed over her that he had remembered that her parents lived in Herefordshire. But the fact that he should have that much power over her made her angry with herself, and her voice matched his for sharpness when she retorted, 'Home—to my flat!'

'We'll see about that!' he said curtly, and just then the ward sister came to remind him that he'd overstayed the minute of 'non-visiting' time she had allowed him. He stayed only to look hard and long at Kassia, then, without a word, he left.

His energy while he had been with her had seemed to revitalise her. But when he had gone, he seemed to have taken that revitalising force with him. Feeling drained suddenly, Kassia faced the fact that perhaps she was not yet quite ready to meet Lyon in some head-on clash.

As if to regain some strength, she closed her eyes, but that only proved effective in bringing his face to mind. Damn him, she thought, and she was all at once on the trail of something which only then struck her. What in blazes had Lyon been doing at the hospital? How had he known she was there? *Had* he indeed known she was there? Had he perhaps been visiting someone in the same ward? Since she remembered the ward sister coming to remind him that she had allowed him only a minute of non-visiting time, though, Kassia had to draw the conclusion that he had known she was there, and that he must have asked specially to see her. Which brought her on to wondering why he would do that, and brought her full circle—how had he known that she was there?

Her head stayed plagued with the same questions until the doctor arrived. But she had been able to come up with not one answer when, sitting up in bed, she gave her full concentration to the questions the doctor was asking her.

Her answers, or so it appeared to her, were satisfactory, so she felt quite confident when, thanking him for his consultation, she added, 'I'll get the nurse to bring my clothes, then you can give this bed to someone who needs it m . . .'

'You're thinking of maybe going somewhere, young lady?' he asked, in a lovely burr of a Scottish accent.

'I'm—not?' she queried, taken slightly aback.

'You should be all right to leave tomorrow. I'll see you in the morning,' he replied and, clearly a busy man, he had disappeared through the curtain screens before she could make one word of protest.

With her prospect of going into work that day just gone up in smoke, although she supposed glumly that Lyon had in all probability let Mr Harrison know where she was, Kassia sighed at her fate. But she had to wait until the consultant's round was over and the nurse she had seen early that morning came to her before she could make any sort of protest.

'I thought I'd be going home as soon as the doctor had been,' she said gloomily, only then realising that she had read much too much in the nurse's noncommittal, 'We'll wait until the doctor comes,' when she had been questioning her about the length of her stay.

'Now why,' joked the nurse, 'is everyone in such a hurry to leave us?'

'I'm sorry,' Kassia apologised, 'but I feel so well,

it just seems crazy that I should occupy a hospital bed when . . .'

'It's not crazy at all,' the nurse told her gently. 'You had a nasty crack on the head, and as sometimes happens in cases like this, when the consultant knows there's no one at home to keep an eye on the patient, he just won't let the patient home until he's satisfied that all is as it should be.'

Kassia reckoned her head was not quite so sharp as it should have been, because it wasn't until after the nurse had waltzed away that she began to wonder—who was it who had told the consultant she lived alone? But for her visit from Lyon Mulholland that morning, she would have naturally assumed that Shaun Ottway had given that information to the nursing staff. But, on remembering Lyon's curt, 'We'll see about that!' Kassia could only wonder.

Why Lyon should go out of his way to contact the consultant to make sure she spent another night under observation in hospital she couldn't think. But, knowing him, the arrogant swine, she wouldn't put it past him!

Loving Lyon with all her being, Kassia nevertheless sent what hate vibes she could find in his direction. Interfering devil, why couldn't he mind his own business?

But, such indignant thoughts only serving to give her a headache, Kassia purposely set her mind in other channels. 'Is there a phone I can use?' she asked a nurse passing by the end of her bed.

An hour later Kassia was sitting out of bed, and having made her phone call she was once more starting to feel like someone in charge of her own life. Since her stay in hospital was likely to be of a brief duration, she saw no point in ringing her parents to let them know where she was. It would only worry them, and—if Lyon Mulholland didn't put his interfering oar in again—she should be out of hospital again shortly after the doctor's rounds tomorrow.

Emma, when she had spoken to her, had been every bit the super friend she had been until their ways had parted when she had started to go steady with Adam Pearce.

'What are you doing there?' she had asked, alarmed, when Kassia had told her where she was.

'It's nothing serious,' Kassia had assured her quickly, and had given a brief outline of how her dinner date the night before had ended. 'The thing is,' she went on, 'I'm in here without a rag to my back except the things I went out to dinner in. They should be letting me out tomorrow, but . . .'

'Say no more.' Emma got the picture straight away. 'Have a list ready and I'll pop in for it and your door-key in my lunch hour. I'll bring your gear in the first chance I have.'

True to her word, Emma called at the hospital at the start of that lunch hour, and she had such an inner glow about her that Kassia just had to comment, 'You look—super,' was the only word that sprang to mind, and had nothing to do with the clothes Emma wore, because she always looked smart.

'Adam loves me,' Emma whispered, and went off to collect—above all—the nightdress which Kassia couldn't wait for her to bring her, leaving Kassia with a lot more thinking to do.

Would she wear that inner glow if Lyon loved her? Pigs would fly before he did, she thought on a sigh, and realised, as she had some time ago, that they did not come much more complex than the man she had fallen in love with. What on earth had made him come to the hospital to see her that morning?

Her thoughts were still with Lyon when, in the middle of the afternoon, a beautiful cellophane-wrapped bouquet of flowers was brought to her bed. 'Somebody cares,' the trainee nurse who handed them to her grinned, and just the thought that Lyon might care was enough to have the colour flush to Kassia's face and for her heart to start hurrying fit to beat the band.

She hit the ground with a bump, and she was overwhelmingly aware of what an idiot she was being when she read the card that had come with the flowers. They were not from Lyon, and she wanted him to be in love with her, and he wasn't, and—she wanted to cry.

A moment later she had got herself under control and she was dry-eyed when she read the card again. 'Don't hate me,' it read, and was signed, 'Love, Shaun.' Kassia thought it was time she made another phone call. She knew the number of Insull Engineering without having to look it up.

From what she had been able to make out, it seemed that the accident which had landed her in hospital had been none of Shaun's fault. But, as she stabbed out the telephone number, she only then realised that Shaun, with that sense of responsibility she had observed in him, could be suffering all sorts of guilty feelings.

'Shaun!' she said brightly when she was ultimately put through to him, 'it's Kassia. I'm ringing to thank you for the lovely flowers!'

'Kassia!' he exclaimed, and for a second or two he seemed quite incapable of accepting that she was actually ringing him. 'Where are you phoning from?' he wanted to know.

'From the hospital.'

'How are you? Are you all right? What do the doctors say?' he shot the cannon-ball questions at her, proving to Kassia that he and his conscience had been having a terrible time of it.

'I'm fine. Perfectly all right,' she assured him, and in the face of the anxiety he had been through, and just in case he knew a little about medicine and had heard that one only normally stayed in hospital for twenty-four hours after a concussion. 'They're letting me out tonight,' she lied cheerfully, so he should not worry any more.

'I was coming to see you tonight,' he replied, swallowing her lie hook, line and sinker, but causing her to have to be more inventive when he re-thought his intended hospital visit, and suggested, 'Shall I come to your flat to see you?'

'Er—no,' she put him off, and knew her head was back in operation when the lie came tripping off her tongue. 'I won't be there—I'm going to stay with friends for a few days.'

She came away from the phone having eased Shaun's conscience a great deal, at the expense of her own. Though the fact that she had lied to him did not worry her all that deeply. For, having refused his suggestion that he visited her at home, she'd had to follow on with another lie if he was to believe the first one.

Having been so busy making up fibs, though, Kassia had entirely lost sight of the question she had been going to ask him—had it been he who had told the hospital authorities she lived alone?

Emma arrived with her long-awaited change of

nightwear when she had finished her stint at her office that day. 'You love!' Kassia thanked her gratefully, and could barely wait for Emma to draw the curtains around her bed before she was disposing of her hospital-issue garment and shrugging into her own cotton nightdress.

'I'll put these in here,' Emma told her, as she bent over to the bedside cabinet to stow away toiletries, underwear, slippers, shoes and top clothes inside. She straightened to place Kassia's dressing-gown over the end of her bed, remarking, 'I guessed you might prefer to face the outside daylight in trousers and a sweater rather than the togs you went out to dinner in.'

'You are thoughtful,' Kassia told her, not having given any consideration to what she would be going home in.

'All part of the service,' Emma grinned. 'Now, are you sure you've got all you need?'

'Positive,' Kassia answered, and could not thank her enough.

Kassia thought her visitors for the day were over when Emma departed to go and get ready for her date that evening with Adam. But, having borrowed a paperback in which to bury her nose while the rest of the ward were having visitors, she had just got hooked into the plot when someone came and halted by the side of her bed.

In that initial second of her head jerking from her book she instinctively knew—maybe because her first thoughts just lately were always of Lyon—that it was him. This time, as her gaze travelled up the long length of her male visitor, Kassia's instincts were proved right. It was Lyon!

Her book fell to the coverlet and, stuck for words

when his grey eyes scrutinised her face, she looked from him, her gaze lighting on the chair which Emma had previously used.

'Take a seat,' she invited casually. 'I'm straining my neck.'

'Hurt anywhere else?' he enquired, and sounded as casual as she, although, as he took the seat she had indicated, Kassia thought that there was still an alert look in the grey eyes that raked her and that missed nothing.

'Not an ache or a pain anywhere,' she told him. If her heart was aching because of him, if her heart was beating like an express train because of him, then he would never know it.

But, as his casual tone had implied, Lyon was not particularly interested in how she was feeling. Showing that she had been right when she had once thought that his eyes had missed nothing, he was suddenly saying, in an accusatory manner, she thought, 'Who's been to see you?'

Cheeky devil! But, sidetracked as she was by his gall, it took a moment or two before the fire and energy which he had always been able to bring easily to the surface was there again.

'Who says anyone's been to see me?' she snapped then, but she was suddenly confused again. Because, as if he was all at once aware of their surroundings, and in that awareness had reminded himself that she was a hospital patient, Lyon lost his aggressive attitude. Stretching out a hand, he touched the short cotton sleeve of her nightdress. And if the fleeting touch of his fingers as they brushed her skin was not enough to weaken her defences, then Kassia had the hardest work to keep herself all of a piece when, with a trace of amusement, he enquired, 'Where did the little Dior number of this morning get to?'

His tag for her hospital-issue nightshirt found her sense of humour, which rose up to again meet his. 'I rang my friend Emma,' she told him, and could not hold down the smile that bubbled to the surface. 'Emma called for my door-key and popped to my flat to get me a few things.'

Lyon had a smile on his face too as, glancing at the floral arrangement which now stood on her bedside locker, he asked, 'Did Emma bring the flowers too?'

'Actually, no,' Kassia told him, but she did not get around to telling him who her flowers were from, because just then he spotted the card that had come with them lying on top of the locker. Without a by your leave, he picked it up.

Stupid though she knew herself to be, Kassia wanted this moment of smiling good humour with him to continue. But, when every vestige of good humour left him as he read his other employee's card, so Kassia knew, without knowing why, that Lyon had taken exception to Shaun sending her flowers. Her heart lifted briefly when the ridiculous notion touched down that Lyon might be jealous. But he soon put an end to all such idiotic notions when he asked bluntly, 'Was Ottway sober when you were knocked unconscious last night?'

'Yes, he was,' she answered equally bluntly, as she hid her bruised feelings that it wasn't jealousy Lyon was showing, but pure and simple displeasure that one of his staff should be drunk behind the wheel of a car.

'You remember that much, do you?' he questioned grittily, clearly not in the best of humours.

Kassia had not recovered any memory of leaving the restaurant they had dined in, and could not even recall being in the car park afterwards. But even so, she might have said more in Shaun's defence, only at that precise moment, her attention to detail woke up.

'How do you know I was out with Shaun Ottway last night, anyway?' she asked as the thought struck her. 'Did the hospital tell you?' she asked when he did not answer straight away. And when Lyon still delayed, all at once a question of early that morning was again in her head. 'And how,' she asked in a rush, 'did you know I was here?'

'There's no particular mystery,' Lyon shrugged coolly. 'Gordon Harrison was in the middle of taking a call from Ottway when I dropped by this morning.'

'Shaun was ringing to tell him that I wouldn't be in today?' Kassia queried.

'Something like that,' he replied without much interest. He went on to kill any last lingering hopes in her heart stone-dead, however, when he cleared up the reason for his visits to her by telling her, 'When Gordon started to show anxiety that you were hospitalised and miles away from your family, I told him that since I had business this way, I'd look in on you.'

'Er—thank you,' Kassia said primly, and because being in love had made her vulnerable and wide open to all sorts of hurt—hurt which Lyon must not see—she dragged up a smile from somewhere, and added, 'But he mustn't worry. Though I'll be able to tell him that for myself when I see him on Tuesday.'

Lyon was not smiling and his charm was very

much absent when he grunted, 'Why break your neck to get back to the office?' And, throwing her into a panic, 'What's the big attraction?' he challenged disagreeably.

Her panic that he might think *he* was the pull almost made her snap something to the effect that it wasn't him, so he need think not that it was. By the skin of her teeth she realised in time that such a response might be a giveaway. Which left her with only one thing to do. Instead of making such a retort, she opted to attack his disgruntled manner. 'With an employer of such charm,' she said, a shade waspishly, she had to own, 'who could bear to stay away?'

Lyon's charming and unexpected, and perhaps slightly ashamed grin at her tart reply had Kassia ready to melt. Fortunately though, before she could go to pieces altogether, he took a glance at his watch and, killing her with her thoughts that he must have a date, he remarked, 'Quite obviously you're improving,' and departed.

Having slept quite a bit that day, Kassia was awake on and off all through that night. With Lyon in possession of her heart, she began to accept that he would be there in her head the moment she drifted up from sleep. Jealousy that he had been on his way to see some female vied with a warm feeling inside her, though. Because even if it was only for Mr Harrison's peace of mind, and even if he did have business in the area, Lyon need not have bothered to call and see her—but he had.

In one of her waking bouts Kassia recalled her panic that, if she was not careful, Lyon might learn that the big attraction at Mulholland Incorporated was Mr Lyon Mulholland himself. Being in love had

made more than a fibber of her, she suddenly
realised. For, whenever she had considered
resigning from her job, and that had been frequently
of late, she had always used Mr Harrison as an
excuse for not doing so. But, she realised, they
didn't come any cleverer than her when it came to
self-deception! Because, although she was very
much aware that Mr Harrison should be spared any
upset he could be spared at this stage in his recovery,
most of her reason for staying on at Mulholland
Incorporated was Lyon. Even though there was
every chance that an age might go by without her
ever catching a glimpse of him, Kassia realised as
she lay in her hospital bed that she had been giving
in to a need to be near to where Lyon was.

To her great relief, the consultant had no
objection to her being discharged when he saw her
on Friday morning. 'No headache, no nausea?' he
queried, after having given her the once-over.

'None at all,' she answered smartly.

'Good, good,' he murmured, and turned to the
attending ward sister to tell her that Miss Finn could
leave. Kassia was out of bed and taking her clothes
out of her bedside locker the moment he had gone
through the screens. She was shrugging out of her
nightdress and getting into underwear and trousers
and sweater before he had left the ward.

'I've heard of keen!' muttered the nurse who
found Kassia dressed and sitting in a chair by her
bed when she pulled the screens back. Then she gave
her a few instructions on what to do if this happened
or that happened, and Kassia was free to go.

'Isn't anyone calling to take you home?' the ward
sister asked when Kassia, having thanked the
nursing staff for their care, went to thank the ward

sister also on her way out.

'Oh, I can easily get a taxi,' Kassia told her confidently, and, because there were a few bits of shopping that she wanted to do on her way back to her flat, she declined the sister's offer to ring for a taxi for her, and thanked her for her care.

With the nightwear and toiletries Emma had brought her and the things she had worn to dine with Shaun Ottway all neatly folded in the plastic bag she carried, Kassia walked along unfamiliar corridors. She did not wish to seem ungrateful, but as she reached the main exit and entrance to the hospital, she could not help but be glad that her short stay was over.

Her hand went down to the door-handle, and she pulled back the door and was ready to go down the concrete steps when abruptly she halted. For there, approaching the steps, was—Lyon!

She was not sure that her jaw did not fall open as she saw him there, but her legs suddenly felt sufficiently weak to cause her to grip hard on to the iron step rail. 'Another minute,' she managed lightly, 'and you'd have been visiting an empty bed.'

'I haven't come visiting,' Lyon replied, his long legs making short work of the steps as he joined her at the top, 'I've come to give you a lift.' With that, he placed a hand beneath her elbow and escorted her down the steps.

Winded as much by the fact that it looked as if Lyon had come especially to take her home as she was to see him there, Kassia was at the bottom of the steps without knowing it. Lyon still had his hand beneath her elbow and was urging her towards where she assumed he must have parked his car when suddenly she stopped stock-still.

'That's very kind of you, Lyon,' she thanked him prettily, 'but I've a few bits of shopping to do before I go back to my flat. I can . . .' She had been about to tell him, as she had told the ward sister, that she could easily get a taxi, but she did not get the chance.

'I'm sure your parents will provide you with everything you need,' he cut her off.

'M-my—p-parents!' she stammered, staring at him with huge green eyes.

'That's where I'm taking you,' he said evenly.

'But—my parents live in Herefordshire!' she reminded him, utterly flabbergasted.

'I know,' he replied, to show that he wasn't suffering from a sudden attack of amnesia.

'But—but . . .' Lyon's taking the plastic bag out of her hand as he endeavoured to propel her in the direction he wanted her to go brought Kassia some way out of her amazement that he was fully prepared to drive her to Herefordshire! 'I'm not going . . .' was as far as her protest got, before bluntly, and regardless of the people having to walk round them as they blocked the direct route to the steps, he stated,

'Knowing the kind of loyalty you have, Kassia Finn, I cannot see you coming from parents who would be anything other than appalled at the thought of you leaving hospital to go straight home to an empty flat.'

He could not have said anything truer, but that was beside the point. 'Well, since they know nothing about my hospitalisation, they . . .'

'You didn't let them know?'

'It seemed pointless to worry them unnecess . . .'

'So I'm right! They *will* worry about you if . . .'

'Naturally!' Kassia told him sharply, wanting to kick herself for slipping up and letting him know that her parents were normal, caring parents. 'But,' she went on stormily, 'since they don't know . . .'

'They will when I tell them,' Lyon said toughly.

'You don't . . .' she broke off, realising the uselessness of telling him that he didn't know her parents' full address or phone number. A man like him would have no difficulty in finding out. 'It's not convenient for me to go there . . .' she protested, feeling she was being blackmailed into doing what he wanted, and not liking it the least little bit.

'Why?'

'Because . . . Because my parents are getting ready to go to—to China,' she told him truthfully.

But she knew he thought she had just made that up when, with amusement lurking around his mouth, he muttered, 'Well, we mustn't do anything to put a stop to that.' His face was deadly serious, though, when, fixing his grey eyes on her fiery green ones, he said, 'I could always take you to Kingswood, I suppose.' And while those words were creating the most tremendous clamour inside her, he added the totally deflating, 'Mrs Wilson would look after you . . .'

Vulnerable to him, Kassia was hurt that he thought he could take her to Kingswood and dump her for his housekeeper to look after. 'If you must take me anywhere,' she cut in snappily, 'then I'll go to Herefordshire!'

She was seated beside him in his car and they were on their way to her parents' home before she faced how instantly upside down Lyon could make her world. Addled-brained wasn't in it! For when there was a question there which had just shrieked to be asked, she had been too stupid to think of it—why should he think *he* had to take her anywhere?

CHAPTER EIGHT

KASSIA was still wondering why Lyon should think he had to take her anywhere when they drove into the county of Herefordshire. Yet there had been plenty of time to ask him. It wasn't even as though the whole of the journey had been taken up with other conversation, she mused, because once she had complied with his plans, Lyon had little more to say to her.

She had at one stage enquired if it was he who had told the powers that be that she lived alone. His tough-sounding, 'Was it supposed to be a secret?' had left her knowing it had been him, and also that he did not care to have his actions questioned.

'Turn off this road, and take a right fork there,' she broke away from her thoughts to tell him. She had no space for her private thoughts after that, because they were nearing her old home and she was fully occupied with giving him directions.

'What are you doing here?' her mother gasped in surprise when she saw her daughter, whom she had supposed to be at her secretarial work miles away in London.

'Hello, Mum,' Kassia greeted her trim and shapely mother, giving her a kiss and a hug. 'Sorry I didn't let you know I was coming, but—I—sort of made my mind up on the spur of the moment.' She avoided Lyon's eyes, and looking at her mother, introduced him as Lyon Mulholland, her employer.

'Lyon, my mother,' she completed the introduction, his first name tripping off her tongue now.

'Come along in,' her mother invited as the two shook hands.

Kassia went first into the house as Paula Finn held the door open. But a glance at her mother's suddenly deadpan expression told her that her parent was remembering that this was the man who had once had the audacity to dismiss her daughter, and who was the man whom that said daughter had once told to stuff his job.

'My—you did make your mind up on the spur of the moment!' Paula Finn exclaimed when, in the pleasant and cosy sitting-room she noticed that Kassia's usual weekend case had been replaced by a plastic carrier.

Kassia had hoped that if she did decide to tell her parents about her brief stay in hospital, that she could pick her moment and perhaps inject a little humour into the telling. But, although the moment was not right, and when her father—with his super sense of humour which could find something comic at the worst of times—was not at home but was at work, she discovered that Lyon was taking the right of decision from her.

'Kassia didn't go back to her flat,' he was telling her mother before she could stop him. 'We came on here straight from the hospital.'

'Hospital!' Inwardly Kassia groaned. Her mother's deadpan expression was a thing of the past. 'What . . .'

'There's nothing to worry about,' Kassia told her quickly. 'I had a spot of concussion and . . .'

'Concussion!'

'It was nothing really . . .' Ten minutes later,

Kassia had told her mother all that there was to tell, and she ended, 'So you see, I'm perfectly fine, and . . .' she threw a hostile glance at the chairman of the company for which she worked '. . . and Lyon should never have told you I'd been in . . .'

'Of course he should!' her mother replied sharply. And, just as though she had started to suspect that her daughter might have returned to London without ever having revealed anything about the accident, she ignored her, and addressed Lyon, to tell him, 'I can't tell you how grateful I am, Mr Mulholland, that you did what you did.'

Mulishly Kassia wanted to remind her mother that she hadn't said that when she had told her that he'd dismissed her. Fed up with the way the conversation was going, she opted out while Lyon—with some charm—asked her mother to use his first name, and her mother heaped more thanks on him for collecting her daughter from the hospital and for bringing her to them for them to look after.

Kassia was of the opinion that she was more than capable of looking after herself, but she had to admit to suddenly feeling considerably mixed up. Because, while she was quite disliking Lyon Mulholland, she experienced a definite pang of disappointment when, after refusing her mother's offer of refreshment, he said that he had to be on his way.

'Don't be in any hurry to get back to the office, Kassia,' he addressed her directly as he prepared to depart.

'I won't,' she said woodenly, if politely in front of her mother.

'We won't let her come back to work until she's fully fit,' Paula Finn assured him, and as she shook hands with him she unknowingly flushed Kassia's sense of humour out of hiding when she drolly added, 'Which, since her father and I are off to China the week after next, had better be before then.'

Lyon had not believed her when she had told him that her parents were getting ready to go to China, Kassia immediately recalled, and she knew, as his eyes left her mother and fixed on hers, that he also had recalled it. Had recalled it and, from the way his eyes were twinkling, had had his sense of humour stirred too.

Oh, Lyon, she thought, and when her mother stepped back and left it to her to see her employer out, Kassia went to the front door with him, her heart filled with her love for him.

There was humour still about his eyes and his mouth at the amusement they shared when, at the door, they stopped and faced each other. Suddenly, though, that amusement was going from Lyon, and suddenly too, as if involuntarily, his head was coming nearer.

His gentle kiss whispered down on the side of her face. It was a brief kiss, a kiss of gossamer lightness, and Kassia could almost imagine that it had never happened. But it had happened, and her face was as serious as his when, straightening, he looked into her eyes.

''Bye, you,' he said gruffly.

''Bye, yourself,' Kassia answered chokily, and when he had gone, she had to stay in the hall for a minute or two to compose herself.

'Now,' said her mother as soon as she returned to the sitting room, 'I didn't want to make a fuss while Mr Mulholland was here, but you must now go up to bed and . . .'

'Mother!' Kassia exclaimed. 'I'm twenty-two years old!'

Half an hour later Mrs Finn had settled for Kassia occupying the sitting-room sofa, but she insisted on having her way in that her daughter must have a blanket over her legs.

'What's the matter with you?' her father asked when he came home from work.

'Nothing at all,' Kassia replied, and to prove it, she smartly left the sofa and went to give him a hug.

In bed that night she relived the moment of Lyon's whispered kiss on the side of her face, and again she wondered why she had not asked him why he should think he had to take her anywhere. Had it been because she was afraid that his answer might be simply that he had been persuaded by Mr Harrison that someone should attend to her welfare?

Was she being stupidly crazy to not want to believe what she had at one time been convinced was the truth—that Lyon did not care for her? Her mother hadn't thought it out of the way at all that a man as busy as he should take the time and trouble to drive her from London to a place where she would be cared for. 'What a pleasant man!' she had exclaimed shortly after she had her settled on the sofa. She had then ignored the fact that he had once dismissed her daughter, and had recalled instead how Kassia had told her that he had the welfare of his staff so much at heart that he had personally gone to see Mr Harrison when he had been ill and away from work.

Kassia turned over in her bed and rejected the idea that Lyon had only brought her to her parents' home out of some concern for the welfare of a member of his staff. She couldn't remember word for word what she'd told her mother in relation to Lyon visiting Mr Harrison, but she could remember that he'd had a special reason for going to see him: to try to establish the true facts about that tender that had gone astray.

Her thoughts started to grow confused as tiredness descended. Surely his threatening to take her to Kingswood for Mrs Wilson to look after if she wouldn't allow him to drive her to her parents had to mean something? Kassia fell asleep on the desperate hope that since she couldn't see him threatening to take every ailing member of staff into his home to be cared for by his housekeeper, then surely that had to mean he cared for her a little.

On Saturday her parents drove her the short way to the next village, where Kassia received more cosseting, this time from her grandparents. Which made her guilt-ridden that, when everyone was being so absolutely marvellous to her, her heart longed to be at Kingswood.

On Sunday her parents mooted that they take her for a 'nice' drive.

'Actually, I was thinking about going to London today,' Kassia ventured.

'I rather think, actually,' teased her father, 'that your mother might have something to say about that.' Which she did.

'I'm fine, Mum, honestly,' Kassia assured her, when her mother drove her to Hereford railway station on Monday.

'You're sure, now?' Paula Finn asked, having doubtfully given in to her daughter's assurances that she felt as 'fit as a fiddle', and her opinion that she really should show up at the office on Tuesday to give Mr Harrison a hand.

'Quite sure!' Kassia told her, and she changed the subject by adding, 'I'll be home at the weekend anyway to say cheerio to you before you and Dad go on your silver wedding trip.'

Kassia was up early on Tuesday morning, and she was eager to get to work. 'Are you fit enough to be here?' Mr Harrison wanted to know when she went in first to see him.

'It was only a slight concussion,' she told him, and had nothing more exciting happen to her that day than having to fend off Tony Rawlings' overtures and take some time out when answering Shaun Ottway's early telephone call. She ended the call having assured him that she was as good as new, and no, she didn't hold the accident against him, and yes, she would go out with him again, but not just yet, because she had several things on.

During her lunch hour on Wednesday she shopped for a silver wedding present for her parents. She did the same on Thursday lunch time, and eventually decided on an antique silver paper-knife which they could both use.

The purchase had pleased her, but still Kassia could not help but feel downcast as she returned to her office. She had been hopeful when she went into work on Tuesday that maybe, if Lyon was still calling in to see how Mr Harrison was faring, he might stop by her desk for a word or two. Yet not so much as a glimpse had she caught of him.

She had dressed with the same attention this morning too, she thought unhappily, as she sat at her desk and took out some work. But again, not so much as a glimpse of him had she seen.

So much for her crazy notion that he must care a little to have done what he had done, to have kissed her in that—lovely—way he had done, when he had said goodbye to her at her parents' home. If he cared even the tiniest iota, she thought glumly, the least he would have done would be to pop his head around the door and ask how she was. Mr Harrison had, Tony Rawlings had, and Shaun had been on the phone before she'd had the cover off her typewriter.

Kassia was busily checking the last of some figures which Mr Harrison had wanted double-checking, unaware that her attention had drifted and that she was staring into space. Gloomily she had just come to the realisation that any caring she had thought that Lyon might have for her must be solely in her imagination, when suddenly Mr Harrison broke into her thoughts and, in consequence, suddenly brightened her whole day.

'I don't want to hurry you, Kassia,' he said teasingly, 'but I should rather like to have those figures ready should our chairman request them when he returns to business tomorrow.'

Kassia took a second or two in which to cover her elation that, by the sound of it, Lyon had not been able to seek her out that week because he had not been in the building. 'Hmm . . . Friday seems a funny day for Mr Mulholland to return from holiday,' she fished.

'He's not been on holiday.' Mr Harrison pleasingly took the bait. 'He's been tied up with one of our other companies.'

Kassia dressed with a good deal of care again the next morning. She went to her office with an expectant air about her, but not knowing quite what she was expecting. She knew that she faced every prospect of going home without ever once having clapped her eyes on Lyon, but she could do nothing to stamp out the hope in her heart as she entered the Mulholland Incorporated building.

Over the next hour her heart jumped into her mouth each time the outer door opened or the telephone rang. At ten-fifteen Kassia, realising that she was going to be a nervous wreck at the end of the day if she carried on like this, tried to get herself under control. But she jumped again when a little while later the phone on her desk rang once more.

'Mr Harrison's secretary,' she said as coolly as she could down the phone, and suddenly she was clutching at the instrument as though it was a lifeline.

'I take it you're well again or you wouldn't be here?' said a well-remembered voice, his tones, though, no warmer than hers had been.

'I'm—fine,' she told Lyon evenly, and disappointedly she guessed, when he had nothing else to say, that he was waiting for her to put him through to Mr Harrison. 'I'm afraid Mr Harrison doesn't work on Fridays yet,' she coolly reminded him as she realised that Lyon must have forgotten that his contracts manager was only doing part-time duties for the time being.

'It isn't Gordon Harrison I'm—interested—in.' Lyon let her know that he had forgotten nothing as he set her straight and made her heart further accelerate at his deliberate choice of the word 'interested', even if his cool tone denied that he had any interest in her whatsoever. 'I'd like to see you in my office,' he commanded. Quietly, the phone went dead.

Kassia was a person who rarely, if ever, flapped. But for the first twenty seconds after Lyon's phone call she did just that. She left her chair, and sat down again. She got up and went to the other door and then returned to her desk for her handbag. With her bag in her hand she went to the door again. But, when she realised that she didn't know if she was going to go straight up to the top floor or to the cloakroom first to check her appearance, she took herself back to her desk again and sat down.

Taking a deep breath, she extracted the small mirror from her handbag and checked her hair. Then, fearing that someone might come in and delay her, she stowed away her bag and, leaving her office, she made for the lift.

She tried not to think at all as the lift took her up to the top floor, but she kept remembering Lyon's whisper of a kiss, his use of the word 'interested', and she just could not think that perhaps he had only summoned her to his office in order to hand back to her the figures which she had typed out yesterday.

Leaving the lift, she stepped along the carpet-covered corridor, telling herself that if Lyon kept her waiting as he had that other time then she could forget entirely the notion that he cared for her at all.

'Mr Mulholland wanted to see me,' she told Heather Stanley as she went in, and she actually got a smile from the severe-looking secretary when she replied,

'You can go straight in.'

Conversely, Kassia wanted a moment or two in which to collect herself, but with Heather Stanley's eyes on her she had no chance to do anything but thank her, and proceed towards Lyon's office door.

The room was as she remembered it, the same large settees, the same easy chairs and the same over-large desk. It was from behind the desk that Lyon rose when she went in. Kassia's legs felt decidedly wobbly as she crossed over the carpet, and she tried desperately to find an even tone from a suddenly dry throat.

'You—asked me to come up,' she reminded him when for what seemed an age he just stood and looked at her.

Then suddenly he was coming round to the other side of the desk. Suddenly he was standing tall, stiff-backed, and suddenly, with a no-nonsense sort of look about him—which she found most off-putting—he was bluntly getting straight to the point.

'You once told me,' he in turn reminded her curtly, 'that you didn't want an affair.' Somewhat shaken, Kassia felt her eyes widen. 'Well,' he rapped, when she had nothing to say, 'does that still stand?'

'I'm—er—not quite with you,' she answered as confusion at his sharp tone mingled with bewilderment to know what he was getting at.

'Dammit, woman!' he exploded, clearly impatient with her. 'You're smarter than that!' And while, with a sensation of shock, Kassia thought she was gaining an inkling of what he was talking about, he went on bluntly, 'That knock on the head can't have numbed your brain so much that you haven't realised I have a need for you!'

'N-no,' she answered faintly. But suddenly she wanted to be miles and miles away. There had she been cosily thinking that Lyon had some feeling for her when, honest as ever, he was telling her in plain language not that he cared for her, but that he lusted after her! She did not want it to be so. And, more because she wanted to be sure she had understood him correctly than anything, she just had to question, 'You asked me up here to . . . So that . . .

in order to—proposition me?'

Far from looking like the lover which she had just asked him if he wanted to be, Lyon appeared more hostile than anything, she thought. 'Put it that way, if you must,' he said shortly.

'What other way is there?' she asked, the let-down part of her wanting to flee, the part of her that foolishly still lived in hope insisting that she stay. 'You want a—a mistress,' she went on, determined that she should not have misunderstood him, 'and I, if I haven't seriously incapacitated my brain, appear to have been elected.'

Lyon did not like her choice of words, she could see that from the way his jaw suddenly jutted forward. But he did not deny what she had said. After long moments of them facing each other across the office, more like adversaries than would-be lovers, he confirmed in the one word that it was just as she had stated. 'Well?'.

'You expect me to answer a—a thing like that, straight away?' she queried, seeing no sense in trying to pretend that he didn't affect her chemistry in a physical way. Especially when she was sure he had perfect recall of the way she had clung to him that night she had dined at Kingswood.

'You can't tell me now?' he gritted impatiently.

Any thrill which Kassia might have experienced at his eagerness to learn if he was going to have the pleasure of her in his bed was negated by just that very thought. Love she did not expect, but it wasn't even caring for her which motivated him! Purely and simply, Lyon lusted after her body. Though even while her head was telling her to give him a downright 'No', she couldn't do it. Not while she was aware that Lyon would not ask her a second time.

'No—I can't tell you now,' she replied woodenly.
'When?" he bit.

'I'll—ring you,' she said, and lest she should give him a firm yes or no without having first thought it over, she quickly left his office.

She spent a sleepless night realising that basically there should be nothing to think over. Lyon wanted her as his mistress, and she had never had it in mind to be any man's mistress. And yet—she had never been in love before, and she was finding that it was the hardest thing in the world not to snatch at whatever crumbs Lyon offered.

Kassia was over her initial disappointment when she drove down to Herefordshire on Saturday morning, just as she was over her confusion at the cold-blooded conversation she'd had with Lyon in his office. But she was no further forward in knowing what she should do. She had gone to his office expecting anything but what had taken place. Not that she had expected him to avow eternal love or anything like that, but it had been like having her hopes plunged into cold water to learn, with no trace of seduction, or any sign of an attempt to coax her to agree, but bluntly, coldly to learn that Lyon wanted a non-caring affair with her.

Kassia was well into Herefordshire when she asked herself just what she *had* expected? The answer to that, though, was simple. She just did not know. It was more hope that had ridden up with her in that lift, and suddenly she was thoroughly confused again, and too mixed up to even know what it was that she hoped for.

There was no clearing of her jumbled up thoughts and emotions for the rest of that day. Nor did she have very much chance for any private thinking of any depth. For once she reached her parents' home, it was all go.

'You're looking better than you did on Monday,' her mother declared when, after she'd given her a hug, she stood back to search her daughter's face. 'Though it strikes me that one or two early nights wouldn't do you any harm.'

'You know what it's like,' Kassia replied with a smile, hoping to convey that her tired eyes came from the constant partying that went on in London, and not from the insomnia that love had given her.

'Well, if you're fit enough to paint the town red, you're fit enough to go over to your grandmother's and wash and set her hair. Your father's decided to take us all out to dinner tonight, and when Nanna knew you'd be home she said she wouldn't bother going to the hairdresser's, and that you set it much better. Are you still going out with that Shaun boy?' she asked all in the same breath.

Because Paula and Robert Finn would be in the Far East on the actual date of their silver wedding day, the meal that night turned out to be a mini silver wedding dinner party. There were about a dozen or so close relatives seated around the table, and at the love that was there to be seen between her parents, between her grandparents, and between a couple of aunts and uncles, Kassia felt quite misty-eyed.

At the end of the dinner her father drove them home and Kassia said goodnight to her parents and went to bed having come to no decision about Lyon. Had he shown her a scrap of affection, of liking, of warmth even, when he had proposed that she be his mistress, then she thought she could more easily have decided what to do.

As it was, she slept badly, and as a result she woke late the following morning. In fact, she was still asleep when some sound in her room brought her awake to find her mother, looking young and girlish, standing by her bed, impatient for her to wake up.

'Come on, lazy-bones,' she said when Kassia opened one eye to find it was daylight. 'Your tea's going cold.'

'You've got a look on your face like the cat that's scoffed the cream,' Kassia replied as she struggled to sit up.

'Are you awake?'

'Yes,' Kassia answered, mystified as to what was coming.

'Properly awake?'

'Honest Injun,' Kassia told her.

'Then look!' Excitedly Paula Finn brought a hand from behind her back to show her the most gorgeous gold bangle.

'Where did you get this?' Kassia squealed, taking it from her and examining the exquisite workmanship.

'Your father! He gave it to me last night after you'd gone to bed,' her mother revealed. 'He was going to give it to me when we were in China, but he heard from someone that one has to declare one's jewellery as one goes into China so, rather than spoil the surprise then, he felt that everything was just right to surprise me last night.'

'Oh, Mum, it's beautiful!' Kassia said softly. And it was. Particularly beautiful was the simple inscription which her father had had engraved inside and which read, 'With my love, Robert.' And that said it all.

The whole relationship her parents had with each

other was beautiful, and, as her mother went happily content from her room, Kassia knew what perhaps she had known all along, that she was not going to have an affair with Lyon Mulholland.

Unable to stay in bed, she went and got bathed and dressed, her doubts and indecision at an end. She had wanted to believe that Lyon cared for her, but he didn't. Never would he give her anything that said 'With my love'. Saddened, she knew that it was like crying for the moon to want a relationship with him that came anywhere near to the loving relationship which her parents shared. What motivated Lyon was purely *physical*.

Suddenly Kassia had accepted—and it had nothing to do with her mother or her father and their special relationship, or anyone else but her—that Lyon did not care. Had he cared for her . . .

Hurrying downstairs, she knew she had made the right decision. She entered the sitting-room in a rush, and promptly she put a teasing smile on her face when she saw that her father was there. 'What's this I see you've been spending your pennies on?' she asked him.

'Amazing what you find in Christmas crackers,' he joked as he lowered the Sunday paper he was reading.

'It's beautiful, Dad,' Kassia told him sincerely, her teasing tone suddenly gone.

'Your mother likes it,' he answered quietly, and Kassia knew that that was all that mattered to him.

She gave them her gift of the antique silver paper-knife over lunch, and she was pleased and warmed that both her parents seemed to love it instantly. It was a happy meal time, but, unsure for how long she was going to be able to keep up the pretence of bubbling over with happiness herself, Kassia made noises about leaving shortly after lunch.

'Have the superest time,' she called cheerfully, as she put her car into first gear. 'Goodbye!' She grinned from ear to ear as she drove away.

Kassia kept a smile on her face until she turned round the corner of the short road where her parents lived, but once out of sight of them her smile faded. Soon too, thoughts of them faded. Soon, Lyon filled her head again.

Back in her flat, she dropped her car keys down upon the table and went to set the kettle to boil to make a pot of tea, and returned to her sitting-room.

The kettle boiled and switched itself off, but she did not make the tea. Her thoughts were elsewhere. Had Lyon spoken with any caring . . . Abruptly she turned her mind away from such thoughts. Though the very fact that he *had* spoken without any caring showed her quite plainly that he would not be waiting with bated breath to hear her decision.

Most likely he thought tomorrow morning, at work, would be about the time when he would get to know if he could expect her in his bed, she thought sourly, and suddenly she wanted it all over and done with.

Lyon's home phone number came readily to mind, though not until she heard the ringing tone did Kassia start to waver. She felt that Lyon had a pride that matched hers, which endorsed for her her belief that he would not ask her a second time.

Her own pride won the day when just at that moment the phone at the other end was picked up, and Lyon's voice said, 'Mulholland.'

She took a steadying breath. 'Hello, Lyon, it's Kassia,' she said, and when nothing but silence came back from the other end, she wished with all she had that he would say something. But, he said nothing. As if he knew that her only reason for ringing him was to give him his answer to his proposition, he left it to her. 'I've—come to a decision about . . .' her voice tailed off, but to her relief, Lyon, his voice even, if still not very loverlike, was there to prompt, 'Which is?'

Kassia had to take another steadying breath before she could end all chance of a personal relationship with him. Pride, which she had to live with, gave her a nudge. 'I'm—sorry,' she said quietly, and she still had the phone to her ear when the click as Lyon wordlessly put down his receiver told her that it was all over.

There was an inner dullness of spirit about her as she drove to work the following morning. Lyon was much on her mind as she parked her car and walked to her office. In candour, she had to admit she did not know if she hoped that he might continue to look in on Mr Harrison on Tuesdays and Thursday, or whether she would rather that she stood as little chance of seeing him as she had before Mr Harrison's illness.

She reached her desk and found some work while she waited for the mail to arrive from the post room. Trying hard to keep Lyon out of her thoughts, Kassia soon discovered the uselessness of that exercise. She was in the middle of re-living her telephone call to him yesterday and, she owned, experiencing the tenderest of feelings for him as she suddenly realised that his lack of answer yesterday had been his way of letting her have the last word, when one of the juniors from the post room sped in.

'Thank you, Maureen,' she smiled, but as

Maureen darted out again, she saw she had dropped off half of the correspondence for Tony Rawlings' department.

'I've got two tickets for . . .' Tony Rawlings called when through his open door he caught sight of her as she handed the wrongly delivered correspondence to his secretary.

'I haven't a free minute this week, Tony,' she told him.

'He never gives up,' his secretary laughed as Kassia made her escape.

Tony Rawlings was far from Kassia's mind as she went back to her own office. Lyon was back occupying her thoughts as she pulled a chair up to her desk. Ready to deal with the day's correspondence, she reached a hand forward, but, as she did so, suddenly, she froze. For during her absence someone, a messenger most likely, had been into her office, and there on the top of the pile she espied an envelope which had not been there before.

But what arrested Kassia more than anything else was that not only was the hand-delivered envelope addressed personally to her, but that it was addressed in a handwriting she would know anywhere! She had devoured the postcard which Lyon had once sent her too many times not to instantly recognise his handwriting the moment she saw it!

Her hand had begun to shake when Kassia moved to take up the envelope, and her mind was in a turmoil when, the envelope in her grasp, she tried to think why Lyon would write to her.

But, unable to glean so much as a glimmer of what the letter contained, she realised that there was only one way she was going to find out. Like a sleepwalker she slowly inserted her letter-opener inside the envelope and slit the edge. Then, with her heart drumming, she extracted the single sheet of paper and opened it out.

The only sound in the room in the following seconds was the strangled, disbelieving gasp that left her throat.

Stunned, unable to believe it, her eyes fell to where he had not hesitated to sign his name. She read through what he had written again, down to the bold black signature of Lyon Mulholland, and she could not credit it. She could just not credit that the man who had asked her to go to bed with him, the man who, not ten minutes ago, she had tenderly thought had let her have the last word, should have written what he had.

For, just to show who had the last word, the handwritten letter from the chairman of Mulholland Incorporated was a short and to-the-point missive—which terminated her employment forthwith!

CHAPTER NINE

WITH incredulous eyes Kassia read a third time the letter to which Lyon Mulholland had signed his name. And still she could not get over the fact that, with no excuse or reason given, he had told her that from this instant she was no longer in his employ!

Numbed by his totally unexpected, unfeeling action, she became some kind of automaton as she collected up her bits and pieces, stowed them in her handbag and left her office. In a dazed state, the words 'How could he?' revolving around and around in her brain, she made her way to the lift, and pressed the call button.

Like someone devoid of life, she stepped into the lift when it came, and, staggered still, she stretched out a hand with the intention of pressing the ground-floor button. Only just then, something violently awoke in her.

Suddenly the 'How could he?' which had been whirling around in her head became a wildly infuriated, 'How *could* he!' And, as her fury erupted, she hammered the button that would take the lift, not to the ground floor, but to the top floor of the building!

How *dare* he! she fumed as the lift carried her upwards. The treacherous, lecherous rat, she raged wildly as the lift doors opened. Storming out of the lift, she charged along to the office which she had been to three times before.

All the time she had been having loving, tender thoughts about him, he had been putting his pen to that insult: no bed, no job! My God, who the *hell* did he think he was?

More incensed by what Lyon had done with every step she took, Kassia reached the door to Heather Stanley's office and went storming in.

'W-wait!' Heather Stanley saw her intention too late. 'You can't . . .!'

But Kassia could; she was already thrusting the door to Lyon Mulholland's office open and, still without a break in her stride, she had marched in.

Two men were in the room when Kassia barged in, one seated either side of the over-large desk. But although she recognised Cedric Lennard as the director who had been with Lyon the first time she had come to the chairman's office, her business was not with him.

It took her barely seconds to steam across the plush carpeting, but Lyon had risen from his chair by the time she got there.

'You—*swine!*' she hissed at him in fury. 'You despicable rat!' she reviled him and, unfastening her bag, she took out the letter he had penned.

Her green eyes were sparking with fury as she began to tear his notice of instant dismissal to shreds. And she cared not that a shaken-looking Cedric Lennard had started to rise from his seat. By good fortune, Lyon had started to move too, and had come round his desk and was standing in perfect position to receive the torn-up pieces of his missive.

'Do you know what you can do with your job?' she said, her voice starting to rise as at the same time as she hurled the pieces in his face, and let go any small hold she had on her temper. 'You can *stuff* it!'

'Er—this, I think, is where I came in,' Cedric Lennard interjected, marginally taking the edge off her anger when she was reminded that he had been there that other time she had told Lyon that he could stuff his job.

'This,' Lyon replied mildly, 'is where you go out.'

Kassia's fury went further off the boil when, to her surprise, he caught hold of the director's arm, not hers, and escorted him, not her, to the door! Put off her stroke a little, she began to feel small darts of panic when, as he saw Cedric Lennard out, Lyon issued his orders to the hovering Heather Stanley.

'I don't want to be disturbed by anyone, or for anything,' he told her coolly, and purposefully he closed the door.

Kassia had not moved, but when he turned and she saw that his eyes held something of a very determined light, she reckoned that she had said more or less what she had come up to his office to say anyway.

She was on her way to the door and almost level with him when, tilting her chin a little higher, she remarked proudly in passing, 'And you can keep your reference too! I'll get by . . .' A small shriek of alarm left her as his hand shot out and he halted her mid-step.

Caught off balance, she fell against him, and as his other arm came round her to save her from falling, her heart began to pound erratically. Her breath caught in her throat, but, weakened by such close physical contact, she had to deny the fast beating of her heart. Hastily she pushed him away and broke his hold.

'In case I didn't make myself clear on the phone yesterday,' she snapped accusingly, 'I'm not interested in an affair with you.'

'You made yourself perfectly clear,' Lyon replied, cool in the face of her heated anger. 'And,' he went on, 'I couldn't be more pleased by your decision.'

'You're—pleased?' she echoed, and conversely she felt momentarily quite peeved that what he was saying amounted to exactly that—that he did not want an affair with her. But the contents of his letter were still fresh in her mind and she was not going to forget in a hurry what had prompted it. 'Like hell you're pleased!' she erupted waspishly, glad to feel a revival of her fury. 'You were so pleased that—when there's absolutely nothing wrong with my work—you turned—er—nasty, and couldn't wait to get to work this morning to . . .'

'Thanks!' Lyon cut in harshly. 'Your good opinion of me does you credit!'

'My stars!' Kassia batted back at him sharply, wondering at his nerve that *he* should be offended that she saw his action in dismissing her for what it was. 'You think I should be *flattered* to be thrown out of my job? Not that I'd work for you again,' she exploded angrily, 'if you paid me ten times the salary I'm getting . . . I *was* getting,' she corrected herself, and as her anger again started to wane, she forced herself to charge on, 'You expected my opinion of you to go up in leaps and bounds after this?' His reply had her ducking for cover.

'It depends,' Lyon answered, fixing her with a steady grey-eyed look, 'where your opinion of me was beforehand.'

Kassia was quick to kill any idea he might be nursing that she had any opinion of him at all. 'Wherever it was,' she shot at him tartly, 'it didn't have far to fall to reach rock-bottom.'

She heard the sharp intake of his breath, just as if her comments had caught him on the raw. But in his next breath he became angry too, and accused, 'You—lie!'

'Thanks!' she somehow found the wit to return his harshly offended exclamation, but she was inwardly panicking madly at the thought that his accusing her of lying must mean he had seen that she had some degree of feeling for him. 'I didn't come up here for a slanging match,' she borrowed some of his arrogance to tell him loftily.

She went quickly to the door, wishing she'd kept her mouth closed, because that was exactly why she had come up to his office. Though, if she had thought about it, she realised, it had been meant to be a one-sided slanging match with Lyon playing no part. That he had answered back wasn't fair! Nor was it fair that he reached the door before her and stood against it and—unless she wanted to try heaving him physically to one side—blocked her way out.

'So,' she said, nervously backing off, 'that's why you dismissed me, is it—because you think I'm a liar?'

'What I think, Kass,' Lyon replied evenly, 'is that you are feeling very unsure of the ground you're standing on right at this minute.'

Trying to hate him for seeing her nervousness, Kassia privately admitted that he was right. The fact that he had used that intimate-sounding shortened version of her name was not conducive to making the ground she stood on any firmer either.

'Huh!' she scoffed, deciding that there was nothing for it but to try and bluff it out. 'Apart from the uncertainty of where I'm going to work next, why should I be unsure of anything?'

Lyon did not move away from the door, but for long, level moments he just continued to stare at her. Then suddenly, and to her immense surprise, he answered quietly, 'Perhaps, my dear, because that's pretty much the way I'm feeling myself just at this moment.'

'You're . . .!' she attempted, but that beautiful-sounding 'my dear' which he had just uttered was getting in the way of her thinking. 'You're . . .' she tried again, and she made it this time, as she added, '. . . but you're always so supremely confident!'

'Maybe so, in business,' he agreed, his voice level still, 'and that was always so in my personal life too,' he added, but he paused and for an age he just stood and looked into her eyes as if trying to read what lay there, and then, very quietly, he said, 'and then, I met you.'

'Oh!' escaped from her faintly, and she struggled hard to get herself together, and to query, 'You mean—that . . . You're saying that, because you want—wanted—an affair with me and because I said no, you . . .' Abruptly, Kassia broke off. Suddenly, sparks were again flashing from her eyes. Because, although she still felt as if she was wading through a quagmire, she thought she saw some light—some disappointing light. 'Tough on you!' she went into battle again and, getting madder by the second, she was able to ignore Lyon's astonished look at the aggressive change in her. 'I don't suppose it's every day that the all-powerful Lyon Mulholland gets turned down, but you can stay as unsure as you like, the answer's *still* no!' With that she has to pause to take a breath. 'Now,' she resumed furiously, *'let me leave!'*

'You'll leave when I say so!' he snarled as his own temper started to fray. 'My God, what a fiery bundle of dynamite you are!' he bit, and, showing that even though his temper burnt on a longer fuse, he had more than enough aggression to match hers, he caught her by her upper arm and propelled her away from the door, pushing her none too gently on to one of the deep, wide settees in the room.

'You can proposition away from now until the return of the dodo,' Kassia had begun to yell, 'and I . . .' when Lyon bluntly cut in.

'In case *I* didn't make *myself* clear,' he chopped her off, 'I'll repeat, I no longer have any appetite for an affair with you.'

'Good!' she snapped, piqued in spite of herself, but not minded to have her nose rubbed in the dirt by him or anyone else. 'Now that we're both happy, I'll . . .'

Lyon's hand firmly prevented her from moving more than an inch or two in her attempt to get up and leave. 'If my suspicions are correct, you're no happier than I am,' he gritted, and as if that comment was not enough to alarm her, he further prevented her from going anywhere by joining her on the settee and effectively hemming her in.

Physically stuck where she was for the moment, Kassia was left to find what sarcasm she could to answer his charge. 'Of course I'm happy,' she said sweetly. 'It always makes me quite ecstatic to be thrown out of my job at a mom . . .'

'Dear God, will you shut up? This has nothing to do with your job!' Lyon roared, and while Kassia grew quite panicky again, he went on, 'If your job, your career, means so much to you, I'll see you have a career. But this, you being here with me, has nothing to do with work!'

'It—hasn't?' Kassia queried warily, her insides all knotted up. 'I thought,' she waded her way carefully through the quicksand, 'that I'd kind of come up to see you because I was annoyed about that letter you had delivered to me.'

'Which is exactly what I'd hoped you'd do,' Lyon replied, to her ears sounding every bit as cagey as she.

'I see,' she said, when in truth she didn't see anything at all. 'So,' she said, and had to play it by ear because suddenly she was in a total fog, 'you had that letter dismissing me delivered and—when it has nothing to do with the fact that you recently pro-positioned me—you hoped that, in response to that letter, I might come up to—er—see you about it.'

'You're—doing well,' Lyon murmured. When he remained cagey, though, and did not let her in on the rest of the mystery, Kassia could not stop herself from showing her exasperation.

'Wouldn't it have been much simpler,' she erupted astringently, 'for you to have picked up the phone and ordered me up here—as I remember, you're quite good at doing that.'

'It would have been simpler, much simpler,' he agreed. 'Only, to tell you the God's own truth . . .' He broke off and, oddly, he seemed to need to take a grip on himself. When he resumed, however, it was she who had to take the most severe grip on herself. For what he resumed to say was, '. . . you've got me in such a state, my dear, that I hardly know what the hell I'm doing any more.'

Starting to doubt her hearing, Kassia stared at him, her eyes growing large in her face. The darts of panic she felt were making her want to get up and run. Yet even when a myriad thoughts chased through her brain—among them, that Lyon might have seen that she cared for him and could be leading her up the garden path for his own lustful purposes—she made herself stay where she was. Rightly or wrongly, she just needed to hear more.

'I've—g-got you in a st-state?' she stammered.

He nodded, his eyes steady on hers as he confessed, 'I've been a stranger to myself, to the person I thought I was, just lately.'

'You—have?'

Again he nodded. 'And it's down to you, Kassia,' he told her.

Kassia swallowed a dry lump in her throat. 'It is?' she queried huskily.

'It is,' he answered. 'You, little hell-cat that you are, have affected me from our first meeting.'

'Oh . . .' she said carefully. 'You mean that first time you ordered me up here and . . .'

'And you told me then what I could do with my job.'

'You *had* dismissed me!' She thought she should set the record straight, although she was not inclined to mention that she was only there now because he had dismissed her for a second time.

'On balance, I rather think you beat me to it,' he replied, which reminded her that before he had told her she was dismissed, she had said she was being paid neither by him nor by Camberham's. 'You slammed out of my office that day in a fury,' he said, and went on to make her weak at the knees by adding, 'and for the next few days, while I was certain I had taken the only action possible, I kept being haunted by the memory of your truly beautiful mouth and smile.'

'Really?' she said faintly, having meant her voice to come out sounding only just this side of interested, but finding that it had come out sounding more like a croak . . .

'Really,' he agreed, and smiled as he said, 'Is it any wonder that I could bring your face instantly to mind when you rang me at home and said you had an interview arranged with Heritage Controls for the following day?'

'I—er—suppose not,' Kassia replied, and she felt as though she was treading on eggs when, as she remembered, she just had to say, 'B-but b-beautiful smile or not, that didn't stop you putting the boot in for me at Heritage Controls. I didn't even get as far as an interview!'

'Be honest, Kass,' Lyon said gently. 'You'd let me think it was you and not Gordon Harrison who'd put that tender in the wrong envelope. You could have done it deliberately, criminally, for all I knew, so what option did I have? What else should I do?'

Put like that, she had to quietly agree. 'Nothing, other than what you did do, I expect.' And, although it had never been her intention to apologise for anything when she had stormed into his office, she found herself saying, 'I'm—er—a bit sorry that I—er—called you a cretinous oaf.'

'Only a bit sorry?' he queried softly, and made her heart pound when he tacked on, 'When I'd made a point of being there at the same time as you?' Kassia could find no answer, and he let her off the hook and instead referred to what else she had shouted at him at that meeting. 'I can only be glad you—hmm—suggested that I should get my facts straight.'

'It was good of you to bother,' she heard her own

voice say, and suddenly she realised she had better get her act together or she'd be in danger of agreeing to any and everything Lyon asked of her.

'You were forceful in your suggestion,' he reminded her, the most fascinating upward curve appearing on his mouth.

Hastily Kassia dragged her eyes away. Lyon was being rather nice to her, and he had said several things which had made her heart beat much more energetically than was normal. But although he had said that her being there in his office with him had nothing to do with her job—or her lack of a job—he had also said he no longer had any appetite for an affair. Which, if she accepted it, made her totally baffled to know not only why he had dismissed her, but also what in thunder was going on! She thought that perhaps she had better find out before his charm made her more confused than she already was.

'Yes, well . . .' she said a shade stiltedly. 'Although you saw to it that I didn't get the job at Heritage Controls, you saw to it that I *did* get the job at Insull Engineering. But . . .'

'Which made you again telephone me at home,' he put in before she could get up a full head of steam to ask him anything.

'You objected to my ringing you at home?' she queried, sidetracked and wondering if she had just been taken to task for daring to ring him at Kingswood.

'Not at all,' he denied swiftly, making her again fall immediately under the spell of his charm. 'I told you at the time that I'd missed hearing from you.'

'You were being sarcastic!' Kassia accused, her eyes shooting wide.

'Was I?' he countered, and she just didn't know

where she was any more. 'I might,' he conceded, 'have attempted to sound sarcastic because, God help me, I just didn't know what was happening to me.'

'You—er—didn't?' Kassia faltered. Instead of getting clear of the fog, she was finding that she was becoming more at a loss than ever!

Lyon shook his head. 'Perhaps I'd become jaded over the years. Bored, even, that life held no surprises any more. Then suddenly you erupted into my world, and life was taking on a new lustre. From that first telephone call, all at once it had a lot more sparkle.' Kassia was giving him rapt attention when he added, 'Is it any wonder that I shouldn't want our subsequent telephone conversation to end?'

'Honestly?' she queried, her eyes still wide on his.

'Honestly,' he replied seriously, and made her heart beat erratically again when he went on, 'When one week went by and then two without my hearing from you, I became irritated at the ridiculous notion that I should be lonely for the sound of your voice.'

'But you were—lonely for . . .' her voice tailed off and she could not finish the sentence.

'Most definitely, I was lonely for the sound of your voice,' Lyon did not hesitate to finish the sentence for her. 'But I was irritated by the notion, as I said, so I let most of another week go by before I took any action.'

'Wh-what action was that?' she asked, having meant to have asked several pertinent questions by now but somehow finding that her intentions were becoming continually diverted.

'I'd asked you to ring me when you got promotion,' he replied promptly, and added without so much as a blink, 'I thought it was about time you started to use your secretarial skills.'

'You . . .' Words failed her for a moment. 'You,'

she said again, and managed to add a more coherent, if astonished, 'You instigated my promotion! You *knew* I'd been promoted when I rang to tell you!'

'Forgive me, Kassia, but I did need to hear from you,' he murmured, sending her heart on another merry dance when he said, 'I then discovered, though, that to hear you was not enough. I discovered that I needed to see you. Which is why,' he confessed, 'armed with your address, I came looking for you.'

Never wanting to wake up if she was dreaming, Kassia let her thoughts fly back to that Saturday when Lyon had called at her flat. She had rung his home that day, she remembered, and had spoken to his housekeeper. Lyon had not been in, but, totally unexpectedly, he had called at her flat that night for the message which she had declined to leave with Mrs Wilson.

'You said you were passing,' she reminded him with the beginning of a smile of her face. 'You . . .' Abruptly she broke off, and her smile never made it. For winging painfully in just then came the bitter memory of an occasion when she had attempted to borrow that self-same phrase. Lyon had been away in Australasia and she, too, had known what it felt like to want to hear someone, to want to see them. But she had received a very different reception when, having driven near his home, she had been bold enough to ring his doorbell. As clear as if it was yesterday Kassia could recall the way she had stood there dumbstruck when Lyon himself had answered the door. But the use she had found for the borrowed 'I was just passing . . .' had not been appreciated. 'Urgh!' she said suddenly on an angry sound, and could not sit still another minute.

With more force than elegance, she pushed her way

away from Lyon's close nearness and the settee arm, and she had moved a good few yards across the carpet before Lyon, moving like lightning after her, caught her.

'What the . . .'

'Take your hands off me!' she shrieked, as she tried to dislodge the iron bands which were suddenly there on her arms to prevent her from going another step.

'What did I do? What did I say?' Lyon asked, looking perplexed. 'My God!' he bit, starting to look aggressive, 'did I say you were a hell-cat? That doesn't cover half . . .'

'What you said,' Kassia put in to cut him off, 'was sufficient to make me realise that you must think I'm stupid! There you were shooting me a line about how you needed to hear me, to see me, well . . .' She had to break off to take a fast pull of breath. But she was furious still, and growing more furious when she thought of how she had sat there like a dummy while he had played ducks and drakes with her heart-strings with every word he spoke. 'Well, all I can say,' she continued hotly, 'is that you might have needed to hear and to see me once, but absence soon cured that need, because you left me in no doubt when you saw me on your return from, Australasia—when you'd already been back in England for nine days,' she inserted vigorously, 'that if you never saw me again it would be a bonus!'

'Oh, Kass,' Lyon breathed softly, his aggression gone as quickly as it had come. 'I didn't want to hurt you. I half thought that I hadn't when you strolled away down the drive at Kingswood as if nothing I could say or do could touch you. But—I did hurt you, didn't I?'

He was still hurting her, and the hurt he inflicted

would last a long time yet, she knew that. But he was never going to know it, not from her. Though since his hands still had a tight hold on her, and since it did not look as though he was ready to let go of her in a hurry, she adopted a disdainful air, to tell him arrogantly, 'I'd very much appreciate it if you'd take your mauling hands off me, and allow . . .'

'I've explained myself badly,' he cut in, not a bit bruised by the terminology she had used for the way his hands gripped her.

'You,' she told him cuttingly, her nose high in the air, 'have explained nothing! Not,' she added quickly, and thereby ruining her high and mighty manner, 'that I'm interested in any explaining . . .' She was still trying to tell him how uninterested she was, when, as he had done before, Lyon moved her to the settee.

'If I haven't explained anything to you, my dear,' he said, his endearment and his gentle tone knocking a great hole in her determination not to listen to another word, 'then it can only be that—as I might have mentioned—you've got me in such a state that I hardly know what I'm doing. But I'd like, more than anything I've ever wanted, for you to stay to hear me out.'

Her head said no, that she had given him plenty of time. Then she remembered how once or twice she had meant to ask him a pertinent question or two, but how her questions had somehow got lost, and how she had not said what she had wanted to say. Perhaps, suggested her heart, she should yield—if only a tiny bit.

'Very well,' she said primly, and she said not another word until, Lyon, having seen to it that she was seated again, seemed at a loss to know where to begin. 'Why not,' she said frostily, as her soft heart sought to help him out, 'begin by explaining how—

when I'd received a postcard from you suggesting that we dine together when you got back—I should suddenly turn into a leper when you did get back.'

For long moments more, Lyon said nothing, but sat half turned, looking into her eyes. Then, on a long-drawn-out breath, he suddenly opened up. 'We'd said goodbye—that day before I took off for my Australasia tour. But my head was still full of you. So much so,' he confessed, 'that but for you thinking me a complete idiot, I would have telephoned just for the pleasure of talking to you.' It hadn't taken Kassia's heart long to ignore the common-sense logic of her head, and she was sitting quietly, tuned in to every word he spoke, as he added quietly, 'I needed to write that card. I needed to have a link when I came back, a reason to get in touch with you again.'

'But—you didn't get in touch with me again! You'd been back nine days when I . . .'

'I know,' Lyon said gently. 'Believe me, I was aware of every one of those days of being back in England and near to you again—just as I was aware that I must not contact you either.'

'Why, dare I ask?' she questioned, and received such an earth-shattering answer that for an age all she could do was to sit and stare at him.

'I knew I must not contact you again for the plain and simple reason,' he said, and paused to take a deep breath, 'that I knew I was in love with you.'

Kassia's mouth fell open. She closed it. But her breath was so taken away that she had to open it to take in some air. 'You—you're in—l-love with me?' she eventually managed to croak out the question.

'You've dominated my waking thoughts for weeks now,' Lyon did not hang back from telling her. 'But only when I was abroad did I acknowledge that this all-compelling emotion I feel for you is love. I've never known an emotion like it,' he went on—but Kassia halted him.

'You realised—acknowledged—that you were in l-love with me while you were abroad?' she queried.

'I did,' he stated firmly, and suddenly her confusion was total.

'Then why were you so—c-cold, so hostile to me when I called at Kingswood that Sunday?' she questioned, trying with all she had to stay on her guard because of the simple fact that she so desperately wanted to believe him.

'I had to be like that,' he told her, making no attempt to look away, 'or I *believed* I had to be like that, because you are so very dear to me that I was afraid of hurting you.'

If his explanation had been meant to clear her confusion, then Kassia felt deeper in the quagmire than ever. But she panicked as she realised that only if he knew *she* loved *him* could he realise that he had the power to hurt her, and so she made every effort to show just how little she loved him.

'What a peculiar way you have of going about things,' she drawled loftily, knowing full well that her condescending air would draw his arrogant fire straight away. But to her astonishment, Lyon did not treat her with his usual superior arrogance, but seemed to be agreeing with her!

'Peculiar, perhaps,' he concurred. 'Though, in my defence, I must say I didn't see that I could behave in any other way at the time.'

'Is—er—that a fact?' she murmured, praying for light, for help, from somewhere.

'I'm afraid so,' he said gently, and went on, 'I was thousands of miles away from you when I realised why

I ached so to be back in England. At first I was fairly incredulous at what had happened to me, but then, in the long weeks of being overseas that followed, I had all the time in the world to realise also that—if you were starting to care a little for me—and forgive me, my dear, but I thought that perhaps you were—then I stood only to hurt you.'

Instantly all Kassia's instincts of self-preservation united. Dearly did she want to believe Lyon when he said that he was in love with her, but as fear beset her that the whole of her being there with him might yet prove to be all part and parcel of some diabolical charade, she was more determined than ever to keep her guard up.

'Really?' she queried, only this time the word did not leave her faintly. This time, so as to disabuse him of any idea that she had ever remotely started to care for him, the word left her as though she was only marginally interested in any of what he said.

But again Lyon surprised her in that he did not take exception to her attitude. 'Try to understand how it was with me, Kassia,' he said instead. 'There was I, a man with ample confidence to tackle anything that comes in the line of business when, for the first time in my life, I'm in love. Without warning,' he continued, 'my supreme confidence has deserted me and, although shouldering responsibility has become second nature to me, suddenly I just couldn't bear to be responsible for extinguishing that inner light that shines in you.'

Kassia had to cough to clear her throat of a sudden constriction. She had never felt more vulnerable, and yet somehow, maybe because Lyon had put in a plea for her understanding, she felt that she wanted to encourage him, that she wanted him to tell her more, and to make her understand.

'How could . . .' she asked chokily. 'I mean . . .' She had to give it up. 'I'm trying hard to understand,' she told him helplessly, 'but I just—don't.'

'I'm not explaining this very well,' he agreed, and he seemed then to make something of a mammoth effort. It appeared when next he spoke that he had decided to go back to the start, for he began, 'I've known for years that I would never marry. In fact, so ingrained in me was it that to marry is something that has never entered my head over latter years.'

Feeling faintly stunned at his introduction of the subject of marriage, Kassia would very much have liked to have asked if the fact that he was discussing the subject at all meant that he had changed his mind about never marrying. But while feeling breathless and suddenly shy she was also feeling ten times more nervous than she had felt, and she was afraid to trust even her own intelligence. So that what in actual fact she did say, was a husky, 'I don't suppose that— marriage—is—er—right for everyone.'

'It certainly has never been right for the members of my family,' Lyon replied, as he feasted his eyes on her face. 'We have something of a track record for ending up in the divorce courts.'

'Your—parents, they're divorced, aren't they?' she asked, and added quickly, 'I don't mean to pry, but that time—when I came to dinner at Kingswood—and you . . .'

'And I acted like a bear with a sore head,' Lyon took over from her, and was side-tracked himself for a moment as he said, 'I should have realised that night, after a week of fighting against the pull of you, what was happening to me, but . . .'

'You fought against what was—er—happening to

you?' Kassia just could not resist asking.

'A lot of energy wasted,' he smiled. 'We'd dined together the previous Saturday and I'd stubbornly let a week pass when, checking my Australasian itinerary, all at once I knew I was desperate to see you again before I went away.'

'You rang me,' Kassia recalled, and was on the brink of going dreamy-eyed at his stated eagerness to see her, when she suddenly recalled something else. 'You didn't appear so desperate to see me from what I remember,' she told him, her tone cooling with every word. 'In fact, when I arrived you'd taken yourself off for a walk just as if you'd forgotten you had ever invited me.'

'Never!' Lyon replied forcefully, and he did send her dreamy-eyed when he said, 'You were taking so long to get to Kingswood that I grew agitated and angry at the number of times I looked at my watch. The only reason I took myself off for a walk,' he explained, 'was because I had to take some physical action or be a nervous wreck by the time you did get there.'

'Truly?' she sighed.

'Truly, my love,' he replied, and set her heart pounding when he following up with the question, 'You are my love, aren't you, dear Kass?'

'I . . .' she choked, and just did not know quite what he was asking, or quite what she should answer.

'Or am I being unfair?' he asked, and he seemed then to think that perhaps he was. For he did not insist that she should answer him, but went firmly back to that Saturday when, at his invitation, she had driven down to his home. 'I came across you half-way down the stairs absorbed by a portrait of my great-grandfather, and I thought you so beautiful,' he confessed. 'But if I could ignore the wild pounding I felt in my heart, then I could not ignore the fact that I grew more and more enchanted by you over that meal.'

Kassia had the hardest job not to swallow at what he had just said. But, while she didn't know where any of this was leading, she did know that, since Lyon was at pains to leave no stone unturned in what he was telling her, she by the same token, had to heed that part of her that would not be dishonest with him—not now.

'But,' she just had to chip in to remind him, 'you weren't so enchanted when, in your drawing-room, you told me I had assumed too much when I thought your parents were dead.'

'Oh, Kass,' Lyon said softly. 'I didn't want to hurt you, I just—wanted to get you off the subject of my family. I wanted to learn more about you, and there you were reminding me of my divorced parents, which brought to mind my sisters, and—I just didn't want any of their unhappiness to touch us.'

'Oh, Lyon,' she said tremulously, and withstood his warm look as she held herself together and remembered how he had once told her that he had two sisters. 'Your parents and *both* your sisters are divorced?'

'My parents split up when I was a youngster,' he did not hold back from telling her. 'I was sent to Kingswood to live with my grandfather—and subsequently inherited the place—but I never forgot the bitterness and fighting nor the recriminations that went on between my parents. When I had to stand by and watch my two sisters go through the same emotional battlefield before their marriages ended in divorce, I just knew that marriage was not for me. And, my dear Kass,' he ended, 'I never had any reason to consider altering that decision—until I met you.'

Oh, Lyon, Kassia silently mourned. While she appreciated that her own parents must have had the occasional spat, she had never heard them exchange a cross word, yet Lyon must have had a very troubled childhood. But, added to her feeling of sadness for him, she began to be enveloped in wonder that, for all the trauma he must have witnessed, he had still gone to the extent of considering asking her to marry him! He must have considered doing so, common sense asserted, as her heartbeats again quickened, or why else was he telling her all this? Her heartbeats evened out, though, when she remembered the outcome of his considerations had *not* been for him to ask her to marry him.

'But, after giving the matter full consideration, you decided to ask me to have an affair with you,' she stated—only she found it had not been that simple for him, when he revealed,

'Not at first. I was in Australia when I decided that, instead of pursuing you as every impulse urged, I should have to cut you out of my life.'

'Hence you giving me the cold-shoulder treatment when I turned up unannounced at Kingswood,' Kassia inserted quietly.

'I was in torment as you walked from me that day,' Lyon owned. 'I'd sent you away, but only to spend the following two weeks in more anguish as I denied my need to see you.'

Kassia did not have to think too deeply to remember her own pain at that unhappy time. That had been before she had been seconded to work back at Mulholland's . . .' She broke off mid-thought, and, remembering how unsurprised Lyon had been to see her back at Mulholland's, she just had to ask, 'Did you have anything to do with my being asked to come back here to work?'

'Guilty,' he admitted unashamedly. 'When I heard that Gorden Harrison was being allowed to come back on a part-time basis to ease himself in, it took no effort at all to convince myself that you, and you alone, with your sensitivity and proven loyalty to him, were the only person possible to be there to help him. Naturally,' he went on, 'I hadn't calculated that my first sight of you back here would make me so incensed.'

'It was downstairs in the foyer,' Kassia put in, but she found she had no need to remind him of anything.

'If the way you looked through me—just as if I wasn't there—wasn't enough to get my hackles up,' he told her, 'then to hear you actually daring to date some other man sent me into near apoplexy!'

'You were jealous—of Tony Rawlings!' she exclaimed.

'Not to mention Ottway. Though I could happily have dropped Rawlings down a lift shaft that day,' Lyon told her. 'But, since that might have been a bit messy, I did the only thing I could.'

'You made him work late. First, though, you ordered me up here—and made me wait to see you,' Kassia supplied.

'You just don't know what you've done to me, do you?' Lyon said quietly, and went on to show a little of his side of the story, when he told her, 'There was I, as furious as hell with you, as jealous as hell of him, and also certain all of a sudden that I was just about to make one gigantic fool of myself. And yet, even though I knew you were waiting out there in my secretary's office, even though I was certain I was going to make a fool of myself, I just couldn't bring myself to tell Heather Stanley that I'd changed my mind about wanting to see you.'

'You were determined to warn me about Tony Rawlings' reputation,' Kassia said huskily.

'Much good did it do me!' Lyon exclaimed. 'My God, jealousy didn't begin to cover the madness that possessed me when you intimated you'd been to bed with him.'

'I'm sorry,' she immediately apologised.

'So, too, am I,' breathed. 'Especially for the way I so cruelly kissed you. I was hating myself at the time, but I just couldn't seem to stop.'

'You did stop, though,' she reminded him. 'You kissed me so gently after that, that I . . .' Her voice faded, and suddenly Lyon's arms were reaching out for her.

Without another word, Kassia moved towards him, and she felt heart's ease when his strong arms enfolded her and, as he had once done before, he laid his mouth over hers in the most beautiful and tender of kisses.

When eventually he broke that kiss to gently pull back from her and to look deeply into her eyes, Kassia felt every bit as staggered by the great tenderness in him as she had been before.

'Oh, Kass, my darling, darling Kass,' Lyon breathed adoringly, 'you must care for me, mustn't you?'

The deep love in his eyes for her, the agony of suspense she saw there as he waited for her answer, left her with no chance of lying to him, even if she were so minded.

'I'm afraid so,' she said huskily, and heard his breath catch before, a moment later, he had pulled her close up to his heart again.

'Don't be afraid, my love,' he instructed tenderly. 'We'll be happy at Kingswood, you and I. We'll . . .' Suddenly, something in her expression caused him to break off. She had never thought to see Lyon panic, but she heard a desperate sound in his voice now when he demanded rapidly, 'What's the matter? I'm rushing you? Am I going too fast? You will . . .'

'Oh, Lyon,' she cut quickly across his torment and, loving him, and knowing now that he loved her, she could no longer hold out against what he wanted her to do . . . For it was not lust that motivated him. 'Nothing's wrong,' she told him. 'And I'm sure everything will be fine. But . . .'

'You do love me?'

'Oh, yes, I love you,' she sighed, and saw some of the strain leave him to hear her say it.

'What, then?' he asked, and he seemed to have an urgent need to know the smallest thing that troubled her.

'I . . . need a moment or two to adjust, I think,' she said, and she was happy to have his arm firmly about her as, talking it out as she went along, she told him, 'I came up here so angry that I was almost beside myself with fury. But now, all in the space of less than an hour, you've told me you love me and suggested I move to Kingswood and—and . . .' Suddenly she had another thought and, 'Oh, crumbs!' she said.

'What . . .'

'It's nothing,' she said quickly. 'It's just that—er— my parents take off on their China tour this week. They're celebrating their silver wedding,' she thought to mention. 'And—well, to be honest, I think I should like some time to—er—break it to them gently that you and I . . .'

'You think they'll object to me?' Lyon queried,

when Kassia thought that her parents were likely to object to any man with whom she told them she was going to live. 'You think,' he added, 'that they'll object to me as a son-in-law?'

'*Son-in-law!*' Kassia exclaimed, and saw shock hit Lyon, the moment before he said astoundedly,

'Good God! You thought I was asking . . . Didn't you hear me say I couldn't be more pleased that you didn't want an affair with me? I wasn't asking you to live with me at Kingswood without first . . .' Suddenly he broke off. Then, very precisely, he articulated, 'I've mentioned that you've got me in such a state that I don't know what I'm doing any more. But I thought when I said we'd be happy at Kingswood, that you'd understood that I want to marry you.'

'Marry me!' Kassia cried. 'But—you don't want to be married! You said that marriage wasn't for you. You said . . .'

'I said,' Lyon cut in, 'that I'd never had any reason to consider altering my decision never to marry. But I qualified that when I added—until I met you.'

'Oh . . .!' she gasped, and looked so taken aback that Lyon, as if at pains to ensure that she should not know another moment of stress, was quickly there to reassure her.

'Believe me, my love,' he said urgently. 'I love you, and I want, more than anything in life, to be married to you.'

'You no longer—want an affair with me?' she choked.

'I don't think I ever did,' he admitted. 'Oh, I told myself it was the only answer. There you were making life hell for me, and . . .'

'How?' she could not resist asking. 'How did I make life hell for you?'

'Apart from making me a raving insomniac on the nights I couldn't sleep for thinking about you, do you mean?' he queried.

'You too!' she exclaimed wonderingly.

'You . . .!' he exclaimed in return, and gently kissed her mouth as though to send any mutual suffering they had known on its way. Then he went on, 'And apart from the lies and deception that . . .'

'Lies and deception?' Kassia queried warily.

'I tried to deceive myself that to stop by to see how Gordon Harrison was progressing every Tuesday and Thursday was no more than I should do,' Lyon answered without hesitation. 'Pure deceit,' he stated. 'I was heart-torn for the sight of you.'

'Oh . . .' Kassia murmured.

'When you weren't in your office one particular Thursday and I learned of your accident, I just couldn't rest until I'd come straight to the hospital to see for myself how you were. I lied,' he told her, 'when I told you not only that I had business which took me that way, but also that I was there out of concern for Gordon Harrison. I was trying to cover up the truth, which was that my concern was for you.'

'Oh, Lyon,' Kassia said softly. 'And,' she asked, 'was it out of pure concern that you came and met me out of hospital?'

Lyon nodded as he told her, 'Dearly did I want to take you back to Kingswood—as I threatened to do if you wouldn't allow me to drive you to your parents' home—but I was afraid.'

'You—afraid?'

'You were getting more and more under my skin,' he told her. 'I spent the whole of the weekend after I'd taken you to Herefordshire trying to forget the compatible way we had parted, and trying to get you out of my head. But you refused to budge, which left me, as I saw it then, with only one alternative.'

'That alternative being an affair with me?' Kassia put in, and she did not need his confirmation as she added, 'You—er—didn't sound very lover-like in your request.'

'Wait until you're thirty-seven and suddenly find out what it's like to feel as nervous as a schoolkid,' he smiled.

'Oh,' she sighed, and it was a loving sound. 'You'll have guessed that I needed to know that you cared . . .' Warmed when the pressure of the arm he had about her increased, she just had to tell him, 'I can't honestly say now how I feel that I rang you yesterday to say no.'

'Be glad,' Lyon said positively. 'I am.'

'You are?'

'Very much so,' he said, 'although I wasn't at first. It came to me over Saturday that since you were definitely not the type to jump in and out of bed with just anybody, and since you hadn't told me right there and then on Friday what I could do with my proposition, that surely argued that you must have some feeling for me. By the time you rang on Sunday,' he confessed, 'I was all over the place with the excitement of being certain that you did care. It was like being hit by a boulder when you said those two words, "I'm sorry".'

'I'm sorry,' she said again.

'Don't be,' Lyon smiled, adding, 'While I don't mind admitting that I don't know where the hell I've been at since your phone call, it brought home to me one very straight fact. It's not an affair with you I want. It's marriage or nothing.'

'Oh, Lyon,' Kassia sighed dreamily, and as if he could not resist it Lyon pulled her closer against him, and rained kisses down on her face and eyes.

'My beautiful Kass,' he breathed, and long moments passed with them content to just delight their eyes on each other. Then they were clinging to each other as though starved. Gently then they settled against each other, with Kassia basking in Lyon's love.

Then a wisp of a memory entered her head, and it was totally without heat that she enquired dreamily, 'Lyon—just why did you send me that letter terminating my employment?'

'God help me, Kass,' he breathed, 'I had to do something! During some of my waking hours last night I realised that the first thing I had to establish was whether or not you did care anything for me. The way to do that, I thought, would be to sack you on the spot; if you did care in any way at all, you would zoom up to my office with all speed. I'll admit,' he went on, 'that that idea didn't seem so brilliant with the arrival of daylight, but it was the only idea I'd had.'

'It wasn't such a bad idea after all, was it?' she teased. 'I was in the lift about to go home when suddenly I got so mad . . .' she broke off to grin at him, 'that I *did* "zoom" up to this floor without having to think about it.' She paused. 'But would you have left it like that had I read your letter and then gone meekly home?'

'I can't see you doing anything meekly, sweetheart,' Lyon grinned. He was serious, though, when he told her, 'Just as I can't see me, feeling about you the way I do, allowing you to walk out of my life without coming after you.'

'Dear Lyon,' Kassia sighed, and all was silent in the room for long minutes as they kissed and held each other.

'And you're going to marry me?' He pulled back to

look searchingly into her enchanted expression.

'You're sure?' she asked.

'For God's sake, say yes,' he said urgently. 'My love for you is strong enough to put paid to any fear that I shall end up hurting you. In fact,' he said, and he was speaking from his heart, 'with my family's example of failed marriages hanging over me, I've never been more certain of anything than that I shall protect you and our marriage with everything that's in me.'

'Oh, my love,' she said huskily, and she could not fail to be impressed by his sincerity. 'If it's of any help,' she went on in the same husky tone, 'you might like to know that I come from a line of happily married people. In fact,' she told him, 'the couples in my family have a history of staying permanently happily married.'

'Then what are we waiting for?' he asked, and pressed, 'Don't you think we ought to join the ranks of the happily married with all speed?'

'Oh, yes,' she sighed.

It was the 'yes' which he had been holding his breath for. 'Darling!' he cried exultantly, and he was bringing her close up against his heart once more when Kassia, her own heart thundering, realised that she had just agreed to marry him.

She smiled, enraptured.

SAVAGE COURTSHIP
by
SUSAN NAPIER

CHAPTER ONE

IT WAS dark inside the big stone house but the lack of light didn't hamper the man gliding silently up the narrow stairway. He moved with the sure-footed ease of someone used to exploiting the full potential of his subsidiary senses. He hadn't needed to be able to see to quietly open the locked front door, double-shrouded in the night-shadow of the portico, and once inside he had found the stairs by instinctively measuring his stride, shifting his double burden to his right hand so that he could plot his upward progress on the smooth banister-rail with his left.

At the top of the stairs he strode confidently into the inky blackness, mentally centring himself between the pale walls to avoid the occasional dark lump of furniture that jutted out into the narrow passageway. Several metres down he turned abruptly to his left, reaching down for a low door-handle and entering the room beyond without even breaking his stride.

When he closed the door behind him the darkness was almost complete and after the briefest of hesitations he walked over to the far wall where he grasped a handful of thick fabric and dragged it aside, revealing a row of narrow windows that overlooked a small, starlit black lake. The smooth yet shifting reflective surface was oddly disorientating, the familiar beacon of the Southern Cross glinted up at him from below, as well as tracing its unique pattern of stars across the midnight vault of heaven.

His hand slowly fisted and then relaxed against the window-frame and, as if the simple action had pumped all the tension out of his body, he slumped, uttering a long sigh of relief as he set the hard, slim case and its soft-sided companion carefully on the floor beside him. He leaned against the windowsill for long moments, an obscure silhouette of dark on dark, his forehead resting against the cool glass. Then, with another sigh, he shrugged himself upright again, rolling his head around on his shoulders in the universal gesture of exhaustion, rubbing his neck with his hand as his soft-soled black shoes padded across the polished wood floor towards a second, shadowy door.

Benedict Savage narrowed his eyes to protect himself against the initial dazzling burst of light in the small bathroom as he flicked on the switch by the door and then leaned over and spun the shower tap to the pre-set pressure and temperature he preferred—strong and almost unbearably hot. He took off his tortoiseshell-framed spectacles and tossed them carelessly on to the marble vanity unit as he rubbed the narrow bridge of his nose.

He couldn't remember ever having felt this bone-weary before—perhaps because usually any tiredness on the return trip to New Zealand was masked by the sense of euphoria generated by the completion of yet another commission. This time the euphoria had been riddled with an indefinable dissatisfaction that had infuriated him, since the work he had produced had been arguably the best of his success-studded career. Perhaps he had just worked too hard for too long on this one—had wanted it too much. There was bound to be a feeling of anticlimax, especially since he had nothing half as exciting lined up to tackle next.

Benedict shook his head to try and clear the miasma of exhaustion that thickened his thoughts.

He stripped off his tailored suit and ultra-conservative shirt and tie, tossing the separate pieces carelessly across the willow-cane hamper in the corner, a grim smile touching his thin mouth as he contemplated the possibility that age was starting to catch up with him. Tomorrow was his thirty-fourth birthday and, although he was confident that he was still at the peak of his intellectual abilities, perhaps his body was telling him it was time to ease up on a relentless regime of travel-work-travel.

This particular flight across the world had been a nightmare of foul-ups and delays, and he had come perilously close to losing his famed cool. That more than anything told him that it might be time for a serious assessment of his priorities.

Benedict stepped into the shower, glancing briefly at his reflection in the steamy mirror as he pulled the glass door closed, noting with a clinical satisfaction that he didn't look as wretchedly jaded as he felt. The eyes that felt gritty and bloodshot were their usual cool, clear blue and he had the kind of olive complexion that didn't readily show the lines of tension that he could feel pulling tightly beneath his skin. His short-cropped black hair might be streaked with premature grey, but his body was as lean and hard as it ever had been, thanks partly to genetics but mostly to his habit of never taking up residence in a hotel or apartment block that didn't have a swimming-pool. His days always started with a mile of laps, the solitary rhythm soothing his mind as it sharpened his muscles.

The hot shower did its job, loosening his aching joints and easing the tightness in skin desiccated by aircraft air-conditioning. His thoughts drifted on a pleasant plateau of mindless fatigue. He stepped out of the shower cubicle and blotted himself roughly with the thick white towel from the heated towel-rail, too sluggish to notice its faint dampness. Dropping it lazily underfoot, he flicked off the light and padded back into the bedroom, rubbing his strong fingers across his sandpaper jaw, grateful that there was no reason to have to shave again before falling into bed. More than one woman had commented on the intriguing contrast between a beard that grew so quickly and his hairless chest.

He snapped on the standard lamp by the window and opened the casements, enjoying the warm flow of fresh air over his damp skin. Auckland in late March could be chilly, but tonight the region was still palpably in the grip of sultry summer. He stretched, slow and hard, prolonging a shuddering yawn as he savoured a pleasurable sense of anticipation. He removed his steel Rolex and dropped it on to the pristine white blotter on the desk which also served as a dressing-table. The prospect of sliding his naked body between cool, crisply smooth sheets was disconcertingly alluring, given the fact that the only limbs waiting to enfold him there were the celibate arms of Morpheus. Perhaps he really *was* getting old!

He turned, a wry curve of self-derision on his lips, and froze.

The high, wide single bed was already occupied.

The pool of light spilling across the floor from the lamp behind him barely reached the blanket trailing off on to the floor but the general illumination was enough to show him that his crisp, tight, pristine sheets were a tangled memory. A woman lay sprawled on her stomach in his bed, one arm splayed across the rumpled sheet towards him, the other folded in at her side, her hand disappearing into the tawny froth of hair that rippled across her shoulders, glinting in the subdued light with the lustre of old gold. Her face was well and truly buried in one of Benedict's rare, private self-indulgences—the super-size down pillows with which he furnished his beds.

He closed his eyes and shook his head sharply, sure that what he saw must be a fatigue-induced hallucination.

He looked again, moving hesitantly towards the bed, still unwilling to trust the evidence of his weary, less than perfect eyesight.

As he got closer he could see the slow rise and fall of her back and hear the faint snuffle made by her breath on the pillow. She was definitely real.

Above the white cotton sheet which draped in modest folds over her hips and legs she wore a wisp of white satin, although judging from the turmoil of the rest of the bed any modesty was purely accidental. One thin white strap had straggled almost entirely off the arm tucked against her body and the consequent lop-sided sagging of white satin revealed a long, breathtaking sweep of graceful back sheathed in lustrously smooth-textured skin the colour of dark honey.

A powerful outrage gripped Benedict. It didn't even occur to his befuddled brain to question who she was; all he felt was a furious sense of betrayal. His precious privacy had been invaded!

This was *his* bed, *his* room, his *home*, God damn it! No matter that he had never called it such before, nor that it was only one of a number of residences he maintained.

And, hell, he was *tired*! All he wanted to do was sleep. Was that too much to ask in a man's own home?

Most infuriating of all was the fact that neither the shower nor the light had woken the feminine invader. Where he desperately longed to be she was already—fathoms deep in contented slumber. Well, not for long!

He bent over and growled savagely, 'Wake up, Goldilocks; Papa Bear wants his bed back.'

There was not a flicker of response. The allusion that had sprung unconsciously to his lips was ridiculously apposite, he thought as he straightened and glimpsed himself in the mirror of the dressing-table on the other side of the bed. Not only was he feeling emotionally bearish... he was physically bare as well!

The little nip of sardonic humour restored a small measure of Benedict's normal equilibrium. He suddenly realised that waking up to find a stark-naked man looming over her was more likely to fling his mystery guest into hysterics than prompt a meek departure. The last thing his exhausted mind and body needed right now was to get involved in a dramatic scene.

He turned, intending to fetch his bathrobe from the hook in the bathroom, when the muted burr of his cellphone distracted him. Tired as he was he couldn't ignore the siren-call of master to technological slave. He detoured to his briefcase and pulled out the humming unit.

'So, are you home yet?'

Benedict raked his fingers over his cropped head as he recognised his friend and colleague's distinctive American drawl. 'Yes, Dane, *just* . . . and you won't believe what I found!'

A lazy chuckle that was Dane Judson's good-humoured trademark vibrated in his ear. 'What do you think of her? Can I pick them, or what? Isn't she the most gorgeous thing you've ever seen?'

Benedict spun on his heel and stared incredulously at the woman on the bed. 'She—I—*you're* responsible for her being here?' he stuttered.

His friend laughed and Benedict could hear the faint clink of bottle against glass in the background. 'Uh-huh. Rendered you speechless, huh? I knew I'd do it one day. I just wish I could have been there to see your face, but I'm stuck here in Wellington until next week.'

'But what in the——?'

'Many happy returns for tomorrow, pal.' There was the audible sound of a toast being drunk.

Benedict cleared his throat as understanding burst upon his sluggish brain. 'This is your idea of a *birthday* present? For God's sake, Dane——!'

'Don't worry, pal, it's all pleasure and no responsibility,' Dane gleefully misunderstood him. 'You don't have to look after her for keeps—she's strictly on weekend loan. I promised you'd return her in perfect nick so make sure you treat her real lover-like——'

'*What*——?' Benedict moved jerkily back towards the bed, stunned by the revelation that the anonymous female body was there purely for his temporary delectation.

Another rolling laugh. 'I keep telling you, all work and no play makes Ben a dull boy. And don't tell me you're not feeling jaded because I know you well enough to read the signs. You need to revitalise yourself with a little hell-raising and, believe me, this babe is guaranteed to loosen you up real fast. A few days with her and you'll feel eighteen again...'

'I wouldn't wish a second time around as a teenager on my worst enemy,' Benedict said sardonically, unconsciously lowering his voice as he leaned against the bedside cabinet, wondering what Dane would say if he knew that his outrageous birthday present had got tired of waiting to spring her surprise and was out cold. Benedict decided not to spoil his friend's mirthful pleasure by telling him. 'Let alone my best friend. I hesitate to inject a dose of unwelcome reality into your adolescent fantasies, Dane, but isn't this kind of arrangement a bit unhealthy these days?'

Dane gave a whoop of delighted laughter. 'Afraid you'll have a heart-attack from the excitement? Come on, Ben—would I give you something that I thought would kill you? When was the last time you had some innocent, macho fun? A year? Eighteen months ago? Trust me, you have nothing to worry about. I had her thoroughly checked over inside *and* out and she's in prime, A-1 condition——'

'For God's sake——!' Benedict could feel the heat in his face, almost as if he was embarrassed on behalf of a woman who was obviously either a high-class call-girl or a free spirit who got her kicks out of having sex with total strangers. He knew it had been quite some time since his last relationship with a woman ended but he had been so absorbed in his work that he had never worried about his inactive libido. Not so Dane, it seemed, whose sex life was as active as his bizarre sense of humour.

'Dane——'

'No need to thank me, pal,' his friend interrupted, ringing off with a breezy, 'Just enjoy! And remember, it's pumpkin time Monday morning...'

Benedict swayed slightly under another rolling wave of fatigue as he switched off the phone and placed it clumsily down on the bedside table. He struggled to keep his eyelids open as he wearily debated his options.

There were plenty of other beds in the house but his proprietary interest in this one was stubbornly acute.

Despite her apparent sprawl, his nameless birthday gift actually trespassed on little more than half of the bed, he noted, her left arm and hip neatly aligned with the far edge of the single mattress. He looked down at her outflung arm, at the long, slender fingers curled laxly over the edge of the bed. Her fingertips almost touched his hair-roughened knee. Gently he encircled her wrist and lifted the sleep-heavy arm, placing it neatly back against her side. There was now an inviting expanse of empty bed available. A man-sized portion, if the man was of greyhound-lean proportions...

Goldilocks slumbered on. She was amazingly still, except for that slow, sensuous ripple of breath down the long, beautiful spine. She made sleep seem like an enchantingly erotic experience and Benedict found himself wondering whether a woman who offered herself up so voluptuously to sleep would be equally hedonistic in her approach to lovemaking.

A lazy stirring of male curiosity piqued his jaded senses, his angry earlier resentment overwhelmed by the knowledge that if he cared to find out he only needed to wake her. She was his to command. He wondered if that fleecy gold hair was as soft as it looked, and whether the colour was natural. He wondered whether her front would live up to that matchless back. Even in the slackness of sleep he could see that her muscles were well-toned. Her waking movements would be strong and supple. He imagined watching that golden back arching and flexing in slow, indolent rhythm with the languid thrust of his hips. He'd take her slow and easy at first... and then... and then...

He looked down at his quiescent body in rueful self-derision. And then... nothing. His mind might be aroused but he was so exhausted he was physically incapable of doing his vivid imagination justice. If he got into bed with her tonight he would be sleeping with her in the strictly literal sense.

Waking up with her in the morning, though, was suddenly an enchanting prospect.

Oh, yes... after a good, solid sleep the birthday boy would be in far better condition to appreciate his very unexpected, and undoubtedly expensive present...

CHAPTER TWO

VANESSA FLYNN was sitting at the scrubbed kitchen table sipping her first cup of coffee of the day when her employer burst into the kitchen and came to an abrupt halt.

Her hands tightened around the cup but that was the only visible reaction that escaped her rigid self-control. Inside she was one huge, all-enveloping blush.

Mrs Riley looked up from the breakfast tray she had busied herself over on the kauri-slab bench in surprise.

'Did you want your breakfast early this morning, Mr Savage?' she asked, her middle-aged face creased with dismay at this departure from routine. 'Only, your office never notified us that you were coming last night, you see, so nothing's quite prepared. I didn't even know that I'd be needed until Vanessa rang me a little while ago——'

'No, no...' Benedict Savage cut her off with a wave of his hand, frowning as he looked at the single setting she had laid on the tray. 'You don't have to rush.'

Vanessa braced herself as his gaze lifted, darted about the kitchen, and reluctantly settled on her.

She willed herself not to let her interior blush show, her dark brown eyes steady as they met his. She had dressed in her best wallpaper this morning—sensible, knee-length grey skirt and white short-sleeved blouse, her damp chestnut hair strictly confined to a neat French pleat, her face made up with the discreet foundation and barest touch of ginger lipstick that she habitually wore when on duty—too little to draw undue attention to her features but just enough to satisfy her feminine vanity.

Not that she had much reason to be vain. She was a shade under six feet but without the willowy slenderness that would have rendered her height fashionable. At least everything else was proportionate to her grand size, but that was little consolation. Her face was what might be politely termed strong-boned, her chin too square, her mouth too big and her wide, dark eyes deeply set and heavy-lidded, so that she was cursed with a perpetually sleepy air which was totally at odds with her practical efficiency.

She swallowed, the sweetened coffee turning bitter on her tongue as she withstood the silent stare of the man she had woken up in bed with that morning.

Behind the tortoiseshell frames she found his blue eyes unreadable. Not that Benedict Savage's expression was *ever* easy to interpret. To her he had always appeared as precise and controlled as the architectural drawings which papered the walls of the studio next to his bedroom.

He was also a very private man, reserved to the point of coldness. In fact it was that very reserve that made him an ideal employer as far as Vanessa was concerned... that and the fact that his visits to his historic house on the east coast of the Coromandel Peninsula were few and far between, and *never* without advance notification.

Until now...

Vanessa's fingers tightened further on her cup. She had an unwelcome premonition that this visit was going to alter the pleasant tenor of life at Whitefield House completely and forever. Already her perception of Benedict Savage had been unwillingly altered. He was no longer merely her employer, he was now regrettably entrenched in her brain as a *man*...

He was still looking at her, and she cringed at what he must be thinking.

If only she could remember what had happened!

Unfortunately, last night was a total blank, from the time she had fallen into bed after imbibing more than her share of champagne over an early dinner with Richard, until the moment she had become aware of the sounds of dawn filtering through a window that she knew she had firmly closed the previous evening.

When she had opened her eyes and found herself almost nose to nose with her naked employer, her arm draped over his hard waist, her thigh trapped intimately between his, she had thought at first that she was dreaming. Not that she had *ever* had erotic dreams about Benedict Savage before; she had always felt utterly safe in that regard. He was just not the sort of man she found attractive. He was too cerebral, too dispassionate, too much of a perfectionist for Vanessa, who much preferred comfort to sharp-edged perfection.

Luckily she had been too muddle-headed to scream when the rest of her senses had confirmed the shocking reality of the bare flesh pressed against hers. She had merely frozen, terrified that her consciousness might awaken his, unable to believe that the supple male hand possessively cupping her soft breast really belonged to Benedict Savage... not to mention the steely hardness that pressed into the hollow of her thigh where it was wedged snugly between his. He might not have roused from sleep but the man in her arms had definitely not been unaroused!

Shame and disbelief had warred for supremacy in the long moments it took for her to realise that she might still be able to extricate herself from the immediate consequences of her folly. The deep, even tenor of his breathing had indicated that Benedict—Mr Savage, she corrected herself grimly, clinging to the flimsy protection that the formality offered—was still deeply asleep, and Vanessa had prayed that he would continue to remain so as she extracted herself, inch by excruciatingly cautious inch, from their tangled embrace, her eyes fixed on his sleeping face.

All had gone well until the final few seconds when he'd shifted and growled an inarticulate protest at the withdrawal of warm, feminine flesh but, blessedly, he hadn't woken...

When she'd finally slithered off the side of the bed, taking most of the upper sheet with her, he had merely rolled further over on to his face with a groan, slinging a long, sinewy arm around the pillow she had vacated and dragging it under his ribs, pinning it there with his drawn-up knee. She had primly flung the sheet back over him and fled hastily, her mortification ridiculously intensified by the knowledge that her presence in his bed was so easily replaced by a shapeless pillow!

It had taken her all of fifteen minutes' hard scrubbing in the shower to feel that she had washed the masculine scent and feel of him off her skin and even now the memory of it returned to haunt her.

Once again, she damned Benedict Savage for taking advantage of an innocent mistake. Why hadn't he woken her up? Or, worse, what if he *had* woken her and, in an alcohol-induced stupor, she had been recklessly wanton...?

She shuddered, looking warily up at him through the protective screen of her lashes. Why on earth was he just standing there like that? Why didn't he say something—an accusation, a joke, a request for an explanation, a demand she pack her bags and never darken his door again—*anything* to break this unbearable tension?

Nervously she tried to assess his uncertain mood. He hadn't shaved and his hair was ruffled—not a very good sign for a man who always presented a perfectly groomed image, even when relaxing in private. His saturnine face had a more than usually shuttered look, his thin mouth a tight slash across the unshaven lower half of his face that emphasised the general impression of indrawn tension. However, his crisp blue and white striped shirt and dark blue trousers were immaculately co-ordinated, so he hadn't been in such haste to track her down that he'd just thrown on the first clothes to hand.

The silence stretched on just long enough for her nerve to break under the strain.

'Did you want me, sir?'

Too late Vanessa realised the suggestive ambiguity of the question and she had to clench her teeth to stop herself gabbling a disclaimer into the ensuing silence. Her neatly buttoned collar suddenly felt chokingly tight.

'I...' He released her from the torture of his sole attention, looking around the kitchen again, as if hunting for his words. 'Er... Am I the only one breakfasting...?'

Vanessa was aware of Mrs Riley's sidelong glance but refused to share her silent puzzlement at their employer's uncharacteristic vagueness. She was too busy worrying over whether he was deliberately prolonging her agony or merely unwilling to humiliate her in front of the housekeeper.

'Why...yes. Vanessa didn't mention that you'd brought any guests with you this time...' Mrs Riley was saying, a faint look of bewilderment crossing her face as she watched her employer's eyes drop as he studied his stylishly shod feet with apparent fascination.

'No, I didn't. So...it's just me, then...' His inflexion rose slightly on the last word, just enough to suggest the possibility of a question. Nobody answered immediately and his gaze swivelled suddenly back to Vanessa, who wasn't quite quick enough to banish her look of apprehension.

He scowled at her. 'Can I see you for a few minutes in the library, Flynn?' He turned on his heel and was almost out the door before he halted, looking back. 'Incidentally, Mrs Riley, I'm really not very hungry this morning, so perhaps just some toast and tea...'

'Oh, what a pity, Mr Savage, and I've just put a nice pot of porridge on the stove——'

'*Porridge*?' He jerked around, looking so shocked at the suggestion that Vanessa, already primed with nerves, gave a jittery little laugh and found herself once again impaled by the focus of his attention.

'In the library. Now!' For Benedict Savage the quiet hiss was the equivalent of a furious shout.

'Yes, sir!' Vanessa muttered to empty air, rising from her seat and unhooking the cropped navy jacket that was draped over the high back.

'Well, I never!' said Kate Riley, crossing her arms over her ample chest and shaking her grey head so that her corrugated perm quivered. 'You'd have thought I was offering him arsenic. He always said he liked my porridge!'

Vanessa, shouldering into her jacket and procrastinating by squaring the cuffs and lapels, soothed her injured pride absently. 'He's probably just in a bad mood——'

'Mr Savage doesn't have moods—he's always a perfect gentleman,' Mrs Riley pointed out with inescapable truth. 'He never gets out of bed on the wrong side but it certainly seems as though he did this morning...'

Vanessa murmured something indistinct in answer to the unfortunate metaphor and rushed out of the kitchen, pressing cold hands to her hot cheeks.

Calm down, calm down, she lectured herself sternly as she walked down the flag-stoned hall. If he fires you, you can charge him with sexual harassment. Or was he planning to charge *her*...? She almost moaned aloud at the thought, its absurdity eclipsed by her horror of scandal. Whatever happened, there would be questions asked because she couldn't possibly continue to work at Whitefield. She would have to leave the place she had come to look on as a quiet, secure haven from the madness of the world. And what was she going to tell Richard? Oh, damn, damn, *damn*!

'Well...?' Thankfully Benedict Savage had not chosen to adopt an intimidating position of dominance behind the meticulously tidy antique desk that fronted the French windows. Instead he was standing just inside the doorway, one hand resting on a walnut shelf of the book-lined wall, fingers tapping involuntarily against the aged wood as she closed the door behind her.

'Yes, sir?' Vanessa stood straight and tall, shoulders squared against the imminent attack.

He cleared his throat. 'I'm sorry if my early arrival has caused problems, but I just needed to get away for a space of time and Whitefield seemed the place to do it. The apartment in Auckland is too accessible and...' he shrugged with a trace of diffidence '...well, I know that Mrs Riley gets in a tizz about these things... Just make sure she knows that I don't expect everything to be as organised as usual...that I don't want any fuss...'

Vanessa was hard put to it not to let her jaw fall open. Mr Perfection was telling her he didn't expect perfection? He was waffling about household arrangements when the real business at hand was shrieking to be settled?

She looked at the tapping fingers. Nerves? Mr Cool was *nervous*?

'So, you'll tell her that, will you?' His fingers suddenly stopped their fluttering with a sudden slam against the wood.

Vanessa's eyes shot back to his face to find him watching her warily. She scrabbled for foundation on a rapidly shifting ground. *He* was nervous of *her*? The notion was mind-boggling.

'Ah, yes, yes, of course, sir,' she assured him hastily.

'Right.' He took off his spectacles, cleaned their spotless lenses with a beautifully pressed handkerchief retrieved from his hip pocket, and put them on again. 'I didn't bring anyone with me.'

'So you said, sir—in the kitchen, just now,' she added as he regarded her blankly.

'Did I? Oh, yes, of course I did.' He pushed off the bookcase and began to pace. 'So...where is our other guest, I wonder?'

Vanessa stiffened. 'If you're suggesting——'

He jumped in, correspondingly quick to suspect. 'Suggesting what?'

'That I take advantage of your absences to invite people to use your house——' she began, angry that he might be trying to make up spurious reasons for terminating her employment. If he was going to fire her for sleeping with him he was going to have to admit it!

'No, no, nothing like that.' His answer was as swift as it seemed genuine, and edged with irritation. 'If I didn't trust you I wouldn't continue to employ you, would I? I just wondered if you knew...'

'Knew what?' She was deeply uneasy now. Maybe she just should have opened up with an apology and explanation instead of leaving it up to him to introduce the subject. But she had never known her employer be anything but direct, sometimes brutally so.

He stopped pacing a mere stride away and turned to her, hands on his hips. This was it, the moment of truth.

Vanessa lifted her chin bravely, gratified to note that even in flat heels she topped him by at least an inch. Whatever he said, she wasn't going to shrink into physical insignificance before him!

'There was a woman...'

'A woman?' Vanessa felt herself beginning to heat up. Oh, God, was he going to try to smooth things over by explaining how last night had only been a spasm of lust and that she wasn't to place any importance on the fact that they had slept together because there was someone else...?

He bit off something that sounded like a curse. Another first. Benedict Savage's words were usually as cool and as measured as the rest of him, precisely weighed and placed for maximum effect with minimum effort.

'Yes, a woman.' His voice roughened sharply at her wide-eyed shock and he raked her with an insulting glare. 'You *do* know what a woman is, don't you, Flynn?'

Her flush deepened at his sneer and she saw his eyes flicker behind their clear lenses, his mouth compress with self-disgust. 'I'm sorry, that was in extremely poor taste...' His hand rasped across his beard-shaded chin as he continued rigidly, 'I mean...last night when I came in, just before midnight...there was a woman—er—in my room...'

'In your room?' She couldn't help it, and when she realised that she had once again inanely repeated his words she bit her lip but this time he ignored the provocation.

'In bed. A blonde.'

'A *blonde*?' Vanessa retreated, startled, visions of sin dancing in her head. Had she taken part in some kind of orgy without being aware of it? Disported herself in some kind of perverted *ménage à trois*? Her employer had never brought a female companion with him to Whitefield before, although he had included unattached women in groups of people whom he had occasionally entertained at weekends. She had thought that his love-life must be as reserved as the rest of him, but now Vanessa found herself regarding those weekend groupings in a suspicious new light.

'Oh, for God's sake!' Her air of silent condemnation caused an explosion that was contained almost as soon as it occurred. His hard jaw clenched as he continued doggedly, 'She had long, fluffy hair...like golden fleece.' Benedict Savage held her mesmerised stare, faint streaks of red appearing on his high cheekbones as he went on,

'Have you by any chance seen her around this morning? She's not anywhere upstairs...'

Golden? Fluffy? Vanessa's eyes widened as she resisted the urge to touch her neat French pleat to make sure that the wavy, sun-bleached ends were firmly rolled into the concealing centre.

It suddenly occurred to her that her employer had never seen her with her hair down. To him she was just Flynn, discreet, sexless, quietly running his household and overseeing the ongoing restoration of the former coaching inn while he jaunted about the world earning a luxurious living designing buildings that were the complete antithesis of Whitefield.

Vanessa, along with the other permanent staff, was merely one of the chattels that he had acquired when he had unexpectedly inherited a distant relative's property and, after initially balking badly at the discovery that the late Judge Seaton's butler was young and female, he had accepted the impeccable references supplied by the lawyer who had handled the judge's estate. He had, however, made it quite clear to Vanessa privately that she was only acceptable in the position as long as the fact that she was a woman never impinged on the job. It never had.

'Apart from being blonde, what does she look like?' Vanessa asked in a strangled voice that tested a wildly implausible theory.

'I don't know,' he said, his bluntness daring her to display any shock. 'It was dark...I never saw her face. And before you ask, no, I don't know what her name is; we didn't get around to introducing ourselves! So, now that your prurient suspicions are confirmed, perhaps you wouldn't mind answering *my* questions?'

His sarcasm went right over her whirling head. She was shattered by knowledge that her outrageous theory was right.

There had only been one woman in Benedict Savage's bed last night and that woman had been Vanessa. But he didn't know that!

'I...but...I——' Relief poured like adrenalin along her veins, throwing her into an even deeper moral dilemma.

As long as he never found out who the woman in his bed had been, Vanessa's job was safe...

'I'm not imagining things!' he growled tersely.

Vanessa licked her lips. 'Oh...of course not,' she said, wondering how long her meagre acting skills would sustain her charade of ignorance.

He chose to take her placating comment as a piece of sarcasm and reiterated tightly, 'She was here, damn it! It was late and I was thick-headed with jet-lag but I wasn't *completely* detached from reality. I *wasn't* hallucinating!'

'I haven't seen anyone except Mrs Riley this morning,' Vanessa said, carefully avoiding any outright lie that could have unpleasant repercussions later. 'Perhaps it was one of the resident ghosts, sir,' she joked weakly.

'I didn't know we had any. Not that I believe in them, anyway.'

His scepticism was only what she expected from such a logical mind. You only had to look at the buildings he designed to see that his imagination was chained to the starkly realistic. 'Oh, yes, people say that there are several——'

'Female?'

She was disconcerted by his persistence over what had been a purely frivolous mention. 'A couple of them, yes——'

'Yellow-haired? Scantily dressed? A seductive siren luring a man towards the gates of hell and damnation?'

Oh, God, now she was *certain* that whatever they had got up to had been deeply sinful.

'Er, I understand one of them was a guest murdered by one of the ostlers here at the inn—a...a dancing girl who was on her way to entertain at the goldfields at Coromandel...'

'You mean a whore?' He cut her gentle euphemisms to ribbons with cool contempt. 'Well, that certainly fits.'

'There's no proof that she was a whore!' Vanessa said hotly, not sure whether it was herself or the ghost she was supposed to be defending.

'What about last night?'

'W-what about last night?' Vanessa quavered. Surely she hadn't given him the idea she had expected money for whatever it was she had allowed him to do!

He looked at her impatiently, mistaking her horror for fear. 'Forget about bloody ghosts. They don't exist. So-called supernatural apparitions usually turn out to be the self-generated fantasies of people who are either gullible, publicity-seeking or deranged. You said you didn't see anyone around this morning. What about last night? You were here then, weren't you? Did you see or hear anything then?'

Oh, God... Her collar tightened again, squeezing her voice into a reedy squeak. 'I was out. I went to dinner over in Waihi...' No need to mention she'd been back, and tucked up cosily in his bed, by ten-thirty p.m.

'Who with?'

In the three years she had worked for him he had never asked her a single personal question and Vanessa floundered, feeling that she was giving away a vital piece of herself with the information. 'R-Richard—Richard Wells.'

'The horse-breeder—from the property along the road?' He frowned. He was obviously trying to remember his fleeting acquaintance with his nearest neighbour; he was probably also wondering what Richard saw in his sexless employee, Vanessa thought sourly, only to be proved wrong as he said sharply, 'Not with Dane?'

Vanessa gasped. 'Mr Judson? Of course not. As far as I know he's at home in Auckland.'

'Wellington, actually. So he didn't tell you about his little arrangement...' He resumed his pacing, looking slightly more relaxed, but Vanessa couldn't allow her vigilance to relax correspondingly.

'Arrangement?'

'It doesn't matter.' He glanced out of the French doors towards the back of the house and suddenly halted with a jerk. 'What the——? Whose car is that in the garage?'

Desperate for a change of subject, Vanessa moved up beside him to look out at the gleaming white car tucked under the open arches of what had once been the coaching-house stables. 'Oh, that! It——'

'What an incredibly beautiful beast of a car!' His envious drawl cut her off, startling her with its hint of boyish eagerness. Benedict Savage, the last word in sophistication—*boyish*? 'Isn't it a——?' He leaned closer to the glass panes. 'Yes, I think it is...a 1935 Duesenberg convertible coupé...just like the one Clark Gable had custom-made. Who on earth...?' He straightened, suddenly letting loose a rare laugh that sounded half annoyed, half admiring. 'My God, I bet *she* arrived in it! That would just be Dane's style. So that must mean she's still here somewhere——'

Vanessa stared at him, confused by this added complication. 'But...I thought it was *yours*.'

His head snapped sideways. 'Mine?' His eyebrows rose in a haughty disclaimer. 'What on earth gave you that idea? You know very well I have the BMW.'

Yes, a precision-engineered, elegantly low-key car that had seemed perfectly suited to his introverted personality. And yet here he was, practically drooling over a flashy, red-upholstered brute whose every gleaming inch was flauntingly extrovert.

'Well...I...it was delivered yesterday in your name, so I naturally assumed... I thought perhaps you'd bought it as an investment...' It was the only explanation that had fitted his coolly calculating image.

'It was delivered? By whom?' As usual he cut swiftly to the heart of the matter.

'Two men. Yesterday afternoon. There was a letter—I assumed from the dealer. I put it there on your desk with the car keys.'

With one last, narrow-eyed glance at the car he picked up the flat envelope and slit the sealed edge with a neatly manicured thumbnail.

What he withdrew wasn't a letter, but a large card of some kind. He stared at the weedy-looking, spectacle-wearing nerd that Vanessa, pretending not to look but unable to restrain her curiosity, could see gracing the front, before slowly opening it and reading the contents. As Vanessa watched, the flush that had lightly streaked his skin a few minutes earlier exploded into a full-blooded, Technicolor blush. He made a strange choking sound in his throat.

Vanessa was fascinated. She had never seen him look so flustered. 'I beg your pardon, sir?' she murmured, her determined coolness rewarded by his dazed regard.

'Dane's given me a *car*...'

'*Given* you a car?' She now understood his helpless amazement. She had known that his friend was wealthy, as were most people professionally associated with her employer, but, even as ignorant about cars as Vanessa was, she realised that the gorgeous specimen in the garage was worth hundreds of thousands of dollars. Dane Judson had a quirky sense of humour and a liking for extravagant surprises, but his extravagances had never been reckless.

'For my birthday.' He scanned the card again and corrected himself. 'No, not given, *loaned*—it's being picked up again on Monday...'

That was more like it. Quirky but grounded in economic reality!

'It's your birthday?' For some reason Vanessa had never thought of her employer having birthdays like ordinary people. He had always been so remote as to be ageless, above such frivolous goings-on as birthdays...

'Today. I'm thirty-four,' he revealed absently, staring down at the card, reading and re-reading the writing inside as if it were printed in a foreign language that he was having difficulty translating.

'Many happy returns,' Vanessa murmured weakly, wishing she had some recollection of the precise nature of the gift *she* had rendered on the eve of his birthday.

He didn't respond, raking a hand over his head, spiking up more of the ruffled strands.

'My God, last night on the phone...all that time Dane was talking about lending me a *car*, and *I* thought he was talking in clever metaphors...'

He groaned and closed his appalled eyes. 'My God, if he ever finds out what I thought I'll never hear the end of it!' His hand covered his mouth as he groaned again, with heartfelt disgust, and his next mutter was almost smothered. 'I must be mad! Ghosts? I could have *sworn* I hadn't imagined any of it...'

'Why, what *did* you think he was giving you?' Vanessa asked, the extreme nature of his reaction spicing her curiosity.

His hand dropped away, and the eyes that had been blue with dismay chilled to the colour of pure steel, but his complexion was still betrayingly warm. 'None of your damned business!'

She knew then exactly what 'arrangement' he thought that his sly-humoured friend had made.

She pokered up immediately, forcing down a rush of humiliated fury at the thought of being used as a sexual birthday favour. At least she had the excuse of being inebriated for whatever licentiousness she might have indulged in. He had no excuse whatsoever! And he hadn't even bothered to look at her *face*! Her woman's body had been all that had mattered. Her normally placid temper simmered dangerously.

'No, sir.'

His eyes narrowed on her, as if he sensed the insolence she so badly wanted to display, but she remained stubbornly impassive and with a shrug he picked up the car keys, tossing and catching them in a gesture that was subtly defiant. 'I think I'll go and check out this magnanimous gift of Dane's.'

'I'll tell Mrs Riley to hold your breakfast,' said Vanessa smoothly as she watched him open the French doors and slip outside.

She knew what he was doing and a small smile of malicious satisfaction curved along her wide mouth.

The imperturbable Benedict Savage was running away. She had witnessed the temporary disintegration of his cynical self-possession and that made him uncomfortable. He knew that she was a shrewd judge of human behaviour—it was what made her such a skilled butler, responsive to the needs of him and his guests to the extent that she seemed able to anticipate their every wish—and he had no desire to be judged on his vulnerabilities. Until now he had been serene in the knowledge that his was the dominant role in the master-servant relationship and now it had probably occurred to him that that balance of power wasn't immutable, that the power of knowledge accumulated over time might make a servant of the master.

Good! It would serve him right to wonder how much she knew or might guess. She hoped he would relive his discomfort every time he saw her for some time to come. Why shouldn't he suffer at least a modicum of the helpless self-consciousness that *she* felt in his presence?

She watched him cross the cobbled courtyard that led to the stables with a smooth, lean-hipped stride, keenly aware of a unique feeling of alienation within her own body and fiercely resenting it. Suddenly she wished that she hadn't been too embarrassed to inspect the body she had briskly scrubbed under the shower an hour ago. Whatever had happened in his bed might have left marks, evidence that might have relieved her fears—or confirmed them—instead of leaving her in this limbo of...

Evidence?

Give that fearsomely logical brain physical evidence to work on and she wouldn't stand a chance!

She stiffened, her heart fluttering in her chest. A fresh surge of panic galvanised her into action. She darted over to the French doors and turned the key in the lock before racing out into the hallway and up the stairs, taking them three at a time, her long legs comfortably stretching the distance.

The door to her employer's bedroom was firmly shut but Vanessa ignored any qualms she had about invading his privacy and skidded inside.

The bed was in exactly the state that she had fervently hoped it would be—abandoned and very much unmade. Vanessa blessed the fact that Benedict Savage's parents had raised him in a rich and rarefied environment that rendered him ignorant of the kind of basic domestic chores that ordinary mortals like Vanessa grew up performing for themselves.

She quickly ripped the top sheet off the bed, rolling it into a loose ball before dumping it on the floor and attacking the pillows, cursing their ungainly size as she struggled to remove the custom-made pillowcases. Her heart pounded as she spotted the long strands on hair that straggled across one of them. She had never realised that she moulted so much at night... or had it been because this time her head had been thrashing to and fro on the pillow in the throes of unremembered ecstasy?

Her mouth went dry at the insidious image of herself writhing beneath a sleekly tapered male body. Who would have thought that under the fashionably loose clothes a man in a sedentary occupation like architectural design would have a body so hard and compact? His skin had been glossy with health, rippling over lean, surprisingly well-developed muscles.

Furious with herself for letting her thoughts run riot, Vanessa wrenched anew at the stubborn pillowcases and shook them out vigorously before turning them inside out and throwing them on top of the sheet on the floor. She stretched across the bed and had just slipped her hand under the mattress to free the far corner of the sheet when the door jarred open, and a voice rattled chills down her spine.

'What in the hell do you think you're doing?'

She could feel one neatly manicured nail catch and tear against the mattress as she jerked upright and around, her sensible shoes skidding on the discarded linen, tangling her feet, so that with a cry of dismay she toppled helplessly backwards across the bed.

CHAPTER THREE

ANYONE else would have reflexively reached out and tried to prevent Vanessa's fall, but Benedict Savage was a law unto himself. He didn't lift a finger to save her.

He merely folded his arms across his chest and watched her bounce and come to rest before coldly rephrasing his question.

'I asked you what you were doing in my room?'

The crisp pattern of his speech was slightly blurred by his rapid breathing. He had been running. What had occurred to her had obviously also belatedly occurred to him; he was here to attempt to sort fact from fantasy.

If she had felt at a disadvantage earlier in his study, it was nothing to what Vanessa felt now.

She pushed herself upright on trembling arms, drawing her knees together and tugging down the skirt over her dangling legs in a vain attempt to recover her dignity. 'I would have thought it was obvious,' she snapped defensively, wishing he would move out of the way so that she could stand up. 'I'm making your bed.'

'Why?'

She bit back the smart-mouthed reply that sprang to her lips and struggled for a respectful monotone. 'Because it's my job.'

'*You* make my bed?'

For a moment he looked as uncomfortable as she felt. He had refused to allow her to perform the more personal services that a butler usually provided, ones that she had cheerfully carried out for the judge—waking him in the morning, running his bath, laying out his choice of clothing for the day. Benedict Savage had informed her squelchingly at that chilly initial interview that he didn't require nannying, and that he would thank her not to invade his privacy unless invited. She had duly kept the required distance, but it wouldn't hurt him to realise that caring for someone's house was, in its own way, as intimate as caring for their person.

'I often help Mrs Riley with the housekeeping,' she said, adding pointedly, 'As you may have noticed from the household accounts, I only employ extra housekeeping staff when you bring guests to stay. It's not economic to have a full household complement idle for most of the year.'

His blank look confirmed a long-held suspicion. She doubted that he ever bothered even to glance at the accounts that she scrupulously presented him with every six months. She could be robbing him blind for all he cared. Once he had decided to trust her, he had given her a totally free hand and however flattering that was to her ego it irked her that it also meant the true extent of her efficiency went largely unappreciated.

Unfortunately he ignored the red herring, and pursued a point she had hoped would not occur to such a supremely undomesticated animal.

'Have I ever given you reason to think I'm so fanatical about cleanliness that I require my sheets to be changed daily?' he said drily. 'This is a home, not a hotel—I've barely had the chance to get them warm, let alone dirty.'

'You do have a reputation for being extremely fastidious,' Vanessa muttered, guiltily thinking of the silky heat that she had been cuddled up to that morning. He had certainly been warming the sheets then. However, she could hardly contradict him.

'But not to the point of being unhealthily obsessive,' he said with controlled distaste.

No, she couldn't picture him being obsessive about anything. That would require a degree of passion she didn't believe he possessed.

'You haven't been here since the beginning of February and your bed hasn't been properly aired because we didn't know you were coming,' she invented hastily. 'I thought the sheets might have been a bit musty.'

'Well, they weren't.' He looked down at the tumble of linen at their feet, his voice acquiring a strangely husky note. 'In fact they were quite deliciously fragrant...'

Vanessa tensed with shock at the thread of remembered pleasure in his voice, finding his choice of words disturbingly sensual for someone whom she preferred to think of as a thoroughly cold fish.

Thank God the perfume she had dabbed on at the beginning of last evening was so expensive that she only wore it when she was going somewhere special! She sought for a way to scatter whatever images were re-forming in that frighteningly intelligent brain.

'Probably from the washing-powder Mrs Riley uses,' she said prosaically, and rose from the bed, forcing him to step back as she summoned a brisk dismissal.

'Well, since I've gone this far I'll have to finish the job. I can't put these sheets back on after they've been trampled on the floor. Excuse me.'

He looked from the bed to her and for a terrible moment she thought he was going to dig his heels in. She bravely stood her ground, banking on his intensely private nature to win the brief internal battle he was evidently waging. The thought of exposing himself to her curiosity again would be anathema to him. She deliberately allowed a hint of speculation to impinge on her expression of polite patience.

His reaction was swift and instinctive. His face shuttered and he inclined his head, saying sharply, 'If you think it's necessary, I suppose I must bow to your superior domestic knowledge.'

Sarcastic beast! In the past his cynical comments hadn't bothered her. Now every word he uttered seemed to grate on her nerves.

'Thank you.' She hesitated, waiting for him to depart. He looked at her enquiringly, raising his dark eyebrows haughtily above his spectacle frames. It had the irritating effect of making Vanessa feel as if he was looking down on her, even though the reverse was true. She had won their little tussle of wills and now she was being made to pay for it.

Vanessa's wide mouth pinched as she strove for the self-effacing politeness that until this morning had been second nature in her dealings with this man.

'I'm sure you must have something better to do than watch me make beds.'

'Not really,' he said unobligingly. 'When you're on holiday there's something very satisfying about watching other people toil.'

'You're on holiday?' Vanessa hoped she didn't sound as appalled as she felt. He had never spent more than a long weekend at Whitefield before. Surely he wasn't staying any longer than Sunday? She didn't think she could take the strain.

An idle Benedict Savage would undoubtedly be a bored Benedict Savage, and when bored he might look around for something to engage his intellect—like solving a puzzle that was best left unsolved.

To hide her agitation Vanessa gave the remaining sheet a huge yank to free it and rolled it clumsily up over her arm.

'More or less,' he replied absently, watching her bend to pick up the rest of the linen. 'You could say I'm in between jobs at the moment.'

She was so used to hearing that euphemistic phrase trotted out by people who came to the door applying for casual work, thinking that domestic service was a sinecure for which they needed no skill, training or enthusiasm, that her soothing response was automatic, her mind occupied with more weighty matters.

'I'm sure you'll find other employment again soon.'

'I'm flattered by your confidence. But if not I suppose there's always the unemployment benefit.' His smooth answer followed so seamlessly on hers that it was a moment before she realised her *faux pas*.

'I'm sorry, sir, I wasn't thinking,' she said, mortified by her slip.

'I thought it was the reverse,' he murmured with dismaying perception, his blue eyes studying her flustered face. 'You seemed to be very deeply immersed in uneasy thoughts. Is there anything worrying you, Flynn?'

Another unprecedented personal question. Now was the moment to confess all and throw herself on his mercy!

Only Vanessa didn't think that he had any. She vividly recalled his declaration at their meeting that he never made an idle threat and she had seen him deal ruthlessly with those who proved to be dishonest or disloyal. Employee or friend, they simply ceased to exist for him. Vanessa was already in over her head in deceit and, in addition, she had broken his golden rule: thou shalt not be a woman.

'No, why should you think that?' Unfortunately her voice cracked on the last word.

'There's a slightly...fraught air about you this morning.'

Oh, God!

'Is there?' she said brightly. 'Well, your arrival did rather catch me on the hop.' She was glad of the ready excuse. 'I'm afraid I don't react well to surprises.'

'Really? Congreve would have it that uncertainty is one of the joys of life,' he said suavely, no doubt trying to intimidate her with his intellect. Well, Vanessa wasn't impressed. Anyone who could read could trot out quotations from classic English literature. She might not have gone to university but she could, and did, love to read widely. With anyone else she might even have enjoyed a foolish game of duelling quotations. As it was she just wanted him to find her dull and boring and totally unworthy of his interest.

'Not mine,' said Vanessa firmly, starting to edge towards the door, clutching her burden. She didn't trust this sudden communicativeness of his. He had never shown any inclination to discuss literature or philosophy with his butler before... or 'household executive assistant' as he had ludicrously suggested she be re-titled.

She had given that idea short shrift. She was a butler and proud of it. It was what she had trained for. It was in her blood. Her English father was a butler and she had grown up in the stately British household that was his fiefdom, fascinated by the day-to-day management of what was not only a home but a family seat, and a three-hundred-year-old one at that. It had been her fond ambition to hold a similar position one day but, as she had discovered, life had a nasty way of subverting youthful ambitions.

'No? That surprises me. I thought that coping with the unexpected was one of your great strengths. You certainly never had any problem accommodating the most bizarre requests of my guests... You didn't turn a hair at the pet lion cub, or the demand to find enough sculls for a wagered boat race on the lake, or, for that matter, the man who collapsed in the soup with a newly developed seafood allergy. Without your prompt action he might have died.'

'I didn't say I couldn't cope,' said Vanessa, taken aback by his easy recall of incidents she had assumed were long dismissed from his mind as supremely unimportant. At the time they occurred she had merely received a cool word of approval, as if she had done nothing more, nor less, than was required of her. 'I just said I didn't react well—personally, I mean. I get churned up inside...'

'It doesn't show.'

'Thank you.' She was already regretting having told him that much. He was studying her with an intentness that increased her anxieties.

Her fingers curled into her palms as she fought the desire to check her hair. As it dried it would lighten several shades to the warm caramel that was so susceptible to the bleaching effects of the summer sun, although thankfully the gel she used to keep the sides tidy would prevent its waviness becoming too obvious. Still, Benedict Savage was an architect, skilled in the interpretation of line and form, observant of small details that might escape others...

'It was a comment, not a compliment.'

'In my profession that *is* a compliment,' Vanessa retorted with an unconscious air of smugness that prompted an amused drawl.

'Being a servant is hardly one of the professions.'

Vanessa bristled at the implied slur. Snob!

'Of course not, sir. I humbly beg your pardon for my presumption, sir.' She would have bowed and tugged her forelock but that would be going over the top. As it was his eyes glinted dangerously.

'You have a devastating line in obsequiousness, Flynn. One might almost suspect it was insolence. Why have I never noticed that before, I wonder?'

Because she had never allowed herself to be so fixed in his attention before. Aghast at her foolishness, Vanessa tried to retrench.

'I don't mean to be——'

'You mean you didn't think I'd notice. Have I really been so complacent an employer?'

'No, of course not,' she lied weakly, and watched his thin mouth crook in a faint sneer.

'Sycophancy, Flynn? Was that on the curriculum at that exclusive English school for butlers that you graduated, drenched with honours, from?'

This fresh evidence of the acuteness of his memory was daunting. She hugged the trailing sheets to her chest and refused to answer, realising that no answer, however cunningly phrased, would please him. He didn't *want* to be pleased. He wanted a whipping-boy for his frustration. The irony was that she had richly earned the position!

'That's right,' he said silkily. 'Humour me. After all, you can afford to. You know I can't fire you.'

'Can't you?' Vanessa said, sensing an unforeseen trap in his goading.

'Well, I could, but that would jeopardise all that I'm doing here, wouldn't it?'

'Would it?' Vanessa was now bewildered.

'You could tie me up in legal manoeuvring for years——'

'Could I?'

Her response was a little too quick, a little too curious. His eyes narrowed. Vanessa straightened her spine and squared her shoulders, lifting her chin in a characteristic attempt to establish her physical superiority.

'I could, couldn't I?' she rephrased with a suitable tinge of menace, but not all the threatening body language and fighting language at her disposal could redeem that brief and telling hesitation.

'Could you?'

'Yes.' Her teeth nibbled unknowingly at her full lower lip.

'And how, precisely, would you do it?'

She was even more at sea, the look in his blue eyes creating a turbulence that reminded her what a poor sailor she was. He looked amused and—her stomach roiled—almost *compassionate*!

'Well, I...I...'

'You don't know, do you?' he said gently. 'You have absolutely no idea what I'm talking about.'

She lifted her chin even higher. 'No.' Her tone implied that neither did she care to find out.

He knew better.

'Did you not understand Judge Seaton's lawyer when he explained the situation to you?' he said, still with that same, infuriating gentleness. 'He assured me that he'd spoken to you directly after the funeral and that you'd appeared quite calm and collected.'

Vanessa frowned, trying to remember, her brows rumpling her smooth, wide forehead.

She had looked on Judge Seaton as not only a saviour but also as a man she had respected and admired and come to develop a fond affection for.

He had rescued her from the depths of misfortune and she, in turn, had travelled across the world with him, rescuing him from the inertia of his unwelcome retirement and the vicissitudes of old age and an irascible personality. Solitary by nature and never having married, when the judge had started having difficulty in getting about and suffering short memory lapses Vanessa had been the one who chivvied him out of his fits of depression and inspired him to start the book he had still been enthusiastically working on when he died—a social history of his adopted home, Whitefield House, and the surrounding Coromandel region.

His death, though not unexpected in view of his failing health, had been a shock, and at the time of the funeral Vanessa had still been numb and subconsciously hostile towards any threat of change in the haven that she had striven to create for herself at Whitefield. She had mentally switched off at any mention of an arrogantly youthful usurper who, it seemed to her, was proposing to take up his inheritance with unconscionable speed, given the fact that he had never bothered to visit his benefactor while he was alive, nor deigned to attend his funeral.

When Benedict Savage had finally made his appearance a week later he had proved totally alien to the late judge both physically and in temperament—something else that Vanessa had fiercely resented.

The fact that the hostility between them was mutual had suited her preconceptions so well that she had sought no explanation for it beyond the superficial. She was safe with male hostility. She could deal with it. It was male interest that made her nervous—self-consciously clumsy, inept and, worst of all, frighteningly vulnerable.

'I remember him rambling on and on about the will,' she said slowly. 'About there being no financial provision for me or some such thing, not that I expected one—I wasn't family and I'd only been with him two years. I don't remember what the lawyer said exactly. I was tired; I wasn't concentrating very well. I was the one who had to make all the arrangements for the funeral, you know. You didn't bother to arrive until it was all over!' There was a touch of querulousness in her voice, the echo of that three-year-old hostility.

'I won't apologise for that,' he said evenly. 'George Seaton and I were only very distantly related on my mother's side. He may well have not known of my existence—I certainly didn't know of his. He didn't leave the house to me by name, he simply deeded it to his closest surviving male blood-relative. Needless to say, my mother was *not* amused at being told she was no more than a mere twig on the family inheritance tree.'

She hadn't known that. It certainly threw a different light on his behaviour. And, having found his parents, on the strength of their single, fleeting visit to Whitefield, even more frigid, hypercritical and self-orientated than their son, she could just imagine Denise Savage's classically beautiful face frozen in an expression of Victorian affront at being confronted with the evidence of her unimportance in the male scheme of things.

A ghost of a smile widened Vanessa's mouth. 'He was an appalling old male chauvinist pig,' she admitted with affectionate disapproval.

'And yet he hired a female butler barely out of her teens?'

For once Vanessa didn't freeze up at the delicate probe.

'I just happened to be in the right place at the right time.' And for all the wrong reasons, extremely sordid ones. 'His previous butler had died after being with him for about fifty years. I don't think he could bear the idea of setting another man in his place and I suppose I appealed to his sense of chivalry...'

'Why do you say that?'

Her mouth twisted softly awry. 'He felt sorry for me——' She had almost forgotten whom she was talking to but a sudden shift in his alertness, causing light to flash like a warning signal off the lenses of his glasses, reminded her. 'I was in between jobs at the time,' she explained blandly.

'Well, he certainly made sure you wouldn't lose this one,' Benedict commented. 'A condition of my inheriting was that I retain the services of the existing butler for at least five years from the date of probate being granted...unless said butler voluntarily relinquished her duties.'

Vanessa's eyes and mouth rounded in astonishment at the revelation. Then a rush of anger flushed her system and her mouth snapped. 'But that first day—you threatened to get rid of me because I was a woman!'

'Untrue. I simply suggested that you would not find me as congenial as the judge to work for, and that you would be happier elsewhere. And I think that "girl" might have been the word I actually used...'

'Suggested nothing! You were deliberately insulting,' Vanessa remembered bitterly. 'You implied I couldn't do the job because of my sex. You implied that I only had it because I had some kind of hold over a senile old man. The judge wasn't senile and you knew it—the lawyer must have been perfectly clear about the validity of that will. You were trying to get me to quit!' she realised explosively. 'Well, I'm glad I refused!'

Not for the world would she tell him that it was cowardice that had held her back, not a determination to prove him wrong. Not even his slimy allegations could winkle her out of the safe little burrow she had dug for herself. Whitefield needed her and she needed Whitefield. Here she was known only by her name and her job, and not by her reputation.

'And I wasn't a girl, either!' she finished angrily, determined to deny him on all counts. 'I was twenty, and I've always been very mature for my age.' It was what had been her downfall—her air of calm self-sufficiency combined with a body that, Everest-like, was a challenge to a particular kind of man simply because it was so majestically *there*. Such splendid isolation had cried out to be conquered...

'You looked like one to me—a big, gangly girl, slow as a wet week, with a surly black adolescent glower and a habit of looking down your nose at me as if I were a lower form of life. No wonder I didn't want to have you foisted upon me!'

She immediately felt thick and ungainly, all elbows and knees, the way she used to feel as an wildly overgrown teenager. It was a long time since anyone had made her so clumsily self-aware and she didn't like it. Not at all. Unknowingly she gave him the same filthy black look that she had given him back then.

'When you're my size you can't flit about like a humming bird,' she gritted. 'If I move carefully it's because I have to calculate clearances that other women take for granted. I doubt if you'd want me blundering about among all these antiques. I'm not, and have *never* been, *slow*. Speed is not necessarily an indication of efficiency, you know. In time-and-motion terms, my way is a lot more energy-efficient than if I was rushing about creating a lot of hustle and bustle over tasks that can be performed simply and without fuss!'

If he recognised his favourite phrase being lobbed back in his face, he didn't acknowledge it. Instead, her vehement lecture appeared to amuse him. She made a tentative move around him and he shifted his weight, blocking her path with the mere threat of further movement.

'Mm, so I very quickly discovered. Why do you think I didn't persist in my efforts to get rid of you? You don't appear to exert yourself unduly and yet the work is always done and this house always runs like a well-oiled machine...' If only he had seen her flying up the stairs that morning. Talk about exerting herself unduly! 'If you had been other than supremely capable I'd never have left the supervision of the restorations in your hands. You've never violated that trust. I wasn't criticising you just now, I was simply telling you what my first impressions of you were.'

'Thank you, but I could have done without knowing,' said Vanessa acidly, thinking that his trust would be summarily withdrawn if he knew the truth about her... not merely about last night but the whole ugly mess that had prompted the judge's job offer and her ignominious flight from England.

She wondered what his reaction would be if she blurted it all out now. He would probably run the full gauntlet: shock, horror, distaste. She had seen it all before, from people far less fastidious than Benedict Savage, people who were supposed to have been her friends.

'I thought it time to get it out in the open—so that I might begin to feel less like an interloper here.'

'Interloper?' Vanessa's impatience got the better of her. 'Don't be ridiculous,' she told her employer. 'The house *belongs* to you; you can't be an interloper in your own home.'

A grim smile twitched his hard cheek. 'Can't you?' His voice lifted from a barely audible irony to that familiar ironic crispness. 'But then, this isn't really my home, is it? If one counts a home as a family dwelling, or a residence one has a sentimental attachment to through regular use, I suppose you could call me effectively homeless. I don't think I've spent more than a month at a time at the same address in the last five years.'

The faintly wistful self-derision in his words gave Vanessa a pang but she caught herself before she started feeling too sorry for him. The man was a millionaire for goodness' sake; he had everything he could possibly want and he had the nerve to complain because his life wasn't perfect! There were people in the world—in this country—who lived in cardboard cartons, or worse, and here he was complaining about having too many homes!

'How absolutely frightful for you,' she replied with a crispness that brought his head up with a jerk. 'Jobless *and* homeless. No wonder you're depressed. If I were you I'd be suicidal.'

'If you were me you wouldn't be having the problems I'm having,' he said cryptically, after a tiny pause and an all-encompassing look that made her extremely nervous. 'And I can't envisage you ever taking the easy way out of your problems. You're the type to go down with all guns blazing.'

'I don't approve of firearms,' she said primly, disturbed by the accuracy of his reading of her character.

'We have something in common, then...other than sharing possession of this house. That is what we do, isn't it, legal ownership not withstanding? You're the one who really makes a home of this house; you're the one who brings it to daily life, who imprints it with personality...'

Vanessa was aghast at the thought that her possessiveness about the house might be the object of amused speculation to others. It was her secret, her little piece of foolish whimsy. Her eyes were stony as she denied her weakness. 'I enjoy seeing the house restored to some of its former glory but I'm the caretaker, that's all. I'm just carrying out your orders.'

'Since I'm hardly ever here to issue them that statement is highly debatable.'

Her eagerness to preserve the state of armed neutrality between them that had made it so easy to treat him as a cypher instead of a human being made her quick to sense criticism.

'If you're not satisfied with my work——'

'I never said that. On the contrary, I'm delighted with the high standards you've maintained in trying circumstances. The restorations are turning out even better than I envisaged. After you've finished your bed-making I'll get you to give me a tour to show me the progress...'

Although bringing him up to date with the work carried out in his absence was a familiar duty that she usually tackled with quiet pride, the thought of spending more time alone in his company while her nerves were still in such a jittery state made Vanessa quail. Fortunately she had a ready excuse at hand.

'I've arranged for some members of the historical society to visit this morning. You did say you didn't mind them being shown around in return for access to their records about the house. Perhaps they could tag along?'

He looked unenthused at the prospect. 'Is Miss Fisher one of them?'

'As a matter of fact, yes,' Vanessa said innocently. The elderly lady, an archetypal twittering spinster, had taken a shine to the elusive new owner of Whitefield and would make a thorough nuisance of herself if she knew he was back in residence.

'In that case I think I might take the Duesenberg out for a couple of hours,' he said hastily. 'You can give me the tour after lunch. If that fits in with your plans, of course.'

'Of course, sir,' she murmured dutifully, heaving an inward sigh of relief as she retreated into the safety of her usual, self-effacing role.

'And don't tell her I'm here,' he scowled.

'Of course not, sir.'

'The woman is a human limpet.'

'Indeed, sir.'

He gave her bland expression a coruscating glare. 'Are you mocking me, Flynn?'

'No, sir,' she lied smoothly.

'Good. Because I can tolerate a lot of things from my employees—insubordination included, if they're good at what they do—but I don't like being laughed at.'

It was definitely an order.

'Nobody does, sir,' Vanessa murmured judiciously. She had noticed that about him—his lack of laughter—it was what contributed to her impression of him as having a somewhat colourless personality. Although he was good-humoured to a fault, he rarely showed any spontaneity. His smile was more of a cynical twist than an expression of warmth. Little seemed to take him by surprise.

Except this morning. This morning he had been caught very much by surprise. The result had been a very distinct loss of that apparently inhuman self-control, and she wondered how much control he had lost last night, when the surprise must have been infinitely greater! She swallowed, her arms tightening possessively on the sheets that bore witness to her own self-betrayal, struggling against the return of her earlier panic. Surely her guilt was stamped all over her face?

Apparently not, because her employer was turning away from her, running his hand rapidly over his chin, the same boyish eagerness in his expression that she had glimpsed in the library, and she realised that his thoughts were running ahead to the birthday present he had been side-tracked from enjoying.

'I don't suppose your historians will be here for a few minutes so it's safe for me to have a shave before I leave. I think I'll take a run up the coast to Coromandel, or maybe even Colville or Port Jackson, if I feel like it. Tell Mrs Riley I'll be back for lunch about one—if you're sure they'll be gone by then.'

'I'll make certain they are, sir,' she assured him. By one o'clock she was sure she'd also be able to persuade herself into a more rational frame of mind.

'Good.' He turned at the entrance to his bathroom, to throw her one more terrifying curve over his shoulder. 'Oh, by the way—don't lock me out again.'

She froze on the threshold of escape. 'I beg your pardon?'

'Downstairs just now. The French doors to the library—you locked them after I went out to look at the car. I had to go around to the front door and knock until Mrs Riley let me back in.'

Vanessa sent up a prayer of thanks. 'Did I? I must have done it automatically. I'm sorry for the inconvenience, sir. It won't happen again.'

Not if she could help it, anyway. The circumstances leading up to her action were, after all, extremely unlikely to recur!

CHAPTER FOUR

'WELL, that should be the last of your rising-damp problem,' Bill Jessop told Vanessa with deep satisfaction as he rose from his crouch in front of the strip of exposed stonework a metre high that ran along the interior wall of what had been the servants' dining-room. 'That last section has dried out nicely. You can get the plasterer to work on it as soon as you like.'

Vanessa followed suit, dusting off her hands as she straightened. 'I just hope we don't find any anywhere else,' she sighed.

'You can't really complain when the place is over a hundred years old,' said the stonemason. 'I think the big problem was that the original builder didn't finish the job. Now *he* was a real craftsman.'

'A pity he succumbed to the gold fever,' said Vanessa with the fine disdain of someone who had never lusted after great riches. 'Instead of drowning in a flooded mine he could have had a long life of quiet prosperity if he'd stuck to his original plan.'

'Maybe it was excitement he was after, rather than the actual gold,' said Bill, a big, stolid man who looked as rough as the materials he worked with. 'Or maybe he was running away from something, or someone. Didn't you say that his wife worked as a cook here for a couple of years after he took off, and had a reputation for being a right old harridan?'

'I don't blame her for being shrewish if her husband deserted her,' said Vanessa tartly. 'Colonial life could be pretty brutal for a woman who didn't have a man to protect her. I'm sure she'd rather have had her husband than the gold.'

'Do you think so? I think she would have been more practical than that. "Gold will buy the highest honours; and gold will purchase love."'

Vanessa spun around, automatically smoothing her hands down the sides of her skirt as she watched her employer pick his way around the ladders and planks that cluttered the doorway.

He had come back from his drive obviously relaxed, his face glowing with wind-burn and his normally economical movements expansive under the lingering effects of high-speed adrenalin. He had described the performance of the powerful car at what Vanessa thought was tiresome length as she'd served his soup, then promptly buried his nose in an architectural magazine while he ate, not even acknowledging the substitution of his empty bowl with a salad, followed by a plate of cheese and crackers. Vanessa had waited until he left the dining-room to take a business call before she'd slipped in to clear the table, congratulating herself that he had appeared to have forgotten his demand for an immediate tour. An oblivious, inattentive and introspective Benedict she was well used to and could handle with ease.

A trickle of dismay slithered down her spine as she realised that she had instinctively referred to him by his Christian name. How had that solecism crept into her thoughts? She glared at him, mentally trying to cram him back into the insulated box labelled 'Mr Savage'. He was not co-operative.

'That's a cynical point of view, Mr Savage,' Bill Jessop said with a conspiratorial male grin. 'I don't think Vanessa is going to agree with you on that.'

She refused to be goaded, folding her hands primly and maintaining a respectful silence as Benedict came to a halt beside them. He had changed, she noticed, into a long-sleeved white polo-shirt which was more casual than anything else she had seen him wear. It must be new, she decided. Something he had brought with him, for she hadn't noticed it in his wardrobe before. The soft draping flattered his lean muscularity, and, tucked into black trousers, emphasised the perfect masculine proportioning of wide shoulders and slim hips.

He looked at her and when she didn't reply his face assumed a bland expression to reflect her own.

'Not me... I was merely quoting Ovid on the Art of Love. That particular piece of cynicism is nearly two thousand years old, but I think that the passage of time has proved the wisdom of his words, wouldn't you say, Flynn?'

She could hardly ignore a direct question but neither did she want to stroke his ego by agreeing with him. 'Then how is it that you're not knighted and married by now?' she prevaricated sweetly, and he laughed.

Vanessa stared. The most humour she had seen him display was a quiet chuckle. His narrow face with its hard, slashing cheekbones, straight, precisely even black brows and high forehead had seemed rigid and austere, the face of a born ascetic. Now, with a sting of shock, she glimpsed a teasing hint of mischief in the warm animation of previously inflexible features, a promise of passion in the relaxed curve of his mouth. In laughter, as in sleep, there was a fullness in his lower lip that was normally disguised by the controlled tautness of his conscious expression. For the first time Vanessa wondered at the origin of that formidable self-control and the faint air of tension that he wore like a cloak—or a suit of armour.

Horrified to find herself studying his mouth with feminine curiosity, Vanessa tore her eyes away, to find that he had stopped laughing and was watching her with an unsettling intentness.

'Perhaps I'm too much of a miser,' he murmured, 'to pay for what I see other men getting for free.'

Bill Jessop laughed at that. 'Nobody who's seen the kind of money you're pouring into this place would call you miserly!'

'Mr Savage looks on it as an investment,' Vanessa pointed out evenly. 'He expects to make a good return on his money by selling as soon as the restorations are finished.' Perhaps it was her very lack of tone that tipped him off, for he was quick to respond, to sense an underlying hostility.

'You think I should be doing it for purely sentimental reasons?' he said. 'Why should I be so altruistic? I have no more historical or personal connection with Whitefield than—than you do.' She stiffened at this casual reminder of her place. 'What would you have me do? Live here permanently myself? The place is far too big for one person, and besides, it's being renovated as an inn. Can you imagine me as a hotelier?'

'Actually, yes,' Vanessa said, stretching her imagination stubbornly. 'You're used to playing host to numerous guests at a time. The only difference is that they would be paying you for the privilege instead of freeloading...' She bit her lip as her true opinion of some of his non-business guests slipped out, but he merely quirked her an oddly considering smile.

'"Playing" being the operative word. I learned a long time ago the value of preventative socialisation as a method of preserving my privacy. A large part of my youth comprised politely displaying for guests. My parents always seemed to be entertaining a continuous flow of friends and new acquaintances. Unfortunately I had no brothers and sisters to take the spotlight off me, so I acquired a fine repertoire of conversational tricks to conceal my shyness and resentment of the instant intimacy that people seemed to think was the required response. I was a Savage and therefore expected to thrive on all the attention. My parents would have been very disappointed in me if they had known how much I hated having to prove myself their son over and over again...'

Vanessa was unnerved by the nonchalance with which he delivered his startlingly frank disclosure. She took an automatic step back, trying to widen the distance between them, but she took with her the mental picture of a quiet, solitary child forced to adopt an adult gregariousness in order to please his parents.

She, too, was an only child but her parents had always made her feel all the more special for being different from them, an individual in her own right. Secure in the circle of their love, she had felt free to rebel and to assert herself, to strike out and make her own mistakes, knowing that any disappointment they felt would be *for* her, not with her.

'It doesn't show,' she murmured.

'I hope that was a compliment, not a comment,' he said smoothly and she realised that he was playing with phrases from their conversation in his bedroom that morning.

'You could always put in a manager and reap the benefits of ownership without the day-to-day hassles,' she said, refusing to acknowledge the significance of his word-play. 'You present the right kind of image: charming yet aloof.'

'Why do I get the feeling that's definitely *not* a compliment?' he murmured back, not giving her time to reply. 'Do I really come across as distant and supercilious? I've always thought of myself as elusive rather than aloof.'

His gaze was engagingly rueful as it met hers, as if he was aware of the inherent romanticism of his self-perception, and was faintly embarrassed by it.

'You can certainly be very elusive when you choose to be,' Vanessa conceded wryly, remembering the numerous times she had had to drag him out for meals. Times when he had shut himself up in his studio with his architectural computer and drawing instruments and left his guests to their own devices.

'No more than you. We had agreed that you were going to bring me up to date on the restorations this afternoon.'

'I was waiting for you to let me know when you were ready,' Vanessa fibbed, conscious of Bill Jessop standing patiently by, his grey eyes bright with interest.

'Really? Is that why I spent ages yanking those damned bell-ropes to no avail?'

Vanessa pinkened at the pleasantly accusing tone. 'I'm sorry, I meant to warn you that the bells have been disconnected while some of the tubing is being replaced.' The vintage mechanical system of zinc tubes encasing sliding copper wires still worked remarkably well and only one or two of the row of bells which hung in the butler's pantry next to the kitchen had had to be replaced.

'Mm, you obviously didn't hear me yelling up and down the halls, either.'

Vanessa raised her eyebrows at him, knowing full well that he had done no such thing. He was too well-trained to stoop to such vulgarity.

'Obviously not.'

'I was beginning to feel like a wraith of my former self... drifting around an empty house with no one to acknowledge my wailing and gnashing of teeth,' he exaggerated lazily. 'I half expected to meet up with my golden-haired ghost again.'

'Ghost?' The stonemason's ears pricked up. 'You've seen a ghost?'

'I told him about Meg,' Vanessa cut in hurriedly, moving determinedly away from the two men in an attempt to draw them apart. 'We won't hold you up from your work any longer, Bill. Mr Savage—shall we start the tour in the drawing-room? It's been papered since you were last here...'

'I certainly saw something in my room late last night,' Benedict said, ignoring her desperate shepherding motion. 'If it was a ghost then she was uncannily lifelike, whoever she was. Have you ever seen this Meg?'

'Well, not myself, no,' Bill replied rubbing his stone-roughened hands together as if to remove a chill. 'But then, I've never been here alone after dark. I've heard tell of some strange goings-on here over the years. Nobody had lived in the place for a couple of years before the judge bought it and it was getting pretty derelict. Personally, I don't know if I believe in ghosts, as such...'

'Neither did I until last night,' said Benedict Savage drily. 'In fact I could have sworn she was as real as you or I.'

'Oh, it always pays to keep an open mind about such things,' Vanessa said quickly. 'The existence of certain psychic phenomena has been well-documented. And if any place can claim to be the site of spiritual turmoil, then Whitefield can. Meg's wasn't the only death by violence here over the last hundred years.'

'You mean I may find myself visited by more apparitions?' He sounded dismayingly intrigued by the prospect. 'How lucky I'm not of a nervous disposition. Perhaps the *Architectural Journal* might be interested in a paper on the subject—the influence of the fifth dimension on architectural conservation. If all my ghosts are as beauteous and willing as the golden-haired Meg I should have no trouble in arousing interest...'

From the corner of her eye Vanessa saw Bill open his mouth to inform him that Meg had been a flaming redhead, not a blonde.

'Yes, I'm sure the historical society would be *very* interested,' she interposed brightly. Willing? What precisely did he mean by *willing*? 'Miss Fisher in particular is a bit of a psychic buff. If she got to hear that you'd had a visitation from the other side, she'd be up here in a flash with her tape-recorder and psychic investigator's handbook, haunting the place herself.'

To her satisfaction her employer blanched, but then he slanted her a keen look. 'For a warning, that sounded distressingly close to a threat, Flynn.'

'I'm sorry, sir,' she murmured with just the correct touch of haughty surprise. 'You told me this morning that you wanted to avoid Miss Fisher and I just thought I should point out the possibility. You know how people in these small communities talk...'

'People might, but since I know you're an utterly loyal and devoted employee, and since Bill here doesn't want to get fired, I don't see how any of this conversation is in danger of leaking out.'

Instead of being offended, Bill laughed. 'I suppose I'd better get back to washing off down that south wall before you decide to fire me, anyway. Nice to see you back again, Mr Savage.' He touched his forelock in a mock-salute as he backed towards the door. 'See you later, Vanessa.'

'Pleasant man,' Benedict Savage commented, running his hand over the mortar in the joints between the grey stone blocks. 'Does a fine job, too. Robert did well to find him.'

Robert Taylor, a specialist restoration architect who worked in the Auckland office of Dane Benedict, had drawn up the plans and a schedule of work for the inn and had been heavily involved in the initial stages...until both he and his boss had realised that Vanessa was more than capable of supervising the ongoing work, even to the extent of employing tradesman as they were required. Now Robert only made a special trip down to Thames as certain, agreed-upon stages were completed.

'Actually, I was the one who found Bill,' said Vanessa quietly. She got on very well with Robert, but he was ambitious and somewhat opportunistic in his eagerness to create a good impression and she thought it did him no favours to let him get away with it too often. 'I'd heard of him through the historical society and seen some of the work he's done in Waihi.'

'I stand corrected.' His casual nod told her that he was aware of his young colleague's failing as he continued, placing a mocking hand over his heart, 'Please, just don't tell me that the ubiquitous Miss Fisher had anything to do with it.'

She couldn't help a small smile escaping the stiffness of her control, her brown eyes lightening with the fugitive gleam.

'No. Madeline's area of expertise is kitchen utensils and cooking-ovens.'

'And ghosts.'

Vanessa's eyes slid away. 'And ghosts,' she conceded reluctantly, feeling herself sinking deeper and deeper in the mire of the foolish deception that had grown out of her choice of diversion. She cleared her throat. 'Where would you like to start your tour?'

'Weren't you anxious to show me the drawing-room a few minutes ago? I was rather distracted last time I was here—I had that Japanese consortium in tow—so I think perhaps you should just show me everything you've done in the last six months. I'm entirely in your hands this afternoon.'

Vanessa looked down at the hands in question. She thought them too large, like the rest of her, but the long, ringless fingers were slender and well-shaped, the round nails short and burnished with natural polish.

He had been in her hands this morning, too, she remembered treacherously. Her palm had been cupped over the rippling tautness of his back, while her left hand had been tucked cosily between their bodies, her fingers curled against his smooth upper chest, measuring the rise and fall of his contented sleep and tingling with the faint vibration of his steady heartbeat. But of course that had been nothing to where *his* hands had been...

'Flynn?'

Her head jerked up and she felt her skin begin to heat up as he regarded her with polite puzzlement.

'Er...yes...good idea. In that case, we'll start with the main dining-room. The marble mantelpiece came back from the workshop last week and you'll be able to see what a difference a professional cleaning job is going to make on that awful one in the drawing-room...'

She was so anxious to escape the intimacy of her thoughts that she rattled on, inundating him with technical details as she took him through the public rooms that were now almost completely restored, albeit with some discreet modern touches necessary for the comfort and healthy well-being of future guests, to what they had been in the former glory years of gold-inspired prosperity.

Judge Seaton had had the enthusiasm and the knowledge but not the financial resources to indulge in more than cosmetic improvements to the old building and Vanessa knew that he would have heartily approved of the changes that his unknown heir had wrought to what had been a sorely neglected piece of local history, whatever Benedict's mercenary reasons for doing so. Perhaps what had happened had been exactly what he had been hoping for when he had written that extraordinary codicil to his will. He had known that Vanessa shared his love of the dilapidated old place, that she looked upon Whitefield as the home she had never really had. He had enjoyed inspiring her with his love of history and perhaps he had been relying on the possessive sense of belonging he had engendered in her to ensure that she would maintain a careful watching brief over Whitefield after he was gone. The thought pleased her far more than did the notion that he might have made that stipulation purely out of pity, or concern that she wasn't strong enough to stand on her own two feet.

Her obvious pride of accomplishment didn't escape the man at her side as he meekly allowed himself to be lectured from room to room like a laggardly schoolboy. At first largely silent, he began interrupting her flow with a pertinent question here and there, just enough to encourage her subtly out of the formal recitation of dry facts into expressing a revealing enthusiasm for her subject. When she forgot herself she even moved differently, her stride long and eager, her hips and arms swinging in an uninhibited rhythm, her head and hands contributing expressively to the conversation.

'I'm glad you don't feel that a contemporary bathroom is an unforgivable betrayal of the integrity of the restoration,' Benedict murmured as he surveyed the chaos of plumbing that sprouted from the tiled wall in one of the small upstairs sitting-rooms which were being converted into bathrooms for the adjoining bedrooms.

'This is going to be a working hotel, not a museum,' Vanessa was quick to defend. 'People expect a reasonable standard of accommodation for their money. Tourists may enjoy visiting museums but they don't want to *stay* in them, especially if it means sacrificing their creature comforts. For the sake of strict authenticity we'd have to offer them a wash-stand and chamberpot or portable commode and I don't see many of them wanting to put up with that! The 1870s were still pretty primitive in this part of the world... I mean, the country had only been settled for a few decades and most of the people's energy was going into scraping a living from the land. As long as the public rooms are restored in their period I don't see a conflict, since the kitchens and bathrooms have to be upgraded to meet modern health standards anyway.'

'Mm, hip-baths in front of the fire do rather lose their rustic appeal when you know you have to haul twenty buckets of hot water up the stairs first,' said Benedict musingly.

'*You* wouldn't be doing any hauling,' Vanessa pointed out sourly. 'Except perhaps on the bell-rope.'

'You don't think much of me, do you, Flynn?' he startled her by saying. 'You seem to think I'm incapable of doing anything for myself. A complete wimp, in fact.'

'Of... of course not, sir,' she denied, not deceived by his mildness. No man who was a complete wimp could have a body that felt like tensile steel wrapped in warm silk, or dominate, as he did, with a mere look. 'I—it's part of my job to make sure you don't have to do manual labour around the house——'

'During holiday breaks when I was studying architecture, I worked as a building labourer—much to my parents' disgust. I may give the impression that I'm a pampered rich brat but I do make some effort to keep in touch with the real world.'

'Of course you do, sir.'

Her soothing tone made his eyes narrow. 'Are you going to "sir" me to death again now?'

'No, s——' She cleared her throat. She hadn't realised how automatically the word sprang to her lips when she was feeling defensive. 'No, of course not.'

'I hate it when you do that.'

'Do what, s——? Do what?'

'Agree with me in that unspeakably pleasant voice,' he said succinctly. 'And don't say that's what I pay you for. I never did have much respect for yes-men. Or yes-women.'

It was unfortunate that he tagged on that last phrase. It had connotations that made her go hot all over. If she had said yes to him last night she had forfeited a lot more than mere respect!

She stiffened at the dawning gleam of predatory amusement in his gaze as her slight flush made him aware of the sexual overtones of his throw-away remark.

'Although, I'll have to admit, there are certain situations where I love to hear nothing from a woman's mouth *but* the word yes...' he added limpidly, for the sheer pleasure of provoking her.

Her tanned cheeks acquired a deeper, carmine tint and her eyes darkened until they looked like smouldering black coals surrounded by a thick fire-screen of gold-tipped lashes. Her first instinct was to flare back at him, but she resisted fiercely.

'I'm sure there are——' She bit off the sentence before it reached its natural conclusion, but the contemptuous 'sir' hovered unspoken in the air between them and it goaded him further.

'You're blushing, Flynn.'

'That's because I'm embarrassed for you,' she said defiantly.

'Oh?' He looked justifiably wary. 'And why is that, may I ask?'

'Because taunting an inferior who can't fight back is beneath you,' she said with icy disdain.

He winced, acknowledging the skilful thrust before parrying quietly, 'I agree, except that I don't happen to think of any of the people in my employ as inferiors. They are people who work with me as well as for me, and there's give and take on both sides. Your job title may *appear* to make you subordinate to my will but I think we both know that you have a degree of autonomy here which puts you in a rather unique position of authority. I wouldn't even be surprised if, where Whitefield is concerned, you actually consider me *your* inferior...'

Vanessa's eyes flickered guiltily and his expression eased. 'As for fighting back,' he continued, giving her a look of wry respect, 'I think you've just proved that you're more than capable of doing that. I'm duly chastened by your polite disdain for my needling.' He moved restlessly over to the small window which overlooked the kitchen garden and low-walled brick courtyard behind the stables. 'Unfortunately I can't promise I'll never do it again. My moods have been rather unpredictable lately. Maybe I'm going though an early mid-life crisis.'

He sounded irritated with himself and Vanessa was so amused by his unlikely depression that she dared to say, 'I found an old walking stick in the attic last week, Mr Savage; perhaps you'd like me to fetch it for you?'

He spun around. 'Now who's being provoking?' But he was smiling the small, cool smile that was his trademark. 'I suppose you still approach each birthday with joyous anticipation. Wait until you hit thirty, then your perspective will change. I'm amazed that someone so young should have such a preoccupation with history.'

'It's an interest, not a preoccupation, and I'm not so many years younger than you——'

'A decade.' Again he exhibited his phenomenal memory for detail. 'You should still be looking dewy-eyed to the future, not back over your shoulder at the cobwebbed past.'

'We can learn a lot about our options for the future from the evidence of the past,' said Vanessa piously. 'I'm not the youngest in the historical society by a long chalk; we even have primary-school children as members.' She paused, then was unable to resist saying tartly, 'And I was never dewy-eyed.'

'Yes, you were,' he said unexpectedly, studying her wide eyes and grave mouth with its hint of repressed emotion. 'I bet you were brimming with painful innocence until adolescence hit you with a wallop. You must have had more difficulty adjusting than most girls. I suppose you were teased about your size by girls and boys alike, and treated as more mature than you actually were by the world in general.'

Now it was his turn to be amused as she backed off, startled by the thumbnail description of her awkward puberty. 'Don't look at me like that, Flynn; it's not sorcery, it's called applied intelligence. I can make an educated guess because I was teased for exactly the opposite reason. I was a late bloomer, both physically and intellectually. I was nearly seventeen when my voice broke, a string-bean with hardly a muscle to my name at an élite boarding-school where physical evidence of masculinity was the main criterion for judging peer status. To add to my misery I had an astigmatism that means I couldn't wear contact lenses. I passed most of my high-school years as a four-eyed wimp. On the other hand being slight did force me to learn the valuable art of talking my way out of trouble, which in the long run is a far more useful life-skill than the ability to thump the life out of someone smaller than you, don't you think?'

As Vanessa remained silent, stunned by yet another startling new facet of her employer's complex personality, he added coaxingly, 'That's your cue, Flynn, to say, Indubitably, sir, in that insufferably stuffy butler voice that you use to squash my pretensions.'

'I wouldn't dream of it,' said Vanessa weakly, wondering why he was opening up with such devastating intimacy to her just now, when it was vitally important to her mental well-being that he remain a convenient cypher, not a living, breathing human being riddled with intriguing weaknesses.

'Oh, well, in that case, shall we soldier on?' He moved to the open doorway and indicated that she should precede him. 'You can tell me more about the original inhabitants of the inn as we go. The extent of your research certainly makes them seem real. Have you ever been tempted to trace your own family tree? The lawyer said that your mother is a New Zealander...'

'She was,' Vanessa was forced to respond reluctantly. 'She died a few years ago.' Just before the storm over Egon St Clair's death had broken over Vanessa's unsuspecting head. It had highlighted her sense of isolation and, not wanting to worry a father already burdened with grief, she had made mistakes that had only added fuel to the ugly rumours that the St Clair family had circulated.

'I'm sorry. Was it an accident or had she been ill?'

'An illness, but it was very sudden.' Uneasy with the continuing thread of intimacy in the conversation, Vanessa distanced herself with a shrug. 'I do have a few great-aunts and uncles and some second cousins around but most of them live down in the South Island, and that's where the family history is. My mother never really kept in touch after she married Dad and went to England.' A fact Vanessa had been extremely glad of when she had first arrived in the country. The last thing she had wanted was to be inundated with family concern and curiosity.

They were coming to the head of the stairs and Vanessa was about to point out the handmade reproductions of the missing balusters when there was the sound of a car tooting in the front driveway.

'Excuse me, I'll just see who that is,' said Vanessa, welcoming the interruption.

'It can't be anyone for me. No one except Dane knows I'm here... and my personal assistant in New York, but she has express orders not to give out the information.' He kept pace with her on the stairs, reaching the front door first and opening it as if he were the butler and she a departing guest.

'Nice vehicle,' he commented as they stood on the stone steps and watched the driver unfold his considerable height from the front seat of a forest-green Range Rover.

'It's Richard.'

'The stud?' murmured Benedict, eyeing the brawny build and handsome features of the man striding across the gravel towards them.

SAVAGE COURTSHIP 65

'He *owns* a stud,' Vanessa hissed, pasting on a smile as Richard approached. Richard usually called before dropping in and if he had done so this morning she could have warned him off. As it was he couldn't have chosen a worse time to turn up out of the blue.

To compensate for her guilty thoughts she strove to sound as welcoming as possible and ended up sounding disgustingly coy. 'Hello, Richard. I didn't expect to see you again so soon.'

Before he could reply Benedict Savage smoothly interposed himself into the conversation by holding out his hand. 'Hello. Wells, isn't it? I was just saying I didn't realise anyone knew I was home.'

'Actually, I came to see Van,' said Richard, smiling pleasantly as he shook hands. Even standing on the second step down he almost topped them both, his bulky oatmeal sweater under the well-worn tweed jacket and working jeans tucked into calf-length boots emphasising his powerful frame. 'She gave me the impression last night that you weren't expected back for a while yet.'

Vanessa tensed. It wasn't beyond the realms of possibility for Benedict, in his present self-confessed state of unpredictable moodiness, to make some crass joke about the cat being away.

To her relief, 'I'm beginning to recognise a certain charm about the place,' was all he said. 'Would you like to come in? We've been looking over the house and were just about to break for coffee.'

That was news to Vanessa, since she would have been the one serving it. He also gave their activities a companionable sound that they had definitely lacked.

'No, thanks.' Richard shook his blond head. 'I just called to drop something off to Van.' He produced the 'something' from his jacket pocket—the tiny vial of perfume that she had filled from the fragile main bottle in her bedroom so that she could carry it in her evening bag. 'It must have dropped on to the floor of my car when you got your keys out.'

Vanessa was hard put to it not to snatch it out of his hand. All it would probably take would be one whiff and Benedict Savage, with his wretchedly superb memory, would connect it instantly with his fragrant ghost!

'Thank you, Richard,' she said, taking it gingerly in her long fingers and tucking it securely in the buttoned breast pocket of her blouse. 'But you needn't have made a special trip.'

'I didn't,' he said in his usual prosaic manner. 'I'm on my way to the vet's and had to go past your gate anyway, so I thought I may as well stop.' His brown eyes crinkled knowingly. 'I also thought it'd give me a chance to check on your health. How's the head this morning?'

Vanessa was aware of Benedict's own head turning her way. 'Fine, thanks,' she said hurriedly.

'Were you feeling ill last night?' Benedict sounded nettled as he studied her profile. 'You could have asked me for the day off. I don't expect you to work until you drop.'

'I was thinking more of her feeling ill *because* of last night.' Richard grinned genially. 'Vanessa had a few too many glasses of champagne.'

'Oh?' Even though she wasn't looking at him she could just *see* the blue eyes sharpen with interest. For the first time Vanessa regretted the qualities that had attracted her to Richard in the first place—his frank openness and the friendly good nature that was incapable of recognising malice. 'Celebrating something, were you?'

'The sale of a stallion of mine...and the pleasure of a pretty lady's company, of course,' added Richard gallantly.

'Of course,' repeated Benedict drily and Vanessa swung her head to glare at him. 'I hope you don't mind accepting second-place stakes,' he said blandly, confirming her suspicion that he was laughing at them.

She forgot that she was only interested in curtailing the conversation. 'I'm flattered that Richard wants to share his successes with me. His stud is developing a reputation for producing some of the best thoroughbred horses in Australasia.' There—now let him try to dismiss Richard as an unsophisticated country hick!

'You mean I can expect my butler to come home legless at fairly regular intervals?' was the droll reply.

'I wasn't *legless*,' Vanessa protested coolly, 'I was merely...' She searched for a properly dignified word.

'Over-tired,' Richard interceded diplomatically, then spoiled it by joking, 'Van is a very quiet drunk.'

'No sea-shanties? No brawling? No dancing on the tables?' Benedict smiled engagingly and Richard's good nature fell for it like a ton of bricks.

'I should never have let her polish off most of that second bottle,' he confided, with a grin of masculine fellowship. 'But since I was driving she said it was her moral responsibility to make sure I didn't stray over the alcohol limit. What could I say? Of course, that was before she began to see the funny side of things. I'm afraid I had to hustle her home early when the dreaded giggles struck.'

'You giggle?' Benedict raised a disbelieving eyebrow at her, as well he might. Her face was perfectly stony, rigid with the fear that Richard was going to mention just *how* early he had got her home...

'I think I'm getting that headache you mentioned now, Richard,' she said firmly.

He laughed and accepted the heavy-handed hint. 'And I must get on to the vet's.'

'Are you sure you won't come in? We could have a chat while "Van" finds her aspirin.'

Vanessa gritted her teeth, but fortunately Richard was proof against further charm. 'Some other time. Will you be staying long?'

'I'm not sure. It depends,' Benedict responded with typical reserve, and then took Vanessa's breath away by saying casually, 'I'm considering sectioning off part of the upstairs as a private apartment and putting a manager in to handle the hotel side of things. The finishing work isn't so far advanced that it couldn't accommodate a few more structural alterations without involving too much extra time and money. So I may soon be here more or less permanently, Wells. At my age a man starts to think about settling down...'

When Richard had gone Vanessa asked him sharply, 'What did you say that for?'

'Because I decided that your idea has definite possibilities after all.' And then he neatly curtailed her desire for further discussion on the subject by drawling sarcastically, 'I can quite see the appeal you two might have for each other. You make a magnificently matched pair, negative and positive, fair and dark—an earthy god and a giggling goddess. If you breed true, your children will be a race of thoroughbred Titans! Shall we get on and do the service areas now?'

He turned on his heel and stalked into the house, leaving Vanessa open-mouthed and furious at his insulting audacity.

CHAPTER FIVE

A WEEK later Vanessa was feeling as if she had been flattened by a runaway truck.

She only had herself to blame. She had known her employer would not be able to bear being bored for much longer than a few hours. He might have decided he *needed* a holiday, but he didn't really *want* one.

What he really wanted, she'd realised after days of watching him restlessly poke and pry and question everything she had done or planned to do, was *change*. He was rebelling against the subtle regimentation of his well-ordered professional life and her impulsive suggestion had provided him with the perfect challenge, an opportunity to be whimsical, since she couldn't believe he really intended to give up his peripatetic lifestyle to languish in the backwater of a small-town inn.

Unfortunately, his method of indulging a personal whimsy had proved to be every bit as serious, meticulously planned and competitive as everything else he did. First, he'd decided that he needed to know every detail of Whitefield's history and reconstruction; he had even called Robert Taylor down for a special consultation, and had gone over all Vanessa's old reports with a fine-tooth comb. Then he had started to prowl.

With the Duesenberg only a fond memory—how Vanessa wished that Dane Judson had leased it for a week instead of merely a weekend—there was nothing to lure Benedict away from the house, and everywhere she'd turned he'd seemed to be relentlessly underfoot. After having had virtual free run of Whitefield for most of the last three years it had been extremely disconcerting to have to confer and defer to a higher power and Vanessa had disliked it even more than she had expected that she would.

She couldn't even get on with her routine daily duties in peace because she was constantly being interrupted with requests for information or assistance. It had been a strain trying to maintain the proper barrier of correctness between them when his own reserve had slipped a little further each day, but somehow she'd managed it, even though it meant her patience was worn to a frazzle. For all his apparent willingness to treat her as an equal, she knew from bitter experience that it didn't do to trust the motives of rich young employers, no matter how benevolent they might seem. Better to be safe in discretion than risk the sorry consequences of being caught out of your place.

Kate Riley, who didn't live in and had only relatively brief face-to-face encounters with their employer, had had a much rosier view of the proceedings.

'He's turning out a bit of a surprise, isn't he—not so stuffy as we all thought?' she said approvingly as she buttered scones for his afternoon tea three days after his arrival. He had told her he would prefer plain, hearty country cooking to the more sophisticated menu of New Zealand delicacies he invariably asked Vanessa to draw up for his visitors—another valuable point in his favour. Country born and bred, Kate didn't consider a man a real man unless he ate plenty of meat and potatoes. And butter, she declared, was what had made the country great!

'You know, I think his real trouble was he never learned to enjoy himself,' she continued, adding lashings of her own blackberry jam. 'What good has having all that money done him, I ask you? Rush, rush, rush...no wonder he never had much to say for himself; the poor man's brain must have been in a constant whirl. This is the first time he's come without his secretary at his heels and look at the good it's done him already! He's as happy as a sandboy, pottering about the place. A real chip off the old block.'

Vanessa, who didn't know what a sandboy was but knew that Benedict's fax-modem had been running hot late into the night, every night, thought that was going too far.

'He was only very vaguely related to Judge Seaton, you know. I don't see any similarities between them at all,' she murmured.

'We'll see,' was all Kate replied, investing the time-honoured phrase with its customary smugness.

He certainly shared at least one of the old judge's less endearing traits, Vanessa had to admit later that day, when she found herself barring the way to the small room which led off the butler's pantry.

Stubbornness.

'I would prefer that you didn't,' she said, using the advantage of her height to block him looking over her shoulder, past the door he had managed to whisk open.

'Why? What have you got to hide?' He had wandered into the kitchen for a cold drink and then lingered to inspect the bells which had just been rehung in the pantry, though not reconnected yet. Vanessa had been polishing a canteen of silver, trying so hard to ignore his disruptive presence that she hadn't been quite quick enough when he had spied the discreet panelled door set back into the far pantry wall, overlooked in his previous glance at the pantry and adjoining larder and scullery.

'Nothing,' she said, hanging desperately on to the door-handle and trying to pull it closed behind her. Unfortunately he had moved too close for her to do so without brushing against his body. 'Because there's nothing much to see. All it needs is a floor-sand and a paint job——'

'Then you won't mind me having a look.'

'You never wanted to look before.' She dropped her shoulder as he attempted to duck underneath it.

He straightened and gave her a quizzical smile. In a white shirt and casual, double-breasted navy blazer, one hand thrust into his trouser pocket, he looked lazily relaxed, but there was a distinct threat in his closeness and the steadiness of his gaze. Her awareness of the sinewy strength that lay under his clothes made her doubly nervous.

'I've never been interested before,' he said simply. 'You complained that I wasn't taking a personal enough interest in the inn. Now that I am you seem to resent it. Did you think you could set parameters to my interest? Defend your own hallowed piece of turf when you have free run of mine? Are you refusing to let me see your room, Flynn?'

Vanessa swallowed at the silken enquiry. She had acted purely on instinct and now she was being made to feel thoroughly foolish.

'And what if I did?' she asked, more out of nervousness than defiance.

'I'd respect your right to privacy.'

He lifted a hand at the same moment as he spoke and she flinched at the sudden movement, then flushed when she saw that he was merely removing his glasses.

She had never seen him without them before and she was amazed at the difference it made to his appearance. Like his laughter, his unprotected eyes made his face look immediately softer, less austere. Younger, too, and curiously unguarded, his pupils expanding hugely to draw more light into his myopic gaze, leaving only a thin outer rim of clear blue iris, of such intensity of colour that it was almost luminous. It was also mildly hypnotic and Vanessa leaned forward in fascination.

'Unless, of course, you changed your mind and moved aside,' he murmured softly, and suddenly his hands clamped mercilessly around her waist and he spun gracefully around with her as if she weighed no more than a feather, setting her back down on the freshly polished pantry floorboards. While she was still wondering exactly what had happened, he coolly replaced his glasses and he strolled unimpeded into her room.

'My God, I can see you wouldn't be able to do much entertaining in here,' he said abruptly, openly appalled at the sight of the single box-bed, dressing-table piled with books and the huge, tasteless Victorian free-standing wardrobe that took up most of the floor space in the cramped room. The single small window looked straight out on to the garden wall. 'Two people in here would be a crowd!'

Vanessa was still trying to get control of her breathing. He hadn't even broken a sweat picking her up!

'It's adequate for my needs,' she said unevenly, hovering back at the door.

'Adequate!' he exploded, turning to look at her to see if she was being sarcastic. She wasn't, which seemed to annoy him further. 'What are you, a masochist? Don't tell me it was the judge's idea for you to live in this...monk's cell. By all accounts he allowed you as much licence as you cared to take—as do I for that matter. You know damned well you could have set yourself up in practically any room in the house!'

She shrugged. 'It's convenient, and since I don't spend much time in there anyway——'

'Oh, I see. So now I should feel guilty because you work such long hours that you don't have any time left over to spend in your own quarters——'

She was impatient now. 'That's not what I meant. I have plenty of spare time, I just don't choose to spend it shut up in my bedroom. You said you didn't want the house closed up like a tomb when you weren't here, that the most efficient way to air a room was to make use of it, so that's what I do. When I read or sew or knit I try to use a different room each time——' She broke off as she realised she was stepping on very thin ice. Any moment she was going to tell him about her methods of similarly airing the beds in sixteen bedrooms, including his...

'What very domesticated hobbies you have, Flynn,' he drawled and she frowned, wondering whether he was insulting her or merely making an innocent comment. There was a small gleam in his eye that made her wish he hadn't put his glasses back on. They were too effective a screen for his emotions.

'Given your insistence of job equality between the sexes I would have thought your interests would have a more feminist bias. At least now I know why I almost spiked myself on a knitting-needle on the drawing-room sofa the morning after I arrived. And I ran across several copies of *Vogue* and *Metro* tucked among the *Architectural Digests* in the library.'

'I was only obeying your instructions about the house,' she said stiffly. 'I always tidy my things away before you come——'

'And thereby leaving the rooms looking as sterile and unlived-in as a *Digest* photographic layout,' he murmured.

'I thought that was what you wanted, Mr Savage——'

'You mean you assumed it was.'

'You never bothered to correct my assumptions,' Vanessa pointed out coldly.

'Probably because I didn't realise myself how wrong they were,' he said, half under his breath. Before she could think how to respond to that cryptic remark he had turned back to view the room critically. 'We definitely have to do something about this room.'

'I told you, it's perfectly adequate——' Vanessa began, thinking that he was introducing radical changes in her life at an ever-increasing rate. Why couldn't he let her get used to one change before initiating the next? Or let

SAVAGE COURTSHIP 75

her have it all at once, so that at least it would be over and done with.

'Adequate in Victorian times perhaps, but hardly these days. Not everyone has your evident taste for spartanism, Flynn. Don't you find it claustrophobic trying to sleep in here?'

It was unfortunate that at that very moment Kate Riley had come into the pantry to collect a casserole dish and she paused behind Vanessa just long enough to chuckle, and say, 'I tell her that myself, Mr Savage, her being such a big girl and all, but Van says she's a very compact sleeper. Mind you, she doesn't sleep in her own bed too often these days—if she had to cram herself into that little bed every single night of the year I'm sure it'd be a different story!'

She bustled away, still chuckling, and for the second time in a few days Vanessa was privileged to see her employer shocked speechless.

For a moment she thought the jig was up and she flushed miserably as his eyes swept incredulously over her from the tip of her practical shoes to the paranoically tamed hair on the top of her head, no doubt mentally stripping and vainly trying to superimpose her over the explicit image inside his head. Then she was the one speechless as he said icily, 'And I thought you lived a cloistered, unexciting life here, far from the madding crowd. Another example of the dangers of assumption. That prim-and-proper air of yours is obviously misleading. You must have quite a reputation if even Mrs Riley accepts your sexual antics—or should I say athletics?—as merely routine.' His expression was very much the ascetic as he continued harshly, 'However, I'm not inclined to be so generous. When I said you were welcome to have friends come here I wasn't issuing you a licence for promiscuity——'

'I am *not* promiscuous——' began Vanessa, with tight-lipped precision. There was something richly ironic in being thought promiscuous because of her fervent attempts *not* to appear promiscuous. And she was innocent on both counts!

'Good. So it's only Wells' bed that you forsake your own for, is it?' he interrupted, adding dangerously, 'At least, I *hope* you go to his place for your little romps, because, when you're here under *my* roof, as far as I'm concerned you're on duty and I'm not paying my caretaker to have sex——'

'Richard and I do not "have sex,"' she hissed furiously, side-tracked by the outrageous crudity of his insult.

'Sorry, *make love*,' he corrected himself sarcastically.

'How dare you——?'

'Prim and proper won't wash any more, Flynn. I dare because I pay the bills here and therefore I get to set the rules of conduct. While you live under my roof I'm responsible for your health and well-being, and I've always taken my responsibilities seriously.' He gave her another narrow-eyed look.

'No wonder you're so tense and jittery lately. My being here is obviously hampering your freedom—you're not getting your usual quota of...*lovemaking*.' He stressed the words with mocking deliberation. 'Well, just be patient. I'm off up to Auckland at the end of this week, to an Institute of Architects awards presentation. I'll stay in the apartment overnight so you'll be able to entertain your lover at leisure. Just remember the rules. I don't care what you do under his roof, but under mine you're as celibate as a nun!'

Vanessa had longed to throw his hypocrisy in his face but the impulse died as swiftly as it was born. Why give him even more powerful ammunition for his pot-shots? Trust him to confuse friendship and genuine human warmth with crude physical desire, she simmered as she watched him leave, wishing she had the courage to heave the canteen of cutlery at the back of his supercilious head. It would give new meaning to the term knifed in the back. She would enjoy seeing him forked and spooned as well!

It obviously hadn't even occurred to him that she might be *in love* with Richard, might be a misty-eyed romantic whose dreams he had just callously trampled into the mire. No, he thought only in clinical terms of lust and appeasing an appetite. No wonder he had never married. He probably wouldn't recognise love if it hit him in the face.

And, to show that his opinions about her personal life were totally irrelevant, she was ruthlessly good-mannered to him for the rest of the week, which sadly had the opposite effect to that which she had intended. Instead of losing interest under the avalanche of politeness he seemed to delight in testing the limits of her patience, tossing personal comments into seemingly innocent conversations like miniature grenades that threatened to blow apart her armoured reserve.

By Friday Vanessa was clinging on to her composure by the skin of her teeth and it was with unutterable relief and a sneaking sense of victory that she watched him depart for Auckland. For the most part she had successfully held out against his flagrant manipulations. But her resistance had taken its toll. In a week he had cranked up her stress level higher than it had been for years and she welcomed the chance for a respite, however brief, in order to rebuild her shaky defences. Perhaps by the time he came back he would have forgotten his game, or be bored by it, and things could return to a semblance of normality.

When Richard rang soon after the BMW had cruised out of the gates and asked her if she wanted to have dinner with him that evening, Vanessa accepted with alacrity.

A nice, soothing night in Richard's undemanding company was just the antidote she needed to a severe overdose of Savage teasing. Since they had decided to eat at a fashionably late hour Vanessa took her time getting ready, pampering herself as she hadn't done in a long time, even painting her nails.

As she got dressed in her newest gown—a black crêpe de Chine streaming out to mid-calf from the fitted, halter-necked bodice—she determined to devote herself to showing Richard that she was now ready to progress from friendly hugs and kisses to something more meaningful.

She ran a brush through her loose hair and then raked it back from her forehead and ears with her fingers and gave it a quick spritz with a firm-hold hairspray to stop the loose strands from annoying her while she was eating. Of course, they probably would anyway, but a woman needed one frivolity in her life and with Vanessa it was her hair.

She surveyed herself in the age-spotted mirror on the wall of her room and nodded as she spun around, pleased with the way the thin crêpe de Chine of the skirt flowed around her legs. It looked just the way the photo did in the *Vogue* pattern book. The stiffened bodice, fastened from waist to collarbone by thirty tiny covered buttons hooked through satin loops and detailed with top stitching, had caused her a lot of trouble when she was making it, but the end result had been worth all her cursing and unpicking. Her bared shoulders were a little unseasonal but she knew the restaurant that Richard was taking her to was small and warm so she merely wrapped herself in a three-quarter-length black mohair cardigan-coat for the car trip.

'Looks rather spooky in the moonlight, doesn't it?' said Richard as they drove away from the inn.

Vanessa looked back at the ragged outline of gables and chimneys, the slate roof gleaming darkly in the light of a richly overripe moon. Crouched in a small valley just off the main Thames coastal-road, with the foothills of the Coromandel Range rising steeply in the background and no other visible signs of the thriving community which existed just over the hill, the inn did look rather Gothic. The main design of the inn was a long stone T-shape, with the kitchen and service areas jutting out at the back, but the uncompromising sternness of the stone shape was softened by the addition of ornate wooden-covered verandas which ran the length and breadth of both storeys, supported on huge pillars of heart kauri milled from the native forests, for which the area was justly famous. The carriage light at the front door which she had left burning only seemed to emphasise the completeness of the shadowy building's isolation.

'That reminds me, has Savage tracked down his ghost yet?'

Vanessa gave him a sharp look. 'How did you hear about that?'

He grinned. 'Word gets around.'

Vanessa gave an inward groan. She might have known that Bill Jessop wouldn't keep his mouth shut. She wondered whether Richard suspected the source of the hoax, but his handsome features were harmlessly amused as he concentrated on negotiating the narrow, winding road.

'He's been into the newspaper office, Melissa says, going through hundred-year-old files. She said he took away photocopies of reports about Meg's murder.'

'Oh?' Vanessa was distracted from her immediate worry by the realisation that Richard had seen Melissa Riley recently. Had it been a date or just a casual meeting? Since she had insisted she wasn't ready for exclusivity the idea of him seeing other woman had never bothered Vanessa before. To her dismay it didn't really bother her now, either. Surely she ought to feel jealous of the man she intended...

Intended what? That was the problem—she still didn't really know what her intentions towards him were. Richard's intentions towards her she could guess; from the gallantly cautious way he was treating her they were of the most honourable kind. He would be happily willing to take her to bed but she had no doubts that ultimately it was marriage that he wanted from her. He was in his mid-thirties and ready to settle down. Unlike someone else she could name. The trouble was that she had a hard time imagining herself in bed with Richard while she was having much difficulty imagining herself *out* of bed where Benedict Savage was concerned!

The small cottage restaurant was filled to capacity. It had a good reputation for excellent food at reasonable prices and was highly popular with local residents who wanted to dress up and eat somewhere a bit more special than the pub or one of the fast-food restaurants that commonly sprang up at normally sparsely populated, seasonal holiday destinations like the Coromandel.

When Richard accepted the wine-list he looked over at her and grinned. 'Champagne, my dear?'

Vanessa's determination shivered. 'What about red tonight? I think I'm going to have the venison,' she said, pretending not to understand the reference.

'Right. But only one bottle this time, OK?'

Vanessa gave him a mock-glare as the waitress drifted away. 'Now she's going to think I'm a lush.'

'I wouldn't blame her. You do look rather lush this evening.' His eyes dipped to the neckline of her dress which she had left unbuttoned as far as the swell of her breasts to give a more casual look. It also revealed more cleavage than usual and, given the way the light boning of the bodice lifted her breasts, she couldn't blame Richard for taking it as an invitation to look. That was what she had intended, wasn't it?

'Why, thank you, kind sir,' she said flippantly, feeling that she ought to blush at the intensity of his gaze but unable to summon the required rush of excited blood. 'You look rather gorgeous yourself.'

To her amusement he produced the flush that had eluded her, visibly moved by her teasing flattery. She felt a surge of tenderness for him. Dear Richard; she couldn't think of one good reason why she shouldn't fall madly in love with him.

To that end she flirted gently with him through the leisurely meal and was waiting for her dessert, sipping the last of the smooth Australian red wine he had ordered, when she suddenly choked.

'Van, are you all right?'

'Yes.' She coughed, blinking her eyes rapidly to clear them of tears. The vision on the other side of the room blurred, then steadied again. It was a delusion; it had to be! Then the man speaking persuasively to the hostess turned full-face to the room. It was Benedict Savage—supposedly safely ensconced at a posh banquet in Auckland—sinfully overdressed in a white dinner-jacket and black tie. Oh, *God*! Furtively Vanessa looked around. The waitress had removed the lavishly large menus when she had taken their order and there wasn't even so much as a pot-plant to hide behind.

'Van, what's the matter? You look as if you've seen a ghost.'

That wretched word again! Vanessa produced a feeble smile. Thank goodness Richard was sitting opposite across the table instead of on the banquette seat beside her, and had his back to the open foyer. With any luck the hostess would just explain to Benedict that the restaurant was full and send him on his way. The kitchen shut down at eleven, and it was nearly that now, although the restaurant itself didn't close until midnight and people usually made the most of their night out by lingering over special coffees or to dance in the small adjoining room where the chef's wife played the piano. Anyway, no one got in these days without a reservation. But if Richard saw him he was bound to acknowledge him in his usual polite way, perhaps—horror of horrors—even invite him to join them!

'Some wine went down the wrong way,' she explained hurriedly, and with perfect truth.

Just in time she saw the light glint off Benedict's spectacles as he lifted his head to look into the room over the hostess's shoulder and she brushed her dessert fork off the table with her elbow and ducked down to pick it up in one fluid movement.

'Whoops, excuse me!' Her head pressed against the bottom of the table, she pretended to grope for her lost implement, her heart thumping as she congratulated herself on her quick reflexes.

'Don't worry about it, Van; I'll get you another one. You won't be able to use one that's been on the floor, anyway.' Too late Vanessa saw the flaw in her impulsive plan. Richard had already raised his voice to attract the attention of their waitress. 'Excuse me, Kylie, could we have another fork here?'

Half crouched under the table, Vanessa closed her eyes and prayed, deaf to the soft hum of conversation and discreet clatter of crockery and cutlery from the patrons around them. All she could hear were the approaching footsteps that sounded like the knell of doom.

'Thanks. Just leave it, Van. Kylie's brought another one.'

Vanessa's panic eased a moment too soon at his quiet reassurance. She was cautiously beginning to ease upright as she heard Richard suddenly rise and say, 'Hello, Savage. What are you doing here? I thought you were up for some big award in Auckland tonight?'

Vanessa froze, thinking stupidly that she hadn't known Benedict was in line for one of the awards, as she listened to the casual reply. She opened her eyes and saw the polished black shoes planted beside the table leg. Shoes that she herself had buffed to their shellac shine the previous afternoon.

'I was. I decided to come back early.'

'Come straight from there, I suppose?' Richard guessed, obviously looking at the white jacket as he ventured another sympathetic guess. 'Missed out, did you? I don't blame you for ducking out early. Those type of things can certainly drag on if you don't have anything to celebrate. But if you called in here for a nightcap on the way home you made a bit of a mistake; they don't run a separate bar.'

'So I just discovered.' There was an excruciating pause, then he said sardonically, 'I hesitate to sound indelicate, but whatever your companion is doing under the table she seems to be doing very thoroughly. That is, I assume it *is* a woman?'

Richard, the idiot, saw it as a joke rather than the subtle insult that made Vanessa go hot all over. 'If you saw her dress you wouldn't ask that question! Are you running out of air down there yet, honey?' he said, his voice threaded with wicked laughter.

It was all so humiliating, Vanessa thought as she clenched her teeth and slowly unfolded herself, the errant fork clutched in her sweaty palm.

She knew that her face was red and her hair was falling all over her face. She was certain that Benedict knew who she was and was just doing this to embarrass her. Sure enough, when her eyes emerged far enough to peep sullenly over the table-top, she could see an expression of malicious satisfaction on Benedict's face as he glanced at Richard.

For her he had a faintly quizzical smile as she reluctantly sat upright, his eyes sinking to the exposed cleft between her breasts before lifting, lifting as she straightened to her full height. The quizzical amusement faltered as his gaze went over the thick blanket of hair that she quickly tucked back behind her ears.

It vanished entirely when he looked back at her flushed face, *really* looked this time, and she knew that he hadn't realised, not until then. He had thought Richard was dining with some other woman.

'*Flynn?*'

Her smile was a mere twitch. 'Hello, Mr Savage; fancy seeing you here.'

Her attempt at bright surprise fell flat as a lead balloon. He stared at her, his eyes leached from blue to sleet-grey as he leaned back so that he got a better look at the hair rippling down between her shoulder-blades.

A nervous tic suddenly began to pull at the skin on his left temple and Vanessa began a fatalistic countdown to the imminent explosion. She could only hope that his rigorous self-control and distaste for emotional display would rescue her from complete public annihilation!

CHAPTER SIX

IT WAS Richard who unknowingly defused the ticking time bomb.

'Why don't you sit with us and have your drink?' he suggested blithely. 'Van and I are just waiting for our dessert. I'm sure the management won't quibble if they know you're our guest. After all, you don't look as if you'll cause any trouble.'

Little did he know, thought Vanessa as, to her horror, the offer was smoothly accepted.

'Why not? Unless *Van* objects. Do you... *Van*?'

She wished he would stop saying her name like that. It was enough to make her hair curl—if it hadn't been a coiled mass of ringlets already.

'Why should I object?' she squeaked bravely.

'I don't know... guilt, perhaps.'

'Guilt?' Why didn't he sit down if he was going to, instead of looming over her like that? There was a perfectly good empty chair next to Richard. She wasn't going to let him bully her with stand-over tactics. 'I've got nothing to feel guilty about,' she lied brazenly.

'No? How about leaving me to come home to a cold, dark, deserted house?'

His mock-pathos made her heart flip-flop in her chest. Perhaps her fate wasn't so cut and dried after all. Maybe she had mistaken that searing look. Perhaps he was just in a foul mood after losing out on an award he had wanted.

'You weren't supposed to be coming home. But as it happens I left a light on—and the oil-fired heating going.' She adopted a conciliatory tone.

'I notice you don't dispute the deserted bit.' To her dismay he didn't take the chair beside Richard. Instead he slid on to the banquette beside her. She felt the heat of his thigh even though he remained a decorous distance away on the upholstered leather bench. 'Unless, of course, you count my ghostly courtesan. Sorry, Flynn, I mean *actress*... What lovely hair you have, by the way,' he continued in the same mild, conversational tone. 'And what a lot of it.'

'She looks quite different, doesn't she, with that mane flying free?' said Richard affably, relaxed by his good meal, and cheerfully oblivious to the undertones.

'Very different. So different, in fact, I nearly didn't recognise her,' said Benedict, shifting on to his hip so that his body was curved towards hers, still a safe distance away and yet suffocatingly close. Vanessa continued to look towards Richard with a fixed smile, her back stiff, conscious that with the blind end of the banquette on her other side she was very effectively trapped.

'Continuing the equestrian analogy, Wells, what would you call that colour?' he mused lightly. 'Golden palomino?'

'Palominos may have golden coats but their manes are always cream or white. Vanessa's colouring is definitely bay.' Richard chuckled.

'Do you mind? This is a restaurant, not a stable,' Vanessa cut in sharply, perversely as annoyed with Richard as she was with Benedict. 'If you came in here gasping for a drink, shouldn't you order one?'

There was a tiny, splintering silence.

'Oh, are you talking to me? I didn't realise—you weren't looking in my direction,' came the purr by her ear and she was forced to turn her head to meet the challenge of his stare.

Did he or didn't he?

Was he baiting her or was her paranoia colouring his innocent words with perilous meaning? He hadn't seen her face, she reminded herself desperately, so he couldn't be absolutely certain, not on such flimsy evidence as her hair.

'Let me buy that drink for you—it'll be easier all round if I just add it to my bill.' Richard interrupted the wordless duel with his customary generosity. 'What would you like? A whisky?'

At Benedict's careless nod he turned in his seat and beckoned the waitress again.

Benedict hadn't taken his eyes off Vanessa and now his voice lowered for her ears alone. 'Is all that hair as soft as it looks, I wonder?' As he spoke he ran a hand lightly down from the top of her skull to the uneven ends of the thick pelt. Vanessa nearly shot out of her seat. Every nerve-end in her scalp seemed to spit and crackle.

'I'm sorry, did I hurt you?' he murmured, his eyes glittering in the light of the flickering candle in the centre of the small table.

'No,' Vanessa gritted. He can't prove a thing, she repeated to herself in a mental chant. All she had to do was hold him off until they got home. Or, better still, until tomorrow, when he might be in a more receptive frame of mind.

'Mmm, it's even softer than it looks.' He stroked again, this time sinking his fingers into the corkscrew ripples and drawing a swath forward over her shoulder. His knuckles brushed the bare skin of her upper arm, sending a fresh shiver of awareness right down to her toes. 'And very attractive against your black dress and pale skin. Such a surprising colour variation, too; it almost looks *golden* in this candlelight. And so light and *fleecy*, such a *fluffy* confection...'

He leaned towards her as he toyed with the captive locks, his nostrils flaring slightly, and her heart jerked in her breast at each tightening of his lethally soft voice on the trigger words.

'Do you mind?' She reached up to push her hair back out of his grasp, discovering to her embarrassment that she was still holding the fork in a white-knuckled grip.

Resisting the temptation to stab him with it, she shifted instead so that her back was to the corner of the banquette, tossing her head so that her hair fell into the shadow behind her. She laid the fork down on the white tablecloth in front of her and then began to fiddle nervously with it as she tried to think of an innocuous starting point for a polite conversation.

When she finally plucked up the courage to give him a quick, sideways glance it was to find him staring down at her hands with their carefully painted nails. Hoping he hadn't noticed their faint nervous tremor, she clenched her fists, and then froze as his fingertip tracked slowly over the white cloth and up over the ring-finger of her right hand.

'That's an interesting ring you're wearing. Silver and jade, isn't it?'

'Yes, a jeweller at a craft commune up past Coromandel made it,' she babbled eagerly, automatically splaying her hand, as much to shake off his touch as to display the large, ornate ring. Local crafts. You couldn't get much more innocuous than that. 'This area is quite famous for the number of artists and artisans——'

'It's an extremely unusual design. One might even say...unique.'

There was something odd in his voice, a note of repressed exultation, that brought Vanessa up short just as she was about to agree. The ring. She had been wearing the ring that night and hadn't bothered to take it off before she crashed into his bed!

'Oh, I don't know, she probably stamps them out by the dozen for the tourist trade,' she said with a hectic little laugh.

But Richard was there to keep her on the straight and narrow, the directest possible route to her downfall...

'Not at those prices, Van,' he said as he turned back from ordering. 'I was with you when you bought it last spring, remember? You didn't want to part with that much until the woman told you everything she did was strictly one-off.'

'Rather like having a personalised number-plate strapped to your finger,' murmured Benedict maliciously. 'Distinctive and gratifyingly easy to trace.'

Vanessa's nerve broke, her hand lifting in a helpless warding-off gesture. 'Mr Savage, I——'

He caught her hand in an unpleasantly tight grip and returned it to the table. 'Is this your dessert arriving with my drink? It looks delicious.'

Vanessa looked at the sticky chocolate concoction placed before her. What had made her mouth water fifteen minutes ago now made her feel ill.

'What's the matter? Digestion playing up?' Benedict taunted over the top of his whisky glass.

Gotcha! his expression said, and like an automaton Vanessa picked up her spoon, deciding she would eat the damned thing if it killed her. Perhaps it would be better if it did!

The decision was taken out of her hands when Benedict intercepted her first spoonful by guiding it, not to her own mouth but to his.

'Mmm, whisky and chocolate, a heady combination...'

She watched mesmerised when his lips slowly parted and his tongue curled under the bowl of the spoon as he took the spoon into his mouth. Her pulse began to thump against the fingers that had encircled her wrist. There was something disturbingly erotic about the way he fed from her hand. His jaw flexed, cheeks hollowing as he sucked the smooth chocolate mousse from the spoon. He seemed to take an inordinate length of time about it, although it was only a few seconds of real time, and when he released the spoon his tongue ran lightly across his upper lip, collecting the residual sweetness. Helplessly she wondered what his mouth had felt like on hers. Had he licked her as delicately and sensuously as he'd feasted on the chocolate? A tingle shot through her body and her lips parted in unconscious imitation of his actions. Her eyes rose, to be captured by his, a fiercely knowing look in them that made her want to sink through the floor.

She knew she was blushing wildly and she looked hurriedly at Richard but he was content, enjoying his own serving of apple pie, blissfully unaware of the sizzling tension across the table. Oh, *Richard*! She felt a fleeting sense of despair for something slipping irretrievably beyond her grasp.

She looked nervously back at Benedict. His eyes had shifted from grey to blue and for the first time she appreciated the true meaning of the phrase 'looking blue murder'.

He looked as if he could cheerfully throttle her, and yet there was another emotion there that was even more terrifying, a tigerish gleam of primitive masculine triumph that hinted that it wasn't her mere death that he was contemplating.

Oh, God, surely she hadn't made any reckless promises to him in the throes of drunken passion? Surely he couldn't expect to hold her to anything she might have said or done in a state of alcoholic irresponsibility?

'Mr Savage——'

His smile was cruelly brilliant at her breathless plea. 'Oh, call me Ben, please... after all, you're off duty tonight and that makes us equals. Besides, such overt formality is rather silly in the circumstances, isn't it—Vanessa...?'

Somehow he made her name redolent with sin, the 's's sliding slowly off his tongue like lazy serpents and coiling seductively around her throat, making it difficult to breathe, let alone defend herself.

'I——'

'One taste just isn't enough...may I have another? I've just discovered an insatiable appetite for your delights.'

He was looking at her mouth and for a moment she misunderstood his husky plea and glared at him in seething outrage.

'The chocolate mousse, Nessie,' he clarified limpidly, guiding her hand with gentle force back to her plate, his forearm brushing the outer curve of her breast as he made her dip and lift the spoon again to his mouth.

She let the handle go and was relieved when he released her without fuss to take hold of it himself.

'You may as well eat the whole thing,' she said, shoving the plate sourly in his direction, realising that his tormenting had only just begun. Well, she might have to take it but she didn't have to like it. If he claimed they were equal then she was going to act it by asserting what little pride she had left. 'And please don't call me by that ridiculous nickname.'

His eyebrows rose, deliberately misunderstanding her. 'Nickname? You mean *Van*? I must admit, it is rather terse and unattractive.'

Richard looked up at the mention, his handsome brow wrinkling with concern as he regarded her irritated expression. 'Don't you like it? But all this time...why on earth didn't you say——?'

'No, I meant Nessie—as he knows very well!' Vanessa struggled not to let her resentment at Benedict spill over on to the only innocent party at the table. 'It makes me sound like somebody's old nanny.'

'I was thinking more in terms of the Loch Ness monster,' said Benedict glibly, taking another leisurely swallow of her dessert. 'You know—mysterious, elusive, appearing when you least expect her...'

'Sounds like rotten butler material to me, Savage,' Richard joked.

Benedict looked at him with a pleasant smile that Vanessa instantly distrusted.

'On the contrary, it makes her ideal. "The noblest service comes from nameless hands, and the best servant does his work unseen".'

'Ovid again?' Richard showed that his memory was much better tuned than his jealous instincts.

'Oliver Wendell Holmes. I'm sure the quotation must be in all the best butler manuals, isn't it, Vanessa?'

She looked him dead in the eye and smiled crisply. 'Why, yes, right next to the one that says that few men are admired by their servants; "Many a man has been a wonder to the world, whose wife and butler have seen nothing in him that was in the tiniest bit remarkable".'

His narrow mouth curved in droll appreciation, as if he knew the extent of dramatic licence she had taken with the quotation. 'I think I'd rather settle for being a wonder to my wife and unremarkable to the world. A much more comfortable affair.'

'"Affair" being the operative word, since you don't have a wife,' she shot sceptically back. He was already a wonderboy in the architectural world so it was unlikely that any wife he took would have any choice but to accept that most of his passion was devoted to his work.

He inclined his head. 'Not at the moment, no. So that only leaves my servants to practise on, doesn't it? Tell me, Vanessa, what more do I have to do to inspire your admiration?'

If he thought to make her blush with his silky invitation he had another think coming, although it was a struggle to resist a torrid rush of blood to her head. What *more*? Was he smugly waiting for her to say what a wondrous lover she had found him?

'Clean your own shoes, perhaps?' she ventured with poisonous sweetness.

He pulled a sour face. 'Actually I had something a bit more challenging in mind. I'm sure there are far more stimulating things you can find for me to do with my hands,' he replied with a diabolical innocence, this time succeeding in making her pinken. He leaned back in his seat like a sleekly satisfied cat. 'You see, Richard, Vanessa and I actually have a symbiotic relationship which works extremely well for both of us, so if you were hoping to gain a butler for yourself by stirring up discontent you're out of luck.'

Richard gave Vanessa a fond grin. 'I like to think I already have one, thank you.'

Vanessa sensed the body next to her tighten, but there was no hint of anything but lazy humour in the voice that drawled blandly, 'Purely at my pleasure, I feel constrained to point out. I'm the one with first call on her loyal and devoted services and I can truthfully state that she is the most obliging creature I've ever had under me. In fact her eagerness to please gives new meaning to the phrase "the butler did it"....'

His sheer audacity took Vanessa's already ragged breath away. She could see that he was working himself into a dangerous mood, Richard's complacent ignorance acting as a goad rather than the soothing tranquilliser she might have expected it to be.

It seemed to make no difference to him that she had obviously not told a soul about what had happened. *She* knew, and that was enough. Richard was good-natured almost to a fault but he wasn't stupid and even he was going to realise that there was more than light-hearted banter going on here if Benedict continued in the same provocative vein. The trouble was, taken at face value, there was nothing in his comments she could object to without bringing the whole embarrassing business out in the open, she thought wretchedly.

'Her insistence on making beds, for one,' Benedict continued relentlessly. 'I thought that sort of thing was against the butlers' unwritten code of rights but Vanessa seems to invent her own rules as she goes along.'

Richard laughed. 'I believe it's called job flexibility these days. So you approve of her game of musical beds? When she first told me I thought she was mad, but when you think about it it does make a nutty kind of sense.'

Benedict's sharply indrawn breath was audible and there was a distinctly grim edge in his voice as he enquired gently, 'In what way, would you say?'

'Well, for myself, I wouldn't like to swap beds every night, but, as Van pointed out, she's always lived in other people's houses so she's never developed any possessive hang-ups about where she sleeps. And in time-and-motion terms I suppose you can't get more efficient than airing a bedroom in your sleep. I've got a reasonably large place myself and my mother is constantly complaining about the amount of effort it takes to keep the spare rooms from going musty with disuse. I tell her she should take a leaf out of Van's book, but she says that it would be too much like living in a hotel. Of course, Van says that's exactly what she's doing—except she doesn't have to worry about paying the bill!'

Richard laughed again and Vanessa smiled weakly as the laser-like blue gaze, intensified by the glass lenses, swung back in her direction. So now he had his explanation. And without her having to say a word.

'Vanessa can be very witty, although her sense of humour sometimes leaves a bloody lot to be desired,' came the biting reply after a moment's screaming pause, but Richard's attention had already been distracted.

'Oh, Van, I see Nigel Franklin leaving over there— remember I said I wanted a quick word with him about a mare he's sending over tomorrow? Would you mind? I won't be a moment...'

Vanessa was aghast at the prospect of his desertion at such a critical moment. 'Oh, but——'

'Of course we don't mind.' Benedict cut across her stammer. 'Don't worry, Richard, I know how to keep Vanessa well-entertained.'

Vanessa glumly watched him go.

'Perhaps you're not so as well-matched as I thought, after all. Rather thick, isn't he?'

Her dark eyes flared defensively. 'No, just uncomplicated.'

The dark head nodded. 'I see...you mean boring.'

'He is not boring!'

'Maybe not below table-level, but then, who am I to judge?'

She bridled with fury. 'I was picking up my fork!' she spluttered.

He sipped his whisky, flaunting his scepticism. 'You were hiding from me.'

'Do you blame me?' She made no further attempt to deny it. 'I knew you wouldn't be able to resist...resist...' Her angry words tapered off as his brows arched.

'Expecting you to admit the truth?'

His smug coolness was infuriating. 'Gloating! Ruining my evening with Richard!'

'Is that what I'm doing?'

'Yes!'

She might have known that would please him. His amusement was tinged with malice. 'Don't you think you deserved a salutary lesson in the dangers of lying?'

'I didn't lie...exactly,' she faltered.

'We both know what a specious defence that is,' he dismissed contemptuously. 'You had every opportunity to correct my mistaken impressions and you didn't. Instead you trotted out that ridiculous ghost story to obscure the issue—tried to make me feel so much like a fool that I doubted my own perceptions. Well, now is the time to make good your numerous sly omissions. And let me warn you—you'd better make it very good!'

'Here?' She looked nervously around. The tables weren't very widely spaced and there were quite a few people here whom she knew. Their conversation had already attracted some curious glances and she hated the idea of generating food for local gossip.

'You had your chance in private and you fudged it,' he said unsympathetically. 'How often can I expect to find you in my bed?'

'For heaven's sake, keep your voice down!' agonised Vanessa.

To her chagrin he immediately lowered his voice to a thready whisper, leaning intimately close so that she could hear. 'Why in the hell didn't you just simply explain your nightly gypsy routine to me? You had no qualms about everyone else knowing. Did you think I'd take exception to an unconventional solution to an understandable problem? For God's sake—I'd have been more inclined to congratulate you for taking such good care of my property!'

'It wasn't that simple——' Vanessa hissed back.

'Why? Because I thought you were an expensive callgirl? You should have been flattered, Flynn.'

She recoiled. 'That's such a typically male thing to say!' she said furiously. 'You think a woman who sells the use of her body to strangers is someone I should *envy*? You think prostitutes do what they do for *pleasure*?' Her voice was choked with revulsion. She had been tainted with that acid brush of contempt once before and the mere memory of it was enough to eat into the scars covering the old wounds.

He looked deeply into her smouldering gaze, his fury stilling at what he saw in the uncertain black depths. 'I'm sorry,' he admitted gently. 'That was a stupid thing for me to say. But I wasn't making a serious social comment, I was just trying to get a rise out of you by being flippant.'

The admission didn't calm her. In her mind she was still fighting that helpless sense of oppression. 'I would never prostitute myself,' she denied fiercely. 'Not for anything or anyone... not for any amount!'

'I know.'

He was no longer angry, she realised with a sting of shock, at least not in the way he had been a few minutes ago. Instead there was a steely determination in his steady gaze that made her swallow hard, suddenly wondering how much her knee-jerk reaction had revealed to him.

He went on, adding to her shock by admitting frankly, 'But I can't deny that it's a common male fantasy—to be seduced by a beautiful stranger who conveniently vanishes afterwards—all pleasure and no responsibility. In real life we all know it doesn't happen that way but we don't have to worry about that when we weave our fantasies. After all, sexual fantasy is the safest sex there is. I'm sure that many women enjoy the reverse of that particular male fantasy in the privacy of their own minds——'

'I don't,' Vanessa interrupted stoutly, trying to stop him before the conversation got totally out of hand.

'Oh? Then what's your favourite sexual fantasy, Vanessa?' He leaned his chin on his hand, that steely glint belying his coaxing expression.

'None of your business,' she said stiffly, bewildered by his swift change of tactics. If he was intent on keeping her off-balance he was doing a damned good job.

'It is if I figure in it,' he mocked her.

'Never in a million years!' Vanessa spat out and he laughed softly.

'You must have been disappointed, then, when you woke up so unexpectedly in my arms?'

She had a fleeting flashback to lean, muscled limbs and rampant masculinity. 'But I didn't wake up, did I?'

she said bitterly. 'If I had a fantasy, it certainly wasn't to be preyed upon by some...some unscrupulous *incubus*...'

'Given the state I was in I doubt whether I fitted the profile of a demon lover, either literally or figuratively,' he murmured.

Did he mean that he'd been so carried away with lust, it had all been over in a trice? Strangely, that thought was even more mortifying. Vanessa had punished herself over and over with speculation that he had enjoyed her helpless body at length and at leisure. She had tossed and turned every night, haunted by the wicked images. Oh, God, if you looked at it like that she *was* having sexual fantasies about him!

'That's a rather odd word to use, though—incubus,' he mused thoughtfully. 'Are you sure you're not getting mixed up with something else?'

'I know what an incubus is,' Vanessa snapped. Now he was calling her ignorant on top of everything else!

'So do I. A demon who makes love to sleeping women. Is that what you're accusing me of—taking advantage of you while you slept?'

'I'd been drinking—you must have realised that; if I'd been in my right mind I would never have acted that way——' Out of the corner of her eye she saw Richard turning away from the tubby figure of Nigel Franklin and his two Asian guests.

'Acted what way?' Benedict persisted.

She glared at him, conscious of Richard's approach. 'If I knew that I wouldn't be worrying about it, would I?'

'Worrying about what?' He continued to be deliberately obtuse as he followed her gaze, watching Richard dip and curve between the tables, pausing to murmur a friendly greeting here and there.

'For goodness sake, what do you care?' she said, smiling brilliantly in relief as Richard neared the table.

'You'd be surprised,' Benedict murmured, turning his back on the other man and rising to his feet to block his view of Vanessa's face. 'But you're right, this isn't the time or place. We're too exposed here.' He let her savour her brief taste of freedom before adding succinctly, 'What we need is a bit of natural cover.' He raised his voice and extended his hand. 'Dance?'

Before she could refuse he had reached down and pulled her out from the banquette, whisking her past the surprised Richard and through the archway into the adjoining room. Applying a delicate pressure to her captured elbow, he spun her deftly against his body and began to move to the throbbing music that poured out of discreetly placed speakers. Several young couples were rocking freely to the beat but Benedict ignored them as he wove a more conservative pattern across the floor, one hand cupping her shoulder-blade, the other firmly pressing hers against his chest.

'But I don't want to dance!' she objected, unobtrusively trying to wrest herself out of his grasp, pushing against his shoulder with her free hand.

'Would you rather I invited Richard to join our fascinating reminiscences about our activities in bed?'

Vanessa slumped in his arms, her physical submission contradicting her defiant words. 'You wouldn't!'

His feet slowed. 'Is that a challenge?'

She turned her head and looked grimly past his right ear, searching for retaliation. 'Don't you feel silly, dancing with a woman who's taller than you?' she said sullenly.

'No. It just means I have a better view of your breasts.'

Her head furiously jerked back and she flushed. He wasn't even looking down into her open cleavage; he was mockingly enjoying the bristling outrage on her face.

'Stop trying to make me feel small. Or rather—smaller than I already am,' he added with rather enchanting diffidence. 'I'm not going to let you dominate me mentally as well as physically. We move well together, don't you think?'

Vanessa's wide mouth thinned stubbornly. 'No.'

His thigh slid between hers as he whirled her around. 'Doesn't this bring back delicious memories?'

'Memories?' she echoed hollowly.

'Of the way we moved together in bed.' The arm across her back tensed, drawing her torso closer so that the tips of her breasts brushed his snowy white chest with every step.

'Stop it!' She arched away and only succeeded in thrusting her hips against his in an even more evocative movement.

'You don't remember, do you?' he taunted huskily, his words blending with the low, sexy throb of the music. He laughed, infuriating her with his perception. 'That's why you were so loath to confess...you didn't know what you'd be confessing to. You don't know what you did during your alcoholic blackout, do you, Vanessa?'

'It wasn't a blackout. I don't know what you're talking about——' she ventured wildly.

'I'm talking about your waking up and finding me naked on top of you...'

Her fingernails dug involuntarily into his jacket. 'You weren't on top of me!'

To her horror he grinned wickedly. 'No, that's right—*you* were on top most of the time, weren't you? Hmm, so you *do* remember something?'

He was enjoying himself hugely at her expense, extracting what, if Vanessa had been in a reasonable frame of mind, she might have acknowledged was a truly fitting revenge. But her frame of mind was anything but reasonable.

'I don't remember *anything*, damn you!' She was driven to admit what he wanted to hear through clenched teeth. 'Nor do I wish to!'

'Liar.' His voice was silky with laughter. 'Don't you want to know exactly how much you have to be embarrassed about? How wild and uninhibited you were in the seamless dark...?'

'No,' she lied fiercely. 'As far as I'm concerned the whole thing was a ghastly mistake. OK, so it was me. I was there, I did whatever you say I did. Now you've got your damned confession we can consider it over and done with,' she gritted.

'Unless you're pregnant.'

'What?' she screeched, stopping dead still in the middle of the dance-floor as if she had been pole-axed. She stared at him in disbelief.

'You mean we didn't——? You didn't even——?' Her mouth quivered with horror as she breathed, 'Oh, God, I don't believe this!' It had never occurred to her that a cautious man like Benedict Savage would not have taken every precaution...and then some!

'I take it this means you're not on the Pill,' he murmured gravely, nudging her back into motion.

'Of course I'm not!' She moaned softly, her body weakly moulding to his as she grappled with this utterly appalling new relevation.

'No, "of course" about it. A lot of women prefer to take responsibility themselves——'

'But I wasn't responsible that night, was I?' she said frantically. 'You must have known I wasn't!'

'How? It was pitch-dark and what you whispered in my ear wasn't exactly calculated to inspire reasoned conversation——'

'Couldn't you smell the wine on my breath?' said Vanessa hurriedly, eager not to hear what she had said.

'Smell, no—taste, yes. But then, you tasted equally intoxicating all over—by the time I got to linger in your mouth I was raging drunk myself...'

Vanessa felt a blush sweep over her from head to toe and quickly got back to the main point. 'How could you take such a risk, with someone you didn't even know——?'

'Oh, Dane assured me you had a certificate of health.'

'He *what*?' She trod on his toe and he winced.

'It turned out he meant the car, remember? Only at the time I thought he was talking about you, you see, so...'

'So you didn't use anything! How *could* you? Didn't you *care* that I might—might——?'

'Have my baby? I'm afraid I was so stunned when I got into bed and found a warm, willing body waiting for me that I completely lost my head. And you certainly didn't give me any opportunity to politely excuse myself...'

'Oh—my—God!' Her head bowed, sinking on to his shoulder. He tightened his grip still further, supporting her trembling body. Her only consolation was that it was unlikely that she would have fallen pregnant at what had been a low point in her monthly cycle. Still, she now faced weeks of horrible uncertainty.

'If you *are* pregnant I suppose Wells will insist on your having tests——'

'What?' Her head jerked up again.

Benedict smiled into her pale, frowning face. 'To see whether the baby is his or mine. After all, I don't suppose either of us would want to claim the other's child. Shall we ask him for his opinion when we get back to the table?'

Her nerveless feet tangled again with his and this time it was her foot that was momentarily crushed. Benedict came to a halt.

'Sorry. Have you had enough of dancing? Shall we go back to Wells?' He began to draw away from her politely and Vanessa reacted instinctively.

'No!' She practically flung herself against his lean strength, unconsciously leading as she forced him back into the safety of motion. She couldn't face Richard yet, not after the way she had flirted madly with him earlier. The beautiful meal congealed like a block of concrete in her stomach at the very thought of him discovering that she had casually slept with someone else during the time she had been acting like a nervous virgin with Richard. 'No... the music's still playing...'

He meekly followed her agitated footsteps, making no attempt to hide his amusement. 'Poor Vanessa, torn between two lovers...'

'We are *not* lovers!' she denied automatically.

'Then what would you call us?'

'Not *us*!' she blurted confusedly. Unfortunately his intelligence was equal to her confusion. He comprehended instantly what she hadn't meant him to know.

'My God, hasn't the stud performed for you yet?'

'He is *not* a stud!' she bit out.

'Apparently not.' He sounded so smug that Vanessa wanted to hit him. 'Who's been holding back—you or he?'

'Richard and I have had an excellent relationship for two years,' she said sharply. 'Just because it isn't based on sex, it doesn't mean it's not intense——'

'Mmm, it must be intensely unexciting,' he agreed glibly and she struggled not to scream. She tried to ignore the slow slide of the hand between her shoulder-blades down the length of her tingling spine. It wasn't until his hand stopped, his fingers splayed across her lower back, curving against the rise of her buttocks, that she found the breath to reply.

'We're both cautious people,' she said blindly, and promptly threw caution to the winds. 'In fact, we're probably going to get married in the not-too-distant future!'

They moved in silence for a few tense seconds. She could feel his eyes crawling over her averted profile.

'He's asked you to be his wife?'

She bit her lip. 'No, not yet, but——'

'But since you've slept with me you've been feeling so guilty about not sleeping with Richard that you've decided it's time to spice up that "excellent relationship" and see if you're sexually compatible enough to marry him when he does ask,' he guessed with devastating accuracy. 'Is that the reason for the sexy-looking dress you're wearing tonight? A tacit signal that you're on heat at last? And where does that leave me? In the role of a "teaser" I suppose, although I thought they were used to arouse hesitant stallions rather than reluctant mares.'

'How dare you?' she spluttered, hating him for reducing her uncertainties to barnyard analogies.

'Very easily, my dear Flynn,' he drawled. 'Just think of me as saving you a lot of wasted energy. If there's been no sign of spontaneous combustion between Richard and you so far, then no amount of desperate fanning is going to create the missing spark.'

'You're talking about sex, not love——'

'You love him?'

She refused to dignify his impertinent surprise with an answer and stared resolutely away from him.

'Vanessa, look at me.' His hand released hers to take her chin in an unpleasantly firm grasp. He turned her face so that she looked fully into his. 'Do you love him?' he demanded, his expression so intent with serious concern that she was momentarily stunned.

'I—yes.'

She was afraid her hesitation had betrayed her, and to cover it she said aggressively, 'I suppose you're going to say that if I loved him I never would have betrayed him by having sex with you, no matter how drunk I was?'

The soft pad of his thumb stroked the corner of her mouth. 'No, actually I wasn't,' he said gently. 'I don't think I have to tell you anything about your feelings for Wells that you don't already know, deep down inside yourself. It's the strength of your own doubts that's the real betrayal, not anything you might or might not have done with me...'

'Oh, and you think you know me that well, of course,' she said with distinctly shaky sarcasm.

'I know that you need to be loved with a reckless abandon and Wells isn't a man prone to recklessness or, from what I've observed, abandon. He's too tame for you. He'll disappoint you, Vanessa, and not only in bed.'

'Damn you, who in the hell do you think you are? I don't have to take this from you!' whispered Vanessa angrily, dismayed at the ease with which he rifled her private thoughts.

'Thinking of quitting on me, Flynn?' he said as the music died around them. 'I wouldn't advise it.'

She flung back her head defiantly. 'Why not?'

'Because if you do I'll make damned sure that you don't have your tame Richard to run to,' he said with silky menace. 'I think he'll appreciate being made a fool of even less than I did.'

Vanessa paled. 'You mean you'd tell him?'

'Not only him. You know what they say, my dear; a lie has no leg but a scandal has wings. I can just imagine the titillating headlines the tabloids could concoct if they got wind of the true identity of the lascivious ghost of Whitefield Inn. Why, we'd open to roaring trade and you'd be the media's latest darling. Shall we return to your ardent swain? I see him looking rather anxiously this way and I wouldn't like him to get the wrong idea, would you...?'

CHAPTER SEVEN

BARELY fifteen minutes later Vanessa was numbly allowing herself to be put into the passenger seat of Benedict's BMW.

Even while a detached part of her brain despised herself for her meekness she seemed unable to fight the old sense of helplessness that had come flooding back at his final verbal thrust on the dance-floor.

When he had taken her back to the table, propelling her blind progress with an iron hand in the middle of her back, Richard had instantly been concerned.

'Vanessa? What is it? You look as white as a sheet!'

'I feel ill,' Vanessa had replied thickly, her dark eyes unconsciously pleading. 'I want to go home.'

'Of course; let me get the bill——' Richard had risen to his feet, extending an anxious hand only to find her moved firmly beyond his grasp.

'No need to rush, Wells. I'll take her home with me. No sense in your making an unnecessary trip. Say goodnight to Richard, Vanessa.'

Even through the veil of her shock Vanessa had sensed the deep satisfaction in the man beside her as he began to draw her away from the table. He was enjoying thwarting all Richard's expectations of a romantic end to the evening.

'Goodnight, Richard,' she'd repeated mechanically.

A scandal has wings... Vulture's wings. She could feel them beating over her defenceless head.

Only when they'd reached the BMW parked on the gravel by some huge pohutukawa trees did Vanessa summon the presence of mind to protest. 'I had a coat——'

'We'll pick it up some other time. They'll keep it safe. Here, take this if you're cold.' He shouldered out of his white jacket, placing it around her trembling shoulders, enveloping her in his warmth and male scent. He opened the door and tucked her fluid skirt over her thighs when it slipped sideways as she swung her legs inside.

'Are you all right?' he asked as he got in beside her and switched on the headlights.

'Yes,' she clipped, looking through the front windscreen at the way the lights were blurred by the faint mist that was drifting in from the Firth of Thames.

He swore under his breath. 'Damn it, stop looking like that. If he really means that much to you I'll take you back inside!'

The rawness in his tone pierced her numbness.

'Who?' She turned her head. His white shirt shimmered in dimness, the dark tie a slash across his throat; what she could see of his expression was tight and angry.

He gave a coldly exultant laugh at her blank puzzlement. 'No, he doesn't, does he?'

He leaned closer to her, so that she could see the fierce glitter in his eyes. 'What is it you're thinking about, then, Vanessa? Where's all that glorious fight gone? What are you hiding? Or should I say, what is it you're hiding *from*?'

That jolted her. Fight? Dear God, she was just beginning to realise how weaponless she was where he was concerned. 'I don't know what you're——'

'Don't! Don't lie to me!' he cut across her sharply. 'I've had enough of it. You know, I always wondered what it was that made you bury your personality under all those layers of stifling pseudo-obedience..."Yes, sir, no, sir, three bags full, sir." And don't hand me that crap about being content with your job. Maybe you were once, but since the judge died you've enjoyed ruling the roost here by yourself too long and too much to relinquish your independence easily to me or to anyone else. I think you're only just beginning to discover your potential. You want something more out of life, but for some reason you're too afraid to reach out and take it——'

She felt too battered to fend off his quiver of questions; she could only stonewall. 'Not everyone has your single-minded ambition——'

'Had,' he corrected ominously. 'You'll be pleased to note I'm rapidly diversifying my interests. At least I look to the future rather than the past for my solutions. That's why you prefer to steep yourself in history, because it's safe, isn't it, Vanessa? No surprises. History can't hurt you. Only what happens in the present can do that.'

She gave a short, painful laugh. What was in the past could very well hurt you, haunt you; she was living proof of the fact.

Her hand crept to her throat, pressing there to halt the rise of burning bile.

A scandal has wings... How aptly that described the way that lies flew from lip to lip, like the innocent childish whispering game, where the distortion of the original message as it progressed further from the source resulted in great amusement. Except that there had been nothing innocent or amusing in the vicious distortions spread about Vanessa. They had had a very serious intent—to destroy her reputation and undermine her credibility.

Unexpectedly his voice gentled. 'I'm sorry if I frightened you with that stupid threat. You must know that it was only my anger talking. I would never betray you like that. I don't want a scandal any more than you do; I enjoy my privacy too much. You can tell me anything... anything at all. I won't be shocked...'

She almost responded to that soft, enticing invitation, almost weakened, almost trusted him, but then she looked into his eyes, saw the ruthless curiosity there, and instinctively shrank from it. For a moment, in his place, she saw other hungry eyes, avid for her version of 'the truth', promising justice but delivering whatever served them best.

'I won't be shocked'. No, given his worldly sophistication he probably wouldn't be, but the sordid little story still had the power to shock Vanessa, to make her feel again that writhing self-contempt and crippling sense of vulnerability.

'I feel ill,' she said through stiff lips.

'Vanessa——'

'If you don't get me home I'll probably be sick in the car,' she said with bitter relish and he hastily turned the keys in the ignition, expressing his frustration with a loud gunning of the engine as he pulled out into the road.

'Don't think this is the end of it, Flynn,' he brooded as they surged forward into the darkness.

'Make up your mind,' she muttered sullenly.

'What do you mean?'

She risked a glance at his dark profile. His hearing was as acute as his perception. 'You call me Vanessa when you want something and Flynn to threaten me. To put me in my place.'

'I have yet to discover what your place is,' he said cryptically. 'Now, be a good girl and shut up while I concentrate. It's been a bloody long night.'

She remembered then where he had been and felt a small flicker of reviving malice. 'Who beat you for the award?'

A flash of light from an oncoming car revealed a sardonic curl to his lip. 'That pleases you, doesn't it—the thought that I didn't win?'

'Of course not.'

'One day I'm going to teach you to stop telling me lies,' he clipped. 'You like the idea of my pride being trampled in the dust. For your information I didn't nominate myself, Dane did. And I didn't lose.'

'But you said——'

'I didn't say anything; your prancing stud made the assumptions. I told you he was a bit thick.'

'You can't blame him!' She flew to Richard's defence. 'You didn't appear to be in a very celebratory mood.'

'I was until I found my butler hiding under his table,' he said grimly, 'and discovered why.'

Vanessa shivered at the reminder and hugged his jacket more tightly around her. He had a one-track mind. 'If you won, why on earth did you leave early?'

'What should I have done? Stayed to be smothered under the avalanche of sycophantic flattery that goes hand in hand with these things? Is that what you think is important to me? It isn't the first award I've won and it won't be the last. I know exactly how much and how little they really mean.'

Vanessa would have taken issue with that breathtaking piece of arrogance except that she knew that in his case it was justifiable. She had seen a photograph of his array of plaques and awards in one of the *Architectural Digests* and read his offhand comment that winning was 'good for business'.

'But your plans. You were going to stay overnight at the apartment——'

'I changed my mind—I know you think I'm rigid and inflexible but I *am* capable of acting spontaneously on occasion,' he said irritably. 'Maybe I just wanted to celebrate my victory with someone who had no axe to grind, about whose opinion I might actually give a damn!'

There was a fraught silence while Vanessa dared to consider what that meant. He couldn't be talking about *her*? While she sought for a delicate way of finding out he made another impatient sound.

'I might have known you wouldn't be impressed. I suppose you'd prefer to think of me as a valiant loser.

As a disappointed man I'm less of a threat, an object of compassion rather than any positive emotion.'

'Don't be silly——'

'Why not? I've already made a fool of myself over you once.'

'This is ridiculous——'

'I agree, totally absurd.' He stopped the car with a skidding jerk and unclipped his seatbelt to turn towards her.

She stiffened, fighting off a dangerous pleasure, all her senses focused on the man now lifting his arm to rest along the back of her seat. He had come back because of her. Because of some boyish desire to impress her with his cleverness... Benedict Savage, who took his enormous successes with cynical casualness, had been proudly bearing his honours home on his shield. She moistened her lips and asked nervously, 'Why have we stopped?'

He was silent for a long moment. Then the furious tension that gripped him seemed to relax. 'So that I can seduce you on a dark and lonely street, Vanessa; why else?'

His words sent a wave of heat rolling over her. 'I—Oh!' She looked out of the window and was mortified to see that they were parked on the gravelled driveway at Whitefield, right before the front door. And she hadn't even noticed! 'Oh.'

'Disappointed?'

She blushed, groping awkwardly for the door-handle and rattling it desperately when she discovered it wouldn't open.

'It's still locked,' Benedict pointed out.

'I realise that,' she said, her damp fingers slipping in panic on the lock as she tried to disengage it.

'Vanessa——'

She heard the rustle of his movement and whirled round in her seat, only to discover that she was still trapped by her seatbelt and that he was leaning across her to deal deftly with the recalcitrant lock.

'What?' To make up for the sharpness of her response she subsided in her seat, reassured by his obvious willingness to let her go.

'Aren't you going to ask me what the award was for?'

'Oh, yes—what was it for?' she asked hurriedly, feeling ashamed of the self-absorption that had led her to misjudge his motives so blatantly badly.

'Are you really interested?'

Typical of the male injured ego—he was going to make her work for his forgiveness. 'Of course.'

'I thought you didn't like my work.'

'Who told you that?'

'Dane. When he was here last year you told him that you thought the Serjeant Building was a boring monolith, exhibiting the kind of concrete-slab mentality that made modern cities universally the same.'

'He just showed me a photo and asked my opinion,' she said weakly, remembering the amusement the other man had displayed when she had unwisely abandoned her customary reserve around her employer's guests and proffered an honest rather than diplomatic response. 'I didn't realise you had designed it.'

Benedict didn't seem in the least offended. 'One of my earliest commissions, when I was still working for my father's firm. He had a stern rule that one supplied clients with what they wanted, not what the architect thought they should want. In that case the client was a hidebound reactionary who thought that Frank Lloyd Wright was a dangerous lunatic. That building fitted him like a second skin.'

'I don't mind some of your later designs,' Vanessa said comfortingly.

'Thank you for that damningly faint praise,' he said wryly. 'I realise commercial architecture is largely a soulless business... precisely because it's such a *big* business, cost-driven to the point that anything new and untried or unusual is usually feared. Plans often have to be approved by a board, and committees are notoriously more conservative and difficult to please than individuals. Only those with real foresight, who want to make a permanent impact on the landscape rather than a smooth turn-around profit on construction, are interested in allowing an architect full artistic freedom. That's why I left my father's firm and branched out with Dane. I wanted to create a separate professional identity for myself...concentrate on smaller commissions calling for greater individualism. I still do the big——' a taunting semi-bow to Vanessa '—"boring" bread-and-butter ones, but these days I supplement the stodge with a good leavening of the off-beat. The award was for a private residence at Piha. Would you like to see it?'

'Go to Piha, you mean?' Vanessa was startled.

His white teeth flashed in the darkness. 'I was talking about something a little more convenient—the plans are up in my studio.'

'Oh. Yes, that would be very interesting,' she murmured, trying and failing to imagine what kind of houses Benedict Savage would design.

Palatial homes for millionaires and pillars of society, no doubt—they were probably the only ones who could afford his magnificent fees. But at least his dangerous mood seemed to have evaporated now that she had given his ego room to flex. 'I'd like to see it, some time when it's convenient...'

His eyes glittered as if he sensed he was being 'handled'. 'I'd better put the car in the garage. Would you like to open up the house? And here, you may as well take this.'

He scooped up something from the back seat and thrust a cool, metallic object into her hands. She found herself looking down at a slender, stylised sculpture. 'Oh, is this your award? It's very nice.'

She heard the smile in his voice. 'Yes, very nice. Run on in, there's quite a chill outside. Have you got your key?'

'I'm not a child.' She opened her door to get out and found herself pulled up with a jerk that made her gasp with pain.

'Here, allow me.' Kindly, Benedict freed her from her seatbelt and she scrambled out in a flurry of black crêpe de Chine, still clutching his jacket around her, conscious of his chuckle pursuing her up the steps.

She was acting like a nervous teenager for no reason at all, she simmered as she flicked on the lights in the foyer and stairwell. He must have known that she thought he was going to pounce on her. But then, what was she supposed to think after the things he'd said to her at the restaurant? Beneath the challenging interplay of words there had run a definite current of sexual awareness, heightened by his obviously vivid recollection of their lovemaking.

Unconsciously she placed a hand over her flat stomach. He had actually sounded quite smug when he'd raised the question of pregnancy, as if the idea of her bearing his child wasn't at all dismaying. In little more than a week he had invaded her body and wrapped himself around her consciousness to such an extent that the certainties that had been her strength and her protection over the last few years had begun to crumble. She was losing control and somehow she had to find a way to regain it.

She put the award carefully on the hall table beside the telephone after studying the engraved plague and was still hovering there uncertainly when Benedict slipped through the front door, which she had left ajar. He must have parked the car with remarkable speed, she thought as he closed the door behind him and locked it, then leant back against the stripped-wood panels just looking at her.

She moved restlessly under that steady gaze. 'I was just wondering whether you wanted me to serve you coffee——' She faltered as he pushed away from the door and began to walk slowly towards her. Automatically she backed away, until she reached a wall and could retreat no further.

It took all her will-power not to shrink back as he came to an unsmiling halt in front of her and reached out to unhitch his jacket from her shoulders with a single finger and draw it away. The slippery silk lining slid down over her bare arms like a caress. He tossed the jacket over the elaborately carved newel post at the bottom of the stairs and casually leaned against the wall, his hand planted beside her tense shoulder.

'Now who's trying to put whom in their place?' he mocked softly. 'After tonight you won't ever dare call me sir again. Get used to it, Vanessa.'

'Used to what?' Her eyes were slightly higher than his but she felt small and surrounded.

'The new relationship between us. If you're going to run this inn for me, you're going to have to do it with authority. You have to decide whether you want to be a butler for the rest of your life or whether you're ready to move on and up.'

'Me? Run the inn?' Vanessa said faintly, pressing herself back against the supporting wall to try and escape the heat of his body.

He had loosened the black tie on the way in from the car and unbuttoned the top pearl stud of his shirt. The white pleated shirt was so thin, she could see the shadow of his torso outlined through the silk. His chin was dark with regrowth. He looked tired, disordered, and disturbingly sexy. It was incredible, but this man, with his only mildly good looks and his spectacles and his studied emotional colourlessness, harboured a smouldering sexuality that was as electrifying as it was astonishing. Vanessa was bewildered. Why had she never seen it before? And why, now that she could see it was so obvious, wasn't he smothered in women wherever he went?

His eyebrows rose. 'Isn't that what you had in mind when you suggested a manager?'

She shook her head. 'No, it never occurred to me!'

'Not even in your secret dreams?'

Her eyes slid away from his. She had no intention of telling him what her secret dreams involved. 'How could I?' she asked huskily. 'I don't know anything about running a hotel——'

'The job you're doing now isn't so far removed from it,' he pointed out quietly. 'You provide accommodation services for my guests, manage staff and purchase supplies. You do accounts and supervise building and maintenance. I think you'd be surprised how well-equipped you are for the job. A small hotel like this needs an intimate, highly individualistic management style, preferably by someone attuned to its unique atmosphere. Who better than you? You love it here, don't you? Wouldn't you like to know that you didn't have to leave? That you could stay on and build it into something that we can both be proud of? If you feel inadequate in any way, there are always courses you can take to improve your management skills...'

It was such a powerfully seductive offer that Vanessa was afraid to question the motives behind it.

'Why me?'

'Because I'm already used to having you around.'

'Oh.'

She was convenient. That hurt and she lowered her lashes against him. From the corner of her eye she watched his free hand move up to finger the velvety loop on the open edge of the neckline which lay against her collarbone, his knuckles almost brushing her chin, and he continued, softly chiding, 'You should be flattered. I don't let people into my life very easily. My mother elevated emotional manipulation to an art form, and to this day I still have a natural disinclination to trust my feelings for fear they'll be used against me, particularly where women are concerned. I think we're alike in that respect—slow to trust—which is why I'm willing to forgive you for playing games with my head. I realise you were only trying to protect yourself. But I'm offering you a unique opportunity here and the beauty of it is, you don't even have to leave home to take advantage of it.'

His finger counted down to the next empty loop and the next, not touching anything but the fabric and yet managing to make her feel as if her skin was being brushed by a thin trickle of fire. At her sharply indrawn breath he looked up from his fascinating tracery and murmured persuasively, 'I do trust you, you see. Will you trust me? If not as a man then at least as a businessman. I'll be totally honest with you, Vanessa. I'd very much like to have you back in my bed, but neither offer is contingent upon your accepting the other. Whether we become lovers or not has no bearing on the fact that I think you're the perfect person to run the inn. I won't make it difficult for you if you choose to make profit with me rather than love, and I certainly won't attempt any emotional manipulation. Ask Dane—I might not like losing, but I'm graceful in defeat.'

His finger flicked down the rest of the open loops to wedge into the fabric V where the bodice was fastened between her breasts and he paused before adding slyly, 'Although you may have to bear with me a little; I'm so rarely defeated that I might be a little rusty about my graces...'

Her mouth came open but nothing issued forth from her parted lips. She was very conscious that the boning of her bodice had made wearing a bra unnecessary and wondered if he had guessed. Her breasts rose and fell, the inner slopes caressing his relaxed finger. He watched the expressions flitting across her face with a faint smile and delicately curved the other fingers of his hand under the smooth edge of the bodice, rubbing his thumb lightly over the top of the fabric. The backs of his fingers moved delicately against the silky swell of her breast in a secret caress that they were both intensely aware of. Only millimetres away from his touch, the soft, satiny peak tightened in an agony of anticipation. Blood rushed to her head, making her feel dizzy with unimagined pleasure.

'This is a very elegant, sexy dress. It looks as if it's melting over you,' he purred, bending a knee so that it touched hers through the folds of her skirt.

'I made it myself,' she heard herself whisper inanely, thinking that it was what was under the dress that was melting.

'Resourceful Vanessa.' His praise curled around her ears and stroked across her senses. 'Your hands are obviously as quick and clever as your tongue.'

She blushed right down into her cleavage and he laughed huskily, his whisky-warm breath teasing her mouth.

'I was complimenting you on your wit, Nessa. What did you think I meant?'

'Exactly what you wanted me to think,' she said, simultaneously hot with excitement and shivery with fear.

Benedict probably thought she was able to hold her own with this kind of dangerous sexual banter but Vanessa knew she was already in over her head. The only other time she had tried it she had been badly hurt. What had started out as a seduction in which she had willingly participated had become little better than rape when Julian St Clair had become brutally impatient with her inexperience. Her slowness to respond to his physical cues had made him lose his temper and abandon any further attempts to arouse her.

He had taken what he wanted and left her bleeding and in pain, telling her flatly that virgins were more trouble than they were worth. This despite the fact that her innocence was what had attracted him in the first place. He had deliberately set out to make her fall in love with him and then abandoned her as just another of life's challenges that hadn't lived up to his jaded expectations.

'I don't know what happened between us so you shouldn't tease me about it,' she said uneasily. 'It's not fair.'

His fingers stilled their delicate by-play. 'Does that worry you?'

She swallowed, pulling her mind back to the present. Benedict wasn't anything like Julian. For one thing he was older and more discriminating, a man who had achieved brilliant success on his own terms, not a spoiled, idle playboy trading on his family name. And he was as patient as he was tenacious, as demanding on himself as on others. He wouldn't hurt her, not physically, anyway...

'Of course it worries me...'

He sighed, and to her aching disappointment withdrew his hand from her dress. He removed his glasses and hung them carelessly from his hip pocket, then curved his fingers around her throat as he looked deep into her eyes. Once again, she succumbed to the spell of his mesmerising gaze.

'I'm sorry,' he murmured meaninglessly as he applied gentle pressure to the nape of her neck, drawing her down to his mouth.

She couldn't have resisted even if she had wanted to; the mysterious shadows in those deep blue eyes were simply too alluring. They made her want to know who the man really was behind his self-controlled mask, to find out whether the strange, shivery sensations that radiated through her body at his lightest touch were real or merely the illusion of desire. She forgot that he was her employer, that there were very sound and sensible reasons why this should not be allowed to happen. She drifted into his embrace with a thrilling knowledge of her own daring. *He* hadn't been disappointed in her as a lover... She had obviously pleased him and now it was time to discover if he pleased her!

It wasn't the fierce, hungry kiss sizzling with passion that Vanessa had eagerly expected, but a long, slow kiss of silky exploration...so long that she nearly suffocated in sweetness before he released her to breathe, only to draw her in again, to taste her with luscious bites of erotic pleasure, his teeth sinking into her swollen lower lip, his tongue unfurling inside her to stroke and linger. A lovely, sensual lethargy dragged at her lower limbs. Her arms slid around his waist to cling to the only solid support in a world of dissolving bliss. She had never known there were so many ways to kiss.

'Why are you sorry?' she whispered in blurred tones as his mouth shifted to the side of her throat and slid lower to the little hollow where her pulse fluttered madly. Her breasts were hurting against his chest, tight and unbelievably tender. When was he going to touch her there again?

Instead his arm slid around her back and he drew her away from the wall as if they were dancing, his mouth still moving against her long, slender neck as he swayed towards the stairs. 'Come with me...'

'Where?' It was a dreamy request, without force or curiosity. She knew where he was taking her. Up to heaven in his arms.

'You'll see...'

He wafted her slowly up into the darkness of the upper floor, stair by stair, kiss by kiss, as if he was afraid that if he let her go for a moment the sensual spell he was weaving would be broken, but, instead of ending up in his bedroom, when he finally wrenched himself away with a soft groan of regret she found herself blinking owlishly in the harsh fluorescent lighting of his studio.

Dazed and trembling, she reached out, but he was already turning away and unrolling something across the draughting-table and clipping the edges flat. His hands, she was glad to see, were shaking as much as hers.

'What are you doing?'

'I want you to see this. The perspective drawings that won the award. And photos of the finished house.'

She stared at him incredulously. He wanted to talk about his work, *now*? 'Ben...'

'Please.' The look he gave her was both searing and pleading. 'It's important to me.' He held out his hand, steady now, and when she took it he drew her hard against his side, his other hand curving possessively over her hip as he firmly directed her attention to the board.

'You see—it's built on a steep hillside covered with native bush. For a couple and their three children. They're both artists. He works with stained glass—that's why there's so much used in the design; they wanted a sense of the bush behind drawn inside the house rather than pushed away by four solid walls. And they didn't have much money, so I had to incorporate a lot of odds and ends that they'd rescued from demolition sites and make sure that a lot of the building work was do-it-yourself capable. What do you think?'

She could hardly think at all, her whole body attuned to the thumb that was stroking her hipbone through the slippery black fabric, but he seemed anxious, so she struggled for a response that would earn his approval. Then, as her interest was caught, she didn't have to struggle at all.

'Why, it's lovely.' She bent over to study the higgledy-piggledy juxtaposition of shapes, the way the house seem to mimic the uneven growth patterns of the surrounding bush, taking on odd tilts and angles obviously to avoid the necessity for cutting down the mature trees scattered over the site. 'It's *fantastic*!' She turned dark, astonished eyes to his. 'You did *this*?'

'I should be insulted by that disbelieving look,' he drawled unsteadily, his expression strangely grave. 'But yes, I did that, although you'll notice it's not signed Savage. I use another professional name for this kind of work, what I call the fun stuff. It's a way for me to let off steam, to indulge myself and yet not compromise Dane Benedict's reputation with our conservative corporate clients... although my identity's no secret in the trade.'

'What are these here?' Vanessa was fascinated by the loving intricacy of his detail. Compared to the slick, water-colour washed sketches of his award-winning commercial work that she had seen these were like illustrations rather than designs, maps of the imagination. 'They look like ladders up the walls. Where do they go? Are these lofts——?'

'Play-lofts and tunnels between the children's rooms.' He gave them a quick, uninterested glance and then deliberately put his hand down over the section she was trying to interpret. 'Vanessa, I didn't bring you here to play twenty questions. I just wanted you to see it, that's all. So that you'd realise that I am capable of being... whimsical and sensitive to interpreting other people's needs, even if they're not completely sure about them themselves. I mean, I may come across as a heartless bastard sometimes but——'

'I never thought you were that——' Vanessa was driven to protest, the lovely warmth of passion beginning to drain away. Was he trying to let her down lightly? To explain that he had responded to her only because he thought that she had needed the flattery of his desire?

'Until now.'

'What's that supposed to mean?' she asked hollowly, not wanting to know the answer.

He turned her, holding her at arm's length by her shoulders, his face grim. 'Just this: unless you lied about sleeping with Wells or have some other secret lover hidden away, there's no way you can be pregnant.'

For a moment she was puzzled and then she realised what he was admitting and why he looked so tense, almost anguished.

'Oh, Benedict, I'm so sorry...' Had he thought that she would think him less of a man because of it? She stroked his taut mouth with tender compassion and he recoiled as if her finger were tipped in poison.

'*You're* sorry?'

'Are you quite certain?' she asked, seeing that she had jolted him with her swift understanding. 'There's a lot that doctors can do about sterility these days——'

He dropped his hands from her shoulders, his eyes blazing with cobalt fire. 'What in the hell are you talking about? I'm not sterile!'

He sounded so furiously certain that Vanessa's heart squeezed in her chest. 'You have children?' She faltered. It had never even occurred to her. Oh, she was so *naïve*!

'No, I *don't* have children!' he shouted at her, so furiously offended that she took a step back.

'Then—then how do you know you're not sterile?' she stammered with what she felt was impeccable logic.

'Because——' He stopped and uttered a word that made her pinch her mouth primly. 'I don't *know*—all right? But I have no reason to *not* believe I'm not——' He ran a hand through his hair in an uncharacteristic gesture of helplessness. 'Oh, hell, will you stop confusing the damned issue while I'm trying to make a confession?'

'*I'm* confusing it?' Vanessa couldn't help an involuntary smile, which seemed to infuriate him beyond bearing. She had never seen him so close to losing control. It was quite fascinating.

As she watched, round-eyed, he took a deep, controlling breath and said very, very carefully, 'What I'm *trying* to tell you, Vanessa, is that there is not the ghost of a chance that I got you pregnant that night——' It was a measure of his mood that there wasn't even the glimmer of amused recognition of his inadvertant pun.

'Oh?' Her limited sexual experience sent her imagination haywire. 'You mean you—er—withdrew...before you...?'

'No, I didn't *withdraw*,' he snarled. 'There was nothing for me to have to withdraw *from*.'

Vanessa looked at him, appalled. Her colour rose, along with her vivid curiosity. 'You mean we just...did it without actually——?'

'We didn't *do* anything in bed that night!' he exploded. 'Correction, we did do *something*,' he amended grimly. 'We slept.'

'Slept?'

He shrugged, easing the motion down through the rest of his body as if loosening it up for combat.

'*Slept*?' She repeated sharply. It was finally beginning to sink in.

'Yes, you know, that state of unconsciousness wherein one is completely relax——'

'We *slept*!'

He bowed his head, awaiting the storm. It wasn't long in breaking.

'Why, you——' Vanessa rounded on him like a furious tornado. 'Are you telling me that I didn't——?'

'Ravish me? I'm afraid not,' he said meekly.

'That you didn't——?'

'Ravish *you*—no.'

'That we just spent the whole time *sleeping*! And you expect me to believe that? What do you think I am, an *idiot*?' she screeched.

'No, an innocent.' He was unwise enough to expand on that. 'If I'd made love to you that night, Vanessa, believe me you would have been in no doubt of it the next morning. You would have been aching and tender in places I'm too polite to mention——'

'You—*polite*?' she spat. 'Was it polite to let me think——? You...you *bastard*!' She went bright red at what she had thought. How he must have been laughing at her!

'Tit for tat, Vanessa,' he pointed out, but Vanessa was in no mood to be fair. Her temper had reached flashpoint and her hand had streaked out and cracked across his face before she even realised her intention.

'That's one,' he said so coolly that she lashed out again, across the other cheek. His head snapped to the side with the force of the fresh blow. Slowly he looked back at her.

'That's two.'

She wasn't foolish enough to make it three but she had a desperate need to goad him out of that infuriating calmness.

'What are you trying to do, frighten me?' she sneered, circling him in a swirling of skirts like a black thunderstorm building up static electricity.

He, perversely, seemed to think he had already weathered the worst. He folded his arms across his chest, slowly rotating to follow her prowling progress. 'I don't have to. You're doing a very good job of frightening yourself. I always wondered what you'd look like in a passion. Now I know. You should lose your temper more often.'

She knew he was trying to distract her. 'And you should be ashamed of yourself!' she spat, clenching her hands in the soft folds of her skirt. All the thwarted passion of a few minutes ago was now channelled into the relief valve of rage.

'I think I should be complimented for my honesty,' he protested. 'I'll even admit that I looked and I lusted but the flesh was sadly unwilling.'

Was he trying to tell her that no man would want her, even served up on a platter? She flinched, then rallied furiously. She wasn't going to let him get away with sexually humiliating her. She had promised herself that no man would ever do that again. 'It damned well wasn't unwilling when *I* woke up,' she flung at him. 'You were certainly plenty aroused *then*.'

He had the gall to flaunt a grin. 'I'm usually at my best in the mornings,' he said modestly. 'And I was probably dreaming about what was to come...so to speak. I had every intention of making love to my luscious satin-wrapped present when I'd slept off my jet-lag. I was very disappointed to find her a figment of my lustful imagination.'

'You're disgusting!' choked Vanessa, coping with a rush of conflicting feelings—relief, embarrassment, forbidden delight...

'I'm a man.'

'You're a pervert!'

'The perversion would have been if I'd brought you up here and made love to you without telling you that it was our first time together. It wouldn't have done for us both to discover you were still a virgin——'

'I've made love before!' she flared defiantly.

'Good. Then I won't have to worry about hurting you——'

She shuddered at the painful memory that that evoked, wrapping her arms around her waist and hugging herself in a revealing gesture that made his eyes narrow and his mouth thin.

'Surely you don't have the gall to think that I'd let you—— ' She choked to a halt as he moved closer, his voice gentling.

'Not *let*, Vanessa. Fully participate as a mature adult. Nothing's changed. You wanted me enough to come this far——'

'No, I didn't, I was just curious.'

His mouth thinned still further. 'Was, and still are. Would you like me to prove it to you, Vanessa? At least I've been honest with you. More so than you've been with me...'

'What do you mean?'

'All this outrage about what I did or didn't do to you. Isn't it really a mask for your own guilty feelings? Didn't it secretly excite you to think about how liberated our lovemaking must have been... neither of us in any state to worry about restraint or inhibition? Weren't you even a little aroused when you woke up to find me beside you?'

She hugged herself tighter. 'I was shocked——'

'Of course you were shocked. But there you were, semi-nude, cuddled up with a naked, aroused man who was completely vulnerable to whatever you chose to do to him. You were curious about me then, too, weren't you, Vanessa? It never occurred to you that it might have been rape, because subconsciously even then you trusted me. So you didn't scream. You looked at me instead. You looked at my body. Did you touch me? Did you *want* to touch me? I would have liked it if you had. I would have liked to have been woken that way, liked it more than anything...'

She couldn't look at him, turning her back and trying to retrieve her badly fragmented composure. 'I——'

'Because I touched you, Vanessa,' he told her with devastating candour as he moved up behind her.

'When I got into bed with you I fondled you a little before I drifted off to sleep—your long, gorgeous back and especially that beautiful, rounded bottom.' His arms came around her body to wrap themselves over hers and gently tug them down to her sides, pressing them there as his voice nuzzled in her hair. 'It was so irresistible... all bare and warm under that flimsy satin slip, like a delicious, downy peach I wanted to bite into... You were lying on your front so I couldn't stroke your breasts, but I knew they must be ripe and full because your slip was loose and I could see the luscious swell at the side where your breast was compressed against the bed. I went to sleep thinking about turning you over and cupping them in my hands, finding out how your nipples would taste, whether they were big or small, cherry-pink or——'

'Stop it!' she cried faintly, far too late for the protest to be effective.

'Why, am I turning you on, Vanessa?' He ran his hands lightly up and down her arms and then, taking her by surprise, spun her around, looking deeply satisfied when he saw her flushed face and cornered eyes, the full lower lip that he had bitten so voluptuously earlier now captured by her own nervous teeth.

He touched her hair with a tenderness that made her eyes sting. 'Don't worry. I'm not going to force you to do anything that you don't want to. Not tonight, anyway. I won't rush you but I'm not going to let you deny your feelings, either, or mine. I give you fair warning that I have every intention of fulfilling my fantasies where you're concerned!'

CHAPTER EIGHT

VANESSA lifted her head and let the stiff breeze float her loosely bound hair off her shoulders. She dug her cold hands deeper into the pockets of her down jacket as she walked along the beach, stepping carefully in her thick-soled trainers to avoid slipping on the piles of loose rocks.

Unlike the silky white-sand beaches of the east coast of the Coromandel, most of the west-coast bays were small, rock-strewn stretches of brown sand scalloped from point to rocky point, the mussel- and oyster-encrusted rocks at the waterline giving way to small boulders than could be overturned to reveal scuttling colonies of crabs and, up past the high-tide line, bleached driftwood and stiffened brown seaweed lay among thick drifts of smoothly weathered stones and pebbles ranging through the spectrum of earth colours.

Vanessa looked up at a sharp cry, but it was only a seagull wheeling above the shallow inshore waters, brown with stirred-up sand. She watched its soaring, wind-tossed flight across the pale grey sky, envying its freedom. There were times she would like to fly free, away from all her problems. But instead she could only drive and walk and even then she wasn't escaping them, because her biggest problem was herself.

She turned to retrace her steps and froze, her heart shuddering in her breast.

Correction, her biggest problem was in front of her, calmly strolling between the rocks as if he had as much right to be there as she did.

She waited until he got into earshot before she asked tightly, 'What are you doing here?'

Benedict shrugged, his black leather jacket sliding open over his cream sweater with the careless movement as he halted on the other side of a shallow rock-pool. 'Walking.'

She snorted. 'You never walk.'

'Only because I don't usually stay here long enough to miss my daily swims. I've decided I'd better get out and about a bit if I don't want to run to fat.'

She gave his lean length a contemptuous look. 'I don't think you have to worry about that.'

'Thank you.'

'It wasn't a compliment, it was a statement of fact,' she said irritably.

'Thank you anyway. You're looking very trim yourself.'

He was looking at her long legs, clad in the jeans that she kept in the boot of the estate car along with her spare down parka and a pair of old sports shoes. When she had left the house earlier she hadn't even bothered to change, just grabbed a cardigan and fled, and now, with her prim navy 'uniform' lying on the back seat of the car, she felt wretchedly defenceless.

She brushed the wind-blown hair out of her eyes, trying to tuck the strands back into the scarf she had used to tie it back.

'Did you follow me here?' she asked bluntly.

'What makes you think that?'

She refused to retreat in the face of his daunting amusement. 'It seems a very strange coincidence, that's all.'

'Since there's only one main road around here, it's not *that* much of a coincidence. I saw the car parked on the verge so I stopped.'

He made it sound like an idle impulse but what reason would he have for driving north from Whitefield? He didn't strike her as a man with sightseeing on his mind. That only left one alternative.

'You said I could have the afternoon off,' she challenged.

'I suggested *we* take the afternoon off,' he corrected gently. 'And you snuck away to hide as soon as my back was turned.'

'I'm not hiding. I just wanted to—to get some fresh air and stretch my legs,' she invented wildly.

Ever since that electric encounter two weeks ago she had been attempting to put a physical distance between them that he had been equally determined to thwart. One night, to her fury, he had invited Richard and his mother to dinner and commanded Vanessa to act as his hostess. She had been forced to smile and act cool and unruffled by his teasing casualness while underneath she had simmered with a temper that had given an unaccustomed sparkle to her looks and prompted some searching glances from Mrs Wells. She couldn't help but be aware, seeing Richard and Benedict together, how dramatically different they were, like light and shadow, day and night, and unfortunately a primitive part of her was far more fascinated by the powerful lure of the hidden and forbidden than the mellow sunshine.

To her further dismay, during dinner Richard had let the cat out of the bag about the work she was doing for Judge Seaton's publisher, completing the book about the colourful history of Thames that he had been working on at the time of his death. Richard had cheerfully recounted the difficulties she had had trying to collate and compress boxes of copious notes and sort through half-scribbled ideas in her spare time and somehow by the end of the meal Vanessa had found that she had been neatly manoeuvred into accepting Benedict's help.

Since then much of her spare time had been spent cheek by jowl with Benedict at the library desk, resolutely trying to treat him like a block of wood while deeply chagrined to realise that his unwelcome expertise was indeed making the book progress much faster.

'Precisely my plan,' he said smugly now. 'We can stretch our legs together. Exercise is boring without company, don't you think?'

'No.'

He regarded her truculent glare with amusement. 'Well, in that case you just carry on by yourself and I'll keep a discreet distance behind.'

'Oh, don't be ridiculous——!'

'It's not me who's being ridiculous, Vanessa,' he said gently. 'What did you think I intended when I suggested you and I play hooky today?'

Vanessa turned away but he had already seen her blush. 'Do I have to tell you my thoughts now? Aren't I entitled to *any* privacy at all?' she demanded fiercely.

'You can have all you want. I haven't brought my thumbscrews with me. In fact, have I *ever* forced a confidence out of you, Vanessa?'

'You're always doing it!' she countered explosively.

'Ah, but by stealth, never by force.'

She gave him a look of immense frustration, aware that he was right. While they had been closeted together over the judge's disordered manuscript she had revealed far more about herself than she had intended, since talking about herself was the only proven way of stemming his tide of threatening confidences about himself.

She didn't want to be lured into curiosity about the velvety-dark contradictions of his character. She certainly didn't want to know that he had worn glasses since he was twelve years old, and that they had fogged up when he had received his first French kiss from a girl when he was fifteen... although she had found herself thinking that perhaps that explained why he had taken them off when he had kissed her!

SAVAGE COURTSHIP 133

She didn't *want* to know those other things about him that touched her heart: that his childhood had been restricted by parental expectations to the point of oppression—an imperious father whose rigid, exacting standards of excellence had raised his son to expect nothing less of himself than perfection and a mother whose social expectations of him had been every bit as stringent and repressive. One didn't express emotions openly in the Savage family circle, one acted with dignity at all times. One doled out affection when it was earned by correct behaviour or academic excellence.

Benedict had learned the lessons of his early childhood well. On the surface he had been the perfect son. He had never rebelled as a teenager, he had performed to expectation at school and at home. He had dutifully joined his father's architectural firm when he had graduated from university and carried on the conservative family tradition, regarding homes and possessions and even people as profitable investments rather than emotional attachments.

Underneath, though, other forces had been at work, the intellectual curiosity and ruthlessly competitive ambition that his father had relentlessly encouraged constantly thwarted by the restrictions imposed by his status within the firm. As the years had passed he'd come to realise that his father's expectations for him, far from being infinite, were quite claustrophobically finite—the pinnacle of Benedict's professional success was to be the inheritance of the company when his father retired and his duty then would be the continuation of the Savage dynasty.

By the age of twenty-eight, Benedict had come to a full recognition that he was not the man his father wanted him to be, and never would be. He wanted more and he wanted it on his own terms.

The split had been achieved with customary Savage dignity, a frigid debate in which both men had obdurately refused to compromise. No emotional outbursts, no public washing of dirty linen, merely a cleverly managed PR announcement that had poured cold water on the choice rumours of a family rift. Benedict had continued to see his parents occasionally on a social basis, although he was left in no doubt from his mother that she was deeply disappointed in him and would deny him the warmth of her approval until he had got over his childish fit of rebellion against his father and returned to the family fold.

Benedict had commented wryly that since his mother's approval was never very warm anyway he could live comfortably without it.

However, understanding him more didn't make him any easier for Vanessa to deal with.

'I think I've had enough fresh air now,' she said desperately, and began to march back down the way she'd come.

Predictably, Benedict matched her stride for stride but he was watching her instead of his footing and a rock shifted beneath his leather shoe, causing him to skid off into a small hollow of sea-water, soaking the cuff of his black trousers.

Vanessa, whose hand had darted out instinctively when he stumbled, snatched it away hastily as he smiled warmly at her in gratitude.

'Thank you, Nessa.'

'Walking over rocks in shoes like that is asking for trouble,' she said, quickening her gait to escape the potency of that stunning smile. 'And now I'll have to send those trousers to be dry-cleaned. Why didn't you wear something practical, like jeans?'

'I didn't know what we were going to be doing,' he said equably. 'And I don't own any jeans.'

That seemed so inconceivable to one of her generation that she stared at him in wonder. 'What do you relax in?' Then she remembered who it was she was talking to. 'Oh, yes, that's right; you don't have time to relax.'

'Until now there was no need,' he commented. 'Perhaps you can teach me to relax, Vanessa.'

She ignored him, remaining stubbornly silent until she reached the car. There she halted, frowning as she saw a vaguely familiar wicker hamper sitting by the front wheel.

'Where did that come from?'

'Kate. It's a picnic.'

'Picnic?'

'Kate said you told her you were going to the beach and then took off before she could pack you some lunch. She said you often had sandwiches on the beach when the weather was fine. She thought you might have had things on your mind and just forgot to ask.'

Vanessa cursed the over-developed sense of responsibility that had made it impossible for her to take off without letting someone know where she could be found. However, she welcomed the realisation that the hollowness in the region of her stomach might not be entirely due to Benedict's unsettling effect on her nervous system.

'I'm not hungry.'

His look was one of amused scepticism. 'Well, I am, so you can just sit and watch me eat before we go.'

'We?' She suddenly noticed that hers was the only car parked along the whole foreshore. 'Where's your car?'

'One of the plasterers dropped me off. He lives at Tapu and was going home for lunch.'

'You took a lot for granted, didn't you?'

'I didn't think you'd be callous enough to drive off and leave your employer stranded.'

Her eyes narrowed. 'Is that a threat?'

'Your paranoia is showing. For goodness' sake, Vanessa, what do you think I can do to you on a public beach?'

He picked up the hamper and began walking towards a huge, twisted pohutukawa tree whose gnarled branches overhung a steep grassy bank below the curve of the road. After a moment she reluctantly followed.

By the time she reached him, deliberately dawdling, Benedict had shaken out a blanket over the long, springy grass.

'I hope you're not going to loom over me the whole time I eat. Sit down. Learn to relax, Vanessa,' he mocked as he sat down on the blanket and shrugged out of his jacket before beginning to rustle about in the hamper.

She sat, and was instantly aware of a strange sense of isolation. With their combined weight the blanket was compressed startlingly deep into the surrounding grasses so that only the sea down the slope directly in front of them remained open to their view. They were totally private from the rest of the beach and the road above. It was also surprisingly warm out of the direct bite of the wind, so warm that Vanessa unzipped her parka and peeled it off, straightening her fleecy grey angora cardigan as she did so.

'Just like a cosy little nest in here, isn't it?' Benedict murmured, echoing her thoughts with unnerving accuracy. 'And look at you. Downy as a young chick. Would you like coffee or champagne?'

She looked at the cut-crystal glass and Royal Doulton cup he was offering, and then at the silver cutlery and starched white linen napkins he had laid on the undulating surface of the blanket. Nothing but the best for Benedict Savage. Always.

'Coffee, please,' she said primly.

'That's right, must keep a clear head,' he said blandly, producing a stainless-steel Thermos flask and pouring a steaming stream of coffee into the cup. 'Milk and sugar, m'lady?'

'No, thank you.'

He handed her a cup and poured one for himself before unwrapping some of the food, which was far more practical than the luxury accoutrements, thought Vanessa in amusement. Kate knew what made a good picnic, no matter how wealthy you were: bacon-and-egg pie; marinated cold chicken; creamy, golden New Zealand cheddar; thick, crusty home-made bread and pickles that Vanessa remembered helping to bottle.

'It's rather disconcerting to realise that while I have to ask you the simplest things about your likes and dislikes you know everything about mine,' murmured Benedict, watching her sip her coffee.

'Hardly everything,' Vanessa contested automatically.

'Still, I feel at a disadvantage.'

As a victory it was a vitally unimportant one but the knowledge that he might feel in any way insecure was a pleasing one. She couldn't help a slightly smug smile as she said lightly, 'Well, now you know how I take my coffee.'

He regarded the infinitesimal lowering of her guard blandly. 'Mmm... You may as well have something to eat, too, even though I know you're not hungry.'

Since she had been practically drooling over the array of food he had spread before her she didn't bother to protest as he cut the bacon-and-egg pie with a chased-silver knife and transferred wedges on to two plates. With a little flourish he snapped out a napkin and leaned over to drape it across her thighs before handing her the plate. 'Do you think I'd make a good butler?' he asked, tongue-in-cheek.

She was startled into uttering the truth. 'God, no!'

'That was very emphatic.' He stretched out on his side, propped up on one arm, munching at his portion of pie. 'Why?'

'Because you're not... you're too——' She stopped, wondering how much her opinion of his character was going to be given away.

'Not what? Too what?'

'Too old.'

He stopped chewing.

'The hell I am!'

Not liking the gleam in his eye that accompanied the growl, Vanessa hastened to clarify. 'Too old to change, I mean. You're used to having everything your own way. I can't see you taking orders without arguing——'

'Are we talking about you or me here?' he interrupted sarcastically. 'I'm an architect; I take orders from my clients every day——'

'I rather got the impression that you only took the orders that you *wanted* to take,' said Vanessa drily. 'Isn't that why you left your father's firm? Face it, you just couldn't cut it in a job that requires you to be constantly deferential. You have to run things, to be in charge. You wouldn't even know where your forelock was, let alone how to tug it!'

'I haven't noticed you being particularly deferential. And since when have I asked for any forelock-tugging from my employees?'

He seemed genuinely pained and she was quick to point out tartly, 'You give me time off and then expect me to be meekly at your beck and call!'

He gave her a grim smile. 'Meekly, no—I'm not that much of an optimist. But if you really didn't want to be here with me now, Vanessa, you would have driven off and left me in a cloud of dust. But you didn't. And don't tell me that it was mere deference to my authority. Your thumb your nose at *that* when it suits you. When we get down to the nitty gritty, this is between Benedict and Vanessa, man and woman, not employer and employee.'

Vanessa gave him a haughty look. 'I really don't want——'

'Yes, you do. You want me and you're afraid of it. You're afraid it makes you vulnerable. Well, hell, men are vulnerable too. Much more so. We can't hide the fact that we find a woman exciting. Look at me, do you think I *like* having such little self-control...?'

He indicated his body with an impatient sweep of his hand from shoulder to hip. Not understanding his reference, Vanessa followed the gesture to its obvious conclusion and felt herself flushing at the sight of his blatant masculinity, her eyes jerking back to his sardonic expression.

'Embarrassed? Think of how I feel!'

She did and her blush deepened. He gave a barking laugh. 'Yes, well, I admit it's not *all* bad. In fact...' his drawl took on a husky note '...some of it is pretty damned good. The question is, what are we going to do about it?'

'We're not going to do anything,' said Vanessa shakily, scrabbling for her battered defences. 'And if you think that you can use sexual harassment to——'

'Sexual harassment!' He jack-knifed to a sitting position, cursing fiercely as coffee spilled across his thigh. He wiped the stain carelessly with the sleeve of his sweater as he continued harshly, 'What in the hell are you talking about?'

'About you using your...your position to...to threaten me——'

'Any threats are in your own mixed-up little mind.' She realised that this time he was genuinely angry and becoming more so with every word he uttered. 'Why should the fact that you work for me have any bearing on the fact that we find each other attractive? So I went off my head a little at first—I think I was entitled, don't you? Did I ever say I'd fire you if you don't have sex with me?'

'No, but——'

'No. I said precisely the opposite, didn't I? And have I touched you sexually against your will?'

He had hardly touched her at all in the past two weeks; that was what had made her so acutely aware of him...the fact that he was making such an obvious effort *not* to touch her. The fact that she had found herself looking at his hands and his mouth and remembering, wondering...

'No, but——'

'Have I made suggestive comments to you while we've been working on that damned book? Have I been anything but casual and friendly?'

'No, but——'

'But what? I've been walking on damned eggshells around you so as not to frighten you off, to give you a chance to get to know me as a whole person, and now you accuse me of *sexual harassment*? My God, do you really think I'm that bloody desperate? That despicable?'

He was shouting. Cool, contained Benedict Savage was shouting at her. And swearing like an explosive teenager.

'No, of course not,' she admitted weakly.

'Then would you mind telling me what *exactly* it is that I do that makes you feel so quiveringly helpless before my slavering lust?' He raked a look down her body that made her feel hot all over.

'It's that!' she blurted out desperately. 'The way you look at me.'

There was a shivering silence. Then, '*Look*? So even looking's forbidden now? I think you'll have to be a bit more precise, Vanessa.'

'I don't want to talk about it——'

'Neither do I!'

Suddenly he was no longer sitting on the other side of the blanket. With a lithe movement he lunged across the clutter between them, upsetting plates and scattering food as he came down over her, straddling her body on his braced arms and knees as she collapsed backwards in shock. 'I'd much rather *do* something about it!'

'Stop it!' she panted, pushing both hands against his chest, holding him at bay.

'Who am I?'

She blinked at him, startled, the nimbus of light around his head making it difficult for her to see his expression. 'What?'

'My name—who am I?' he demanded, allowing her the illusion of being able to keep him at arm's length as he hovered over her. 'You don't call me sir any more and you can't quite bring yourself to say Mr Savage either. But you refuse to call me Benedict. I don't like being a nobody. So why don't you try Ben? You called me that once before, remember? Short, sweet and intimate. Try it. Say Ben, Vanessa.'

'For goodness' sake——'

'Say it.' He took off his glasses and threw them away in a gesture of reckless intent that made her heart pound.

'All right, damn it—Ben!' she retorted wildly. 'There, I've said it. Ben, Ben, Ben——'

Her provocative chant was suddenly smothered. There was no tentativeness, none of the explorative gentleness that had characterised his last kiss. This time he was all aggressive, dominating male. The kiss was hot and hard, swallowing her anger and feeding it back to her piece by defiant piece. In the first few savage moments of contact he didn't even allow her the luxury of a response—biting, licking and sucking at her mouth as if he were a starving man driven to extract every scrap of nourishment from the sensual feast before it could be snatched away from him.

But even as her mouth parted helplessly under the greedy onslaught Vanessa knew that she wasn't going to deny him anything. Only Benedict could make her feel like this, so furious, so frustrated, so wildly aroused that she no longer cared about the rules and petty restrictions that she had carefully worked out to build and govern her peaceful life.

'Say it again,' his husky voice growled into her moist depths. His tongue caressed hers, stroking his name along her trembling taste-buds, teasing it out of her in an aching sigh of pleasure.

'Ben...'

He gave a low grunt of triumph and the kiss changed, hardening even further as he came heavily down on her, his lithe body crushing her into the cushioning grasses with a powerful surging movement that dislodged her feverish grip on his sweater. Her hands slid up over his shoulders and curved down over his straining back as he settled his full length intimately against her, pushing insistently at her knees until he had nudged them far enough apart to insinuate himself between them.

'God, I love the way you say my name...' He cupped her head in one hand, pulling at her scarf with the other until her hair fluffed out across the blanket, and then he nuzzled at it before returning to her mouth, this time paying thorough attention to her every response.

As his tongue licked at her senses his free hand smoothed down the side of her soft cardigan and over her denim flank to hook behind her knee, bending it up to rest alongside his hip, increasing the intimacy of the undulating pressure between her thighs in a way that made her moan.

'Am I hurting you?' he whispered harshly, lifting his mouth from hers to study her dazed expression.

'Yes...' Her eyes were closed, her face stiff with an agony of bliss that he couldn't fail to misread.

'Then let me help you, heal you...' He shifted his torso sideways and her eyes fluttered open as she felt a pearlised button between her breasts suddenly give way.

'Why is it you always wear clothes with so many damned tiny buttons?' he growled, so intent on his task that he didn't notice her watching him through wondering eyes. His face was flushed, the tip of his tongue tracing his swollen lower lip as he concentrated.

She looked down at what he was doing, shocked to discover that he wasn't bothering to undo the buttons in a proper sequence but was merely exposing her breasts as quickly as he could. Somehow it seemed more indecent that way. Instinctively she put a hand to the top button only to have it impatiently brushed away.

'No. I want to do it. I want to see.' He looked up then and his eyes were hot and dark and at least as indecent as her thoughts. He deliberately held her gaze as he undid another button and then paused, splaying his hands possessively over the twin swells of soft angora and contracting them just enough to make her gasp.

'Someone might come,' she whispered threadily, arching helplessly as his hands contracted again.

'No one can see us here. We're safely tucked up in our little nest,' he murmured, not taking his eyes off her vulnerable face as he undid the rest of the buttons by touch and slowly began to draw the loose edges of her cardigan aside, stroking the downy wool across her sensitive skin. 'You want me to look at you, don't you, Nessa, to stop this ache we both have...?'

She stopped breathing, wondering whether he would be disappointed when he finally saw the plain white bra she was wearing, serviceable rather than seductive.

He looked down and stilled, a tiny smile sizzling at the corner of his mouth at the sight of the smooth, seamless cups and the intriguing shadowy outline of her areolae traced against the silky fine fabric. 'Where does it fasten?'

It was her willingness he was requesting, not operating instructions, Vanessa realised and she responded breathlessly. 'H-here.' She pulled her arms from his neck to touch herself nervously between her breasts, her voice nearly as thick as his.

'No.' He stopped her tentative movement, catching first one wrist and then the other and pressing them down against the rug on either side of her head. She lay quiescent as his fingers trailed slowly away to deftly unclip the tiny catch and delicately ease her breasts free from their aching confinement. His eyes blazed like blue fire.

'Oh, yes...oh, darling, just look at you...' He leaned forward and his forefinger drifted across her bare nipple in a whisper-light caress. She flinched and he touched her again, and again, until she was arching into the maddeningly light caresses, needing more than this exquisite teasing.

'So soft and smooth...' he murmured, absorbed in his erotic entrancement. 'And such beautiful, velvety pink rosebuds...look how they darken and furl so sweet and tight when they're plucked...' His thumb and forefinger moved skilfully, sending sharp splinters of abandoned pleasure streaking to the core of her being. He let her experience the thrill over and over again before he finally gathered her into his cupped palms, admiring the frame his masculine fingers created around her overflowing ripeness, lifting her, praising her with his eyes and words and finally, to her unbearable delight, his mouth.

Her fists opened and closed helplessly beside her mindlessly tossing head as he suckled his way up the warm, creamy slopes, seeking the peaks that he had meticulously teased to rigid excitement, nuzzling them hotly, licking and sucking at each swollen bud in turn, at first with extreme delicacy and then with a ravishingly raw hunger, working on her with his teeth and tongue until her whole body pulsed with the same powerfully driving rhythm that rode him between her raised legs, stroking her with his growing hardness until she was aware of nothing else but a terrifying pressure building up inside her.

A wave of primitive fear increased the pressure as her body jolted with the impact of another bunching male thrust. He was ready for her but she wasn't ready at all—she would never be! She couldn't see him but she could feel how big he was—much bigger than Julian had been and that meant that when he lost control the pain would also be worse and the pleasure that he had given her would be nothing in comparison. She was mad, insane to think she had wanted this...

She wasn't aware of the frightened little sounds and hectic movements she was making until he reluctantly abandoned her glistening flesh to soothe her frantic cries with his mouth.

'It's all right, darling, it's all right.'

'No, no...' She was almost sobbing as she writhed beneath his thighs, torn by the devastating conflict of desire against doubt. 'It hurts——'

'I know.' He kissed her, misunderstanding, holding her tightly and groaning as his body was racked by a long shudder. 'I'm sorry, I didn't mean for us to go so far... Here, let me at least do this for you...'

She felt his hand on her bare belly, the tug on the snap of her jeans, the metallic slide of her zip, and then the long, skilful fingers were brushing through the soft thicket between her legs, finding her secret source, touching her where she was hot and damp, sliding inside with a shocking ease that sent a piercingly erotic thrill of terror shafting to her brain. She wanted it all in that instant—the pleasure, the ramming pain, the brutal, bleeding emptiness...

'No!' She went rigid and blackness came swirling in on her, the way it had that other time when the agony had been so intense that she had momentarily passed out, but this time she fought it, determined not to give in, not to be completely helpless. The darkness swirled hot and suffocating, clinging around her eyes and nose and mouth until suddenly it dissolved with an icy shock.

Her eyes flew wide and she found herself staring up at Benedict, who was kneeling over her on the rug, bathing her face and neck with a napkin dripping with champagne.

'What a dreadful waste,' she croaked automatically as she saw him clumsily slop another splash of vintage bubbly into the napkin and she gasped as he applied its wet chill to her throat.

'It's not going to be wasted, believe me.' He lifted the napkin and shocked her by applying his mouth to her foaming skin, lapping it dry with delicate, rasping strokes of his tongue. 'There. Happy? Now tell me who the hell Julian is!'

'Julian...?' The colour that had leached from her face flooded back.

'The man you seem to have got me mixed up with just now. The bastard whom you begged not to hurt you.'

She tried to struggle upright, pulling her cardigan over her bare breasts. 'I'm sorry——'

He pushed her flat again with an implacable hand. 'So am I. I want to know what he did to you. Did he rape you?'

'I...n-no.'

His mouth thinned at her uncertainty, his blue eyes glowing with ruthless intent. 'We're not leaving here until you tell me, Vanessa. I'm not going to be made to pay for someone else's crimes. Who is bloody Julian?'

She held his gaze, just. 'A man I used to know. In England.'

'Were you in love with him?'

Her eyes fluttered away from his. 'No! Yes—I don't know——'

'This isn't multiple choice. Which was it?'

He was angry, but she had the sense to know that it wasn't with her. She looked back at him pleadingly. 'Please, let me do up my cardigan first...'

For an awful moment she thought he was going to refuse, his eyes growing hungry again as they roved over her flushed, well-loved breasts, but then he muttered something violent under his breath and swivelled to rake through the debris of the picnic and find his glasses. He put them on and watched broodingly as she fumbled first with the fastenings of her bra and jeans and then started on the tiny buttons of her cardigan. When it was evident that her shaking fingers were tackling a task that was temporarily beyond their capability he took over with an impatient growl, making her painfully aware that her nipples were still stiff and throbbing from his mouth. When he had finished he caught her chin in his hand.

'Now, Vanessa. Talk.'

He was brooking no refusal and after the devastating intimacy they had just shared her resistance was wretchedly weak.

'Julian was the son of the man I was butler for in London,' she said wearily. 'He liked a challenge and I was naïve and stupid enough to present him with one. It was my first really independent job and I had no family or friends in London and the whole situation was pretty nerve-racking—Egon St Clair and his wife were going through a fairly spectacular marriage break-up and their two grown-up daughters and Julian used to turn up at the house every now and then and contribute to the shouting matches.'

She pulled herself out of his grasp and sat back, trying not to notice that Benedict's casual elegance was now sexily rumpled, the coffee-stained fabric of his trousers stretched tautly across his thighs, the sleeves of his sweater pushed up to reveal the dark hair on his arms and the steel watch glinting on his strong wrist. 'So when Julian suddenly started plying me with attention I was grateful for his kindness, and flattered... he was thirty, rich, handsome and sophisticated—what insignificant nineteen-year-old *wouldn't* have been impressed? And he presented this image of himself, you see, as a tortured romantic, a misunderstood poor little rich boy who secretly longed to have his rakish life redeemed by the love of a good, plain woman. Like an idiot I fell for it. But all he wanted was a one night stand, a chance to flex his ego...' All her wretched humiliation was in her voice and in the bitter smile that bracketed her wide mouth as she looked unflinchingly at Benedict. 'So you see, it wasn't rape because I went with him willingly.'

'But you changed your mind somewhere along the line, didn't you?' he said shrewdly. 'Vanessa, if he forced you at *any* point, it was rape.'

Her mouth twisted in a painful attempt to be honest. 'I told you, I *wanted* to... I *tried* to enjoy it but he—I just couldn't seem to——' She broke off and shrugged miserably, looking out to the white-capped sea. 'I don't wonder he got furious in the end.'

'Did he hit you?' he asked in a peculiarly clipped monotone.

'Oh, no, nothing like that. He was very strong; he just held me down while he—he——' She shuddered, her eyes hauntingly dark. 'I—I was badly bruised, that's all,' she ended up lamely, cringing away from the memory of the clinical details. 'And I was sick for a couple of days...' To recover just in time for the fresh storm to break over her unsuspecting head.

Benedict was too acute an interpreter of the language to miss the glaring subtext. 'He was your first, wasn't he?' he said ferociously. 'Your first lover and the selfish bastard botched it!'

Vanessa was disturbed by his relentless intensity. 'It happened years ago. It really has nothing to do with you——'

'It does if you're going to faint with fear every time you approach a climax in my arms.'

'*Benedict*!' She folded her arms protectively across her breasts as they surged back to aching life. Tiny cramps of treacherous pleasure ripped through her body, causing an immediate panic. 'I can't let it happen again,' she said desperately. 'I can't afford to get involved with you——'

'Why? I'm free, I won't cost you anything.'

His attempted lightness caught her on the raw, lancing another festering boil. 'That's what *he* said, and in the end it cost me everything I had!'

'What are you talking about?'

It was time he knew. Perhaps then this awful agony of indecision and apprehension would be over. He would reject her finally and completely before it was too late. He would fire her and she could crawl away with her pride in tatters but her fragile heart still intact.

'I'm talking about why I left England when I did,' she said in a hard voice that matched the shellac shine in her eyes.

'I had to. You see it wasn't just Julian I slept with. Oh, no. I had sex with his father, too, even though he was fat and ugly and old enough to be my grandfather. I didn't care because I knew he was rich.' The words began to pour from her in a brittle avalanche, gathering an icy momentum of their own. 'I had it all perfectly planned, you see. I insinuated myself into Egon's household and then I seduced him in the marital bed and persuaded him to kick his wife out into the street. I made sure he alienated the rest of his family and then I convinced him to write a new will that disinherited them all and left his entire fortune to me. Then he conveniently died of a heart-attack, probably because I injected an air bubble into his veins one night when we were having sex. Only the autopsy never proved it, so I got away scot-free.'

'What in the *hell* are you talking about?'

Behind the mask of his bewildered shock she knew what was happening. His fastidious mind was already beginning to recoil from the muck-racking lies. Mud sticks. That was what the St Clairs had relied on when they had started their sordid rumour campaign—Julian included. He had robbed her almost simultaneously of her virginity *and* her virtue. By the time the furore had died down she had been a social and professional pariah, clean only in the eyes of her father and Judge Seaton, who had been a personal friend of Egon St Clair and knew the greed and viciousness of which Belinda St Clair and her offspring were capable. The judge had been as shocked and angry as Vanessa that Egon had chosen to make her an unwitting accomplice to his posthumous revenge on his estranged wife by naming her as his heir, thereby setting her up as the sole target of her furious malice. He had suggested that she sue the St Clairs for slander and the papers for libel, but Vanessa had just wanted to put the whole horrible nightmare behind her. She couldn't face more prying publicity; the snickers and the pointing and the leering curiosity had sickened and sapped her spirit almost to the point of breaking.

'Oh, don't worry. I didn't prosper from all my sordid crimes,' she flung at Benedict in wretched defiance, hating him for sitting there so silent, so still, unquestioning, accepting. 'The fortune turned out to be wildly inflated and I had to sign away my claim to avoid financial litigation. I'm surprised you don't recall the juicy details; it made the tabloids all over the world. It was a story with everything—kinky sex, blackmail, fraud and murder. You should ask to see my scrapbook some time! Nothing ever came to court, of course, but that's only because I was too clever for the cops—the police couldn't dig up enough solid evidence to bring charges. But this is probably no surpirse to you, right?' she goaded, at the end of her tether. 'You always thought there was something suspicious about me and the judge. Maybe you were right. A woman with my background——'

She broke off. His head was bent, his shoulders were shaking. He was erupting with rage, with outrage; he was going to slice her heart out of her chest with a few brutal words and sling her into an exile far worse than the oblivion she had already endured. But then he threw his head back and she saw that he was laughing—*laughing*...

For a moment she thought she was going to vomit with the pain. She leapt to her feet, black dots dancing nauseatingly in front of her stinging eyes. 'Oh, so you think it's funny, do you?' she choked. 'My life being ruined is just a big joke to you——'

She whirled to run but he was up, catching her by the elbow, still laughing. 'No, Vanessa! Listen——'

'*Listen*? You——' She tried to hit him and he twisted her arm behind her back.

'I wasn't laughing——'

The blatant untruth made her twist violently. 'Let me go, you filthy liar——'

'Vanessa.' He shook her panting form roughly. 'You can't fling things like that at me in a temper and expect me to take them seriously. Besides, if that farrago of ridiculous nonsense bears any relation to reality I'll eat my hat. Of course I laughed. To anyone who knows you at all the idea of you being an evil, gold-digging vamp is totally risible. What you know about seduction can be written on the head of a pin! You have no idea what turns a man on. Now, why don't you just calm down and tell me about your deep, dark, dreaded past properly, instead of waving it in front of my face like a red rag to a bull? You got exactly the reaction you damned well deserved...'

And so had he, thought Vanessa savagely a few fraught moments later, looking in her rear-view mirror to see the masculine figure standing in a cloud of sandy dust as she accelerated recklessly away from the beach. Was he shaking his fist at her? He was certainly furious, his last frustrated yell ringing in her ears.

'You can't run away from your emotions forever, Vanessa. I won't let you use Whitefield as your private bolt-hole to avoid life's nasty human complications——'

At least she had got the final word in. As she'd slammed the car door, almost catching his fingers in the process, she had yelled back, 'Why not? *You* are! I never believed you decided to come down to Whitefield out of the blue just for an innocent holiday. You said you needed to get away and Auckland was too accessible. You're running away from something, too, so don't preach your self-serving sermons at *me*!'

CHAPTER NINE

IT WAS a miracle that Vanessa didn't kill herself on the drive back to Whitefield. She could hardly see the road for tears and she was shaking so badly that the gears ground fiercely with every change.

She wasn't a masochist, she told herself fiercely. She wasn't going to set herself up for another lesson in the miseries of unrequited love. Back there on the beach she had realised, to her horror, that she was even more vulnerable to her emotions now than she had been five years ago. Julian's charm had been largely superficial, his character incapable of a great depth of emotion, and at some instinctual level she must have realised that, for, although his rejection and betrayal had been wretchedly painful at the time, she had survived it by despising him and forgiving herself for her immaturity.

Benedict—clever, cultured, cloaked in layers of intriguing emotional complexity—was impossible to despise. Such a serious man would never love easily—or feign love where it didn't exist—and he was cruelly honest about his intentions. He was looking for a lover, not a lifelong companion. He was rejecting her love before it was even offered.

Well, this time she was going to be the one doing the rejecting, Vanessa told herself as she spun the car recklessly into the gates at Whitefield. A volatile cocktail of temptation and challenge had temporarily deranged the molecules of her brain, that was all. Her feelings towards Benedict were pure chemistry—and she was a stout opponent of chemical dependencies.

She wasn't in love with him. She *refused* to be. She would stick to her original plan and fall in love with Richard and he would be kind and tender and never terrify her with feelings she couldn't control, or force himself into every crack and corner of her consciousness until she felt her life wasn't her own any more!

Suddenly Vanessa slammed on the brakes, fish-tailing the car on the gravel as she almost rear-ended the snazzy yellow left-hand-drive Corvette parked crookedly with its boot open on the forecourt.

A short, stocky man with rusty brown hair ran down the steps from the house to jerk open her door so suddenly that Vanessa almost fell out at his feet.

'My God—is that you, Flynn?' he said, his incredulity turning to frank amusement. 'I thought it was Mario Andretti!'

Vanessa recovered herself and straightened to her full height. 'B—Mr Savage didn't say that you were expected, Mr Judson.'

He grinned at her stiffness, his twinkling brown eyes curious as she tried to smooth back the curly, wind-swept mass of her hair.

'I live to surprise him,' he murmured, pretending not to notice the tear-stains on her cheeks. 'Though I get the feeling that this time I'm the one in for the surprise. Mrs Riley said you two were on a picnic. Didn't Ben come back with you?'

'I didn't ask,' she snapped with perfect truth and flushed as his curiosity intensified. She was searching for some innocuous comment to temper her rudeness when a woman emerged from the house behind him.

She was in her late twenties, petite and perfect, a dainty, slender woman who looked as fragile as she was beautiful, her flame-red hair emphasising the pale translucence of her skin and the brilliance of the slanted green eyes. Her classic suit matched her eyes and screamed Chanel.

'Have you found out where Benedict is yet, Dane? Goodness, who on earth is this?' The amused drawl and the slow, critical sweep of the green eyes made Vanessa's hackles rise instantly.

'I'm Mr Savage's butler,' she said crisply.

'You're kidding? She's kidding, right?' The woman arched incredulous brows at Dane who shook his head with a grin as he lifted a suitcase out of his car.

Vanessa found herself on the receiving end of a careless shrug of dismissal. 'Oh, well, I suppose Benedict likes to have his little eccentricities. What does he call you?'

Darling, Vanessa was tempted to reply caustically.

'Flynn.'

'Well, Flynn, if you *are* a butler you'd better help Dane bring in the suitcases.'

'You're *staying*?' Vanessa blurted inadvertently.

'Of course we're staying,' the woman answered impatiently. From her accent she was an American and Vanessa wondered if she and Dane were an item. It was fortunate that Vanessa had assumed her professional mask of polite rigidity because the next comment came as a searing bolt out of the blue.

'I certainly didn't come all this way to be fobbed off on any hotel. Benedict and I have a lot of planning to do. He's under a lot of pressure and I can understand him needing a break, but he has to make some decision about our engagement——'

'Engagement?' Vanessa echoed helplessly.

'Yes. I'm Lacey Taylor.' She said her name as if she expected thunderous applause, or at least a glimmer of recognition. She got neither.

'He—Mr Savage never mentioned a fiancée,' Vanessa managed to say.

'Benedict is a very private man. I don't suppose he sees any need to discuss his personal relationships with domestic staff,' she was informed pointedly. 'Now, perhaps you'll direct me to my room so that I can freshen up before he gets back from wherever he's disappeared to. Come, Dane.'

Then she was gliding away, her high heels crunching prettily over the gravel.

Vanessa looked at Dane Judson blankly.

'Why do I feel like a dog being called to heel?' he said ruefully. 'If you see Ben before I do, tell him not to blame me. When Lacey gets an idea in her head it's pretty tough to shift and I didn't think Ben would appreciate her turning up here on her own.'

'But... who is she?' Vanessa was trying to come to terms with the knowledge that all the while that Benedict had been stubbornly burrowing his way into her heart he had already been committed to another woman. So much for not being able to despise him. He was *worse* than despicable!

'An architect—a very clever one, too. She works for his father's firm. Her parents are great friends of the Savages.'

Oh, great. Loaded with brains as well as beauty, and almost part of the family already. If Vanessa hadn't been so furious she would have burst into tears.

'How long have she and B—Mr Savage been engaged?'

'Ask me that again in a couple of hours and I might be able to give you an answer,' Dane said drily, picking up the two heaviest cases and carrying them up the steps, leaving Vanessa to trail behind with the other one as she turned his cryptic words over in her head.

Did he mean that the engagement had been secret, even from Benedict's best friend? Come to think of it, she hadn't noticed any engagement ring on those slender fingers...

She found out why a couple of hours later as she served afternoon tea in the drawing-room.

Whatever Benedict's relationship with Lacey Taylor, he wasn't in love with her. His body language spoke volumes. While Lacey leaned into his every word, smiled at him and laid her hand on his arm every chance she got, Benedict was all but rolled into a defensive ball of armoured politeness. Yet Lacey behaved as if his cool reserve were a gushing welcome. She didn't so much flirt as brazenly assume, and Vanessa found herself almost admiring her for her gall.

Dane, sprawling sideways in his chair, winked at Vanessa as she bent to offer him a slice of Kate's Madeira cake.

'Lucky I'm here to act as chaperon. As you can see, loverboy can hardly keep his hands off her,' he whispered wickedly.

Since Benedict had moved to stand against the window on the far side of the room to Lacey, his hands clasped firmly behind his back, the comment made Vanessa bite her lip to hold back an unprofessional smirk.

As she straightened she caught Benedict's smouldering gaze and hastily returned her mouth to its former primness.

She didn't know how he had got back to the house from the beach but it had taken him an hour and he had arrived in a full-blooded fury, slamming the front door so that the whole house had seemed to shudder and yelling for her in a voice that had promised savage retribution. Fortunately, his unexpected guests had promptly appeared to thwart his temper and since then Vanessa had been grateful to Lacey for sticking to him like fly-paper.

Now he beckoned her with an ominously grim expression, and, holding the plate in front of her like a shield, Vanessa approached him warily.

'What was he saying to you?' he demanded in an undertone as Lacey replied to some remark of Dane's. 'Whatever it was, don't believe him. I had no idea they were going to turn up.'

She looked at him serenely. 'I don't imagine you did. It must be very awkward to have your intended mistress and future wife under the same roof.'

Her cool whisper made his eyes narrow but she immediately turned away to pour the tea before withdrawing, nervously aware of Benedict's brooding gaze following every step of her dignified escape.

Later, when she was clearing away the tray, he managed to extricate himself long enough from his guests to waylay her outside the door. 'It's not what it looks like, Vanessa. Lacey's not my fiancée, damn it!' he said fiercely.

'That's odd. She seems to think she is!'

'We went out together a few times. All right, more than a few,' he admitted raggedly as she stiffened. 'But that's all we did. Go out. It was a mistake. I never asked her to marry me. You have nothing to be jealous of——'

'Jealous?' she said with coolly calculated surprise, as if the idea had never even occurred to her, and watched his eyebrows twitch sharply together into a scowl.

'Benedict——?'

He jerked, cursing under his breath at the snip of heels that accompanied the plaintive call.

'You'd better run along, Benedict,' Vanessa goaded, enjoying his harassed expression. 'Your fiancée's getting anxious.'

Dinner was even more enlightening. When Vanessa ventured into the room with the soup tureen Benedict turned to Lacey in an excellent imitation of a man to whom servants were wholly invisible and stated deliberately that, as he had already told her a number of times, he had no intention of pandering to their parents' archaic notion of a dynastic marriage between their offspring.

Her answer was to pat him condescendingly on the hand.

'Now, Benedict, aren't you carrying this rebellion against your father too far? So what if he told you he would like to see us married? That's no reason to sacrifice our future. And it's rather insulting to both of us to suggest that the only reason I could want to marry you is to consolidate our inheritances. Why, I've always adored being in your company and we get on splendidly. I don't think we've ever had an argument in all the years we've known each other! And you can't deny that our backgrounds and careers are incredibly compatible. Don't you agree, Dane?'

'Oh, incredibly compatible,' murmured Dane obediently, earning himself a ferocious look from his friend.

And so it went on throughout the entire four-course meal, Benedict baffled at every turn by Lacey's unshakeably confident belief in their shared destiny.

Seated between two men in elegant dark suits and looking quite stunning in a simple green cocktail dress, Lacey was obviously in her social element but, by the time she brought coffee, Vanessa no longer wanted to scratch out the gorgeous green eyes. She actually felt sorry for the beautiful and bossy Miss Taylor. Benedict had done everything but yawn in her face to demonstrate his lack of interest and she hadn't even noticed.

No wonder she and Benedict never argued. Lacey had obviously never roused the man behind the smooth manners and seamless sophistication.

It was evidently only with Vanessa that he was a savage, for, when she had served the final liqueurs and requested permission to retire, Benedict leaned back in his chair and asked silkily, 'Are you sleeping in your own bed tonight, Vanessa?'

The atmosphere in the dining-room dropped ten degrees in two seconds.

'I thought her name was Flynn?' said Lacey sharply.

'Flynn is her surname,' supplied Benedict smoothly, not taking his eyes off his quarry. 'Vanessa?'

She could just imagine what was going through the other woman's head. And Dane Judson's. If his eyebrows rose any higher they would disappear into his hairline.

'Yes,' she bit off, and then breached one of the cardinal rules of etiquette by delivering a gratuitous little speech about how she *used* to air the empty bedrooms.

'May I go now, sir?' she said woodenly, when this small exercise in embarrassment was over.

To her horror Benedict rose and sauntered towards her.

'Don't be so stuffy, Vanessa; we don't have to pretend to be formal in front of my friends.' He slid his fingers under her elbow and turned her towards the door, tossing casually over his shoulder, 'Excuse us for a minute, won't you?'

Out in the hall Vanessa wrenched her arm away and stormed off to the kitchen. Kate had left after she had dished up the main course and there was no one to hide behind as Benedict followed hot on her heels.

'Get out of here! Do you know what they must be thinking?' she raged at him. 'Especially after that stupid remark about where I was sleeping. I've already had my reputation stolen once by some spoiled young buck and I don't intend to have it happen again. Go back to your fiancée!'

'Oh, no, you can't convince me you still believe that canard,' he dismissed contemptuously. 'Not after you've seen her in action.' He leapt back as she angrily turned on the tap over the kitchen sink full-blast, sending a jet of water bouncing off the dessert plates, nearly drenching the front of his pale grey silk shirt.

'For goodness' sake, Vanessa, this is not about your reputation—or mine,' he said, reaching across her to turn the tap off so firmly, she couldn't get it to budge again. 'Stop trying to frighten me with your lurid past. I don't *care* what happened back in England—except that whatever mess you got tangled up in obviously hurt you badly enough to colour your whole attitude towards love and sex. I'm sorry if I seemed to treat your *alleged* notoriety lightly, but I was angry at your lack of faith in me. Whether it was a mix-up or a set-up I know you could never have done the things you claim you were accused of. That's an example of *my* faith in *you*.'

Vanessa was in no mood to be coaxed. She turned and, finding herself trapped against the sink, lifted her chin belligerently. 'So?'

'So...that pot-shot of yours on the beach about running away wasn't entirely off-target. I did desperately need a break, but for the last few weeks Lacey's been popping up wherever I go and I thought she'd never follow me here. Lacey hates small towns. Even Sydney isn't big enough for her.'

Detecting a hint of softening in her rigid expression, he moved in closer again, using the husky, confiding tone that turned her bones to wax. 'She doesn't love me, Vanessa. My parents have egged her on to think that I'm secretly dying to be drawn back into the family fold and Lacey is ambitious; she can't bear to fail—in *anything*...'

'She can't *force* you to the altar, for goodness sake,' said Vanessa, torn between anger and unwilling sympathy. Lacey Taylor did seem to be an oppressively single-minded woman. 'All you have to do is say no...'

'I have. And she tells me I'm just gun-shy about giving up my selfish, bachelor independence——'

'She's an intelligent woman; she'll get the message eventually——'

'Yes, if I'm sufficiently brutal about it in a public enough way I'm sure I can humiliate her into never even speaking to me again, but she doesn't deserve that kind of cruelty. I'm not in love with her but before she was encouraged in this fixation we had a good platonic friendship, and as a professional she still has my greatest respect.'

He took off his glasses and blinked at the harsh fluorescence of the kitchen lighting, and Vanessa was sunk. 'You can understand my wanting to avoid beating her over the head with her pride, can't you, Vanessa?' he said softly, placing his hands on either side of her on the bench. 'If she knew I had someone else tucked away in my life she could blame me instead of herself for her failure to pin me down...'

His hips had crowded her buttocks against the stainless-steel bench and the tip of his tongue was stroking the seam of her primly sealed mouth.

'You want to pretend that we're involved?' she murmured distractedly.

'I don't think any pretence will be necessary,' growled Benedict, nipping at her lower lip, his thighs grinding lightly against her.

Vanessa shivered. 'I won't lie——'

'I know. You won't have to...' He nuzzled into the prim white collar above her jacket to kiss the betraying pulse-beat in the curve of her throat, his hands holding her hips as his left knee flexed, pressing inexorably forward against the constriction of her skirt, pulling it taut between her thighs until he was resting his knee against the cupboard door behind her.

'She won't believe you're serious about me...not when you could have someone like her...'

'She'll believe.' His mouth was back on hers, this time demanding entry, his own voice thick with sensuous abstraction. 'If I appear to be madly in love with you her pride will *demand* that it be very serious——'

It was like a dousing with icy water. 'If I appear'... He only wanted the outward trappings of love, not the sincerity that was in her heart. A lie implied was as damaging as a lie spoken, as Vanessa had good reason to know.

Lies had destroyed her ability to trust, had infected her relationship with Benedict from the start. Secrets and lies. She was even starting to lie to herself now, telling herself she didn't love him. And if she weakened and became his lover, who would he use in turn to get rid of Vanessa when her love became an embarrassing inconvenience?

'No——' She pulled sharply at his hair to make him release her and when he staggered back in surprise she twisted away and darted behind the kitchen table. 'No, oh, no! I'm not playing *that* game. Lacey Taylor is *your* problem, *you* deal with it. Don't expect me to help you do your dirty work!'

Something in her expression must have warned him how close she was to full-blown hysteria, because he backed off hastily, uttering soothing noises as he retreated which poured salt into her invisible wounds. She didn't want to be soothed, she wanted to be *loved*—for herself alone, without guilt or guile. And for no other reason than that she was *worthy* of being loved.

Over the next two days, however, Vanessa found her sense of proportion returning as Lacey Taylor gave no sign that she noticed anything odd in the way that Benedict and his butler cut at each other with insulting politeness. Of course, she was so busy complaining about everything from the lack of air-conditioning to the smallness of the bathrooms that Vanessa doubted Lacey had time to notice anything but her own discomfort. She made it clear that she only tolerated Whitefield because Benedict was there, although he was spending most of the day shut in his studio with his nose buried in a sheaf of 'urgent' contracts that his colleague had handily produced.

Dane Judson was quite another kettle of fish, however, and Vanessa became resigned to the casual irreverence with which he insisted on discussing Benedict with her. Dane was a cynic about life in general and love in particular, but he made Vanessa laugh and she was not unaware that he had deliberately set himself up to be an entertaining buffer. Benedict noticed, too, which didn't improve his mood, and his retaliation was to invent some entertainment of his own.

'Celebration? What kind of celebration?' Vanessa asked remotely as she faced the animated trio in the drawing-room on the third afternoon following Lacey Taylor's arrival.

Benedict's mouth twisted at her rigid lack of expression. 'What kind do *you* think it might be, Vanessa?' he taunted cruelly.

'It's a birthday party—for this creaking old inn that Ben seems to have fallen in love with.' Dane's swift reply rescued Vanessa from her vocal paralysis. A birthday, not an engagement! 'He says it opened a hundred and twenty years ago next Saturday so he's decided to have a party to mark the occasion.'

'A costume party,' Lacey announced gleefully. 'I'm going to get mine sent from the States. I know a fantastic little place in the Village...'

'Don't go overboard, Lacey; I'm throwing a casual party, not the social event of the season,' said Benedict drily. 'This is strictly for the locals who've been involved with the inn over the years so I want the atmosphere to be very relaxed and informal. Mrs Riley has said she'll arrange the catering with a community organisation that needs the funds and members of the historical society are going to rent theatrical costumes——'

'You've spoken to someone from the historical society already?' Vanessa asked, suddenly feeling a creeping sense of paranoia. Why all this sudden sociability? She didn't think he was just pandering to Lacey's boredom with the bucolic joys of small-town living.

Blue eyes gleamed, as if he knew what she was thinking. 'Mmm. Miss Fisher, actually. Such a charming, enthusiastic old lady!'

This of the twittering spinster he had driven for *hours* to avoid on the day that he arrived! Now she *knew* he was up to something. Gone was the moody, sullen stranger of the last couple of days and in his place a man who looked dangerously back in control.

'But—next *week*?' Vanessa stuttered. 'You'll hardly have time to organise invitations, let alone extra staff——'

She might have known that he'd have all the exits covered. 'The invitations can be verbal and we won't need staff. I told you, it's going to be casual, a BYO affair where everyone can feel comfortable, like a block party—except the whole community'll be involved. Most people will be happy to pitch in and help where they can. So, you'll be here, Vanessa, but in costume like the rest of us.' He leaned back in his chair and inspected her from neat crown to sensible toe. 'And I think I have the perfect costume for you...'

Right. Perfectly dreadful, no doubt! Vanessa didn't trust that crocodile smile. Before she was sucked completely into the whirlwind of activity that Benedict's brilliant idea generated, she made sure that she obtained a suitably sedate costume from Miss Fisher and had tucked it safely away in her room well in advance.

By the time seven o'clock the following Saturday evening rolled around Vanessa felt so distracted by the million and one calls on her attention that she had actually half wriggled into her chosen dress before she discovered that it refused to fit.

That was because it wasn't the dress she had originally hung carefully in her wardrobe. That one was plain and decorous, as befitted an authentic Victorian lady. This one was all crimson satin flounces with black piping, with a neckline that made Vanessa's eyes widen and a waist that made them water.

The other dress was nowhere to be found and when Vanessa found a box in the bottom of her wardrobe containing a stiffened black basque she knew why.

The crisp, precise writing on the lid of the box needed no signature.

> I'm sure you recognise the dress. It's from the daguerreotype of Meg on the copy of the Playbill in the judge's files. I had to guess the colour, but the dressmaker assures me that the rest of it is copied faithfully from the original—hence the need for this...

And then, as if written merely as a careless afterthought, 'Do you dare?'

As if she could be manipulated by a childish challenge! Even as a child Vanessa had never been one to accept a dare without carefully weighing the risk against the all too likely consequences.

But sometimes the choice wasn't so simple, she thought, nervously remembering that Benedict had ruled that anyone not attending the party in costume would be required to pay a public forfeit. She had a feeling any forfeit he demanded of her would be considerably more trouble than taking up his stupid challenge. Maybe he *expected* her to choose the forfeit. After the difficult week she had just had, the last thing she wanted to do was to face another fraught decision.

She almost chickened out when she saw the results of her eye-watering battle with the hooks down the front of the rigidly boned corselet. Hourglass wasn't the word. From the generous flare of her hips her waist was nipped in to breathless smallness, her pushed-up breasts almost brimming over the satin demi-cups of the bodice. Against the black satin her skin looked starkly pale, the erotic contrast even more intense when she had donned the black stockings that were supported by crimson garters at mid-thigh.

'You have no idea what turns a man on.'

She certainly did now. The thought of Benedict personally choosing this time-honoured instrument of feminine torture and male titillation made her go hot all over. Practical application apart, the undergarment was frankly indecent.

Perhaps Meg wasn't a totally innocent victim of unsolicited male aggression after all, thought Vanessa as she donned the dress which now fastened easily over her compressed flesh. Thank goodness the dressmaker had included a very unauthentic zip under the arm!

Even with the dress on Vanessa found she couldn't forget what was underneath; it was physically impossible. Every breath she took was sharply curtailed by the curved bones pressing against her abdomen and the lush over-abundance crowding the low neckline kept catching her eye when she looked down. She couldn't even see her black buttoned half-boots unless she craned her neck past the wanton obstruction, she realised with a little *frisson* of wicked amusement as she brushed her loose hair and applied her make-up with a heavier than usual hand.

She was startled by the numbers already present when she had finally psyched herself up sufficiently to emerge shyly from her room a few minutes before the party was officially due to begin. It appeared that no one intended to miss a single minute of fun, and consequently masses of people had arrived early 'to help', and then decided that the best help they could provide would be to create an atmosphere of raucous conviviality!

After she had briefly checked that the women from the local school's parents' association had everything under control in the kitchen and their husbands had the bars up and running, Vanessa allowed herself to be quickly swept up in the noisy ebb and flow of friends and acquaintances and strangers, the mutual hilarity over costumes providing just the ice-breaker that Benedict had planned.

The night was fine and summery, and it wasn't long before people began abandoning the crammed house and the garage where a small stage had been set up for the band, to spread out over torch-lit grounds. The sprawling chaos provided the perfect camouflage as far as Vanessa was concerned and for the first hour, until dusk turned to velvety darkness, she flitted in wary circles, only once stumbling across Dane pouring punch behind a potted orange tree for a giggling shepherdess. His green breeches and flowing white shirt were in studied disarray—he was Don Juan, he informed her with a wink and an amused leer at her plunging neckline.

A little while later she saw Lacey at a distance, holding glittering court as an extravagant Queen Elizabeth I under the spreading elms by the lakeside bar. Benedict was one of her courtiers, unexpectedly dressed in the starkly plain black and white garb of a Puritan, and Vanessa was maliciously pleased to see how jarringly out of place he looked beside his flamboyant, red-headed Queen.

Some time later she was watching the dancing inside the cavernous garage, waiting for Richard to return with another glass of pleasantly intoxicating punch, when a black-clad arm suddenly slid around her tiny waist, drawing her sharply back against a lean, hard body.

'Hello, Meg.'

For the briefest instant Vanessa allowed herself to lean against his welcome strength.

'Benedict.'

He didn't move and she didn't turn. This tiny moment of possession was too precious, too private to be shared... even with him.

'I'd accuse you of being elusive,' he murmured, 'but in that dress I suppose it's the last thing you could be called.'

She tossed her head, barely missing his chin. 'Whose fault is that? I didn't want to wear it!'

'But you did.' His arm tightened.

'I—didn't have any choice.'

'There are always choices, Meg. The ones we don't take are often as revealing as the ones we do. Dance with me?'

He spun her in his arms and looked down at her. Not at her breasts but at her red-painted mouth. He was kissing her with his eyes. Even though he had his glasses on she felt the full impact of that look. His hand fluffed her hair. 'Dance with me, Meg?'

'I'm waiting for Richard,' she said breathlessly, sure it was the wretched basque that must be starving her of oxygen. 'He's away getting me a drink...'

He looked over her head. 'He's talking to Lacey. Let him stay away. Besides, he's not in costume.' He looked back down at her, taking off his tall buckled hat and casting it carelessly aside, revealing the cropped darkness of his hair which so suited the austerity of his garb.

'He didn't have time—he's just come back from ten days in Melbourne. He only got back tonight. He's virtually come straight from the airport.'

'Tough!' Benedict looked triumphantly unimpressed. 'He has to surrender something of value for his transgression. You can be his forfeit to me, Meg.' He began to sway, drawing her into his arms and slowly blending into the passing flow of couples.

'I didn't think Puritans did anything as frivolous as dance,' she said shakily as she instinctively matched his languid rhythm.

'Oh, we can be seduced into the sins of the flesh like any other mortal. We just take leave to feel more guilty about them afterwards.' He had both hands at her waist now, holding the centres of their bodies lightly together as he moved, the brush of his legs in their thick black breeches catching at her satin skirts.

'I'm afraid what I know about seduction could be written on the head of a pin,' Vanessa responded haughtily.

His steps faltered, but not his gaze as his mouth crooked wryly. 'What fool phrased his compliment to you so badly? True seduction isn't about *knowing*, it's about *being*...'

His eyes gravitated inexorably to the plunging neckline of her gown. His nostrils flared, his sensual memory recognising the distinctive scent rising from the warm texture of her flesh, the scent that had lingered in his bed. 'Just be you; that's all you have to do to seduce me.'

'You mean, be Meg,' she said wistfully. In this dress she wasn't supposed to be her ordinary self, she was his erotic fantasy come to life.

'I mean be Vanessa,' he told her huskily. 'Infuriating, irresistible Vanessa. Do you know why I asked you to dance?'

She shook her head dizzily, and he answered his own question with a frank explicitness that made her breathing sharp and shallow.

'I wanted to see your lovely breasts move for me. I wanted to watch them sway and ripple like cream with every tiny, delicious motion... every breath, every sigh. I remember how hot and spicy they tasted in my mouth, how taut and swollen they felt when I cupped them in my hands... Do you think any one would notice if I bent and put my mouth just *there*... in that milky soft crevice...?'

'*I* would...!' Vanessa clutched at his forearms, her shallow gasps turning to a startled moan as her head fell back and her knees sagged. The tiny red spots in front of her eyes turned black.

'For God's sake, Vanessa, don't play the swooning Victorian maiden on me *now*!' he said with rough amusement that turned to rueful dismay as she continued to sink, her back arching limply over the span of his strong hands...

SAVAGE COURTSHIP 171

He uttered a harsh sound of dismissal as someone offered assistance, half lifting, half carrying her wilting figure off the makeshift dance-floor and through the brick archways lining the back of the garage, to one of the old stable loose-boxes, kicking the bottom of the dilapidated half-door shut behind them. Here at least they were private, if not peaceful, the open half of the door letting in a flood of yellow light along with the insistent throb of music and cacophony of voices.

'Vanessa? You're not going to actually pass out, are you?' he asked with ragged humour as he propped her against the wall, protecting her bare shoulder-blades from the rough wood by sliding his arm behind her.

She pressed a hand to her compressed stomach and shook her head muzzily as she panted, 'No... I just couldn't breathe for a moment. It's being trussed up in this dress—I can't seem to breathe and dance at the same time. Thank God women liberated themselves from their corsets years ago!'

She took several more quick, heaving breaths before she became aware of the carnal expression on Benedict's face as he slowly removed his glasses.

'It wasn't the dancing that took your breath away,' he said hoarsely. 'It was me.' And having uttered that literal truth he abruptly did what he said he had wanted to on the dance-floor. The feel of his mouth sinking voluptuously into her mounded breasts made Vanessa briefly panic again and then her eyes fluttered closed and she gave up worrying about breathing altogether.

Oh, what a lovely, lovely way to die, she thought as wave after wave of suffocatingly sensual delight clogged her heart and lungs and set her blood pulsing thick and sluggish in her veins. The faint bristle on his chin rasped erotically across her tender skin as his fist caught the bottom edge of her gown, dragging it up past her calf, her knee... holding her upright against the wall with his body as he slipped his hand further up under the crushed satin flounces to stroke the strip of satiny inner thigh laid bare between the garter and basque. Rivulets of fire flowed wherever he touched and lingered...

'Open your mouth; I need to be inside you,' he groaned, pulling his arm from her back and cupping one half-exposed breast possessively as he sought her surrendering lips hungrily.

Even through layer upon layer of satin she could feel his all-consuming need and suddenly nothing mattered but to assuage it. She ran her hands up his arms to cup his head, guiding him to the pleasure of them both, gripped by a fiercely erotic tenderness, her heavy eyelids lifting just in time to see——

Richard's mixture of pained regret and embarrassment as he turned away, gallantly trying to shield the couple inside the box from the shimmering figure at his side. He wasn't quick enough. In a split-second Lacey's beautiful face ran the gamut from curiosity to shock, disbelief and anger before she spun on her heel and stalked away in defiant disgust.

Vanessa stiffened and pushed at Benedict, whose realisation that they weren't alone had done nothing to bank his desire.

'Oh, God—Richard and Lacey,' she whispered despairingly. 'They must have seen us leave the dancing, and wondered what was wrong——'

'They had to find out some time. Now maybe Wells will stop sniffing around and find his own woman...' Benedict's crudely gloating satisfaction was like a slap in the face.

She stared at him in horror. 'This was all part of some clever plan of yours, wasn't it?' she accused wildly. 'That we be seen to sneak away and Lacey follow us—that she catch us in a flagrantly compromising position...' She realised what she must have looked like with her skirts hiked up around her waist and Benedict's hand between her thighs, and on her breast. 'Oh, God, you *planned* for this to happen...'

'The hell I did! How was I to know you were going to swoon in my arms?'

'You *used* me. You promised you wouldn't, then you *used* me!' Vanessa cried. 'How can I ever believe anything you say? Oh, God, I *hate* you!'

She lashed out with a viciously closed fist and he caught it in an iron grip, jerking it behind her as he ground out savagely, 'That's *enough*!'

He caught her other wrist and clamped it with the same hand, and then dragged a weakly struggling Vanessa out of the ramshackle back door of the garage and across the unlit rear courtyard to the French doors of the library, the only downstairs room that was shut off to the party-goers. While Vanessa panted and squirmed he searched for his keys in the narrow pocket of his breeches and unlocked the door, thrusting her inside and locking it again behind him, drawing the curtains and turning on the lamp on the desk before striding to the door to the hall to make sure that that too was firmly secured. The soundproofing that had been installed with the new wall-linings created a hushed, exotic quietness as Vanessa stood, rubbing her wrists and summoning her courage finally to demand imperiously, 'What do you think you're doing?'

'I know exactly what I'm doing.' Benedict turned, stripping off his tunic and shirt as he came towards her. 'Creating the strictest privacy in which to make love to you. No distractions, no interruptions, no possible grounds for a misunderstanding later. Perhaps I can teach you to trust the pleasure I can give you, if nothing else. At least it'll be a start. Will you take off that dress—or do you want me to do it?'

Vanessa put her trembling hands to her breasts to quiet the tumult that rioted there at the sight of his powerful chest and flat belly sheened with a light perspiration that defined the lean wedges of curved muscle as they rose and fell with his ragged breathing. He looked as if he had been running, his body pumped with adrenalin, his control so finely balanced that she could see faint tremors as opposing bunches of muscles strained against each other in anticipation of the next explosive burst of movement. He was the brutal image of a man primed for sex.

He was unbuttoning his breeches now, watching her become aware of the violence of his arousal as he exposed himself blatantly to her shocked eyes. He bent to pull off his boots and the narrow black breeches, his hard flanks flexing and bunching, and then he straightened again, completely naked. Completely vulnerable. Glistening with his need...

'Give me this one chance, Vanessa,' he demanded, the angry edge of his ruthless intent blunted by the flushed fascination with which she was still staring down at his jutting body. 'Let me show you that when I'm with you, as far as I'm concerned, nobody else in the world exists...'

Her eyes flickered up to his. Her hands fell away from her breasts. He reached for her...

The cataclysm struck.

One moment Vanessa was standing before him, fully clothed, and the next her dress was on the floor and she was lying on the rug beside it covered by a trembling, groaning man in the throes of urgent passion, her long legs wrapped around his powerful hips as the excruciating pleasure that was concentrated in the thrusting fullness that parted and penetrated her escalated to a series of violent convulsions.

There had been no time for fear, no time to register anything but the glory of his manhood as he had reacted with frenzied delight to the sight of her in the satin basque, rolling over on to his back and seating her astride his engorged loins so that he could enjoy the sensuous sight of her arched above him as he roughly dealt with the row of hooks, releasing her pointed breasts to the lascivious attention of his hands and mouth as he undulated beneath her, letting her control the pace until she began straining and shuddering, unsatisfied by anything less than his complete possession.

There was no pain as he turned her on her back and mounted her in one fluid movement, stretching her with his fingers to fit him, only a ferocious relief at being able to take the full length of him, to absorb and milk him of his maleness until he jerked and stiffened and uttered hoarse, guttural cries of violent gratification as she joined his fierce upheaval.

Afterwards, while they still lay co-mingled, he gentled her out of her state of shell-shocked bliss, making her blush with his lavish praise.

'You see, at least we can speak honestly to each other with our bodies,' he murmured as he reluctantly helped her to dress, kissing her breasts in tender acknowledgement of her passionate exhaustion as he zipped her up and then pulled on his own clothes, his manner redolent with possessive satisfaction. 'What could be more honest than sustained mutual passion...?'

Vanessa looked at her sinfully dishevelled Puritan as he stretched contentedly, then strolled over to unlock the hall door. He was signalling that their lovely private idyll was over already. Her heart ached for all that she now had of him... and all that she never would. Unless she risked one final dare...

'Mutual love, perhaps?' she ventured bravely.

He stood, his hand on the door-handle, looking so utterly stunned at the suggestion that Vanessa knew instantly that she had made a bad mistake.

Before she could retrieve the betraying words Benedict staggered as the door was suddenly thrust inwards against him.

Moments later, just *how* bad Vanessa's mistake had been was being forcefully rammed home to her as they were confronted by Benedict's horrified parents, who wasted no time in pointing out the appalling implications of Benedict's allowing himself to be publicly associated with a woman of Vanessa's deeply dubious background and morals. And Benedict seemed to be tacitly agreeing with every doom-laden word!

CHAPTER TEN

IT WAS dark inside the hilltop apartment and Vanessa cursed at the lack of light as her trembling fingers dropped the doorkey and she had to grope around on the cold marble floor to find it.

Then she had trouble finding the light switch and when she finally clicked it on she had to blink in disorientation as she was confronted by the white-on-white, ultra-modern room. It took a few moments for her to remember to cross to the long narrow window on her left and wave in silhouette to the man waiting on the city street below.

The yellow Corvette took off with a throaty roar and Vanessa watched the red lights glow as he took the corner at the end of the street.

She wondered why Dane was in such an all-fired hurry to get wherever he had suddenly insisted he had to go, when he had done nothing but procrastinate, delay and dawdle all the way from Thames to Auckland. What should have taken no more than an hour and a half had taken over three. He had driven at least twenty kilometres per hour under the speed-limit, stopped for petrol and oil at two different petrol stations and pulled over twice to check his 'pinging' engine.

Then, just past Huntly, he had decided he was ravenous and had pulled into an all-night truckers' restaurant and ordered a huge meal which he had taken ages to eat, all the while plying a white-faced Vanessa with coffee and trying to persuade her to reinterpret the scene which had prompted her midnight flight from Whitefield without even so much as a change of clothes or a toothbrush. She had even had to borrow Dane's car-coat to cover the crumpled satin costume she wore in order not to create a riot among the truckers.

Somehow it had seemed symbolic that she had left Whitefield as stripped of possessions as she had been of pride. Lacey's malicious introduction of Vanessa to Benedict's parents as his lover-cum-butler couldn't have been better timed to create maximum shock and embarrassment... especially since it was obvious to them all what had been going on in the locked library.

The older couple had heard of the party from Lacey and had duly decided to make a flying visit, expecting to be able to offer their congratulations on what they assumed to be their son's engagement to a most eminently suitable young lady. Instead they had been confronted with graphic evidence that he had fallen into the clutches of an appallingly unsuitable, social-climbing hussy.

Vanessa had had to bear the shame of hearing Aaron Savage tell his son, 'For God's sake, if you want to sleep with the servants at least have the decency to be discreet about it!' and his mother frigidly suggest that whatever he was paying her it was obviously too much!

'A female butler! I always wondered what possessed you to agree to such a questionable arrangement,' Denise Savage had said in cut-glass accents of brittle disdain. 'And now my worst fears have been justified!

'Don't you care about the pain you're causing your father and I? Do you know the damage this could do to the family's reputation if it got into the papers? Goodness knows, there are certain people who would leap at the chance to use a scandal to embarrass your father. Whatever you do inevitably reflects directly on us... And you're not really being fair to this... this *person* either. Is she really someone you'd be comfortable introducing to our friends? Of course not... because it's all in such appalling bad *taste*, Benedict. Even if you're temporarily blinded by infatuation you must realise that we'd be a laughing-stock if you tried to introduce her to society...'

There had been more in that vein and Vanessa had kept waiting for an angry Benedict to leap in and defend her honour. But he had remained silent and when she'd finally tried to interrupt on her own behalf Benedict had coldly told her to be quiet and let him hear everything his parents had to say.

In the end, she had walked out in such a blind agony that she had nearly trampled Dane as he hovered by the door. Benedict had been so absorbed in what his parents were saying that he hadn't even noticed her go and, looking back over her shoulder one last time, Vanessa had numbly realised the true extent of the family resemblance.

Benedict's face had worn the same expression of pale hauteur that his mother's habitually did and his arrogant stance had been so similar to his father's that it had been almost like seeing the same man reflected through an age-distorting mirror. Perhaps his fling with her had been just one last act of rebellion against the inevitable genetic trap.

She'd been walking down the driveway towards the gates of Whitefield in a zombie-like state when Dane had caught up with her, and when no amount of desperate pleading could divert her from her obsession with getting to the airport in Auckland by whatever means she could, hitch-hiking—even walking every step of the way if she had to—he had eventually agreed to drive her. She had to go home, she'd kept repeating. She was running to the only haven left to her, the home of her heart—her family—to the love and understanding of her father in Los Angeles. *He* had never been ashamed of her...

She had fiercely refused to go back to the house even to pack, nor would promise to wait for Dane while he did so, and in the end he had given in to her fragile mental state and got his car.

While he drove he had talked incessantly, telling her what a great guy Benedict was, deep down, and how, if Vanessa was in love with him, she owed it to him to give him the benefit of the doubt; that Benedict's parents were knee-jerk reactionaries; that she shouldn't do anything rash, like leaving the country, without talking to Benedict first.

Vanessa had refused to respond until he had pointed out to her, when they were nearly to Auckland, that since she had neither money nor passport she couldn't leave the country immediately anyway. He had kindly insisted she stay at his apartment for the rest of the night, until she could call her father and 'reorientate' herself. By that time all Vanessa had wanted to do was crawl into a bed, bury her head in the pillow and have a good, long, private bawl!

She was a bit disconcerted that, after hours of relentless over-concern, Dane had casually dumped her on his doorstep with his key and a casual 'good luck', but she supposed he was respecting her desperately obvious need for privacy. Equally obviously he would have no trouble finding a bed elsewhere.

Bed...

Wearily, she turned towards the spiral staircase that Dane had included in his verbal sketch-plan and plodded upwards. She couldn't ever remember having felt this hopelessly bone-weary before. She shook her head to try and clear the miasma of exhaustion that thickened her thoughts.

The first room at the top of the stairs was a bathroom and when she clicked on the light and caught sight of herself in the mirror Vanessa shuddered. She looked even worse than she felt. The crimson dress was tawdry and garish against her bloodless skin and she could see several faint, reddened marks on her breasts from Benedict's lovemaking. Was this what his parents had seen? This...brazen doxy. No wonder they had been so horrified!

Vanessa was suddenly acutely aware that she was still perfumed with the fragrance of her abandon. She could smell Benedict on her skin. With shivering haste she shed the wretched gown and the indecent garment underneath.

The hot shower did its job, easing her aching body and cleansing away the intimate evidence of passion, although nothing could wash away the tiny, tender abrasions on her breasts and stomach and thighs. Weak tears mingled freely with the pulsing water over her face as she began to wonder what she had forfeited by her cowardice. If Benedict hadn't fought for her honour, neither had she made any attempt to fight for his. What if he, too, was alone and hurting right now...?

Pushing away the painful thought, Vanessa blotted herself on the thick white towel from the heated rail and rubbed half-heartedly at her steam-damp hair, discarding the towel listlessly on the floor with uncharacteristic untidiness before padding naked into the only other room on the mezzanine floor.

In the hint of clouded moonlight from the window she was aware of the vague, shadowy outline of a bed by the far wall but she ignored it, drawn across the room by the melancholy sight of the sleeping city. The view led in a direct line across the bricks and blocks of the central commercial district to the moon-struck waters of the Waitemata Harbour. Moon-struck. That perfectly described Vanessa. She wallowed for a moment in her splendidly miserable, self-induced isolation.

She turned on the standard lamp that she had nearly knocked over as she approached the window, and unlatched the fastening on the casement so that she could open it wide, breathing in the faintly metallic air of the city and momentarily enjoying the faint tightening of her bare skin at its cool touch. She must start to do this now, appreciate the small joys of life, since she was making such a mess of the larger ones.

She turned, a wistful smile of self-derision on her lips, and froze.

The big, wide double bed was already occupied.

The pool of light spilling across the floor from the lamp behind her was more than sufficient to reveal that the occupier was a man. He was sprawled on his stomach, his arms spread-eagled, his face buried in one of four huge pillows that were propped up in a row against the headboard.

Vanessa closed her eyes and shook her head sharply, sure that it was a fatigue-induced illusion.

She looked again, moving hesitantly towards the bed, still unwilling to trust the evidence of her tear-swollen eyes.

Above the white silk sheets, which were bunched carelessly low on his hips, the interloper's long, naked back was lean and densely muscled, faintly gleaming in the muted light, as smooth as tan-coloured satin and rippling faintly with each slow, sensuous breath. Under the arm outflung towards her she could see a thick drift of silky-soft black hair and, just above the edge of the sheet, the taut rise of the twin globes of his buttocks revealed a dusting of similar, very fine black down.

A powerful sense of bitter outrage gripped Vanessa. How *dared* he?

She began to bend and suddenly every muscle in that long, sexy, naked male back tensed and he rolled over and she found herself staring into a very wide-awake pair of grave blue eyes.

'Hello, Goldilocks. What took you so long?'

She was stunned by the warmth of desiring in that soft, whimsical growl. 'W-what are you doing—how did *you* get here?'

He shook his head back and forth against the pillow.

'Oh, ye of little faith,' he murmured, with such aching gentleness that she felt weak. Her knees swayed against the mattress and he came up on one elbow and caught her wrist, applying just enough pressure to sit her down on the edge of the bed, facing him. In her shock she forgot that she was nude and he ignored her state of innocent unawareness with gentlemanly tact.

'Where else should I be but here—with the woman I love?' he asked quietly.

It was a dream, a wishful dream.

'This is Dane's bedroom——'

'Oh, no.' His mouth curved at one corner. 'My friend has much better preservation instincts than that. This is *my* apartment, Nessa. That's where you were always going to eventually end up. In *my* bedroom, in *my* bed...in *my* life.'

The last was the most devastating. She trembled, brushing at her damp hair with her free hand, unaware that her bare body was revealing the welcome that she could not yet dare admit. 'But...you can't be here——'

He kissed the strong, slender wrist that he held, watching her intently as he drew her hand down to his chest and she couldn't help noticing that he had a number of reddened marks which were the feminine version of the brands she wore. He held her hand against his strongly arhythmic heartbeat. 'Does this feel like an illusion?

'Dane called me on his cell-phone from the first garage he called at. I made him promise to bring you here but to delay long enough to let me get here first. Thank God the pilot who flew your dress down is a teetotaller, because I'd invited him to the party and I just grabbed him and made him an offer he couldn't refuse. I wouldn't even let him stop to change on the way to the airport. It's the first time I've ever flown anywhere with a giant bat at the controls.'

Vanessa almost giggled in spite of herself. Then she remembered, and her face acquired a painful stiffness.

'W-what did your parents say?'

He sat up, the sheet dipping dangerously in his lap, his faint smile fading as he said, choosing his words carefully, 'They're my parents, Vanessa. I may not like them very much sometimes but they'll always be my parents. If you're going to be a permanent part of my life then they'll be a permanent part of yours, and we'll have to learn to deal with them together. But last night I had to let them run out of steam before I had any hope of getting them to listen. I know from bitter experience that trying to argue with them point by point only lets *them* control the confrontation. So they stated their ignorant misconceptions, and afterwards I set them straight. I told them that I loved you. That if it came to forcing me to choose between them and you, you would *always* win. They probably won't speak to us for a couple of years after we're married—in fact, if we're lucky, for *more* than a couple of years—but I'm their only son and I doubt if they'll risk cutting the ties completely...'

Vanessa's eyes were dark with anguished desire. He was talking about permanency...about loving *her*. About *marriage*...as if they both knew they were foregone conclusions. 'The things they said—— When you told me to be quiet, let me go like that, I thought——'

'I told Lacey to leave, too,' he interrupted flatly. 'There were some things that I needed to say to them in private—old scores to settle, you might say, and some groundrules to lay for the future. They won't ever speak to you or of you like that again.' He sighed. 'I suppose I should have realised that any mention of the fatal word "scandal" was bound to spook you badly. My only excuse is that at the time I was so euphoric that you had trusted me enough to mention love that it never occurred to me that you would suffer another crisis of faith so soon afterwards...'

'I—you just looked so shocked when I said it——'

'I was. I couldn't believe it was so easy. I knew I could make you feel passion, and I was using that for all I was worth, but I didn't think that I had yet impressed you sufficiently to winkle your heart out of its tight little refuge...'

'Oh, I found you very impressive!' Vanessa teased, suddenly brimming with confidence as she ran her hand down the centre of his chest to his navel, and below to where his skin began to pale. 'Arrogant, but extremely impressive.' Her fingertips dipped under the sheet.

He sucked in his belly with a savage hiss. 'Brazen hussy,' he said thickly, reaching out to cup her breasts and massage the stiffened nipples. 'No wonder you create a scandal wherever you go. You won't have to inject me with anything lethal, darling; just keep on doing what you're doing with that hand and I'll have a little death all on my own...'

He had thrown out the metaphors deliberately, but Vanessa's radiance remained undimmed. Her certainty that she was loved gave her the security to laugh at her former fears. Her eyes gleamed with wicked, sultry knowledge as she chuckled huskily. 'Is that your idea of trying to desensitise me?'

He groaned, his hips arching off the bed, thrusting himself into her hand. 'I think it's me who needs desensitising. I meant to take it very slow with you that first time because I was afraid of hurting you, but then you were so damned responsive, I got carried away. I was afraid you might think I was no better than that bastard who hurt you... that you were disappointed...'

'It all happened so fast, I didn't have time to be disappointed,' said Vanessa, so blandly reassuring that for a moment he took her seriously and looked deeply chagrined.

Then his smile was every bit as sultry as hers as he kicked off the sheet and pulled her full-length on top of him. 'You know, Goldilocks, you haven't said you'll marry me yet; maybe I should threaten to withhold my favours until you agree.'

'If you do I'll haunt you,' Vanessa said huskily, wriggling experimentally and making them both shudder.

'Oh, yes, please...' He groaned expressively. They both laughed and he kissed her. 'We'll live at Whitefield, shall we? You running the hotel and me designing eccentric little houses. And who knows? Maybe...' He stopped suddenly and his eyes flickered. He nudged her nose with his. 'Nessa... remember how I teased you in the restaurant about being pregnant...?'

'Yes.' She knew what was coming and turned her face into his chest to smile. A few weeks ago, even an hour ago, it could have been a potential tragedy; now it was a symbol of the joy they would share in the years to come.

'I—er—when we... in the library... I know this was incredibly irresponsible... but I forgot to, you know...'

She was tempted to tease him for his unaccustomed coyness but she regarded him with tender brown eyes instead, watching an insufferable smugness settle over his beloved features as she said pertly, 'I suppose I *had* better agree to marry you, then. It wouldn't do to add illegitimacy to all the scandal I'm bringing down on the Savage family.'

'The only scandal around here, Nessa, darling, is that I love you so much I'm going to disgrace myself if you don't let me demonstrate it *right now*...'

A DANGEROUS LOVER
by
LINDSAY ARMSTRONG

CHAPTER ONE

'I NEED a pair of twins. Preferably redheads with freckles, and I'd like the boy to have a particularly mischievous look and—no, let's make it the other way round. The girl should be a real tomboy and the boy a bookish type—what's so difficult about that?'

Verity Wood grimaced as she strode down the corridor, for her boss's voice was clearly audible and his mood all too familiar; and she guessed he would be surrounded by several anxious, nervous people who had not the slightest idea of how to deal with Brad Morris on these occasions.

She was almost right, she discovered as she entered the office. There was the girl from the typing pool whom she'd asked to deputise for her this morning and who was close to tears. There was Tim Cameron, office manager, looking very stern, and William Morris, Brad's brother and head of the Morris Advertising Agency, wearing a dark suit and waistcoat and the lugubrious expression he so often wore when confronted by his brilliant but erratic sibling. And finally there was Primrose Carpenter, the only one looking faintly amused, but stunningly beautiful as always.

No one noticed Verity enter as Brad Morris continued in a mixture of tones that was both sardonic and scathing with a dash of plaintiveness thrown in for good measure. 'I mean to say, you are asking me not only to advertise this very ordinary little household item, but also to persuade sixteen million Australians to dash out and purchase one, yet you treat my simplest request as if I'm asking to go to the moon. Indeed, it would probably be easier *to* go to the moon...'

Verity raised her unusually golden hazel eyes heavenwards and stepped forward. 'There is no problem, Mr Morris,' she said evenly, and restrained herself from adding 'apart from yourself'.

Everyone swung round, although in Brad Morris's case this merely involved swivelling the chair he was reclining in a couple of notches. He did not remove his long legs from the desk, nor did he remove his hands from behind his head. And he said nothing for a long moment but he used that moment to full effect as he scanned Verity from top to toe, from her cropped golden-red hair, *her* freckles, her white fitted jacket, her short black skirt and her long legs encased in sheer black stockings to her elegant court shoes with little heels and back to her hands with their short nails and no nail polish. Then he drawled, 'I do believe Mrs Wood has deigned to grace us with her presence. How fortunate we are!'

During the two years she'd worked for him Verity had longed to hit Brad Morris on occasions, and this was another of them, she discovered, and was not helped by the fact that she'd spent a difficult morning, but she breathed deeply and sought for the cool formality with which she normally treated him. 'I was not aware you were coming in this morning, Mr Morris, otherwise I would have been here,' she said equably and then found she didn't feel particularly equable. 'In fact,' she continued, 'in lieu of any information to the contrary, I assumed you were still holidaying in the Whitsundays. However, if after six weeks of procrastination you've finally decided to get to work on the Pearson account, may I say that, considering how much time I've spent fobbing Mr Pearson off, not to mention actually lying to him, it's not *before* time?'

The silence was electric. The girl from the typing pool seemed incapable of closing her mouth and even Primrose looked startled.

As for Brad Morris, he unwound his tall, wiry frame from chair and desk and stood up leisurely. As always, he scorned his brother's more conventional attire and wore khaki trousers with a check shirt and suede boots. His brown curly hair looked as wild as it usually did and his rather Roman nose prominent. Yet there was something amazingly attractive about him to women, Verity had discovered. She'd put it down at first to his tall, thin gangliness arousing their maternal instincts, but had had that apparently disproved to her often enough to strenuously doubt it now. But he doesn't attract me, she reminded herself, and she waited for him to retaliate as she knew he would. Then she thought—why wait?

'After all,' she said casually but with a cutting little edge, 'we all *know* you're a genius of a kind. We all know you have a remarkable talent for handling children and animals and their owners and their parents and that you make wonderful ads, but they *are* only ads, here today, forgotten tomorrow, and it really doesn't, one would have thought, entitle you to act like a cross between Shakespeare and Van Gogh. It can't be that weighty a muse, surely?'

There was no electric silence this time. Tim Cameron moved restlessly, the typist shut her mouth with an audible click of her teeth and William Morris cleared his throat preparatory to speaking, but his brother beat him to it.

'Don't bother to defend me, Billy,' he said sweetly, causing William to look momentarily pained. 'Unfortunately, since *Mr* Wood's—er—untimely demise, whoever has been sleeping with Mrs Wood hasn't been doing a great job of it. Either that or no one has. But,' he gestured genially, 'I'm quite used to dealing with these frustrated, spinsterish outbursts. Primrose, darling,' he turned to her, 'I was going to take you out to lunch, but as you can see things are a little out of control here, so would you mind getting yourself a cab home?'

Primrose Carpenter withdrew her lovely violet gaze from Verity with an effort and said with a tinge of exasperation, 'Brad, we were on the way home from the airport in *my* car when you became infused with inspiration and insisted on coming here!'

'That's true,' he replied gravely. 'I'd forgotten. But that even simplifies things. If you could retrieve my bag from your boot and give it to—Tim?'

'Brad—yes, of course,' Primrose said but with a tinge of confusion and something else darkening her eyes.

'I'm sorry things have happened this way, Primmy,' Brad Morris said and stopped rather abruptly, with the lines and angles of his face set into an expression that was curiously withdrawn for a moment. Then it was as if he made a conscious effort to break that moment, and he said lightly, although there was no mistaking the look of deep affection and tenderness in his grey eyes as they rested on her, 'But chin up, darling! I'll give you a buzz tonight.' He turned to Tim Cameron. 'Tim?'

'Yes, fine,' Tim Cameron said hastily. 'I'll come and get it, Primrose. Er...' But he didn't have to say any more; perhaps Verity's expression said it all, because everyone then trooped out with alacrity, excepting perhaps Primrose, who cast Brad one last, lingering glance.

Brad Morris waited until the door was closed, then he leant his fists on the desk and said, 'Before you hit me, Mrs Wood, why don't you tell me what's biting you?'

'*You* are what's biting me, Mr Morris——'

'I can assure you, Mrs Wood,' he drawled, 'I am not. I don't go around biting women unless I'm invited to, and then I do it in the nicest possible way.'

Verity ground her teeth in frustration.

He went on when she found it impossible to speak, 'Is that really the problem? I mean, the lack of some man to bite you nicely? If so, why is it such a problem? By my reckoning, you've been a widow for over two years now and no one would expect you to remain faithful to a memory forever. Particularly if it's interfering with your state of mind——'

'Mr M-Morris,' Verity still had difficulty articulating, so angry was she now, 'I must warn you not to continue in this vein, because I'm liable to do more than hit you, believe me.'

He looked her up and down with a satirically raised eyebrow. 'All right, have a go,' he invited. 'It might just relieve some of the pressure. Are you a black-belt karate expert in disguise, though? Because if you are I don't think that would be quite fair. I'm not, you see. And, on second thoughts, I might object to being tossed over your shoulder and thrown heavily to the floor. What I had more in mind was for you to pound your fists uselessly against my manly chest—something along those lines.' He grimaced. 'I—er—might have miscalculated.' His gaze roamed down her body again. 'To the extent that you're not exactly a fragile little flower of a girl—how could I have forgotten?' he marvelled. 'But our very own trim, fit, athletic Mrs Wood—much more a fitting Jane-for-Tarzan-type, really. I will retract that offer, Mrs Wood,' he said gravely. 'But, should you like to pound the desk instead—be my guest.'

Verity stared at him for a full minute, during which she fought a pitched battle with her emotions and was further incensed to see him watching the way her breasts heaved beneath the white linen; then she swung away and strode to her desk. 'That's the last time you'll insult me, Mr Morris,' she said precisely, and sat down and started opening drawers and relieving them of their contents with fiercely controlled movements.

He looked slightly amused and strolled over to lean against the wall next to the desk. 'Which bit?' he queried after a moment.

'*What* bit?'

'Was so insulting?'

'All of it!'

'Ah. Then you don't see yourself as having the kind of figure Tarzan would have enjoyed? Perhaps I was a bit unkind there. To tell the truth, Mrs Wood, you have a wonderful slim, lissom figure, with incredible legs, and I should imagine few men alive could resist it.'

The phone rang before Verity could reply, and in fact she picked it up only because she was afraid of what else she might do. 'Hello!'

'Mrs Wood? It's Len Pearson here!'

She took a breath and lay back in her chair. '*Hello, Mr Pearson*,' she said brightly. 'How are you today? I'm sure you're ringing to find out if I've been able to pin Mr Morris down and actually get him to start work on your account,' she went on without waiting for a reply. 'Unfortunately I have some bad news for you. He is here—oh, by the way, he was never as busy as I've led you to believe these past weeks, I was simply covering for him while he lazed in the sun in the Whitsundays. But the bad news is, although he *is* here now, I've decided to—er—part company with him. Now that might not seem an earth-shattering event to you, Mr Pearson, but, believe me, it's going to be an absolute disaster. Mr Morris is incredibly difficult to work for, and without me to do the ground work for him in this advertising campaign he will be simply lost. Incidentally, to make matters worse, he actually views your *wonderful* invention as "a very ordinary little household item", quote, unquote, so—well, be that as it may, it will also take him ages to find someone to replace me. Not that there aren't plenty of people out there who could do the job, but people who could actually tolerate working for Mr Morris would have to be as rare as hens' teeth. So I would suggest, Mr Pearson,' she said sweetly, 'that you give serious consideration to taking your account elsewhere. Goodbye. Do have a nice day.'

She put the phone down and looked up at Brad Morris defiantly, to see that he was laughing silently.

Then he said softly, 'Bravo, Mrs Wood. In this game of tit for tat, that was a stroke of genius. I salute you!'

Verity closed her eyes then stood up, heaved the shopping bag she'd brought to work on to the desk, shovelled her belongings into it and looked around for her bag.

He straightened at last. 'Oh, come now. Can't we call it quits? Believe me, you've routed me utterly. Can you just imagine the lengths I'm going to have to go to soothe Pearson's wounded vanity? He seriously believes he's come up with the eighth wonder of the world.'

'If I thought for one moment you *yourself* would go to any lengths——' She broke off with a disgusted sound. 'No, I'm going anyway, I've had enough——'

He moved closer—so that he was standing right beside her, in fact. At six feet two to her five feet eight, he was nearly a head taller than she was, but she raised her eyes to his and there was a clear warning in them; also a lot of anger.

But he studied her unworriedly and with a glint in his grey eyes she recognised only too well—the advance notice that he was about to do something outrageous. She stiffened and started to say something, but he put his hand on her wrist and overrode her, 'There is another way we could resolve this, Verity.'

She stilled. 'Don't call me that.'

'Why not? How ridiculous is it to work with someone for two years and insist on being called "Mrs Wood" all the time as if you were at least sixty and a genuine spinster into the bargain? To my mind it's all part of the problem, and it's about time I did something about it. So you may call me Mr Morris until the cows come home but I shall call you Verity from now on—and I'll also do this.' He paused and smiled faintly. 'Do note that I have you boxed into a corner, Verity, in the cowardly interests of my wind and limb, I must admit, but also in *your* best interests.'

And, as she only had time to take a startled breath, he pulled her into his arms.

'No...' she whispered incredulously, stunned into immobility.

'Yes,' he murmured. 'In fact, quite definitely so. How does it feel?' His grey gaze rested on her parted lips, the colour flooding into her cheeks. 'I have to say that for me it feels rather good, but it would be even better if you could relax.'

Verity made a convulsive movement and at the same time made a discovery that surprised her: Brad Morris might be tall and wiry but he was also stronger than she was, a lot stronger—so much so that without exerting much effort at all and without hurting her he was quite capable of holding her in his arms against her will.

'Let me go,' she said shakily.

He shook his head, his eyes amused. 'Not until I've done what I set out to do.' He moved his hands and gathered her closer so that her body was resting against his. 'An amazing handful, Mrs Wood.' His lips twisted. 'That just slipped out, sorry. The Mrs Wood bit. The rest is all too true. *Do* you sleep with anyone these days?'

Verity stared up into his eyes and knew from the suddenly heavy-lidded way he was looking at her that, however this had started out and whether or not Brad

Morris had intended merely to tease her, he now fully intended to kiss her.

She gathered all her resources and warned herself to stay calm. 'No. I don't intend to, either, so you may as well let me go, Mr Morris. If nothing else, wouldn't you say it's a little undignified what you're doing?'

He laughed quietly and slid one hand up the back of her neck and into her hair. 'I never rested on my dignity, Verity. You of all people should know that.' And he bent his head and started to do just what she'd feared.

She did struggle then, and despite the uselessness of it—at least the uselessness of trying to free herself— she managed to evade his mouth quite successfully. But he merely lifted his head until she stopped struggling and said gravely, 'Not a good way to begin, apparently. Tell me how you like to start. I shall bow to your preferences.'

Verity was breathing heavily. 'My current preference,' she said raggedly, 'would be to see you struck down by a bolt of lightning before my eyes!'

He grinned, then his eyes sobered. 'I'm going to do it, you know. You could always close your eyes and think of England, not that I would dream of going that far, but all the same...' He shrugged and loosened his arms slightly and simply waited. But his eyes never left hers.

Verity swallowed, then heard herself saying huskily, '*Why*?' And immediately coloured again and bit her lip.

'Why?' He considered and allowed his long fingers to roam through her hair again. 'There is this spontaneous sort of combustion flowing between us today,

Verity,' he said musingly. 'You took one look at me and were obviously possessed of an uprush of emotion that made you want to, if not kill me, squash me as flat as you could. And almost simultaneously I was moved to retaliate as humiliatingly as I could. Since we have no real reason to hate each other, it occurred to me that the cause of all this,' he smiled slightly, 'overheatedness might be something else altogether. It generally is between persons of the opposite sex. Have you ever worn your hair long?'

'Yes. And no,' Verity said. 'I——'

'Why did you cut it? It's a wonderful colour and I like the texture.'

Verity closed her eyes frustratedly and then flinched as he drew his fingers down her cheek.

If he noticed he made no comment. 'As for your freckles,' he went on, 'they're like a gold-dusting on your skin. I know this is a very obvious question, but are they all over you?' His hand left her skin, but only briefly, to slide under her jacket. 'You were saying?'

She opened her eyes and stared into his. 'Don't you ever give up, Mr Morris?'

He grimaced. 'Not often. But tell me. You said yes. And no.'

'Yes, I have worn my hair long, and no, I don't believe this "overheatedness" has to do with anything other than the fact that you are impossible sometimes. You must *know* you are.'

'Sometimes,' he agreed, and then as her eyes glinted an ironic gold he said wryly, 'All right, often. But normally *you* never have any trouble coping with me. Why not today?'

Verity sighed unwittingly and then, because he had a point, and because she didn't seem to be getting anywhere by any other means, said, 'I had some awkward business to settle this morning. It left me in a—very tense mood.'

'What was it?'

'Nothing.' She bit her lip at his sardonic look. 'It was private.'

'I wouldn't shout it from the roof-tops.'

'Nevertheless, it is *my* business, Mr Morris. If,' she continued with an effort, 'I allowed it to... colour my dealings with you this morning I apologise, but you were also going out of your way to be provocative.'

'Provocative,' he mused, and Verity suddenly realised that he was now trailing his fingers up and down her spine, lightly, beneath her jacket, and almost absently, and it was—she swallowed—oddly reassuring.

His lips twisted. 'Then, I, too, apologise,' he said, 'with a flourish! I mean,' he explained, 'there is surely no better way for two people to make up after an argument than this!' And he bent his head and kissed her lightly on the lips.

Verity neither protested nor responded, but she did feel herself relaxing a little—and that proved fatal. A trap, she had to acknowledge, as much for herself as it might have been for him. But as her taut body softened slightly it was as if the full impact of being in his arms hit her. It was as if her senses were being bombarded with the sheer potent attraction of Brad Morris that she'd tried for so long to deny or to decry.

It was as if they were suddenly caught in an electromagnetic field that caused all else to fade by comparison, the office, the building, the noises outside the door, everything but this amazing awareness of each other. In fact, all Verity could think was how right his hard lines felt against her, how the feel of his arms around her and his hands on her back and hips were causing her body, which had been so chaste for so long, to flower within and without and to tremble with anticipation. How she seemed to be drowning in his clever, intent gaze and how her mouth suddenly felt luscious and kissable, her breasts achingly sensitive—and how not to be kissed and caressed would leave her feeling like an empty void.

And, as it all hit her, her lips parted, and she flushed hectically this time, and he said something inaudible and claimed her mouth.

It was a deep, searching kiss, and when she finally broke away he let her, but moved his hands more and more intimately on her, flicking the buttons of her jacket open and cradling her body to his.

'No...' It was more a breath of sound than anything as the feeling of his fingers on her skin, slipping beneath her bra, brought her back to some sanity.

'Yes,' he murmured and started to kiss her again, and somehow, she wasn't sure how, their positions changed so that she had her arms around his neck and he was free to find the front clasp of her bra and to release it and span her waist beneath the swell of her breasts, then move his hands slowly upwards until he could touch her nipples with his thumbs and inflict a kind of gasping delight on her that ran right through her body.

What would have happened next was something Verity refused to allow herself to dwell on, but at that moment someone knocked on the door.

She froze, and her eyes flew open as Brad lifted his head and she found herself looking into his eyes and seeing the wry expression in them.

She closed hers briefly with a look of horror and moved convulsively.

'It's all right,' he said quietly, adroitly clasping up her bra, running his fingers around its upper edges, then smoothing her jacket and buttoning it up and turning his head at the second, timid knock. 'Come in.'

It was the girl from the typing pool, Verity saw before she turned away hastily. Come to collect some papers she'd left, she said. On Mr Morris's desk, she added very apologetically, and yes, she could see them and she could just nip in and out and get them and leave them in *peace*. This she said with an unmistakable kind of significance and a hurried look at Verity, who had turned back, and then blushed.

'By all means,' Brad said pleasantly and sat down on the corner of Verity's desk.

She was as good as her word, except that she tripped on the way out, and if she'd looked embarrassed before it was nothing to how she looked as she closed the door.

Verity drew a deep, quivering breath and started to blush herself.

He smiled faintly and reached over and took her hand. 'Don't.'

She tried to pull it away and said tautly, 'Why not? It will be all over the office before you can say Jack Robinson!'

He grimaced. 'She actually saw nothing, Verity. Although she might have got the vibes,' he conceded. 'But who cares?'

'*I* care——'

'Why? It happened—to my mind the much more important thing is why it happened. I think we should discuss that, don't you?' He raised an eyebrow at her, his grey gaze alert and slightly quizzical, and he moved his fingers on the inside of her wrist.

To her horror, that action caused her to feel as if it was happening to her all over again—What is happening to me? she wondered frantically. 'You,' she licked her lips, '*you* caused it to happen, Mr Morris.' And gained momentum as a rather sick feeling invaded her and caused her to feel both frightened and angry. 'You must have a remarkably short memory if you don't recall that your hurt pride led you into an exercise of sheer male chauvinism!' And she snatched her wrist away.

His eyes narrowed. 'Well, now,' he drawled, and his gaze dropped to her breasts, 'is that how you always react to exercises of sheer male chauvinism, Mrs Wood? Or was I right all along? Have you starved yourself of love for reasons best known to yourself, and frustrated yourself in the process to the extent that you just couldn't help yourself? It's just as well we were interrupted then. Otherwise I could have had you on the floor, couldn't I?' He looked up at last and his eyes were a cool, mocking grey.

Verity went white, causing her freckles to be really noticeable and her eyes to look a dark, molten gold. She started to speak, swallowed, then said, 'Goodbye, Mr Morris. I'm resigning.' And she picked up her two bags then realised she was still boxed into a corner, in a manner of speaking, and she added through her teeth, 'Get out of my *way*, damn you!'

He did, unhurriedly.

CHAPTER TWO

'Verity!'

'Hello, Mum.'

'What are you doing home this early in the day? Are you feeling sick, darling?'

Verity put her bags plus a plastic bag full of groceries on the kitchen table. 'No.' She sighed. 'I've quit.'

Her mother, who was small, grey-haired but chic and lively-looking, laid the letter she'd been reading down and stared at her daughter, open-mouthed. 'Why?'

Verity gestured. 'It's a long story. I've told you how difficult he is to work for. I just—blew my top today.' She flinched inwardly as she thought of all the other things she'd done, things she had no intention of revealing to her mother or to anyone else.

'Well, darling, yes, you have told me, but it's an extremely well-paid job and——'

'There are other jobs. In fact, I've had several approaches from other advertising firms, so—don't worry.' She smiled at her mother reassuringly. 'Where's Maddy?'

'Gone shopping with Tanya and her mother—it never rains but it pours,' Lucy Chalmers added vexedly.

'It's actually fine, and lovely outside,' Verity murmured, and started to put the groceries away.

'No, I mean *this*.' Lucy waved the letter she'd been reading agitatedly. 'It's from Helen. Would you believe, she's broken her ankle?'

Helen was Lucy's sister, Verity's aunt, a genuine spinster, Verity thought—perhaps because she had those thoughts rather prominently in mind—and headmistress of a country school. Who lived on her own, moreover, and would be seriously handicapped with a broken ankle, her thoughts ran on as she began to perceive the other cause of her mother's distress.

'Ah,' she said slowly. 'Well, it couldn't have worked out better. I can look after Maddy while you go and look after Auntie Helen. It really *couldn't* have worked out better, in fact!'

'Verity,' her mother looked at her seriously, 'you'll want to be out and about, looking for another job. I know you've done marvellously well financially, but there's still the rent to pay and the repayments on the car, the electricity bill came today, together with the telephone bill, and they're due on the same day—I don't know why, but they always are——'

Verity grimaced. 'I have got a bit put aside, Mum.'

Her mother looked supremely dubious; then she brightened. 'Look, I've thought of the perfect solution! I'll take Maddy with me. She'd love a little break in the country, and you do know she's as safe with me as she is with you!'

'Oh, Mum,' Verity looked at her with deep affection in her eyes, 'yes, and I don't know what I would have done without you, but... it'll be so much work—Maddy, and Auntie Helen with a broken ankle. No, no, I'll cope——'

'You will not, Verity Chalmers—sorry, Wood,' her mother said, drawing herself up to her full height, which was all of five feet two. 'I'm as strong as a horse anyway. And supposing you do find another job and they want you to start work straight away? What then? You'd have to put Maddy into a crèche of some kind—you know how I feel about that! No, this is the way we'll do it. You could even drive down to see us on the weekends—of course, you'll miss Maddy and she'll miss you, so that will solve that, and Helen would love to see you as well. Unless the Woods...?' Her mother stopped abruptly.

'They did not,' Verity said drily. 'Nothing has changed there. Mum,' she paused and bit her lip and considered that she really couldn't afford to be unemployed for very long, 'if you're really sure?'

Lucy relaxed. 'Of course I am, pet! Now tell me what Mr Morris did to upset you so greatly?'

Verity's face thinned and she was silent for a moment; then she grimaced and managed to say fairly lightly, 'I shouldn't know where to begin.'

'Well, he is a very clever man apparently. I mean, you just have to look at his ads, and then there's the journalism he does on the side—I love his travel column in the paper! It's so witty and different... and didn't you tell me he writes school textbooks? Books with such an ingenious approach that kids just can't help understanding things better?'

'I have never tried to deny that he's clever, astonishingly versatile and a whole lot of other things, Mum. It doesn't alter the fact that he's quite impossible,' Verity said with finality.

That evening she persuaded her mother to go to the pictures with a friend. 'It might be your last chance for a while,' she said with a grin. Lucy was an avid film-goer, and all the arrangements for their departure the following day had been made. Once Lucy Chalmers made up her mind about anything, she was an amazingly fast worker, and Verity was to drive them down and spend one night with them.

'It will help to settle Maddy in,' she'd said, 'and give you a bit of a break, but then you really ought to get stuck into finding a job!'

Verity couldn't help smiling to herself as she and Maddy, who was bathed and in her pyjamas, did a jigsaw puzzle—or rather, Maddy concentrated fiercely on it. They were sitting on high stools at the kitchen counter and, although it was officially winter in Brisbane, no one had told the weather, and the front door of the small duplex was open to admit some balmy night air. They'd had dinner and there was a pot of coffee percolating gently on the stove, filling the place with its aroma. And Verity was smiling, despite her traumatic day, because not only was her mother an incredibly fast worker but also because she herself was incredibly lucky to have a mother like Lucy, whom Maddy adored and felt quite safe with.

She looked down and gently plucked one of her daughter's springy fine red-gold curls without breaking her concentration, and felt her heart contract as it so often did when she thought of the miracle that was Maddy. And she didn't know what alerted her, but after a moment or two something did, although she heard no sound, and she looked up and saw Brad Morris standing in the open front doorway.

She stayed arrested, a curl still wound round her finger, and felt suddenly suffused with a hot, blushing sense of shame. Then she released the curl and stood up. 'What do *you* want?'

Maddy looked up, wide-eyed, as he stepped over the doorstep into the lounge, then she turned and buried her face in Verity's loose-knit top. Verity picked her up. 'It's all right, honeybunch,' she said softly, regretting her harsh earlier tones but shooting Brad Morris an angry glance.

He stopped in the middle of lounge. Then he shook his head as if to clear it, and said, 'Why didn't you ever tell me?'

'It's got nothing to do with you,' Verity said stiffly.

'That you have a child? No,' he agreed, 'not *per se*, but I don't see why it should be such a deep, dark secret, either.'

'You did say, when you interviewed me, that it wasn't the kind of job that would suit anyone with encumbrances,' she reminded him with a bitter little smile.

He considered. 'It's not. You managed very well, all the same. But tell me, what other disinformation did you pass on? *Was* there ever a Mr Wood? I mean, are you a widow or a single parent?'

'Oh, there certainly was a Mr Wood,' Verity said with irony. 'And I am a widow and a single parent, as it happens, but be that as it may—what do you want?'

He stared at her and the child in her arms. 'What's her name? She's very shy, isn't she? But you must know, Verity,' he raised his grey eyes to hers, 'that I do not go about frightening children.'

It was all too true, Verity had to acknowledge. How he did it was something of a mystery; he certainly made no overt approaches, he wasn't a patter of heads or a pincher of cheeks, he offered no bribes, although he could do a few things that fascinated kids—but in fact he often indicated a lack of interest that one would have thought would turn them off. Yet it had the opposite effect. The only analogy that she'd been able to come up with was her own aversion to cats and the discovery that if you set out to ignore a cat it would be piqued enough to want to climb on to your lap and no one else's.

'She's more than shy,' Verity said abruptly.

'Oh? Why?'

Verity looked at him frustratedly. 'She doesn't trust men—not that it's anything——'

'To do with me,' he finished for her, and added with a faint smile, 'I wonder if she gets it from her mum? But look,' he went on before Verity could respond, 'why don't you put her down and let her finish her jigsaw, you can sit right next to her as you were, and we could... continue our discussion?'

'There's nothing to discuss. *If* you've come to beg me to return——'

'I have,' he said blandly and wandered over to the counter, where he idly picked up a piece of jigsaw and after a moment fitted it into place. 'Not precisely beg, but point out the mutual benefits; that sort of thing.'

Verity was conscious of two things: the creeping knowledge that Brad Morris didn't ever give up, and the fact that Maddy had raised her head and was watching what he was doing interestedly. I might have known, she thought exasperatedly, and was further exasperated when Maddy suddenly indicated that she wanted to get back to her jigsaw. Verity put her down on the stool and avoided Brad's eyes.

'You haven't told me her name. Or why she doesn't trust me,' he said quietly.

'Her name is Madeleine. She's three, and that's all I intend to tell you, Mr Morris,' Verity replied equally quietly but with clear intent.

'All right,' he said mildly. 'Well, now she's settled, why don't you offer me a cup of coffee? I can assure you I could do with one. I have spent the entire afternoon with Len Pearson. I'm exhausted, wrung out, talked out, I haven't eaten—and, despite your conviction that I wouldn't personally do anything to return him to the fold, he is returned, and it was entirely due to my heroic efforts. Are these biscuits?' He picked up a barrel on the counter, opened it and sniffed appreciatively. 'Home-made shortbread, I do believe. Is that another of your talents, Verity? May I help myself?'

'My mother made them. Oh,' she muttered and turned away to the stove. 'One cup of coffee and then you leave,' she said as evenly as possible, and only for Maddy's sake.

'Of course.' He waited patiently, pulling himself up a stool and munching shortbread as if he really was starving. 'Thanks. By the way, I've changed my mind,' he said conversationally as she passed him a steaming mug and pushed milk and sugar towards him.

'Good. I'm surprised, but it would be impossible to go on——'

'Not about that. No, I've decided to give the red-headed twins a miss. I'm going to use a cockatoo instead, a talking one, naturally.'

Verity groaned then coloured.

He went on, waving a biscuit, 'Len Pearson gave me the idea actually. Did you know the man is a multi-millionaire and that he's recently started a charter-boat company in Port Douglas? You can hire his boats and everything is provided—skipper, crew, et cetera.'

'I know a great deal about Len Pearson and he knows a great deal about me,' Verity said a shade wearily. 'After all, I've spoken to him nearly every day for the last six weeks. He also owns a frozen-food empire, a sixty-foot yacht, his wife died a year ago, he's very lonely and he's been an amateur inventor for some time.'

Brad cocked an eyebrow. 'Has he been making telephonic passes at you, Verity? I must say, he was most disturbed to hear that we had—parted company. He more or less told me that unless I got you back he *would* take his account elsewhere.'

'As well as everything else, he is sixty-two,' Verity pointed out acidly. 'And I thought you said you had got him back——'

'That was never a safeguard against anything— being sixty-two——'

'*Mr* Morris——' Verity bit her lip as Maddy moved restlessly then yawned.

'Looks like bedtime to me,' Brad murmured. 'And not *before* time,' he said with a charming smile, 'if you intend to get all heated again, Verity. May I make some shadow faces on the wall for her before she goes? I've added a new one to my repertoire. Let me show you.'

The net result, and it was all about as flattening as an encounter with a steamroller, was that Maddy went to bed charmed and delighted and fell asleep almost as soon as her head touched the pillow.

And by the time Verity returned to the kitchen Brad had freshened their coffee.

'Where was I? Ah, yes, we were discussing Len Pearson, but if that's a painful subject we could get on to the cockatoo——'

'No. Look here,' Verity said, 'I'm not coming back.'

'Mr Morris,' he drawled.

She blinked at him.

'You forgot to say it in that frozen way you usually do, that's all. Why?'

Verity took a deep breath and took refuge in her coffee for a moment. 'I must be slipping, Mr Morris,' she said drily then.

'I meant, why won't you come back, Verity?'

'I should have thought that was obvious,' she said shortly.

'Well, it's not, actually. By the way, I haven't entirely given up on redheads. I would also like to include a red-bearded, kilted, bagpipe-playing Scotsman and a boat—as well as a talking cockatoo.'

'Isn't that a bit hackneyed?' Verity said before she could stop herself. 'I mean, people have been making fun of kilted Scotsmen for—a long time probably.'

He sat forward. 'That's what you don't understand. So few do! It's those wonderful, hackneyed things that people love... Mind you,' he sat back reflectively, 'I have had other ideas. I have this image of a mediocrely pretty woman but one of those incredibly tenacious ones with all the mediocre ambitions in life—tiled patios around bungalows, cooking in woks, fondue parties—and the kind of woman who persists in calling her husband Douglas or Richard or Michael when everyone else, their mothers included, calls them Doug or Dick or Mick.'

'That's diabolical,' Verity said slowly, but she couldn't help smiling. 'On the whole, I prefer the Scot.'

'Do you know any?'

'No. Anyway——'

'Verity, can I tell you something else?' he queried and proceeded to do so. 'Len Pearson is contemplating a major *international* advertising drive for his frozen foods as well as something for this fleet of charter boats that takes tourists to the Barrier Reef from Port Douglas. But, being no fool, he's not prepared to part with his hard-earned dollars on any old campaign, he wants the best, so he's come up with this—test drive, you might call it, on his own... quite clever little invention, and I *refuse* to laud it any further.' He grimaced. 'But the gist of the thing is, get this one right and we get the other two. How,' he looked at her earnestly, 'could you possibly even consider deserting the camp at a time like this? Have you any idea what it will mean to the Morris Advertising Agency? The frozen-food one alone is like manna from heaven. It's already a household name—all we'll have to do is jazz up its image slightly and the——'

'Don't go on,' Verity said quietly. 'There is nothing so indispensable about me that will make or break this campaign, so you're wasting your time playing on my finer feelings, it's just ridiculous!'

'It's not. You yourself put it all in a nutshell only today. I'll be lost! Do you have any idea how many people I interviewed before I came up with you? Do you imagine I would have been half or even a quarter as productive as I've been over the past two years if it hadn't been for you? How many people do *you* know who can come up with a cockatoo, a red-bearded, kilted, bagpipe-playing Scotsman and a boat without all *sorts* of fuss and then keep us all happy into the bargain——?'

'Even I might have trouble with that,' Verity said drily.

'The cockatoo or the Scotsman?'

'Both.'

'Verity——'

'Mr Morris, I hesitate to say this, but why are you deliberately ignoring what happened this morning? If it demonstrates nothing else, surely it does demonstrate that our days of being able to work together so productively,' she said ironically, 'are gone?'

He eyed her alertly. 'I wasn't sure that you'd want that resurrected,' he said after a moment.

'Believe me, I don't. I——'

'By the way, I do apologise for the "having you on the floor" bit. That was unforgivable, not to mention horribly ungallant.'

Verity felt the warmth stealing into her cheeks but resolutely ignored it. 'And the next time it happens? Will you be able to refrain from being horribly ungallant again? And again?' she said gently.

He looked at her thoughtfully, then raised an eyebrow. 'If you don't kiss me back the next time, I might.'

Her fingers curved about her coffee-mug, but she restrained herself and said in a colourless voice, 'There will be no next time—that's what I'm trying to tell you.'

He looked her over in silence, taking in her slim yellow trousers and loose white cotton top, her flat yellow shoes and absence of any make-up, which was as informally dressed as he'd ever seen her, then said with a faint frown, 'Do you honestly think you were entirely blameless this morning, Verity?' He gestured with a tinge of irritation. 'Blame is not the right word, but you know what I mean.'

She closed her eyes. 'I don't want to discuss it. It *happened*, and it makes it impossible for us to work together; that's all there is to say.'

'What about anything else?'

She opened her eyes. 'What about it? What else?'

'Well, you seem to be seriously suggesting that, although it *happened*, we pretend it didn't—we ignore it, in other words. Yet I can assure you, for all my sins, I don't normally go around doing that kind of thing willy-nilly.' He smiled without amusement. 'Nor, I'm equally sure, do you. Not,' he added quietly, 'as passionately as we did it, Verity.'

It was a moment before Verity spoke, and it took a great deal of will-power to not only frame an answer when she would have preferred to fall through a handy hole in the floor, but also to utter it with a semblance of composure. 'I think,' she said slowly, 'we will just have to put it down to being one of those mysterious things that can be neither explained nor should be... agonised over. That's what I really think, Mr Morris.' She raised her golden eyes to his and there was a kind of bleak defiance in them. Then she couldn't help adding with some irony, 'What, as a matter of interest, do you think Miss Carpenter would have made of it all?'

His mouth hardened. 'Let's leave Primrose out of this, Verity. It——'

'Oh, I see,' she mocked, and their gazes locked in a way that was about as combative as two people could get without coming to blows—which gave Verity a curious sense of satisfaction. Got you there, Mr Morris, she thought.

But he merely said with a flash of something in his eyes that was gone before it was decipherable, 'I doubt if you do see, but if that's how you really feel then all more the reason for us *not* to break up a wonderfully successful *working* relationship all because of a—what would you call it?—a non-event, really. Particularly as I intend to offer you a rise, and a further one if we get Pearson's other account and——'

'Mr Morris——'

'I *wish* you wouldn't keep calling me that,' he said, really irritably this time. 'And may I make another point? We've been discussing this for,' he consulted his watch, 'an hour now, during which time neither of us has shown any inclination to leap on the other and none of that naughtiness of the *non-event* kind has surfaced at all. Or has it?' he challenged, looking every bit as autocratic and unamused and wildly impatient as only he could.

Verity opened her mouth to deny that it had, but her mother chose that moment to walk in.

Verity groaned inwardly then said to Lucy, who had stopped in the kitchen with a surprised expression, 'This is Mr Morris, Mum. He's just leaving,' she added flatly.

'Oh, please don't leave on my account, Mr Morris,' Lucy said hastily. 'I'm quite ready for bed, actually. I've just seen this *exhausting* movie. No, do stay and talk to Verity. Especially,' she said, taking Verity supremely by surprise, 'if you've come to talk her into staying with you.'

The result was entirely predictable. Brad Morris slid off his stool and advanced upon her mother, exuding the charm he could also turn on like no other from every pore. 'I can't tell you how delighted I am to meet you, ma'am! And I do hope you'll forgive me, but I've eaten just about all your absolutely delicious biscuits, and I *am* here to talk Verity into coming back, but I'm having little success.'

'Ah,' Lucy said, and subjected Brad to a penetrating scrutiny, and it was obvious from what she then said that she approved of what she saw. She said, 'Between you and me, Mr Morris, Verity can be a very determined person sometimes. However, I see that as a character asset, on the whole.'

'So do I,' Brad agreed ruefully.

'Had you, then, considered apologising to her for whatever it was you fell out over? Or perhaps promising to mend your ways somewhat?' she queried a little sternly. 'All Verity has told me is that you're...just impossible.' Her expression relented slightly as she added, 'Men so often simply don't realise they are, you know.'

For just a second Brad Morris stared at her, transfixed, and was without words. Then he swung around to Verity so that only she could see the little glint in his eye as he said very seriously, 'I apologise for *everything*, Verity. And I shall certainly try to mend my ways.'

'Now, Verity, it would be churlish not to at least allow Mr Morris a probationary period,' Lucy Chalmers said gently to her daughter. 'Wouldn't it?'

'Darling, are you still cross with me?'
'No,' Verity said and changed gear.

'Because I talked you into going back to work for Mr Morris?'

'Mum, I've just said I'm not cross with you.'

'Unfortunately I know you well enough to know that you're annoyed about something!' Lucy said humorously and glanced over to the back seat to see how Maddy was. 'But I found him quite charming—oh, I'm sure he can be difficult. I mean, you can *see* the energy and the intelligence—I wouldn't be surprised if the air literally hums about him at times.'

Verity winced and changed down again.

'But I really couldn't help feeling that you have *great* prospects with him. After all, considering how inexperienced you were in advertising when he hired you, he's already done great things for you, and, well, the devil you know, especially one who pays you as well as he does and proposes to pay you even *more*...' She didn't finish that bit but started on another thought. 'Besides which, you like advertising, don't you? I mean, you find it interesting and challenging and would like to make it your career, and, from what I've read, Brad Morris is about *the* most exciting person in the game today. Did he make a pass at you, Verity?'

Verity turned her head to study her mother briefly, then sighed. 'Something of that nature occurred, yes,' she conceded formally. 'How did you guess?'

Her mother chuckled. 'Why do one's offspring always imagine one came down with the last shower, particularly in romantic matters? Were you being very superior, dear? About men in general or something like that?'

Verity was silent.

'Well, I won't probe any further,' Lucy said brightly. 'But I do think one should forgive men the odd pass from time to time. I mean, it obviously couldn't have been the ongoing, obnoxious, bottom-pinching kind of thing or you'd have left ages ago. I would take it as a compliment if I were you. They just can't help themselves occasionally, even nice ones, you know, poor dears. And you should also bear in mind that you're a bit sensitive on the subject of men, anyway. Not without cause,' her mother said soberly. 'But not all men are like *that*.'

Verity drove for a while in silence, then she glanced at her mother and smiled wryly. 'You're so sane. I'm sorry I've been like a bear with a sore head.'

'Didn't you tell me he has this fabulous girlfriend?' Lucy said relievedly.

'Yes. Primrose Carpenter. She's that model I pointed out to you in a magazine. They've been together for quite a while now. As long as I've worked for him—at least, I've been sending her flowers and chocolates and all sorts of wild and wonderful things since I started working for him.'

'What kind of wild and wonderful things?' Lucy asked with a laugh.

'Well, I told you about the giant panda bear—toy, of course—then there was the bicycle made for two and,' Verity paused, 'as a matter of fact, a talking *cockatoo*...'

Lucy laughed again. 'He does sound like an exciting person to be in love with. Will they marry, do you think?'

'I think it's only a question of when.'

Lucy pursed her lips. 'She might be wise to get him to the altar sooner rather than later.'

Verity had to smile herself. 'To curb these outbreaks of—whatever it is even nice men can't help from time to time? You could be right. I think we're here.'

Her mother squeezed her arm fondly. 'That's my girl. You look much better now.'

But that night in bed, with Maddy snuggled up to her, and even with the comforting knowledge that Maddy had taken to her Great-Aunt Helen's country establishment like a duck to water—there were some ducklings and chickens, a lamb and a kitten, all of which had fascinated her—Verity didn't feel much better, she discovered. In fact, there seemed to be an aching little void around her heart that, much as she wished to, she couldn't solely attribute to missing Maddy, as she undoubtedly would. And she dared not, she found, allow herself to dwell on what other causes there might be for it.

CHAPTER THREE

IT WAS, two days later, impossible to be unaware of the discreet buzz of speculation as Verity arrived for work. Not only had she to run the gauntlet of the receptionist and an unusually large number of employees in Reception, but she also ran into both Tim Cameron and William Morris on the way to Brad's suite of offices.

Tim was looking more his usual urbane self, and he said heartily, 'Great to see you, Mrs Wood! So glad you changed your mind.'

William Morris, however, drew her aside. 'Mrs Wood,' he began earnestly, 'I can't tell you how glad I am to see you. And I'm only sorry that I didn't take the opportunity to tell you, before—er—your little run-in with Brad, how much we value you at the Morris Advertising Agency. Not to put too fine a point on it, you've coped with Brad admirably, better than anyone else we've ever had, and at this point in time, with the prospect of the Pearson account tripling itself, it would be a disaster to lose you.'

'Thank you, Mr Morris,' Verity murmured.

'I'd also like to say, if you,' he gestured uncomfortably, 'have any more problems with Brad, please do come to me with them. I'm sure that between us we could sort them out!'

Verity controlled an insane desire to laugh hysterically as she visualised herself telling this staid, middle-aged man, who was so different from his brother, the exact nature of what had occurred between her and Brad Morris. 'Thank you,' was all she could find to say again.

'He's not... a *bad* person, really,' William persevered. 'In fact, the main problem is he's just been too darned bright for his own good ever since he was born, virtually. He exhausted our poor mother, who was always convinced he would come to a bad end; as a child at school... well, let's just say he exhausted them too, several of them. But we'd be a bit lost here without him. My wife...' He paused and grimaced, and Verity was assailed suddenly by Brad's 'mediocrely pretty woman' with pretensions who could have been Gloria Morris to a T, although of course she didn't have to confine herself to bungalows or cooking in woks now, and who couldn't, it was a well known fact, tolerate her brother-in-law. 'My wife,' William repeated, 'has always maintained he needs a really good woman to sort him out. My own opinion is that she would need to be a cross between a saint and a brigadier-general, but perhaps that's what Gloria means,' he reflected with a sudden look of surprise. 'Anyway, do remember I'm always available, Mrs Wood.'

'I will, Mr Morris.'

Consequently, as Verity entered the office, with curious visions of Brad Morris as an energetic, uncontrollable schoolboy in her mind, it came as even more of a shock to find her boss sitting behind his desk in an upright position, something he rarely did, and dressed in a neat dark suit, a pristine white shirt and a conservative royal-blue tie, which looked suspiciously like an old school tie—a quite famous old school tie, she recognised as she came closer.

She raised an eyebrow and couldn't help smiling faintly.

'Good morning, Verity,' he said promptly, and added, 'What, may one enquire, is the cause of your mirth?'

'Hardly mirth,' she responded, and turned away to her desk.

'You're surprised to see me dressed like this?'

'I am indeed. I'm more surprised by the tie, however.'

He grimaced. 'It's my old school tie—did you imagine I was born fully educated?'

'Not at all. But I have just been given to understand you—er—well, exhausted several schools as well as your poor mother, which led me to believe that you mightn't be a rightful recipient of an old school tie.'

Brad Morris lay back in his chair and looked entirely unperturbed. 'I did have a few changes but that was in my primary days,' he conceded. 'Who passed on all this startling information?'

Verity shrugged, sat down and began repacking her drawers from her shopping bag.

'It had to be Bill.' He chuckled. 'What else did he say?'

Verity shrugged evasively again.

'I see. Well, if you're wondering why I'm dressed the way I am, there are two reasons: I'm trying to reform, as I promised your delightful mother, and I thought therefore that looking the part of an advertising executive could only help me to act like one; and I'm meeting my publisher for lunch. You're looking very smart yourself, incidentally.'

Verity was wearing a straight, soft jade-green dress with a matching jacket—all very simple but well cut—with bronze accessories. 'Thanks,' she said briefly without looking up.

'How is Maddy?' Lucy had confided quite a few details to him at their legendary meeting, including their plans for the next few weeks.

'Fine.'

'I see,' he said again, and when she did glance up at last it was to see him looking perfectly serious, except for his grey eyes, which were glinting with amusement.

And she cautioned herself suddenly against overreacting and said much against her will, 'She's settled in really well, actually. My aunt has a small menagerie of young animals and I shall be amazed if she doesn't come home with a kitten at least. Talking of animals or those kind of things,' she opened a fresh notebook and wrote 'Pearson Account', then raised her golden-flecked eyes to Brad Morris, 'are you still of the same mind? Regarding Scotsmen, cockatoos and boats?'

'I am.' He looked at her a little more narrowly. 'Have *you* been clobbered with inspiration?'

'Not precisely. But it did occur to me that only six months ago you gave Miss Carpenter a talking cockatoo—I remember it because I actually found it for you and it was a magnificent specimen. I wondered if she'd mind—lending it to us for the ad?'

'Ah.' Brad Morris drummed his long fingers thoughtfully on the desk for a moment, then said unusually laconically, 'No.'

Verity couldn't help looking surprised. 'Did it die? Or fly away? Or stop talking?'

'None of those things. Well, it will soon be common knowledge, I suppose,' he said drily, 'but the fact of the matter is, Verity, that I've been thrown over for a member of the English aristocracy—no less than an earl,' and for a fleeting moment his eyes were hard and grim.

Verity stared at him, open-mouthed, until she reminded herself of the girl from the typing pool. But even then all she could say feebly was, 'What?'

'It's true.'

'But—I mean—only days ago you were...'

'That was our swan-song.' He sat back, the grimness replaced now by a deliberate kind of lazy world-weariness. 'Primrose and I—well, put it this way, Primmy was a bit undecided for a while. It is a giant leap forward for her, but she had some reservations; one would be a fool not to be aware that any aristocracy doesn't take too kindly to losing their earls to models, especially with Australian accents, however beautiful, but in the end she decided she had every attribute to be the Countess of So-and-So and to go for it. She has gone,' he added succinctly.

'But—you *let* her?' Verity was still having trouble with her voice and a tendency to look shell-shocked.

A definite look of irony crossed Brad's eyes before he remarked, 'Talented as I am, indeed, everything that I am, I'm still a long way from being a peer of the realm.'

'You could be as unhappy as the Countess of So-and-So as anyone else,' Verity said slowly as, for the first time in nearly two years, she tried to look into Brad Morris's soul and discover how he *really* felt. 'I mean, if you love each other and——'

'Verity, Verity,' he drawled. 'Are you that naïve? Let me explain the real dilemma of truly beautiful women to you. I mean that kind of matchless beauty that you see quite rarely, and you'd have to agree Primmy has it?' He raised an eyebrow at her.

'Yes. Yes, of course,' Verity agreed, trying not to sound even faintly tart.

'Well, it's their everything, you see. It's their entrée into all sorts of society, it can be a substitute for brains, although I wouldn't say Primmy was brainless, but it's such an asset above all else that they'd be...foolish if they didn't seek and strive for the right setting for it, didn't find a place for it where it could be cosseted and treasured and receive the right amount of exposure, which is like a form of nourishment to truly beautiful women—believe me, she'll never be quite as unhappy as the Countess of So-and-So, whatever he's like, as she could be looking back and thinking of what she *might* have been.'

Verity opened her mouth, hesitated, then said uncertainly, 'Have you any idea how cynical that sounds?'

He shrugged. 'I think it's a fact of life.'

Verity was silent beneath the weight of her thoughts—the sudden memory of the way he and Primrose had looked only a few days ago in this very room, the...yes, she reflected, the tension that had flowed between them, albeit briefly, and then the affection and tenderness in his eyes that he'd not been able to hide, the totally impossible mood he'd been in, even for him. And she remembered that fighting glance they'd exchanged and what he'd said when she'd mentioned Primrose that same evening and implied that he was being faithless if nothing else, and her unspoken surprise, unspoken even to herself, that Brad Morris was that kind of man... Why didn't he tell me then? she wondered. Because even the fact that he can't have her doesn't change the fact that he loves her? Of course... He didn't deny it just now, he embarked instead on what had to be a bitter and cynical discourse, even though he tried to make light of it...

Her eyes widened as it crossed her mind to wonder then whether the kiss they'd exchanged had been the unforgivable but perhaps only human reaction of a man who had been passed over for a peer of the realm?

'What,' he murmured, 'is crossing your mind, Verity?'

She blinked and coloured slightly, then raised her eyebrows at him with some hauteur. 'I'm surprised you can't read my mind. You seem to have set yourself up as quite an authority on women.'

'You don't think I'm right about Primrose?' he queried.

'I...' She stopped and started again. 'I would rather not go into it any further. How am I to know anyway?' she added crossly.

He shrugged. 'I got the distinct impression you were speculating, all the same.'

'No—that is to say, it's futile for me *to* speculate. *All right*,' she added to his look of scepticism, 'let's say I was human enough to do so briefly——'

'I would have thought you more than anyone would be in the position to speculate.'

Verity stared at him. Then she said, 'I'll tell you what position I am in, Mr Morris. One of being able to end the bargain we made any time I choose. So now either we drop the subject and get back to business or I leave. Where were we? Ah, yes: cockatoos, painful a subject as they may be——'

'They aren't.'

Want to bet? Verity said, but to herself, and wrote down 'Cockatoo' on her pad, and thought, Perhaps I could borrow someone else's? I've got the feeling if I buy one I'll be landed with it, and anyway, as I know from previous experience, it's not that easy to buy talking cockatoos... Then she raised her head as the silence lengthened, to see her boss staring at her broodingly.

'Is something wrong?' she asked involuntarily. 'I mean, something else?'

His expression didn't change for a moment, then he looked at her with such sardonic amusement that she took a startled breath. But, before she had a chance to say anything, he sat up. 'We have to go to Port Douglas to make this ad, Verity. I don't know if I mentioned it, but it should only take a week at the most, unless *everything* goes wrong, so it won't interfere with your visits to Maddy, but if we do get caught up there over a weekend I will naturally give you time off to compensate. We'll be going up by train, the *Queenslander*, which will kill two birds with one stone for me, and we'll fly home. So far as boats go, one of the reasons for us going to Port Douglas is that Len Pearson happens to have a plethora of them up there—and he was rather charmed at the thought that we might be able to use one of his boats, thereby giving that area of his operations some free publicity as well as establishing a link between his commercial operations and his inventive genius. He has also decided to start off the campaign on his charter boats in a poster and pamphlet form, so we'll be able to do the photography at the same time—thereby killing another two birds with one stone,' he said wryly. 'The Scotsman I'll have to leave up to you, Verity. If necessary, we can take one with us, but I think I'd rather find a local. You have three days to organise it. How does that suit you?'

Verity again closed her mouth, but this time she threw her notebook on to her desk and stood up, her eyes a deep molten gold. 'It doesn't,' she said crisply. 'How long have you known all this?' she demanded.

'Since I spent an exhausting afternoon with Len Pearson. I had to make some reparation for your damning comments, such as conceding, against my better judgement, as a matter of fact, Verity, that Port Douglas would be a good place to do all this—the man is simply fanatical about the place and he is paying so——'

'And you didn't see fit to tell me all this that *evening*? In other words, you lured me back under false pretences, Mr Morris——'

'I wondered when we'd get back to that,' he drawled.

'Did you?' she shot back at him. 'Well, now you know. And here's something else for you to know! I have no intention of spending weeks away with you, let alone being closeted on a train with you for *days*, so——'

'What are you frightened of, Verity?' he said softly but with a significant look. 'Yourself?'

She picked up the notebook and threw it at him. He dodged it lazily and eyed her quizzically, which incensed her all the more.

'There's nothing I'm frightened of,' she spat at him. 'What I object to is your incredible thoughtlessness, your unbelievably high-handed ways—"you have three days to organise it all, Verity",' she mimicked. 'Port Douglas has to be at least a *thousand* miles away! How the hell am I to know what facilities they have up there? Or whether there are any wandering Scots minstrels up there?' she said witheringly, and added, 'If you must know, the mere *thought* of kilts and bagpipes is starting to give me the heebie-jeebies, but, that aside, it could be an absolute nightmare trying to organise things up there, especially *your* kind of...things, which are inevitably a nightmare anyway! Why can't you just do something *simple* and close to home?' she said passionately. 'Why does it always have to be these three-ring-kind-of-circus deals?'

He took his time about answering, time he spent examining her extreme state of agitation, including her heaving breasts. Then he said mildly, 'I thought I'd explained why, but, that apart, anyone can do simple, ordinary things close to home. My inspiration comes from a much wider source, which is why my ads are such works of art. We have also been away from home, before, Verity, not to mention the fact that you haven't got anyone *at* home at the moment. And short notice has never been a problem before—that's how I work.'

'Your modesty is also unbelievable,' she ground out, and sat down with a disgusted sound. 'Three days,' she marvelled. 'No. I refuse to do it. I don't choose to be that *far* away from home anyway.'

'You didn't make any such stipulations when you agreed to come back to work.'

'I didn't *know* you were planning to turn this into an extended safari——'

'So it would have affected your decision?' he queried, with a lazy glint in his eye that should have warned her but didn't.

'Yes,' she said shortly.

'Then I think the events that passed between us several days ago have to be the cause,' he said with the sort of lazy mockery that was equally stinging as the more overt kind. 'You've never before objected to my *modus operandi*, you see.'

Verity took a furious breath. 'And *I* can't help thinking Primrose Carpenter is well shot of you, you know. I'm sure even an earl would find it difficult to have an ego as large as yours! Had you taken that into consideration, Mr Morris? That you might have actually sent her flying into the arms of her earl because you are such a monumental egotist?'

Apart from the knowledge that she'd been possessed of an unbelievable desire to wound him or his vanity or something, and had given way to it in an unforgivably personal manner—and it struck her as soon as the words left her mouth—she was almost immediately assailed then by the knowledge that she might as well be hitting her head against a brick wall. Because he made no movement but sat there studying her with nothing more than a little glint of curiosity in his eyes, as if viewing with a sort of universal cynicism now yet another genre of the female species—not, she couldn't doubt it, the *truly* beautiful type, but probably the hysterical, bitchy type... She raised her hands to her face frustratedly.

Then, at last, he sat forward and said meditatively, 'Verity, I've got the feeling some man made your life hell once, and *I* can't help speculating that it might have been the late, possibly *unlamented* Mr Wood.'

She took her hands away. Then she took several very deep breaths and said tonelessly, 'Would you please explain why it's necessary to go up there by train? If what I've read is true, it takes two days and a night.'

His eyes narrowed and for a moment he looked as if he was in two minds, but perhaps the bleak, cold look in her eyes helped him to decide. He said, drily, however, 'The paper I write for wants me to do a series of articles on Australian trains, starting with the *Queenslander*. It occurred to me that at the same time it might be a very peaceful way to—finalise my ideas on Len Pearson's thingumajig.' He started to look irritated and picked up one of Len Pearson's 'thingumajigs', actually called a Kneg, from the desk, and stared down at it so balefully that it suddenly occurred to Verity that this ad was causing her brilliant boss some problems.

'I rarely doubt myself,' he continued, 'but how anyone can get so worked up over a fiddling sort of cross between a clothes-peg and a penknife is enough to make me start. Anyone would think he'd invented the original safety-pin!'

'Ah, but,' Verity said, 'if you were a Scotsman caught on a windy boat who had lost his safety-pin but not his penknife, it could be a lifesaver.'

'Verity!' For a moment he looked totally entertained—indeed, he looked so vitally alive that it caused her heart to contract in a manner that was acutely disturbing. 'You've read my mind!'

'I have had a bit of practice,' she said as prosaically as she was able. 'As a matter of fact, it is quite a useful little thing, and it did occur to me that it might have some impact if it *didn't* have a name. I mean, perhaps you could devise three or four scenarios instead of just the one, where someone who doesn't know what it is finds it useful in bizarre circumstances then looks at it perplexedly and asks what it really is. And then you could flash the name across the screen with a sort of "don't leave home without one" message.'

There was dead silence for a long moment, during which Verity started to feel uncomfortable and as if she'd overstepped her mark or suggested something stupid to say the least, and she grimaced and murmured, 'Not terribly original, probably—it was just a thought.'

'My dear,' he said softly, but his grey eyes sparkled magnetically, 'I don't know why I'm sitting in this chair instead of you. Unoriginal be damned—it's brilliant!' He frowned. 'Why didn't I think of it?' he demanded. 'I've been racking my brains for bloody weeks!'

'Perhaps you had other things on your mind. And you did come up with the Scotsman,' she consoled him.

'So I did.' He grimaced, then brightened. 'This calls for a celebration. I'm taking you out to lunch, Verity, whether you like it or not,' he said with all his old assurance, and stood up.

She sighed and struggled to keep a straight face. 'It's only nine-thirty in the morning, Mr Morris,' she pointed out gently. 'Besides, you're lunching with your publisher.'

He glanced at his watch, pursed his lips and sat down again. 'That's true—tell you what, though, you'd enjoy meeting my publisher, so I shall still take you out to lunch. But in the meantime, could you get me Len Pearson on the phone, please? If he invented the thing he must have some idea of all the bizarre uses it can be put to.' And he pulled a pad towards him, which happened to be the one she'd thrown at him, read what she'd written, glanced across at her with a wicked little glint in his eye, then tossed it back gently so that it landed fair and square in front of her. 'Put the damned cockatoo on hold,' he said. 'You're right, I've suddenly decided I'm allergic to them.'

An hour later such was the level of activity in the office that Verity was quite confident that her boss would completely forget about his lunch invitation, if not the lunch itself. She was wrong.

At twelve-thirty he looked at his watch, reached for his jacket and tie, which he had discarded, ran a hand through his disordered hair and said to everyone in the office, 'That's it, folks. I'm taking my assistant out to lunch. Ready, Verity? You can titivate at the restaurant if necessary.'

His brother William, who had been made privy to the latest developments in the ongoing saga of the Pearson account, and who was looking pleased and genial, suddenly looked even more pleased and genial. 'What a good idea!' he enthused. 'Don't rush back, you two. I'll draft someone from my office to do a bit more of the groundwork for you, Mrs Wood.'

'This is unnecessary,' Verity said as they left the building. 'What could I possibly have in common with your publisher?'

He looked down at her amusedly. 'That's one of the delights of life, surely? You never know what you're going to have in common with strangers, do you? But you will have one thing: your sex.'

'She's a woman—I might have known,' Verity muttered.

'Now why would you say that, I wonder?' he queried as they stopped at a traffic-light. 'Or have you really decided I'm a womaniser of the worst kind, given,' he remarked quite audibly, 'to taking serious disadvantage of my assistant whenever the mood takes me? I notice,' he added with a significant downward glance, 'that you're wearing the kind of clothes it would not be so easy to slide my hands beneath today, Mrs Wood. From the top, that is.'

There were about six people around them at the junction but they all exhibited the same reaction— quick, disbelieving sidelong glances and then deliberately blank expressions.

Verity tightened her mouth and refused to budge when the light changed until everyone had moved on. Then she said as she started to walk, 'You fight incredibly dirty, don't you?'

He shrugged. 'I—retaliate, yes. And I guess I'll keep doing it while you continue to hold this distorted view of me, my motives and *your* total lack of involvement.'

'You also apologised for everything once—how false was that?' she marvelled.

'As a matter of fact, I thought you were far too intelligent to go on believing I *could* apologise for some things.'

Verity looked up at him and was a little stunned to see that he looked reticent and reserved, not mocking nor even amused, and that as he loped along, instead of looking incongruous in his beautifully tailored suit, there was something dynamic and intensely masculine about him, something completely at home, and it was not lost on most of the women walking towards him—they were even giving him backward glances. But, for reasons buried too deep for her to take into account, she continued to fight.

'I don't know how you can—I mean, if you still wish to harp on what happened, as you obviously do, may I present it to you in another light? Primrose had not even *gone* when you... when you——'

'When I succumbed to the intense attraction that was flowing between us that day, Verity?' he supplied, stopping in the middle of the pavement. 'Ah, but you see, I'd known Primmy was a lost cause for quite a few weeks. I was merely being a good friend in need while we were away. Also, contrary to your belief that it was an idyll for two in the Whitsundays, we were, in fact, part of a group, and *I* was working, hard as you may find that to believe as well, but if you care to read the Saturday paper for the next few weeks you could even find yourself quite entertained by my lively, witty, utterly refreshing view of the Whitsundays, which had been done to death in sheer banality by everyone else. We're here,' he added gravely.

The restaurant was small but beautifully appointed, and when he suggested a drink at the bar while they waited for his publisher to arrive she excused herself instead and looked around for the powder-room.

'Over there,' he pointed. 'Don't try to leave by the fire escape, Verity. That would be rather craven, don't you agree?'

What amazed her as she rinsed her hands and stared at her reflection in the mirror was how well she looked.

A seething state of anger must have subtle but beneficial properties, she reflected as she touched up her make-up, and decided it was more a matter of aura than actual looks. Because her hair usually shone and held its bouffant short shape with a fringe with no more than a flick of a comb—it was that kind of obliging hair—her skin was usually smooth and golden with its bloom of freckles, and her figure beneath the elegant jade outfit had not altered a centimetre in any direction. So why? she wondered. I mean, why should I look as if I've spent all morning preparing for this lunch instead of looking harassed and hard-worked? Why should I look clear-eyed and alert and as fresh as a daisy? Could it be that I was beginning to... *feel* dull and a bit deadly, and Brad Morris, if nothing else, has shaken me out of it? She grimaced, then looked at herself very soberly and said softly, 'Keep fighting, Verity. Don't let him wear you down, and above all it might be wise to remember that passive resistance could be more helpful to you than—the other kind.'

A few minutes later it struck her as rather ironic that his publisher of all people should be instrumental in helping her to continue the fight.

And it was obvious that Sonia Mallory was as surprised to see her as the opposite was true.

'So you two know each other?' Brad said as they sat down. 'I told you you might have something in common with each other,' he added to Verity.

Sonia, who was in her late thirties and one of those very refined, elegant women, although obviously with a sharp brain beneath it all, said languidly, 'Verity was married to my cousin Barry. You must have met Barry, Brad. You went to the same school, although he was years behind you—well, perhaps he missed you—he would have been only... twenty-five now, Verity?' She looked at Verity for confirmation.

'Yes.'

'Ah,' Brad murmured. 'No, I don't remember him, but——' he too turned to Verity '—you didn't tell me you were one of *those* Woods, Verity!'

There was a short, sharp silence. Then Verity said with commendable restraint, 'Only by marriage. And they didn't approve of me, so I don't claim any kinship.'

Sonia grimaced. 'I have to say, Verity,' she commented, 'that I always felt his parents—my uncle and aunt—did go out on a rather extraordinary limb over you, my dear, but it was such a very *young* marriage that surely, in retrospect, you can see their point? It wasn't terribly successful, after all, was it?'

Verity picked up the glass of wine that had just been poured for her and stared down into its golden depths for a moment before she said, 'If that was all they'd had against me, yes, I have to say, if nothing else, history proved them correct. But there was much more to it, Sonia. From the moment they laid eyes on me they decided I wasn't good enough for Barry; they never once considered that *he* might not have been good marriage material for *anyone*; they never ever acknowledged that he had a serious drinking problem—yes,' she said as Sonia's eyes widened, 'I wondered how much they'd played that down, but it was one he acquired before he met me, and somehow or other he managed to hide it from me as well until it was too late.'

Some doubt expressed itself in her late-husband's cousin's eyes, and it was because of that that Verity decided to continue, 'And it was the ridiculous pressure they put on him over me that exacerbated it. They also refused me any kind of help when I needed it desperately, they cut him out of their wills and told him it would stay that way so long as he stayed married to me—of course, the awful irony of that was Barry predeceasing them both and dying virtually penniless and with not a cent to pass on to his child, their only grandchild. And finally they virtually accused me of *driving* him to drink and thereby driving himself into a tree. Oh,' she said gently and put the wine down, untasted, 'one last thing—they do want to help with Maddy now, they've decided. I got a summons several days ago—do you know how they put it, Sonia? They told me that, in return for specified amounts of time she spent with them, they would be prepared to contribute to her schooling.'

Brad, who had been following all this with a growing frown in his eyes, said suddenly, 'Was that the morning you took off work? The day I got back?'

Verity looked at him sardonically. 'None other.'

'But why weren't you good enough for him?' he asked.

'If anyone should understand that, *you* should,' Verity said.

'No. No, I don't,' he murmured, the light of obstinacy that she was all too familiar with entering his grey eyes.

Verity waited until their meals had been served, during which time she debated whether to go on with this conversation, let alone the lunch, then decided she might as well be in for a pound as well as a penny. 'The English aren't the only ones who have an aristocracy. There's one right here in Brisbane and they generally live in Ascot or Hamilton, or that's where their parents live, and they too don't take too kindly to surrendering their sons, even if they aren't earls, to girls who didn't go to the right schools, who had to work to put themselves through college and practise all sorts of petty economies——'

'But your mother is absolutely delightful, Verity,' Brad objected. 'Cultured and——'

'She may be, but she's also been a widow for nearly twenty years, she brought up three children single-handedly and my father before he died was only a lowly primary-school teacher. At a state school. Funnily enough,' she paused, 'I didn't think it made any difference either until I met Barry. But now I see it every day. I see it in your old school tie, I see it in the people you know and associate with, I've sent flowers to your mother, so I know she lives in Ascot—so is the Carpenter family mansion, for that matter—and we all can't help knowing that your brother William, for reasons best known to himself, committed the social solecism of marrying outside the clique, which is a bit of a trial, even for as determined a woman as your beloved sister-in-law. And you yourself only a few moments ago alluded to *those* Woods—need I say any more?'

For a moment Brad looked faintly stunned, and it was Sonia who broke the impasse.

She said with a chuckle, 'Ouch! Well said, my dear. But I do feel I can add something here. We aren't all the raving snobs you take us for. And,' she sobered, 'there were other factors to be taken into account regarding Barry's parents. He was their only child, conceived after years of trying—so yes, I have to concede they were blind to a lot of his faults and they probably put enormous pressure on him to succeed, although I *hadn't* realised he was such a drinker. His father has also built up this impressive empire and, in the manner of most fathers, probably counts its ultimate worth in its family continuity.' She stopped, then looked at Verity. 'It's quite possible that your little girl could be a very rich little girl one day.'

'I don't have any ambition for Maddy in that regard.'

Sonia picked up her knife and fork, but then she looked across at Verity and held her gaze for a long moment. 'I see,' she said finally. 'Well. Brad, dear, shall we talk business?'

'Are you—seething with anger?' Brad said as they walked back to the office.

'No. Should I be?'

'Sonia can be a very reserved person, but she did express a desire to see Maddy.'

'She expressed an unspoken desire to reserve judgement,' Verity said coolly.

'I don't think she would go along with anything unjust,' he replied judicially.

Verity walked in silence for a time. Then she said, 'It doesn't matter to me one way or another.'

He stopped walking—they'd arrived at the office anyway—and said, staring down into her eyes, 'Did you love him, Verity?'

'Look,' she answered quite calmly, 'I apologise for airing all my dirty linen at your business lunch, but it doesn't give you the right to harass me for any further details. And would you mind if we got back to work? We have an appointment with the copy-editor in—exactly five minutes.'

'All right,' he returned obligingly. 'Perhaps now is not the time nor place. Like the cockatoo, I'll put that one on hold—I take it you are coming to Port Douglas, by the way?'

Verity took an exasperated breath. 'If I had any sense I'd run a mile,' she said crossly.

He stood back and smiled a shade maliciously. 'No one's stopping you.'

CHAPTER FOUR

THE *Queenslander* pulled out of Roma Street Station at ten past nine on the dot, not three, but four days later, which had given Verity the chance to spend the previous day with Maddy, but, apart from that, little chance to relax over the preceding days at all. In fact, she'd worked late every evening as the ideas she herself had activated had rolled off her boss's brain in a seething mass.

She grimaced as she sank down on to the comfortable seat of her double sleeper and watched the Brisbane suburbs roll by gently. There was no doubt that Brad had come up with three more hilarious scenarios for Len Pearson's Kneg, and there was equally no doubt that Len Pearson was absolutely delighted with the whole concept and was flying up to Port Douglas himself—a town not only dear to his heart because of his charter-boat fleet but also because he grew up there, and to have it as the background for his inventive genius was, to quote him, really tickling him pink. It was not only tickling him pink, Verity mused wryly, it was also loosening his purse-strings quite amazingly, for they were having to fly just about everything, including one bearded Scot, the real McCoy, into the little town for the making of the ads. Not that it was such a little town either any more, he'd assured Verity with palpable pride. With the opening of the Cairns International Airport only seventy miles away and the Port Douglas

Sheraton Mirage, together with its beautiful four-mile beach, its proximity to the Great Barrier Reef and the World-Heritage-listed Daintree Forest, it attracted tourists from all over the world yet still managed to retain its small-town charm.

'I wonder,' she murmured, and turned her head as her door clicked open.

'Wonder?' Brad Morris said, coming in and cocking an eyebrow at her. He'd reverted ever since the day they'd had lunch with Sonia Mallory to his casual attire.

'Nothing,' she said, and yawned.

He grinned. 'Know how you feel. Ever been on one of these before?'

'No. Only suburban trains.' It amazed her slightly that she suddenly didn't even have the energy to feel the usual wariness and annoyance with which she'd viewed this trip from the time it had been mooted, but the fact of the matter was that all she wanted to do was curl upon this comfortable seat and sleep like a log.

'Then I can demonstrate a few things to you. Take this notice, for example,' he said sternly and tapped it. 'Only the conductor can release the upper berth, and no one should be in the lower one when it's being done.'

'I can read, and I have no need of the upper berth.'

'All the same, don't even be tempted. Now here,' he tapped a panel and released it, 'is your wash-basin, your vanity mirror, et cetera, you can hang a few things up in here,' he opened and closed two doors, 'very few,' he added whimsically, 'and right beneath where you're sitting is a portable table that you pull out and stand up in this groove, so. There are two footstools, as you see, pillows up there, and, for complete privacy on the corridor side, this blind that you pull down. What else? Ah,' he turned in the small space, 'facilities. There's a shower in each carriage up that end and toilets at either end, Ladies' down that-away. We are about four cars away from the club car and the dining car, and morning tea will be served soon. And I am right next door, should you require any information about locomotives; it's an electric one at this stage, but we change to diesel at Rockhampton—— I don't think I've ever made you laugh before, Verity!'

Why she should find herself giggling like a schoolgirl was not altogether clear to Verity herself, but she couldn't deny that she was. 'I think,' she attempted to explain, 'it's because I've just realised you're something of a train buff, which is the last thing I would have thought. And something of a little boy about them, too.'

He sat down and stretched out his long legs. 'It never ceases to amaze me, the curious things you believe of me, but yes, I do love trains, they—relax me. It was also an ambition of mine once to be an engine driver.'

'I see what you mean about being relaxing,' she murmured, turning her head to the window. 'I don't know how I'm going to keep my eyes open.'

'Come and have tea first—then I'll leave you alone until lunch.'

He was as good as his word, and after tea she watched the lush, hilly countryside of the Sunshine Coast hinterland pass by with its variety of flowering subtropical trees, banana and pineapple plantations, and those unusual formations known as the Glasshouse

Mountains. She even managed to stay awake until lunchtime and couldn't help being most favourably impressed by the *Queenslander*'s cuisine. She had a seafood platter for lunch that was fresh and excellent and most artistically served. But it and a glass of wine took their toll, and, as the landscape gradually changed to the more common Australian variety of grass and gum-trees, back in her cabin she stretched out and fell dreamlessly asleep.

It was five o'clock when Brad woke her, knocking on her door. She sat up, looked around dazedly then let him in, still flushed from sleep and still looking dazed. He grinned and set the tray he was carrying down on the table.

'Lie back again,' he advised. 'It doesn't do to wake up too quickly. I've brought us a sundowner.'

She grimaced down at her crumpled jeans and ran a hand through her hair, and subsided obediently, although not full-length, and not because she was being obedient. 'I feel awful!'

'One usually does after sleeping during the day on top of a big meal. Unfortunately you can't run it off because we don't stop anywhere long enough until after dinner, but this is the next best thing.' He handed her a glass and sat down himself.

'What is it?'

'Vodka and lime basically. It's my own concoction, a guaranteed pick-me-up that I've perfected over the years. Cheers!'

Verity stared at the tall frosted glass suspiciously, then thought, What the hell? and sipped it. It tasted delicious. She took another sip and sat up.

'See what I mean?'

She had to laugh. 'Can you also guarantee that it won't have me falling flat on my face?'

'Not if you take it slowly. What will complete the cure is a shower and a change before dinner.'

Verity groaned.

'Now, that we *will* be able to walk off, as I mentioned. We stop at Rockhampton for twenty-five minutes. Do you know what they used to call Rocky?'

'No. Tell me,' Verity invited.

He looked at her with a wicked little glint. 'A city of sin, sweat and sorrow. I believe it's improved over the years.'

'I'm glad to hear it.'

They were silent for a time, sipping their drinks idly and watching the sunset cast its pink glow over the landscape while the wheels clicked rhythmically over the rails, until Verity said, unthinkingly, 'This was a better idea than I would have believed.'

He turned his head and studied her comprehensively, with a different glint in his eyes this time. 'Most of my ideas are.'

She tried to regroup her thoughts as she felt her skin prickle beneath that grey gaze. 'I meant, I could become a fan of train travel. That's all.'

'What did you think I meant?'

She swallowed some vodka and lime. Then she sighed and laid her head back. 'I thought you might have meant... something along the hoary old lines of *you* knowing what's better for me than *I* do. You would be wrong, Brad.'

His lips twisted. 'Would I? I wonder. But anyway,' he shrugged, 'that's a first. Nearly two years to get one use of my name,' he marvelled. 'You really can't accuse me of being a fast worker, Verity.'

'I wish——' She stopped and bit her lip.

'That I wouldn't joke about it? Then I shall desist,' he said gravely.

'I wish you'd *forget* about it. We might even end up friends, that way.'

'I hesitate to mention it, but in this case you brought the subject up, not me, Verity.'

'Boloney,' she muttered. 'You *looked* at me...'

He stretched his legs out sideways and made himself even more comfortable. 'That's interesting. I mean, that you can interpret my looks so accurately. Wouldn't you say it indicated a certain similarity of thought processes? As if we are of the same mind about some things?' he added softly but with his eyes alive and dancing with dangerous little sparks.

'My dear Mr...my dear Brad,' she rephrased coolly, 'all it indicates is that most women can recognise when they are being mentally undressed by a man.'

He laughed and raised his glass in a salute to her. 'I was right about these, wasn't I?' he also said. 'It's quite restored you. And, on the subject of mentally undressing you, I have to be perfectly honest, Verity, and admit that it's becoming a bit of a problem.' He paused. 'I suppose if I told you you have the kind of figure that lends itself to that kind of thing you would take instant umbrage and you'd tell me you can't be held responsible for your body but,' he said humorously, 'there is——'

'Don't go on,' Verity interrupted wearily, and added with asperity, 'You and my mother make a good pair!'

He looked genuinely surprised. 'We agree on that subject?'

'On the subject of—men will be men and even *nice* ones should be allowed a pass or two because they can't help themselves,' she said tartly.

He lifted an amazed eyebrow. 'You actually told your mother what happened? She didn't appear to know, though.'

'Of course I didn't tell her,' Verity said impatiently. 'She... guessed.'

'After she met me?'

Verity looked at him darkly. 'If you're going to say that she must have concluded you're a nice man, she did. She's also one of those people who believes *most* people are nice, so don't get too carried away about it.'

'I'm suitably demolished,' he murmured.

'And I'm the Queen of England,' Verity replied witheringly.

He rested his head on his hand and studied his drink for a time, until eventually he said idly, 'Of course, that's not the problem.'

'What isn't? I don't know what you're talking about,' she said, but with less asperity, mainly because some curious instinct was prompting her to defuse her emotions—or perhaps it was the vodka, she reflected rather wryly.

'Those wandering impulses even nice men are subject to,' he said thoughtfully, 'as I was about to postulate before you cut me down—verbally this time, which, I suppose, I should be grateful for, although,' he mused, 'you're very handy with your verbs, so I don't know why I should be that grateful, but it probably is less dangerous than having things thrown at one.'

She grimaced, because she'd obviously left her decision to defuse things until too late, and said with what she hoped was a nice touch of boredom, 'I still don't know what you're talking about—not that it matters.'

'Well, it matters to me—it's my reputation that's at stake, after all——'

'I would have thought you'd be content,' she cut in swiftly, completely unable to help herself, 'to rest on my mother's judgement of you. There certainly can be no kinder interpretation that I can think of, even if she's quite wrong!'

'Don't work yourself up, Verity,' he advised. 'Have some more vodka——'

'Look,' she ran a hand through her hair, 'I just don't know why we have to indulge in this adolescent sort of... mating talk!'

'Ah,' he said mildly, but his eyes mocked her, 'at least you recognise it for what it is. But, while mating rituals might have become more civilised—I'm not about to club you on the head and drag you by the hair to my cave—the primitive urge can be less susceptible to civilisation, I'm sure. Adolescent?' He smiled at her, a dangerous little movement of his lips. 'Do you mean unspecific? Then I'll try to remedy that—I was trying to make myself clear anyway. You are not the subject of wandering impulses of the nice kind from my point of view, Verity. I want you—I want to take you to bed, to be *perfectly* specific, and I'd be extremely surprised if you didn't want it too. But I must say in my defence that I've seen hundreds of pretty girls with great figures and, beyond doing what your mother is quite right about occasionally, it's a totally different thing from this. In other words, dear Verity, it's the sum total of *you*, not just your stunning body. And, to further establish my bona fides,' he drained his glass and stood up, 'I'm prepared to wait before I make any more real gestures of the—mating kind until you're prepared to confide in me about your traumatic marriage. Finish your drink; I'll put the tray outside the door,' he added.

Verity stared up at him with such a conflict of emotions chasing through her eyes that he laughed softly, removed the two-thirds-empty glass from her fingers and said softly, 'I think I'll have it before you're tempted to throw it.'

'You're...' But she couldn't go on.

He raised an eyebrow and said with tormenting gravity, 'Not nice at all? Perhaps not, but I don't think niceness really enters this arena. No,' he reflected, 'there's a magnificence about it that goes way beyond anything as pallid as niceness. Why don't you ask yourself why you're in such a magnificent rage, after all?' he suggested. 'I suggest we have dinner at six-thirty. So why don't you also use the shower first? I'll be having a cold one, incidentally. Maybe you should too.'

The shower was steel-lined, the water was lovely and hot, and it was quite an experience on a speeding train going around a series of bends. It also proved to be of assistance to Verity in controlling her temper and dealing with the shocking discovery that she would very much like to scream and scratch as well as throw things.

And, on returning to her cabin, she locked herself in securely, pulled all the blinds down and had a serious heart-to-heart chat with herself as she dressed.

But, despite the palliatives she offered herself and all the insults she offered her boss, she finally sat down rather forlornly and knew she had to acknowledge at least one thing: those minutes she'd spent in Brad Morris's arms, being kissed and kissing in return, had been—breathtaking...

She lay back with her eyes closed and, for the first time since it had happened, allowed herself to remember it all. And it was no consolation to find that the fierce resistance and will-power she'd used to block it out of her mind, the anger and blame she'd directed at him—none of those things had the power to diminish the recollection; the way the fine hairs of her body stood up and her nipples tingled told their own tale.

She took several deep breaths and got up to pour herself a glass of water. 'All right. All right,' she whispered, 'he got you in the end. And, if you're completely honest, the only way you can block the effect he has on you is by attacking and being angry all the time—and even that may be a curious form of provocation. You wouldn't be here, stuck on a train with him, miles from anywhere, otherwise. You would have left him, and no amount of persuasion would have made you change your mind. So what does it all mean?'

She sat down again and hugged herself almost protectively and stared at nothing in particular for a long time. 'I'll tell you what it means, Verity,' she said to herself suddenly. 'This has happened to you before. This kind of sensual betrayal, even just possessing a body like this. And look where it got you. Into an abyss of misery you didn't, at times, ever think you'd be able to climb out of. You'd be mad if you ever trusted it again. And while we're on the subject,' she added to herself with a bitter little smile, 'after nearly two years of treating me like a—well, the way I wanted to be treated, but all the same, why is Brad Morris suddenly possessed of this... urge to take me to bed, let's be *specific*?'

She didn't have to articulate the answer, it was so obvious. All she had to do was call to mind Primrose Carpenter's exquisite features.

Then she shrugged and decided what she needed to do next was formulate a plan of action for the next week, let alone how to deal with being closeted on this train with him. And that provoked a spark of anger, although she refused to allow it to mushroom into anything more. But really, she did think, he always intended to use this train trip for these purposes. How low is that?

In the absence of any knock on her door at six-thirty, she took herself down to the dining car and discovered the object of her scorn already in the club car and looking at his watch.

'Ah. Thought you might be going to skip dinner, Verity,' he murmured, and added with a roving glance over her fresh grey linen trousers and ivory knitted top, 'You look very nice.'

Verity smiled—well, it felt more like baring her teeth, to be truthful—and murmured, 'Flattery will get you nowhere, Brad.'

He raised an eyebrow but merely returned, 'After you. I've been able to secure a table for two. Aren't we lucky the train isn't full this trip? It usually is.'

'Very lucky.'

He grinned.

* * *

But as they sat opposite each other, separated by the white napery, gleaming silver and glass, it was as if Brad Morris had also formulated a new plan. In other words, he set out to be a charming companion, introduced no sexual overtones—it was she who did that unwittingly—into the conversation, and was almost impossible to resist without Verity's resembling a sullen boor. Of course, the attractive stewardesses were also having a hard time resisting him, and their service was little short of inspired.

'Do they know who you are?' Verity queried at one point.

He shook his head. 'I prefer to travel incognito.'

'That seems a bit sneaky,' Verity commented.

'It's actually the other way around—it obviates the possibility of bribery and corruption.'

'Are you travelling under an assumed name, then? I should have thought the whole country would prick up its ears at the mention of Morris in a travel context.'

He laughed. 'I'm not that famous, although I do get recognised from time to time.'

'I see.'

He looked at her interrogatively. 'What does that mean?'

She looked down at her cheese platter then up into his eyes with a faint, wry smile. 'I was just—well, contemplating the nature of certain things.'

'You're going to have to be more specific than that, Verity,' he said amusedly.

'Well, why these girls should be fluttering around you like moths, for example.'

He grimaced. Then he shrugged and smiled a devilish little smile. 'Search me, Verity. Perhaps their antennae have picked up that I know how to treat women? That I like them and respect them and often regard their bodies as works of art. It certainly can't be my looks,' he said virtuously. 'I know I'm no oil-painting.'

'Yes, well, I guess I walked into that one,' Verity conceded, plucking a bloomy red grape and popping it into her mouth.

'You know,' he leant back thoughtfully and twirled his glass, 'anyone would think I was the only man who'd ever undressed you mentally. I mention it only since *you* expressed the desire to discuss the nature of certain things, of course. I had planned to avoid the subject altogether for a time.'

'I've just lost that desire,' Verity said lightly. 'Apologies for...' She gestured.

He regarded her with a curiously unsmiling glance for a moment. Then he said, 'Should we have our coffee and a liqueur at the bar? And I thought, after Rockhampton—where you could ring your mother if you wanted to, incidentally—we might... do a bit of work?'

Verity held his gaze with a narrowed glance of her own. 'Why not?' she said at last.

Maddy was fine, so was Lucy, and both thrilled to hear from her so far away. And, due to Brad's knowledge of the train-travelling public's habits—he'd made sure they'd got off as soon as the train had stopped and were first at the public phones before the queue formed—they still had twenty minutes to exercise.

'I really need this,' Verity said as they strode briskly down the platform in the cool, late May night air.

'So do I. You're a fast walker, Mrs Wood.'

'I was once a fast runner, at school. Oh, look, you were right! They're changing the engine.'

'I've mentioned this before, but I'm often right. Tell me,' he went on hastily, 'about your childhood.'

She shrugged. 'There's not a lot to tell. My father died when I was four, I have two older sisters, one lives in Hong Kong and one in Perth, which really kept my mother on the trot as the various grandchildren were born, until, well...' She tailed off.

'You needed help with Maddy?'

They came to the end of the platform, and Verity turned abruptly. 'Something like that.'

'Where was your mother when you first needed help so desperately and the Woods wouldn't come to the party? Doing the rounds of the other grandchildren?'

'She was in Hong Kong. My sister there was having a very difficult pregnancy, besides hating the place and finding it difficult to come to terms with the fact that her husband would always want to be roaming around the world,' she finished in an end-of-subject tone of voice.

'All right,' he said mildly.

But Verity stopped suddenly and stared at the sad little tableau being enacted on the platform. Two policemen and a policewoman were escorting a passenger off the second-class section of the train, a girl in her late teens or very early twenties, crying helplessly while the policewoman carried what was obviously her baby. 'What are they doing?' she whispered.

Brad sighed. 'She was smoking marijuana. They were afraid she wouldn't be able to look after the baby, let alone herself, so they had to call ahead for assistance.'

'How do you know?'

'I was talking the train manager before dinner.'

Verity closed her eyes and turned away. And, as if it was the most natural thing in the world, he put his arm around her shoulders. 'Does it bring back—memories?'

'It shouldn't. I never resorted to drugs, and who knows what her circumstances are? But—if she's alone and trying to cope...'

'You know how she feels. Do you think I don't feel sad, watching something like that?'

Verity raised her eyes to his, and what she saw and felt was like a blow to her heart. What she saw in his eyes was the weary sombreness of someone who did feel compassion for other human beings, despite their weaknesses. What she felt was the almost overwhelming urge to rest gratefully in his arms and to submit not only to that compassion but also to anything else he cared to do to her. She was, she discovered, achingly aware of him again, and she had to wonder how she could ever have pretended to herself that he did not attract her, that his cleverness did not intrigue her, that you couldn't know him without knowing he'd be a superb lover even before you'd felt his hands on your breasts... How it was suddenly so tempting to think that this might be different.

She turned away abruptly and stumbled.

'Verity.' He took her hand and swung her back. 'Tell me.'

'No. I mean, it's nothing,' she said raggedly. 'I think we're about to leave. Let's...get to work. On second thoughts, I've got more than enough I can do on my own, so—I'll say goodnight.'

He stared down at her, taking in her unusual lack of colour and agitated eyes, and she couldn't tell what he was thinking at all. But finally he released her hand and said, 'Off you go, then. Goodnight.'

She did work very late for two reasons: to take her mind off Brad Morris and to make sure that she slept. But what she couldn't take her mind off was how she was going to cope with the next day. They didn't reach Cairns, the end of the line, until late afternoon, and then they had an hour's drive to Port Douglas. But surely, she thought, once we're there the pressure will ease a bit? At least the *proximity* must.

In fact, the pressure eased the next day, although not the proximity. But her boss, for reasons best known to himself, was in a businesslike mood for most of the day, thereby lulling Verity into a false sense of security. But also causing her to again feel that cold little void, which in turn was the cause of some bitter self-directed mockery.

'I think that just about sums it all up,' she said that afternoon. 'I'm still worried about a couple of things, but they're outside my jurisdiction, I guess.'

'What are you worried about?'

'The weather, for one thing,' she said wryly. 'It's all very well, talking about filming boating segments, or any outdoor segments, for that matter, but the weather is always a hazard. And it's raining in Cairns, at least,' she added.

'How do you know that?'

'I listened to the weather report on the radio.' She indicated the one built into the wall. They were in his cabin, which was surprisingly tidy. Whatever else he wasn't, Brad Morris was obviously an organised traveller, with all his belongings fitted into one small grip.

'What would I do without you?' he murmured. 'But it never pays to worry too much about anything, you know. We will find a way.'

'You mean, I will have to find a way,' she said a shade tartly. 'The last time we were held up by weather, you and the film crew played cards and left me to deal with all the postponements and cancellations and rebookings—I know,' she gestured, 'it's my job, but I was a nervous wreck by the time it was finally done.'

He looked amused. 'You didn't show it.'

She turned her head away and stared out of the window. They were deeply into sugar-cane country by now, so the view was rather monotonous, but just at that moment she felt as if she could watch it all day—at least it was a respite from the turmoil of her emotions. What was to cause her some surprise was the fact that this was not obvious—that her emotions were in turmoil despite certain resolves she'd made overnight.

'What are you thinking, Verity?' he queried after a few minutes.

She schooled her expression and turned back. 'Nothing much.'

'Is that going to be the answer, do you think?'

She licked her lips but refused to be put out by the narrowed, rather autocratic way of old he was looking at her. 'I don't know what you mean.'

His eyes glinted sardonically. 'That you're going to try to—blank yourself off from this. I can't help wondering what tactics you employ—with yourself, I mean—and perhaps I should warn you that such rigidly self-imposed celibacy on someone who is not of a truly celibate nature can have harmful side-effects.'

Her eyes glinted gold but she restrained herself. 'You can make as much fun of me as you like...' She shrugged.

'I was merely offering advice.'

She smiled faintly. 'I wonder how many men over the millenia have offered that particular bit of advice,' she mused. 'But then again you did tell me once you had a penchant for the hackneyed, didn't you?'

'And *you* once, Verity, melted into my arms and kissed me about as deeply as I've ever been kissed, and you moved your body against mine with a kind of yearning, and you gasped with sheer delight when——'

'Stop it!' she commanded, her eyes now a blazing, angry gold. 'I have no idea what makes you think you have the right to torment me like this——'

'Because it is a torment,' he said with soft mockery and suddenly looking quite relaxed. 'For both of us. That's why——'

'All right!' she flashed. 'So I did...I did what I did, but you're also right about something else! Even hardened celibates probably find times when the flesh is weaker than the spirit—that's all that happened to me, and not without considerable pressure, may I remind you, from you. And considerable expertise, I have no doubt,' she said scathingly. 'But the only conclusion to be drawn from that is—I'm not a block of wood.'

'Are you saying I could seduce a block of wood?' he drawled. 'I doubt it——'

'Oh!' Verity ground her teeth and stood up. 'Stop...'

'Stop working you into a rage, Verity?' he said softly and eyed her quizzically.

'Yes.' She bit her lip but couldn't help adding a little helplessly, 'You really—you really *enjoy* it!'

'I sure do. I'd hate to see you going back to the petrified and perfect Mrs Wood!'

'But we can't—I can't go on like this!' she protested angrily. 'It's just not fair——'

'Maybe. It's not necessary either,' he said with a shrug.

She stared at him. 'And I know what your solution is—don't bother to enlighten me, but the answer is no! How many times do I have to say it?'

'I had in mind another solution for this impasse, Verity,' he murmured. 'It's not new, but during the course of last night and this uncomfortable day my feelings that it is the solution have strengthened. I really think you should tell me about your marriage. Confide in me, in other words. Ever done that?' He lifted an eyebrow at her. 'And then,' he continued, 'we might be able to make a rational and mutual decision as to whether there is any hope for the attraction between us, the mutual attraction, my lovely block of wood,' he said precisely and with no small tinge of irony.

CHAPTER FIVE

'THIS is it?' Verity looked around incredulously.

They'd arrived in Port Douglas after being met in Cairns and driven up by a representative of Len Pearson's charter-boat company in a company four-wheel-drive vehicle. This was standard practice, apparently, for clients of the company to be so met and transported, and Len Pearson had insisted that they avail themselves of the facility. It had been too dark to make much of the scenery along the way or Port Douglas itself, but it could be truly said that the room she now stood blinking on the threshold of in the Club Tropical complex was stunning.

Club Tropical was a new hotel in Port Douglas, Len Pearson had explained in the course of one of his lengthy telephone conversations with Verity. And, wonderful as the Sheraton Mirage was, Club Tropical had the advantage of being in the heart of town, of being very comfortable and modern—indeed, quite imaginative, he'd said with a chuckle, I do advise you to stay there, Mrs Wood, I'm sure Mr Morris will love it...

'This is the Bali Suite, Mrs Wood,' the manager of Club Tropical said proudly to Verity. 'We've put Mr Morris in the Reef Suite.'

'Mr Morris' was, in fact, leaning against the doorframe, behind the manager, laughing silently as the manager proceeded to draw Verity into the room and demonstrate all the virtues of the Bali Suite. He was

A DANGEROUS LOVER

still laughing, but only with his eyes, when the manager left them, having been assured that Mr Morris, whose Reef Suite was right next door, didn't need a guided tour of his facilities.

And he straightened and murmured as the door closed, 'Verity, if you could see your face...'

She tightened her lips and turned away from him exasperatedly.

'What's wrong with it?' he queried then. 'I think it's quite wonderful—a marvellous four-poster bed, complete with draperies,' he gestured towards the bed, 'sumptuous couches, rugs and delightful artefacts, discreet lighting, a subtle blending of colours—pinks and brown and cane—fans and screens, your own louvred patio on to the jungle and just about every mod con, including a video and CD-player and a spacious and luxurious bathroom. I don't understand your reservations.'

'Then I'll tell you,' Verity said precisely and unwisely. 'If ever I've seen a setting more geared towards seduction I can't call it to mind, and if that's what *you* had in mind——'

'I had nothing to do with it!' he protested and started to laugh again. '*You* booked it——'

'Only on Len Pearson's advice,' she shot back. 'I had no idea...it was like this.'

'Perhaps that's what *he* had in mind, then,' he drawled. 'I believe he is due to descend on us some time or another. But how come your thoughts are so irrevocably tuned in to seduction, Verity? I mean, I will admit it would be a nice place to seduce someone in, but to be hit on the head by that very thought the moment you laid eyes on the place is—a little curious, wouldn't you believe?'

'Go away,' Verity said through her teeth. 'Go away before I brain you with one of these delightful artefacts. And don't dare show me your face until tomorrow morning because I would be—it would make me quite sick!'

Of course, he didn't go immediately. He strolled up to her instead and took her wrist and said with sudden dispassion, 'For someone with a name like yours, you display a remarkable disregard for the truth, *Verity*. Have a pleasant evening.' And he released her wrist and left leisurely.

Verity stared at the closed door and then did something totally out of character. She threw herself down on the magnificent four-poster bed, clutched the wonderful pillow in the shape of a butterfly, and had a good, old-fashioned cry.

Presently, and not feeling much better, she got up and unpacked her things and had a long soak in the bath that was the size of a spa. Then she ordered herself something to eat, which she only picked at, and finally, and disconsolately, she went to bed.

She woke at dawn, looked through her 'jungle'—in fact, a wide tropical window-box backed by the leafy environment of Club Tropical—and knew that she desperately needed some exercise. She pulled on jeans, trainers and a white sweater and slipped down the cool, tiled corridors and across the water gardens out into the street.

Club Tropical faced a park that was bounded by the port inlet and the sea, and the grass was wet with dew, there were some wonderful, huge old trees and a sense of freshness and serenity that was something of a balm to her troubled soul. There was also not another person in sight as she explored the park and then the main street of what could still be called, she decided, a rather charming small town. A mixture of old and new, and different, she reflected. It was a while before she could pin down the difference; then she realised it was to do with being in far north Queensland, being in the tropics probably, which laid its own stamp of individuality on things. Such as a warmth in the air, despite its being winter, and the knowledge that this warmth could become a tormenting heat in summer; the lush, tropical vegetation and prolific birdlife, the realisation, she was sure, that life would be lived much more slowly up here. This thought caused her to grimace, and as she walked back past the old wooden pub opposite Club Tropical she advised herself to have her wits about her.

She reinforced this advice with a spa and a brisk swim in the hotel pool before breakfast, and she was feeling considerably better when her boss made his appearance in the Bali Suite—she was on the phone and already drawing together the threads of the operation, as she thought of it, when he tried her door, found it unlocked and walked in.

And one look at his expression was enough to tell her that she might need more than her wits about her today—she would probably need all William Morris's virtues of a saint and the discipline of a brigadier-general rolled into one. Good, she thought with a flicker of humour as she turned away wordlessly while he helped himself to a cup of the coffee she'd brewed—Club Tropical provided not only a coffee maker but fresh beans and a grinder—good. I can handle him like this.

Little to know how wrong she could be.

* * *

By the evening of the next day she was in no doubt at all, though. Not only had just about everything that could go wrong gone wrong, but Brad's irritability, which had a low threshold at best, had become little short of catastrophic. But not only that... Where before she'd coped with these situations, not exactly blithely but with assurance and competence, now, despite every effort, she too was tense, and no amount of advising herself helped. And, if anything could be worse than all that, she knew why she was so tense. Not because he was irritable and impossible, not because some essential camera equipment had disappeared into the vast maw of the commercial-airline system and one of the camera crew come out in a mysterious rash which proved to be chicken-pox, to name but a few of the disasters that had befallen them, but because of her new and intolerable awareness of Brad Morris as a potential lover.

She couldn't believe what was happening to her. How could she be struck breathless and lose the thread of what she was saying and doing just by catching sight of his hands or watching him stride across a street? Even worse was the discovery that, while he appeared tall and gangly in his clothes, without them, in the swimming-pool, his body, still tanned from his sojourn in the Whitsundays, was finely made and discreetly muscled, with wide shoulders and narrow hips—and a joy to behold, she thought bleakly once as she watched him surface and pull himself out of the pool with the grace and strength of someone superbly fit.

The other goad to her flesh was the way, unless it was absolutely necessary, he ignored her and treated her as if she were a robot, and she couldn't help herself from raging inwardly about it even while she knew it was only a slightly ostentatious display—had she not indicated that that was how she more or less wanted to be treated?

In her later, saner moments she admitted to herself that it all had to come to a head. At the time, however, on that third evening when they got in from an abortive day's shooting, when she was tired and wet, it had started to rain, and she longed for a bath and a chance to sit down, she couldn't imagine what prompted her to bring it to a head; in fact, it all bubbled up and there didn't seem to be a thing she could do about it.

Because as Brad came into the Bali Suite behind her, slammed the door and opened his mouth to say something damning and cutting, she had no doubt, she turned on him like an angry lioness and hissed, 'Don't say a word! If you're going to blame me because anything resembling a boat makes him seasick——'

'I am,' he countered curtly. 'Why didn't you check?'

'Because it didn't enter my head!' she all but shouted. 'I checked his bagpipe-playing ability, his Scots accent, I checked that he owned a kilt and all the paraphernalia that goes with it—I even got you a redheaded one with a red beard, since you're so hooked on redheads. The last thing that occurred to me was that a man built like an ox would...go to water like a kitten once you got him in a boat!'

'You can't help seasickness or a fear of the sea, and you're mixing your metaphors,' he said coldly. 'Look, you goofed; why not admit it?'

It was the last straw. 'If that's how you feel, see how you get along without me, then,' she blazed.

There was a moment's silence as they stared at each other, he with his eyes dark and moody, she suddenly looking white and exhausted and unaware that her thin blue blouse was moulded rather revealingly to her figure. Then he moved his shoulders restlessly and said drily, 'That old gauntlet? It's becoming a bit of a paper tiger, isn't it? How many times are you going to hold me up to ransom——?'

'I'm *not*——'

'Oh, yes, you are, my dear. And all because you *can't* cut the last tie and walk away.'

'No,' Verity whispered and put the back of her hand to her mouth.

'Yes,' he insisted. 'Why do you think we're fighting over something that should be quite funny really? I mean, you're right in some respects. He is built like an ox, he has legs like tree stumps and he'd be the last person you'd want to meet in a bad temper on a dark night. So this inordinate fear of the sea and boats is—well, it shouldn't be so hard to see the funny side of it, with all due respect to his feelings.'

'You were the one who just said I'd "goofed"...'

'Because I'm suffering from the same problem, Verity,' he said deliberately. 'The only difference is, I'm not trying to hide behind a façade of pretence and indifference. A façade, moreover, that does your intelligence and integrity no credit. No, don't,' he gestured as she tried to speak, 'don't give me the old platitude about that being a typical male sentiment over the *millenia* or whatever. Surely we're two adults who can be honest with each other if nothing else? Or are you as rigid and restricted in your thinking to really believe that all men are the same? If I was to generalise about women like that I can just imagine your scorn.'

She took her hand away. 'You...you have some pretty rigid theories on truly beautiful women,' she said huskily.

'Ah, Primrose.' He smiled without humour. 'What I neglected to tell you is that her earl is twenty-five years older than she is, she will be his third wife, neither of the others being deceased and she's the same age as his eldest daughter—would you, in all honesty, be uncritical and not question her motives in a situation like that?'

Verity turned away abruptly, buried her face in her hands briefly, then turned back and said starkly, 'All right. All right. I'll tell you what it was like, and why I'm the way I am; then you might *understand*...'

He started to say something, paused, then said quietly, 'Have a shower and get changed first. You're soaked. I'll make us some coffee in the meantime.'

'So are you.'

'Not really. Well,' he grimaced down at himself, 'I'll change my shirt. Go ahead.'

She showered and donned her jeans and the white jumper she'd worn earlier. Then she stared at herself in the mirror as she heard him move around, making the coffee, and saw that the tension was still there in her eyes and her mouth and that she looked a bit pale so that the golden red of her hair appeared darker; and it occurred to her that she had never really confided in anyone, not the sordid details of it all—was that what he would expect to hear? she wondered. And would it be good for her? Or would it lead to other things that only a fool would get involved in?

* * *

'So, where to start?' she said brightly, sitting with her bare feet curled beneath her in a corner of one of the couches, a cup of coffee in her hands. He was about as far away as he could be on the opposite couch and he'd changed into a cotton-knit top and brushed his hair. His feet were also bare, and he'd adjusted the lighting so that it was soft and gentle and closed the glass doors leading to the louvred patio, thereby closing out the sound of the rain.

'At the beginning,' he suggested.

'The beginning was quite commonplace,' she said drily. 'Boy meets girl—well,' she conceded, 'Barry was charming, good-looking, and he had an aura of sophistication, although he was only a year older, that intrigued me. I've asked myself many a time whether it was his money that also intrigued me, and I can't deny that it was pleasant to be driven around in a sports car and taken to good restaurants, to actually be able to go to concerts and sporting events, not just watch them on television, even,' she grimaced, 'to be the object of envy among members of my own sex, but he also had a laid-back approach to life that was...' She shrugged. 'Life wasn't easy for us after my father died—I don't mean it was joyless. My mother is the kind of person who can breathe joy even into the sort of genteel poverty we lived in, but we always had to be so careful, so Barry's attitude was actually refreshing.' She broke off and glanced across at Brad. 'That might be hard to understand unless you've worn hand-me-downs, et cetera, et cetera,' she said ruefully.

'Go on,' he responded idly.

She sipped her coffee then put the cup down. 'It didn't seem to be long after we'd met that I...began to think I was in love with him. But I was very cautious, and for a time he went along with it. Then... things,' she plaited her fingers, 'began to get out of hand, and it became harder and harder to say no, and that was when I made a tactical error: I told him I didn't believe in love without marriage, and he pointed out the difficulties of a nineteen-year-old and a twenty-year-old getting married against their parents' wishes, and we had a blazing row—several—and he said finally that I was being ridiculous, and I said if he thought that then we'd better not see each other again, so we didn't for about a month... And I was miserable and I couldn't help wondering if I was being ridiculous, but I was also piqued because he'd never taken me to meet his parents. For some reason I had it in the back of my mind that it would make things more proper if his parents approved of me, that an intimate relationship might be on the cards then, but anyway,' she gestured, 'he came back and said he couldn't live without me, so marriage it would be, and I... I went out and did it. Without my mother's knowledge too. You must,' she smiled painfully, 'be wondering what kind of an idiot I was.'

He considered. 'I think it's one of our age-old dilemmas. How to protect young people who have all the feelings of adults but not the wisdom from those kind of mistakes. I mean, you obviously had a good Christian upbringing that was at odds with these liberated times.'

'Kind words; thanks,' she murmured.

It was his turn to smile. 'You also, at nineteen and carefree, spirited, possibly,' his lips twisted, 'a bit headstrong, with a stunning figure and legs like...' he gestured '... would be enough to turn even Barry

Wood's head, despite what he must have known would be his parents' reaction. My dear, you're right, it's a commonplace story because so many of us are just human.'

She laid her head back and sighed. 'But to be *so* blind.'

'You mean about his drinking?'

'Mmm... as well as everything else.' She lifted her head and looked at him. 'I must admit, I was a bit amazed at how much they all drank at first, his crowd, but he never seemed to have any trouble holding it and I suppose I put it down—my amazement—to a lack of sophistication—do you know, he started drinking when he was fifteen? No, you wouldn't, of course, but I really didn't have any idea that whenever he was depressed or frustrated he would literally try to drown it all in alcohol.'

There was a long silence. Then Verity sat up and said briskly, 'I suppose the rest is not hard to guess.'

'No. An unplanned pregnancy,' he raised an eyebrow at her and she nodded, 'his parents' reaction, his allowance cut off—that kind of thing?' Again she nodded. 'I suppose the gradual slide towards him turning violent was only a matter of time. Is that why Maddy doesn't trust men?'

'Yes,' Verity whispered and cleared her throat. 'That was another mistake I made. To let it go on for so long, to ever have let myself live in hope that I could change him. I even threw up college and worked at anything I could get so he could finish his degree and so that what little money he did have we could save towards a home.'

'How long did it go on for? The physical violence?'

'He only attacked me twice; unfortunately, Maddy was old enough the second time to have some understanding of what was going on, and fortunately I had the sense then to just... leave. But that's not the only kind of violence, is it?' She looked away and shrugged. 'I have to admit there were times when I indulged in forms of mental cruelty.'

'But—was your mother away all that time?' he queried with a frown.

Verity realised her fingers were still plaited and she unwound them slowly. 'No. If there's one thing that's harder to admit than admitting to yourself you've made a dreadful mistake, it's admitting it to a parent, I've decided. I think it's the guilt, so I tried to brazen it out—well, pretend everything was fine.'

'But——'

'No, Brad,' she stood up and looked through the glass doors, 'it's not possible to tell yourself you're entirely blameless of a serious error of judgement if nothing else. You can't blame it all on being nineteen and a bit headstrong or having a mixed-up set of values, not that kind of disaster.'

'And you don't admit that most people make mistakes?' he queried.

She turned slowly and stared at him for a full minute, with her eyes golden and shadowed, before she said evenly, 'Yes, I do. You see, it's because I know what mine were, that I—am determined not to make the same ones again. I'm not, in fact, as you seem to think, tarring all men with the same brush. I'm simply saying—certain things are not to be trusted. They can mislead you; they certainly misled me, anyway.'

'Ah,' he said slowly, 'I think I begin to see the problem. If you mean what I think you mean, about not being able to trust the sensual side of your nature,' he stopped and smiled faintly, 'join the club, Verity!'

She breathed exasperatedly. 'What do you mean?'

'Just that it's a notorious problem most people suffer from to a greater or lesser extent. What,' he looked at her quite seriously suddenly, 'you're discounting altogether, though, is that we make our mistakes and *learn* from them——'

'I've just told you I *have*,' she pointed out.

'No. You've told me that one mistake has caused you to block off all those very natural impulses and lose faith in them entirely—or at least try to block them off.'

'Brad,' she said very quietly, 'believe me, when you find yourself making up wild and implausible stories to explain away a black eye and a split lip not only is your self-esteem at rock bottom but also your faith in just about everything. But be that as it may, I'm not,' she said, paused, and went on with an effort, 'able to deny any more that I'm...affected by you. But the very way it sprang up out of...well, nothing, leads me to make two judgements.' She stopped and her lips moved into the semblance of a smile. 'Firstly, I'm not as immune to my hormones as I thought I was, and secondly, *you're* not as immune to losing Primrose as you might have thought you were. And that's...about all it amounts to.'

He stared at her narrowly. 'In other words, you think I'm on the rebound?'

She shrugged and nodded.

He swore beneath his breath, then said quite audibly with all his old arrogance and with almost tangible mockery, 'What do you propose we do about it, then, since you've set yourself up as such an expert on these matters?'

It stung, that mockery, she discovered, and she replied in kind without really thinking, 'Why don't you find someone else to—rebound upon? As a matter of fact, I could point out at least two girls who would be delighted to help you get over Primrose: the one in Len Pearson's charter-boat office—she's quite young, but obviously willing—and——'

'Fine. And what will you do?' he shot back. '*As* a matter of fact, I've thought of the perfect solution for you, Verity. Ever thought of taking a "toy-boy" lover? Someone who could help you with your hormones but whom *you* could lay down the law to, say, someone about twenty who you could dazzle with your wonderful legs and breasts—like the kid handling Len's boat today, for example. He couldn't take his eyes off you and all he wanted to do was fetch and carry for you all day—yep, I reckon you could handle him, Verity, and a short interlude with him might just be what you——' He stopped only as she went to hit him, and deftly gathered both her wrists in his hands in an unbreakable grip. 'Now, now, Verity,' he drawled, 'you should try to curb these violent impulses——'

'And you should curb your filthy insults,' she spat. 'Let me *go*.'

'In a moment. Why was my insult any less acceptable than yours? I would have thought we were advising each other to do exactly the same thing and you actually got your advice in first, dear Verity.'

She opened her mouth to dispute that anything she'd said could be as insulting as being advised to take a 'toy-boy' lover, but a sudden spark of honesty compelled her to admit that there was something in what he'd said...

She breathed deeply and tried to veil any acknowledgement of this revelation from her eyes. 'Just let me go,' she said tautly. 'If you think *this*,' her gaze swung to her wrists and back defiantly to his, 'kind of treatment is liable to advance your cause an inch, you haven't listened to a word I've said to you.'

His teeth glinted in a sudden, mocking little smile. 'You're not frightened of me, Verity,' he said softly. 'You know damned well I'm not about to resort to blacking your eyes. You're only afraid of yourself and living and loving and laughing again because you haven't got the guts to say to yourself, "OK, it happened, but that doesn't mean to say I have to spend the rest of my life like a zombie."' He opened his hands and she reacted like lightning.

She hit out at him, but because she lost her balance at the same time it wasn't that hard or accurate, and she would have fallen over if he hadn't grabbed her about the waist.

'So,' he drawled as she went still, 'I touched a nerve, did I? Let's see if I can do it again—I mean, channel all that furious, nervous energy more productively, or where it belongs, if nothing else.'

But Verity had come to her senses. 'Don't make me kiss you again,' she whispered, and hated herself for the pleading note in her voice.

'It's not a question of making you; I'm inviting you to reciprocate, that's all. It seems to be about the only thing left to do.'

'I hate you,' she said despairingly as he nuzzled the top of her head.

'I know,' he murmured, tilting her chin so that she could see the wicked little glint in his eye. 'Hate away. There are times when I'm in two minds about you. It doesn't seem to change this.' He touched his fingers to her mouth. 'Or the feel of you, the taste of you—which is beginning to haunt my waking and sleeping hours, believe me—the longing to slide my hands right up those long legs, to have time to undress you properly, not just mentally. Seeing you swimming is a special torment, incidentally, despite your very proper togs,' he said, and smiled slightly at the tremor that ran through her body. 'Can you imagine just the two of us in some very private pool late at night, swimming naked? And coming back to a bed like this, relaxed and refreshed?' He paused, and there was no amusement in his gaze as her eyes widened; then she fastened her teeth on her bottom lip. 'So, it's all still there and more so now, and it just won't go away, call it what you will. Is there anything you'd like to add?'

'I knew it!' a delighted voice said behind them, and Verity saw Brad's own teeth shut hard as she started convulsively before his hands fell away and he turned.

'Len,' he said flatly. 'Delighted you could come, but you really should knock, mate.'

Len Pearson was not one whit abashed. He advanced his bulky, balding, pink-jowled personage further into the Bali Suite, saying jovially, 'I did knock! Guess you two were too—er—preoccupied to hear me. But this is excellent!' He rubbed his hands together delightedly. 'I guessed the kind of problems you and Verity were having, you see, and I said to myself, I said, "Len, those two need a push in the right direction and I'll be damned if Club Tropical isn't the just the kind of wonderfully romantic place to do it." How right was I?' he queried ingeniously but didn't wait for a reply. 'Well, now that you've got that settled, boyo, I'm sure you'll be able to produce some stunning ads for me. I'm not too old to appreciate that when the fillies are proving troublesome it can put you off your work, your sleep and all sorts of things.' And, so saying, he gave Verity a paternal pat on the bottom. Then he added the straw that broke the camel's back. 'Your brother agrees with me, by the way. He said that in his opinion the one way to keep you happy was to keep Verity with you—and keep you happy too, of course,' he added to Verity.

Of course, Brad saw it coming, but he couldn't keep the reluctant amusement out of his eyes and he started to say something, but Verity beat him to it.

'I don't believe you,' she said to Len Pearson with magnificent, entirely unsimulated scorn and grabbed the back of the couch for support as every last little import of his words sunk in and her eyes started to burn that molten gold. 'What am I?' she demanded. 'Some carrot to be dangled in front of an unwilling horse? Some sort of,' her teeth chattered, 'c-concubine set out to tempt a jaded sheikh? Who gives a damn if he's happy? I don't, and I don't care if no one ever buys a Kneg or the Morris Agency goes out of business or all your charter boats sink and your frozen foods defrost at one and the same time. You can't *use* me like this! How *dare* you? As for you,' she turned to Brad, 'you put me in this impossible position. It's because of *you* that people are talking about me and...and...using me—I could kill you for that——'

'Verity,' he said grimly, 'where's your sense of humour? Gone west with all your other——?'

'Er—sorry to intrude,' yet another voice said, 'but the door was open.' They all swung round, and it was Bob, who was in charge of the filming operation. 'The thing is,' he continued, 'Hamish, our very own Scot, is in the process of putting together a blinder across the road.' He jerked a thumb in the direction of the pub. 'From the odd things he's said, I gather he's rather mortified about the number of times he threw up today. Especially in front of you, Mrs Wood. A bonny, bonny lass, he—er—called you, strong and shapely and a credit to some place called Lothian, if I've got it right. He believes your ancestors must have come from there anyway. And he seems also to think,' Bob paused and looked embarrassed, 'that you don't treat Mrs Wood properly, Brad. That you were *verry*,' he rolled his 'r's mightily, 'rude to her today.'

There was an incredulous silence. Then Brad drawled, 'You might have been right, Verity. For everyone's peace of mind, we'd have been better to leave you at home.'

CHAPTER SIX

'Mrs Wood—or may I call you Verity?'

'You can call me what you like, Mr Pearson.' It was the next morning, it was pouring, and Verity had just finished breakfast. She had no idea what had transpired with Hamish the night before and she had been just about to pick up the phone to organise transport for herself to Cairns, where she fully intended to catch a flight back to Brisbane.

'I would love a cup of coffee,' Len Pearson said, and sat down in the Bali Suite with every evidence of good humour as well as of being a man with a mission.

Verity sighed, then rose and poured him a cup.

'I came to apologise,' he said earnestly as she handed it to him.

'You don't need to.'

'I most certainly do. To make you feel like a carrot or a concubine was unforgivable!'

Verity winced inwardly—it was impossible not to see, although grimly, the humorous side of it when put like that. She shrugged. 'I probably over-reacted there, Mr Pearson. All the same——'

He sat forward. 'I've had an idea. It occurred to me that you all could do with a day off and that's what I'm going to give you. My yacht is moored in the marina, my crew is standing by——'

'A day off?' she said incredulously. 'Out on the water? Forgive me, Mr Pearson, but that would be like a day in purgatory. It's also raining, in case you hadn't noticed.'

'It will stop.'

Her eyes widened. 'I beg your pardon?'

He waved a large hand. 'I didn't grow up in this part of the world for nothing, Verity, and anyway, I contacted the lighthouse-keeper on the Low Isles and it's lovely out there. It would take us about an hour to get there and then we could have a picnic lunch on the beach, swim, snorkel—you name it, we could do it. I've even persuaded Hamish.'

'Hamish!' Verity raised her eyes heavenwards.

'Uh-huh. You see, it so happens that my mother was a MacDonald from Lothian—Edinburgh, to be precise—and we had a long chat last night about, well, all the things dear to Hamish's heart. What's more, he's now of a much *stouter* heart to do with all things maritime, and if we keep him busy enough and out in the fresh air enough I'm sure we can overcome his *mal de mer*. We might even, although it's ostensibly a holiday, get everyone relaxed enough to do a little shooting.'

'But he's bound to have a hangover—Hamish, I mean—and then there's——' She stopped a bit helplessly.

'Och, as they say back in the Lothians, Verity,' Len Pearson smiled widely, 'he has a very hard head, our Hamish, and I got to him before he did too much damage to it. He also is unaware that *you* might be aware of his sentiments, I've explained that Brad is a little temperamental, and I've sworn Bob to secrecy.'

Verity stared at him. 'You amaze me, Mr Pearson,' she murmured. 'And all in the cause of a Kneg.' She shook her head bewilderedly.

He brightened. 'I'm like that, Verity. It's how I've come to make so much money. Once I get an idea, I just can't let it go. I'm also,' he sighed and looked downcast for a moment again, 'a fairly new widower with no children, so I like to keep busy and *involved*. Will you come?'

'No——'

'Please.'

Verity got up and paced around. 'You might,' she said after a moment, 'have solved Hamish's *mal de mer* but the aversion I'm suffering from towards *Mr* Morris is another matter, and——'

'Ah! Well, Verity,' he broke in genially, 'I've had a bit of a rethink there and I've come to the conclusion that you're right. If there's *anything* you object to in Brad's—er—well, his approach or whatever, if you can see no future for any kind of personal—um—relationship with him, then stick to your guns!'

Surprise caused Verity to pause mid-stride. Len Pearson rose and added, 'I've already seen him, by the way, and told him that he may be a genius in the advertising world, but to force his attentions on any woman is not really the done thing and I'm not too happy about having my Kneg or my frozen foods associated with that kind of behaviour.'

After what seemed like an age Verity closed her mouth, then said, 'You're joking!'

Len Pearson merely looked curiously wise.

'What did he say?'

'Well, it was touch and go for a moment, I suspect, but in the end all he said was something rather strange. He said I should meet your mother.'

Verity blinked.

'Will you come, please, Verity? You see,' he hesitated, 'I used to drive my wife mad with all my inventions, but when I perfected the Kneg, which was just before she died, she said to me, "Len, I think you might have come up with something worthwhile at last."'

The Marina Mirage at Port Douglas was its usual colourful self, despite the rain, which was undoubtedly easing, but Verity couldn't help thinking she would rather have spent the morning browsing through some of the wonderful shops and having an early lunch at the waterside restaurant that overlooked the marina itself and all the boats moored there. Or doing anything but once again being closeted with Brad Morris, even on such a splendid yacht as Len Pearson's *Jessica*. But Len was so proud as he personally gave her a guided tour of its teak, brass and velvet below-decks magnificence, and so happy to have come up with his idea of a 'holiday', even if it was a busman's one, that she couldn't help feeling touched and as if she should make the best of things.

She had no conversation with her boss as they all arranged themselves comfortably up top beneath an awning for the trip, and Hamish, not wearing his kilt but with it in a bag and stowed with the camera equipment, actually joked about getting his sea legs, and quaffed the 'wee dram' Len had had the foresight to offer him as the *Jessica* slid gracefully out of the marina and up the inlet towards the open sea. She'd been unable, however, to stop herself from directing Brad one searching glance to try to divine the nature of his mood. But, if he viewed the day as anything other than a happy diversion, he was not showing it, she decided.

And in the hour—during which the sun broke through and there was just enough breeze to put up the sails—it took them to get to the Low Isles he only addressed one comment to her that would not have been for public consumption. Otherwise he included her quite naturally as he literally held court, and she witnessed Brad Morris, for reasons best known to himself, displaying the magnetic, charming side of his nature so that even Hamish appeared to be won over.

And his one private comment hadn't been all that trenchant, considering what he was capable of. He'd surveyed her as she sat bare-legged on the deck, wearing white shorts and a navy and white spotted blouse with her face raised to the sun and her hair glinting red-gold, and said, 'I've been told you're off-limits today, Mrs Wood. I wonder if he warned everyone else off too?'

She'd simply closed her eyes and examined the sun-shot shadows behind her eyelids.

They did everything Len had said they could—swam and snorkelled and explored the small island with its lighthouse and coral reef, with its amazing variety of tropical fish, and then had a wonderful picnic lunch and lazed on the beach for a while.

It was while they were doing this that Hamish stood up suddenly and announced that if he didn't get it right today he never would.

A concerted groan went up, but Brad cocked an eyebrow at Len. 'It's not quite what we had in mind— I mean, its not one of your charter boats with your insignia plastered all over it—but if we could use the *Jessica*, which is much more solid, from Hamish's point of view, to be standing upon, playing the bagpipes in a breeze——'

'You got it, boyo,' Len said joyfully.

'Now, Hamish, all you have to do is stop playing your bagpipes, look down with obvious distress at your kilt, which, if you stand this way, should blow up like so—don't worry, we won't show the world your underpants—and Pete here——' Pete was a regular television performer and he was dressed as a fisherman, complete with rod '—will hand you a Kneg and say, "Get up in a bit of a hurry this morning did you, mate?" Then you give him a withering look but take it, look at it with a frown then flick it open and clamp your kilt up with it just as it starts to blow open again. Now that's all quite simple. The important bit comes next: look relieved, then scratch your beard and say, still looking down at it, "What the devil is it?" in your best Scots accent. Got that?'

Hamish nodded with dignity.

'Good.' Brad turned to Pete.

But Pete pre-empted him with a laugh. 'Then I say in broad Aussie and with a shrug, "No idea, Jock. Thing that puzzles me is what you're doing on this flaming boat anyway." And turn away disgustedly as Hamish goes back to his bagpipes.'

It won't work, Verity thought. To get the timing right, to convey the latent comedy of a fisherman and a kilted Scot playing his bagpipes and stuck on a boat together for no apparent reason with only the sketchy kind of rehearsals we've had so far—it won't work, the wind will die...

But it did. In fact, it worked so well that everyone broke up into helpless laughter as the last skirl of the bagpipes faded away and Hamish, still dignified, stared across the boat out to sea.

'Brilliant, Hamish,' Brad called. 'You've done it! You too, Pete.'

Len offered Verity, as the only woman on board, the exclusive use of the main state-room, which had its own shower, to get changed and 'freshen up' if she wanted to. Verity accepted the offer gratefully and closed herself into the luxurious cabin all done out in pink and gold and even boasting a double bed. She had a shower and changed back into her clothes, then as sounds of revelry filtered through she discovered she only felt tired and depressed, lonely and filled with visions of a long, lonely life, visions she'd never before allowed herself to contemplate, and of course with Maddy around it was always easier to batten down on them, but now... She sighed, slipped off her shoes again and lay down on the bed. Just for a few minutes, she told herself, but she fell asleep almost straight away.

It was Brad who woke her. She opened her eyes sleepily and he was standing there with two glasses of what she recognised as vodka and lime. But for a moment they simply stared at each other before he put the glasses down beside the bed and pulled up a stool.

Then he said, 'We thought this might have happened.'

Verity slipped her hand beneath her cheek and glanced at her watch. 'Did you? We must be nearly there.'

He shook his head. 'Everyone was enjoying themselves so much that we took a bit of a detour. We won't be back for another hour. You're missing out on quite an experience.'

She said nothing but propped herself up on her elbow and took a sip of her drink.

The silence lengthened, then he said, 'Funnily enough, I'm not in the mood for,' he gestured upwards, 'all those fun and games any more.'

'I know,' Verity said involuntarily.

He raised an eyebrow and she took an unsteady breath because she could tell from the lines and angles of his face the vague sense of let-down he generally felt after the euphoria of a successful shoot. 'What do you know?' he queried sombrely.

'How you feel.'

'I thought it went well.'

'It did. Despite my reservations, it went wonderfully well.'

He smiled at last. 'Didn't you think I could do it?'

'Not that.' She sipped again then shrugged. 'I'm not in a very positive frame of mind, probably. No, I meant that you always feel a bit let down afterwards, not immediately, but——'

'An hour or so later,' he said with some self-directed mockery. 'How well you know me. And what a cross I must be to live with.'

To her horror, Verity suddenly discovered she had tears on her lashes. She sat up impatiently, dashed at her eyes and took refuge in her vodka and lime, saying after a serious swallow, 'I'd better not take any more afternoon sleeps—I could get addicted to these pick-me-ups.'

'Verity,' he said very quietly and took the glass from her suddenly nerveless fingers, 'why are you crying?'

'I'm not—— I don't know.' She licked her lips despairingly.

'Could it be because this is one of those moments when, irrespective of all the whys and wherefores and dos and don'ts, there might just as well be only you and me on this planet—we can't stay away from each other; we can't even tear our thoughts away?'

She looked at him and couldn't deny it, and it was a long, silent look and she couldn't even tear her eyes away.

He reached out a hand at last and curved it round her cheek and brushed a tear away with his thumb, and it was such an unexpectedly tender gesture that she was lost, quite lost. So that when his lips met hers there was no resistance. And after a deep, searching kiss when his hands moved on her body she felt that wonderful sense of languour that came before the need to give, but she hesitated and hid her face in his shoulder and he merely stroked her hair for a while. Then she looked up with the words framed to tell him she didn't want go any further—and found she couldn't do it. That the rapture was no longer just warm and languorous but becoming electrifying, and she couldn't control her breathing or her pulse-rate or the way her skin shivered of its own accord. It was as if the very centre of her being was linked at that moment to Brad Morris and there was no way she could sever the connection. And instead of saying no she found she could only stare into his eyes, mesmerised and yearning for the warmth and the tenderness to continue so that that part of her soul that had been so brutalised not only by the trauma of her marriage but also by Barry's parents' rejection might heal a little and take some courage from it.

So it was that, with her skin feeling like warm silk beneath his touch, she moved softly as one by one he discarded her clothes then his own, and they might as well have been on another planet as they made that timeless kind of acquaintance new lovers did. She gloried in the way he stared down at her breasts with an indrawn breath, then cupped them and laid the lightest touch on their sensitive peaks with his fingertips. She loved the feel of his hands under her arms and the feel of his long back and broad shoulders beneath hers.

She was helpless when he laid her on the bed and lay beside her and trailed a path of devastation with his lips down her throat and lower and stroked her thighs and her hips. And she touched in return and moved against him at last and more and more urgently at the stunning, wonderful feel of it. And in an equally wonderful way they needed no words; they seemed to know instinctively what pleased, and, as the tempo altered, it did so for them both. And as a kind of wild abandon started to claim her his strength was her saviour, and, once he had entered her and his own kind of abandon took over, she didn't falter but wrapped her arms and legs around him and met and matched his deep thrusting rhythm until an explosion of pleasure claimed them both.

They came back to earth slowly, still wound together and breathing deeply until he lifted his head at last and stared down into her eyes and she stared back. But that was when she began to comprehend, as his gaze held hers captive, that she had no secrets from him now, he knew her most intimate depths, her very essence as a woman and she'd have no defences left—

and the full realisation of what she'd done began to dawn on her.

Perhaps he saw it in her eyes, because a split-second before she moved convulsively he said, 'Verity, don't——'

But she did. 'Let me go!'

'No. Not like this. There's no need——'

'Yes!' she whispered desperately. 'What have I done?'

'Nothing terrible—something quite wonderful, actually, and——'

But, if her own doubts weren't enough, someone chose that moment to knock on the door and call through that they were nearly there, and the full horror of the situation burst into her mind. Of being caught in what could only be called an indiscreet and indelicate situation, to say the least, and using someone else's bed, someone else's boat... She closed her eyes and broke into a cold sweat as she waited for the door to open, but it didn't and she heard footsteps retreating, although that didn't lessen her anguish a lot as Brad sat up abruptly.

'Bloody hell,' he swore softly. 'I'm beginning to think we're jinxed. Why can't people just leave us alone?'

'If he'd opened the door...' She put her hands to her face, going as hot as she'd been cold.

'He couldn't. I locked it. Do you think I *wanted* an audience?'

She took her hands away. 'When? When did you lock it?'

'When it appeared that what happened was inevitable,' he said evenly. 'I didn't come down here with the express purpose of seducing you, Verity, if that's what you had in mind.'

'Oh!' She sat up and pulled the bed-cover over her. 'All the same, can you imagine the... looks and the speculation going on up there? The "wonder what they're doing behind locked doors" kind of comments? I must be mad!'

'No.' He took her wrist and stared into her agitated eyes. 'Marvellous and warmer than I'd thought possible, generous, exquisitely sensual,' he said deliberately, 'but lost and lonely—well, there's no need to be that way any more, and there's no need to give a damn about what anyone else *thinks*.'

But she tore her wrist free. 'And what about what *I* think?' she shot at him.

He sat back. 'Tell me,' he said with a twisted little smile but a glint of something darker in his eyes. 'I've no doubt it will be a revelation.'

For a wild moment Verity contemplated telling him that he was responsible for what had happened, he had seduced her or exercised some strange power over her—but only for a moment, as a stronger voice within her told her to be honest at least. So, what to say? she wondered a little frantically. It can't work for us, you can't be held responsible for the fact that I'm battered and bruised mentally, and *I'm* not interested in an affair and I still believe you're trying to exorcise Primrose anyway? Don't forget, I was the one who not only sent her the flowers and whatnot, but I also knew what you did, how *together* you were for so long, how you looked at her in the office...

She breathed deeply and said merely, not looking at him, 'If you think I'm going to walk off this boat arm in arm with you, you're mistaken.'

'Verity?'

She looked up at last.

'Say that again!' he commanded.

A flood of colour rose up her throat. 'Just go away, Brad,' she whispered.

He smiled slowly, a savage, tigerish smile that didn't hide the contempt in his eyes. 'Do you really have such a small, trite little soul?' he marvelled. 'Is that all you can say after an experience like that? Believe me, I've done my best not to be typically cynical about women.' He paused and reached for his trunks and shorts, then shrugged on his T-shirt. 'But I'm beginning to wonder what does go on in their minds. I shall relieve you of my presence, Verity,' he added, strolling over to the mirror and running his hand carelessly through his hair. 'And I shall go up top and compound the,' he paused again and swung round to look at her with an incisive glance that seemed to cut her to the quick, 'sacrilege by telling everyone we were working on the next riveting chapter of the Kneg saga.'

And he left, closing the door with almost insulting gentleness behind him.

There was a church in the park that skirted the Port Douglas inlet. A little white wooden non-denominational church called St Mary's-by-the-Sea with a long history, although the building had been moved and restored several times after cyclone damage.

What she hoped to gain as she walked up the steps and into its simple interior, Verity wasn't sure. She'd slipped away and decided to walk back to the hotel from the marina and left everyone still carousing on the *Jessica*. Brad had not even looked in her direction as she'd made her excuses to Len. In fact, it had appeared to her that most of them were rather careful not to look at her too closely.

She stood for a while, staring at the stained-glass window depicting someone picking up sea shells, and then out through the open wooden shutters behind the altar that framed a lovely view of the inlet bathed in the golden light of the setting sun. Then she sat down, leant back and closed her eyes and tried to defend herself against certain charges: of smallness and triteness of mind, for example, not to mention committing sacrilege. But the only thing that came to mind was an overpowering sense of melancholy and the feeling that he might have been right. At least, about *her*. She'd given herself with an intensity that made all her earlier, even happy recollections of sex before it had become like a war pale by comparison. And then she'd drawn back from it...

But for him? she wondered. Could it have been such a momentous experience? That he was unlikely to find with any other woman?

She opened her eyes and stared down at her hands and was surprised to see them gripped tightly together—she couldn't remember doing it, although she did understand why she might have done it. Because she was staring one fact in the face at last. She'd done the one thing she'd thought it was impossible for her to do, and she was terrified. Of herself and whether she was once again making a terrible mistake; of him and whether he knew what he was unleashing...

She trembled and tried to resist it, the memory of their lovemaking, but couldn't, so she got up and ran out of the little church and all the way back to Club

Tropical, where she sat down and immediately made her daily phone call to Lucy and Maddy—the only thing she could think of that would restore her to some sort of normality.

CHAPTER SEVEN

'THE Daintree Forest—the Wet Tropics World Heritage Area, in other words,' the guide said proudly, 'contains the oldest surviving rain forests in the world. They've been around for more than a hundred million years!'

Verity stared out of the window of the deluxe four-wheel-drive vehicle at the towering forest on either side of the saturated red ribbon of mud that passed for a road and assimilated some other interesting facts about the Daintree—that sixty per cent of Australia's bat species, sixty-two per cent of the butterflies lived in this point-one per cent of the continent, as well as two species of kangaroos that were very rare and different, kangaroos that climbed trees and moved backwards. There were also crocodiles, as one couldn't fail to be aware of from the moment you drove aboard the ferry that took traffic across the Daintree River and you observed the signs similar to no-smoking signs but with a swimmer and rampant crocodile featured. As for the varieties of plants, the list was endless. And she could believe it all as the dripping, impenetrable-looking foliage passed slowly by. The road was not only waterlogged but very narrow, very steep and winding.

The problem was, she just couldn't raise much enthusiasm for the Daintree; in fact, she found it rather claustrophobic and menacing. Perhaps a dry, sunny day might have helped, she thought with a sigh, but knew in her heart it was not so. And then there was the irony that their destination, Cape Tribulation, so called because Captain Cook happened to be sailing past in 1770 when he ran into the Great Barrier Reef and holed his ship, so aptly echoed her situation in name. Deeply troubled, to put it mildly.

The beach at Cape 'Trib', as the locals fondly called it, had been chosen for the second in the Kneg series, and it made Verity feel incredibly weary just to think of it.

But it too went well, so well that she couldn't help feeling that the Kneg ads were beginning to have a classic feel about them, and it made her smile faintly to think that Len Pearson just might go down in history as an inventor. It also was impossible not to appreciate that Brad had moved into another gear, so to speak. If he'd been inspired with Hamish and the boating sequence, he was even more so on the beautiful sands of Cape Tribulation, where the rain stopped and the sun shone and a thirst-crazed wanderer—a spare member of the camera crew who was an amateur actor in disguise—found a Kneg on the beach and managed to carve a hole in a coconut with it and drink the milk, then stare down at it with acute puzzlement.

On the way back they stopped at the lovely and aptly named Coconut Beach Rain Forest Resort for lunch—they were obviously not going to be allowed to escape any feature of the area, so great was Len's pride in it—but the day was fast approaching a nightmare for Verity and again she was unable to find any real enthusiasm... for anything, food included.

So she decided to go for a walk along the beach, and so deep in thought was she that when she came to a creek bed that cut a swath of rippling channels across the beach, and wound behind it was a shallow, dark, tree-lined chasm, she stopped walking and just stood there, staring at nothing in particular, thinking in circles. Bitter little circles around herself and Brad, but with most of the bitterness directed at herself.

But I don't know why I should feel this way, she reflected. I don't really know why I can't get out of my mind his accusation that it was a trite, small-minded way to behave. To even feel guilty...

Something moved up the creek bank, she just caught it out of the corner of her eye, and instantly she was filled with a churning sense of panic and but one thought on her mind—was it a crocodile? And for a frozen moment her legs wouldn't work. Then she spun round and ran straight into Brad.

'Whoa!' he said, fielding her. 'I didn't mean to frighten the life out of you.'

'You didn't!' she gasped. 'I thought—something moved back there. I thought it was a crocodile.'

'I doubt it——'

'Why?' She said frantically, trying to evade his grasp. 'Everywhere you go up here there are warning signs about crocodiles!'

'So there are, but, assuming it was one in the first place, it would have been upon you and attacking you by now, if that's what it had on its mind, and in the second place, while people have undoubtedly been attacked, it's a very uncommon occurrence. It was probably a lizard.'

Verity looked over her shoulder fearfully but there was absolutely nothing to see, which not only made her feel foolish but correspondingly cross. 'It *might* have been a crocodile,' she said witheringly.

He smiled down at her, a mocking little smile. 'A lot of things *might* have been, Verity. The trouble with you is, you see problems where there aren't any, and——'

'Let's not get personal,' she broke in tautly. 'And would you mind letting me go?'

'When I'm ready,' he responded. He had his hands on her waist and he leisurely inspected the cream cotton blouse she wore with khaki knee-length shorts. 'After all,' he said finally as a tinge of pink came to her cheeks, 'we're not exactly strangers, are we?'

'What's that got to do with it?' she countered.

'Well, despite the fact that I find your...ways somewhat strange, I can still appreciate that you got a fright. In fact, I can still feel your heart banging away merrily, although I'm tempted to wonder if it's because of your crocodile now—or me.'

'Don't pride yourself on too much, Brad,' she warned angrily. 'It's not every day I see, even mistakenly, a salt-water, possibly man-eating crocodile——'

'And it's not every day that *I* get made love to so wonderfully and then have the door slammed in my face, so to speak. Almost as if I were a man-eating,' he paused and smiled, not pleasantly, 'make that a *woman*-eating monster. A curious analogy, but, I'm sure you'll agree, in the circumstances, quite appropriate. You really should have stopped me, you know, if you were going to feel like this.'

Verity stared up into his grey eyes, suddenly arrested, because, of course, there lay the root of all her guilt and confusion. She closed her eyes briefly. 'Well, I didn't,' she said tonelessly and then, with more spirit, 'Do you really believe that makes me——? I'm sure there's a name for it——'

'There is,' he agreed, and said no more, but the way his gaze dwelt lazily on her mouth then her breasts beneath the cream cotton was at the same time so intimate and so insolent that Verity felt seared, and also at the same time as if she were back on the *Jessica* with him, lying naked beneath him, revelling in all he did to her.

She took a despairing breath and wrenched herself free, her emotions in such a turmoil that her heart had started to beat in a way no mere crocodile would have induced it to. 'All *right*,' she said through her teeth, 'it was a stupid thing to do. But the stupidity wasn't only on my side. It was actually a crazy thing to do! I know you take a pretty casual view of things, but to allow ourselves to get so carried away, to...to,' she stuttered, 'lay ourselves open to more or less being caught...caught——'

'*In flagrante delicto*?' he drawled. 'We didn't. I told you, I locked the door.'

'And you don't think that was as good as shouting it from the roof-tops?' she said sardonically. 'Have you not noticed how everyone is looking at us—or refraining from looking at us?'

'Verity, we had this out yesterday. I'll grant you, it was unfortunate, but it's not the real issue,' he said grimly.

'Oh, but it is, Brad.' She hesitated, but the words were building up in her and, rightly or wrongly, she couldn't help herself from saying them. 'I've never behaved like that in my life and I just hope to God I'm never tempted to again! I...it's madness, a kind of madness, and I wish you'd just forget it all, let alone...' Something stopped her then, though too late.

'Let alone leading you astray? Is that what you were going to say?'

She bit her lip and had to look away from his cool, suddenly almost clinical gaze.

'What a fraud you are, my dear,' he went on softly but with an inlay of sheer contempt. 'You loved it, you'd love it again and again, wherever and whenever—is that why you're running so scared? Because once you start you're insatiable?'

It was so cruel that every vestige of colour drained from her face, and she swayed slightly. Then she was prompted to cry that she *was* running scared, but of falling desperately and irrevocably in love with him; that was what she feared was being unleashed within her. But finally pride came to her aid. She said huskily, 'Brad, if you honestly believe that, to ever want to have anything to do with me again would be—no better than what you think I am.' And she turned on her heel and walked surprisingly steadily back to the resort. He made no attempt to catch her up.

Back in the Land Rover, she steeled herself to try to act normally, but it was an incredible effort and she had no idea how she was going to cope while they made the rest of the series or whether she should even try...

And she was never more relieved than when she was at last able to close herself into the Bali Suite as darkness claimed far north Queensland. In fact, she sat slumped on one of the couches for an age in the dark before she wearily got up to run a bath.

The phone rang just as she stepped out of it and she was about to ignore it, then thought it might be

Lucy, so she ran over to answer it, wrapped in a towel. It was Brad.

'Verity?'

'Oh... Yes?'

'Look, I'm having a conference—rather, I'd like to have a conference—but you have most of the paperwork, the art lay-outs and copy, et cetera for the charter-boat literature, so I thought we might as well hold it in the Bali Suite,' he said with unmistakable irony.

'What—now?' she replied incredulously.

'What's wrong with now?' he drawled. 'The sooner we get this wrapped up, the sooner we can all go home.'

'But I'm not even dressed...' She broke off and bit her lip. 'I haven't eaten,' she added.

'None of us has. I'll order something to be sent up. As for being undressed, did you have anything particular in mind? If so, I hope you've chosen a partner wisely, someone who understands all your little quirks—mightn't it be an idea to send him along to me first? I could tell him what to expect.'

'You can also go to hell, Brad Morris,' she said coldly and with incredible restraint. 'But do stop in on your way,' she added cordially. 'There's nothing I'd like better than to get this ghastly roadshow over and done with, even if it means working night and day.' She slammed the phone down.

It was a mistake, of course. It was like flinging the gauntlet down to a highly superior enemy, one much better versed in the art of warfare—in this case, the subtle art of a war of words—and by the time the conference was over she had, through every other emotion, to marvel at how he'd done it. How he'd contrived without exactly saying so to let everyone know that a state of war existed between them, to make everyone thoroughly uncomfortable and glad to be able to escape, and to make her feel like a limp rag.

In fact, all she could do as they left was retreat to the patio with a tray of coffee-cups, and assume as she heard the door close that he had left too. She stared down at the counter she'd placed the tray on, then turned to the open green louvres and took several deep breaths to compose herself as she caught that familiar feeling creeping in, that lonely, melancholy feeling. And she clenched her fists and wondered bitterly and with a little flicker of anger why she should feel like this about a man who could humiliate and had humiliated her publicly once again, let alone who could say what he'd said to her in private. There could be no doubt in anyone's mind after tonight that something deeply and darkly personal was going on between them. Even if they hadn't caught the implication of his words, the sardonic glint of his eyes every time they'd rested on her had made it all abundantly clear.

He really is a bastard, she thought, and tensed as one by one the lights clicked off behind her. The last to go was the one on the patio, and she swung round incredulously. But it took a moment or two for her eyes to adjust to the relative darkness—there was some faint light coming up from the water gardens below. Then she could distinguish his outline silhouetted in the doorway only feet from her, and gradually more details. He was standing with his hands shoved into his pockets, his shoulders relaxed, but he was watching her steadily.

And as the first shock passed it was replaced by another. Because her first instinct—to retaliate as cuttingly and contemptuously as she knew how—was curiously swamped by something else. It was like a rising tide, she discovered as they stood staring at each other, of singular awareness not only of him but also of herself and everything around them—such as that there was also moonlight filtering through some clouds, and the haunting perfume of a tropical shrub wafting on the faint breeze. It was the feel of all the fine hairs on her body standing up and the divining that she felt restless and unfinished, still angry and not to be placated, but once again as if there were only the two of them in the world. And, to put it even more simply, she reflected, to be in the awful position of being incredibly attracted to a man you often hated.

He broke the silence. He said in a cool, clipped voice, 'Are you feeling the way I am, by any chance, Verity?'

She made no gesture; her pride wouldn't allow her to. 'I'm not sure what you're feeling, Brad. But—and you may accuse me of further pettiness of mind when I say this—things are not so simple between us as you seem to think, and to make the whole world privy to...' She hesitated.

'Our problems?' he supplied drily.

'...our problems,' she agreed with irony, 'is, to my mind, extremely petty, not to mention trite, and the sign of a severely wounded ego, if I may say so.'

'You may,' he responded, 'not that you'd be right.'

She did make a helpless little gesture then, and she turned away.

'Not entirely right—I'll amend that,' he said. 'Yes, my ego was somewhat wounded, since you mention it. To be so—good together and not to be able to repeat the experience is naturally galling, and I suppose it's only human to ask yourself what you might have done wrong. And then human also to go on the defensive and exhibit classic symptoms of a bashed-up ego—perhaps you were about halfway right,' he conceded, and waited until she turned with a reluctant smile playing on her lips before adding, 'I'm glad I've amused you.'

She put a hand on the railing. 'You haven't. Not really.'

'You were smiling.'

She shrugged. 'A momentary weakness.'

'As was the other?' he queried with a lifted eyebrow.

'As was the other,' she agreed, not with defiance and not caring how she would be judged again, but with simple honesty, and she stared down at her hand gripping the railing then lifted her gaze to his, but there wasn't enough light to make out the expression in his eyes. And she tensed as he took a few steps towards her. 'Brad...' she said, but her voice got caught in her throat and she found she could only stare helplessly up at him.

But he made no move to touch her, his hands still pushed into his pockets, and at this range she could look into his grey eyes but be unable to decipher them. And he said with little inflexion, 'But that's only half the story, isn't it, Verity? You've made up your mind this is not to be. You've probably cited to yourself a dozen good reasons why it couldn't work, shouldn't be allowed to exist—you're ignoring one basic fact: it *exists*, whether you like it or not. Right now, for example, you're terrified that I'm going to touch you because that would weaken your resistance and allow your senses to speak for you.'

He stopped, then as she stirred restlessly he went on in the same even voice, 'Don't imagine the same isn't happening to me—I'm tired but I know I won't be able to sleep. I'm—fed up and wishing to God I'd never heard of a Kneg let alone been roped in to promote it, but then again if someone dropped the world rights to promote Coca Cola in my lap right now I'd feel the same. Because of you.'

'Brad——'

'Let me finish,' he said quietly. 'Of course, that would be no concern of yours—if you weren't standing so still in the moonlight, if you didn't look tired and strung up, haunted and hauntingly desirable—for the same reason. So, we're in this together. It's that same basic fact.'

She licked her lips but forced herself to speak. 'And do you believe that that one simple fact is going to take care of all the problems between us, Brad?'

'No,' he said sombrely. 'That would be naïve. But to deny it is like killing something before it's had a chance to live, it's like denying hope—and that's a dangerous way to be.'

'Have you any conception of how I might be if I have an affair with you that... that ends negatively?' she whispered.

'Why are you so automatically assuming it has to end negatively, Verity? What *is* your definition of a negative affair, by the way? One that doesn't end in wedding bells? I would have thought you'd learnt that lesson the hard way.'

She gasped. 'That's as good as saying it won't!' She stopped abruptly.

'No,' he countered. 'It's saying that a lot more can exist between a man and a woman than an *automatic* progression to the altar. It's saying that, whatever happens between us in the future, right *now* we're inextricably bound together and you're running away from it for no good reason——'

'Are you sure you're not rehearsing good copy in favour of promiscuity?' she broke in mockingly.

He took his hands out of his pockets at last and folded his arms. 'Are you sure you shouldn't be wearing a placard saying "Don't look, don't touch unless you're prepared to tender a marriage licence", Verity?' he drawled.

She was unable to conceal the flash of pain in her eyes, and a spark of confusion.

If he saw it he made no direct comment, but then she knew he must have because he said differently, 'You don't honestly believe I'm *toying* with you, do you?'

She bit her lip.

'Or that this has anything to do with promiscuity?'

'I...' Her shoulders sagged suddenly. 'No. It has to do with not wanting to be hurt again, I guess,' she said huskily and starkly.

'And you think I have a record of going around deliberately hurting women?' He smiled, a brief, chiselled movement of his lips. 'I'm prepared to admit to a lot of faults, but that's a new one to me.'

She blinked several times in an attempt to evade the compelling grey glance, but it was no good. She sighed. 'No. But it doesn't change the fact that,' her voice quickened in a kind of desperation, 'I don't know what to do! I...' But she couldn't go on and she bowed her head and fought back humiliating tears at the same time as she wondered why she hadn't cited the one thing that was her biggest stumbling block, the one person, to be exact—Primrose. Because, she thought, I just know he's not going to admit he's on the rebound—I doubt if he's even admitted it to himself. Or was that an admission of a kind? The bit about all the things that can go on between a man and a woman—such as wanting me but still *loving* her...

He watched and waited.

'There are times when I hate you, like this evening.' She looked up tautly but with no more than a suspicious brightness in her eyes.

'I don't think that matters,' he said gravely.

'Of course it must!'

'No. Not when it's the other side of this.' He took the last step and put his hands on her shoulders then let his fingers roam up the slender line of her throat.

She couldn't help herself. She tilted her head back and shivered with pleasure, and when he looked into her eyes it was to see the mute acknowledgement that her senses were trapped before she closed them wearily.

'Don't look like that,' he said barely audibly and touched her lips with one finger.

'I must. And I'll probably want to fight you again,' she whispered raggedly. 'Don't imagine——'

'I won't,' he promised but stifled any further speech by the simple expedient of kissing her.

'I think you should go.'

He stirred beside her. They were covered only by a sheet, and the Bali Suite was in darkness. 'To protect my reputation or yours?'

'Ours,' she said. 'Besides which, I'm plagued by memories of people knocking on doors.'

He linked his fingers through hers. 'I know what you mean. But it's far too late—or early—for that.'

'Don't you believe it,' she said ruefully.

'I hope you don't always associate that—with this.'

'So do I.' She bit her lip.

'Was it any good?' He let go of her hand, propped himself on an elbow and reached out to switch on a lamp.

Verity blinked several times and drew the sheet up further, causing an absent smile to flicker across his lips, but he didn't attempt to disrupt it. 'Isn't that akin to asking—was I any good?' she said barely audibly.

He looked wry. 'All right. Was I?'

'I meant,' she hesitated, cursing herself, 'I don't think we need to indulge in post-mortems.'

'You may not,' he replied, 'but don't forget my bashed-up ego. It would be kinder to tell me.'

She sighed, then had to smile reluctantly. 'You were fine and it was...' But she broke off and turned away abruptly to lie on her back as patches of heat started to steal up her throat. 'Don't make me do this,' she said huskily. 'It's quite juvenile.'

'I have to disagree—you certainly couldn't call what we did juvenile, therefore any discussion of it shouldn't be juvenile—perhaps humorous, if you'd let it be—but not to say anything at all,' he murmured and tucked the sheet in around her solicitously and in a way that made her feel foolish, 'is rather denigrating it, wouldn't you agree?'

'No, obviously I don't,' she responded with an effort. 'Anyway, it must have *been* obvious what I thought of it.'

'You're not ashamed of being wild and wonderful, are you, Verity? What I said earlier today was the words of a deeply frustrated male person and——'

'I'm not.' But she sat up jerkily again and it wasn't quite clear to her whether she was ashamed and denying it or calling a halt to any further discussion on the subject. Probably a bit of both, she thought gloomily. 'Look,' she said rather drily, 'it was...wonderful, as you very well know, and you were...the same, but I reserve the right to...to... Oh!' She turned to look at him exasperatedly.

'Keep your thoughts to yourself?' he said lazily.

'Yes. I did warn you.'

'So you did,' he said softly and drew his fingers idly down her spine.

She trembled in spite of herself, and had to make herself go on. 'I also reserve the right not to have you getting caught leaving my room at a questionable time and in compromising circumstances—and please don't start on about sacrilege again,' she warned, 'because I don't care what it makes me or how small and trite but I prefer to be very private about these things. I also have to work with you tomorrow. We have an early start, moreover, and, if that's not bad enough, we have to hike up Mossman Gorge and perform miracles with a Kneg on a suspension bridge over the raging Mossman River—— Don't do that,' she said in quite a different voice.

He laughed softly and took his fingers from her spine. 'What am I allowed to do?'

'Just go,' she said with an effort. And added in a voice that quavered ridiculously, 'P-please.'

'OK. I'll consider myself banished, Verity. Well, when I've done this...' Which was to kiss her lingeringly then tuck her up again. 'But I'll be back.' He pushed the red-gold strands of her fringe off her forehead and stared down at her with a sort of quizzical amusement, and added, 'It's just as well I'm not really possessed of a wounded ego, isn't it? I could go out and shoot myself—had you thought of that?'

'I never for one moment believed you were.' But she couldn't stop herself from answering that amusement in his eyes with a faint curve of her lips. She sobered almost immediately, though. 'Brad, tomorrow...?'

'What the hell do you imagine I'm going to do?' He sat back with his old look of impatience and she flinched.

'It's going to be difficult enough to do this as it is,' she said stubbornly, however. 'And I do have to get back to Maddy.'

He narrowed his eyes then said quietly, 'She means an awful lot to you, doesn't she?'

'The world,' Verity answered simply.

He said, after a few moments, 'She's a lucky kid.' And left not long afterwards.

But it was a while before Verity got to sleep; she found herself hugging the spare pillow and staring into the darkness for an age as she tried to contemplate the future.

CHAPTER EIGHT

'ANOTHER good day's shooting,' Len Pearson said excitedly. 'If these ads don't sell my Kneg, I'll eat my hat.' And, 'Only one to go, boyo!' as he slapped Brad heartily on the back. 'I know you were dubious about doing the whole caboodle up here, but it's worked a treat.' His face fell. 'If only my Jess had lived to see them. She grew up in Port Douglas too, you know. She loved it.'

'As a matter of fact, I've thought of putting something into the last one that clearly shows it is Port Douglas,' Brad said rather gently.

Len brightened, and they got into an earnest discussion on what was the best way to do it.

Verity watched them for a moment then turned away with her heart beating erratically. It was not yet twenty-four hours since they'd slept together for the second time, and, although it was she who had insisted they give no intimation to anyone that they had, it was she who had had difficulty concentrating all day. And not so much, curiously, because of the serious misgivings that were lying just below the surface of her mind, but because of the visions that had plagued her all day: of lying in his arms, mute but consumed by desire, memories of the things she'd done, although she'd kept such strict control on what she'd said, thoughts of the night that lay ahead...

She closed her eyes and took herself to task and was consequently brisker than absolutely necessary as she made her excuses—they were all having a sundowner in the pub across the road to celebrate the successful shoot.

'Stay a while, Verity,' Len pleaded.

'I can't,' she said but softened it with a smile. 'We left too early for me to ring Maddy this morning, so she'll be waiting for a call.'

'Oh, well, I guess we should let you go—what do you say, Brad?'

'By all means.'

To her dismay, Verity found herself hesitating, but he said no more and turned to Bob.

She left, but as she crossed the road she found herself wondering what 'by all means' actually meant. That he would come? That he wouldn't because he found the secrecy she'd insisted on ridiculous? He'd gone along with it all day, however, although there'd been times when she'd discerned a devilish little glint in his eyes—damn, she thought. *This* is ridiculous.

She had a long chat with Maddy and Lucy, and they were both delighted with the postcards they'd received, and Lucy let slip that her sister Helen was getting about more and more.

'It should only be another couple of days at the most, Mum,' Verity said. 'Is Maddy——?'

'Maddy's fine, darling. Missing you, of course, but there's so much here for her to do. I must warn you that she's adopted a kitten!'

'I expected no less,' Verity said with a laugh. 'Not that I'm crazy about cats, but it could have been a lamb or a duck.'

'And how is it going up there? Are you coping with Mr Morris?'

For a split-second Verity was plagued by an image of herself and Mr Morris entwined on the four-poster bed, and she had to swallow hard before she said, normally, she hoped, 'Yes. He hasn't been too bad. Um... apart from the odd day.' And closed her eyes and felt herself break out into a sweat that was to do with lying by evasion as well as a lot of other things.

But it was when she put the phone down at last that everything that had been lying just below the surface of her mind all day rose up to torment her. How to tell her mother, for example. How to go on working for him in less rarefied circumstances than these. And it was over an hour before he came. During which she showered and washed her hair and blow-dried it, and changed into a pair of oyster trousers and a long-sleeved, silky cinnamon blouse, tucked in and belted round the waist by a leather belt with an intricate brass buckle. She even put on some make-up. But as she stared at herself in the mirror and decided she looked groomed, slim but taut, she had also to ask herself what she thought she was doing. Making a statement of some kind? Trying to deny that all day all her senses had been homed in on this time, when he'd come to her or with her and take her in his arms and...

She shook herself slightly and tried another tack— You're on the right track, kid, she told herself with totally false humour. You might have laid down some arms, but you don't have to lie down and beg——Oh, *hell*, is that why I'm feeling all churned up? Because he hasn't dropped everything and come...? If that's so, you better change your tune.

But that, although she didn't know it, was to prove unexpectedly difficult.

He came not long afterwards, neither changed nor showered, and it was not hard to guess that he'd come straight from the pub.

'You didn't have to,' she said coolly and winced inwardly as she let him in and led the way.

'Didn't have to what?' he queried.

'Tear yourself away,' she said over her shoulder before she could stop herself, and gritted her teeth and sat down on a couch.

'It was the opposite, actually,' he replied, coming to stand directly in front of her and flexing his shoulders as if he'd been sitting too long. 'I, speaking figuratively, had to bolt myself down. Otherwise I would have got up and run after you across the road like a lovesick teenager. Which I didn't think you would appreciate.'

'I wouldn't——'

'On the other hand, if I'd known you were working yourself into a state because I wasn't here I would have thrown caution to the winds.'

'I'm not. Do you have to tower over me like this?' she asked irritably.

He laughed and sat down next to her. 'You are, you know. Why?'

She plaited her fingers and stared down at them silently, feeling defeated and foolish.

'I like your hands,' he said at last, and freed one to take it into his. 'I can't stand women with long, talon-like nails.' And he folded it into a fist and raised it to his lips. 'As a matter of fact, there's so much I like about you, Verity, that it's hard to know where to start.'

'Don't,' she said huskily.

'Don't what?'

'Flatter me...shower me with compliments,' she said drily.

'I wouldn't dream of telling you anything but the truth.' His smiled faintly. 'I also feel we should go about this a bit differently.'

'What?'

His eyes laughed at her. 'This.' He touched her cheek then spread his fingers through her hair and leant closer. 'Mmm. Smells lovely. Clean and fresh.'

'How differently?' Verity asked with dogged determination.

'I think we should talk. Talking while you're making love is—makes it extra-special. Adds another dimension of intimacy, if you like. So far we've been unusually silent.'

And so far it's been by design, Verity thought. She said, just a little ironically, 'So you gave me to understand last night, but perhaps some people are talkers and others not. Is there a sort of set pattern of excellence for it?'

'By no means. What works for some doesn't for others, but talking is a fairly spontaneous reaction, and you, for example, are seldom lost for words in other respects.'

'Brad...'

He waited.

She bit her lip, tried again, then said, 'I can't. I mean, I wasn't trying to...to...'

'Make verbal love?'

'Well, no——'

'Come up with some more objections, then?'

She winced.

'Well, yes?'

'I... Oh, yes,' she agreed a bit exasperatedly.

'Then I definitely did stay away for too long. Are you hungry?'

'No—I mean, I hadn't thought about it yet.'

'Ah. I really thought you had dinner first in mind, and I was going to suggest, seeing as you look so fresh and tidy and quite stunning, that I take you out for it—I happen to know where the rest of the mob are eating, so we could avoid it like the plague—but on second thoughts you could be right; I think we should stay here and forget about food, and that way I could reassure you and——'

'Take me to dinner,' she said with a sort of gloomy decision. 'That way I might...I don't know.' She grimaced.

'Delay the evil moment?' he suggested with perfectly wicked gravity.

Verity laid her head back with a sigh. 'If you must know, yes. What does that make me?' She turned her head to stare into his eyes.

'A fighter, my dear,' he said after a long moment. 'And a gallant one at that.'

They ate at Oskar's, which was part of the Club Tropical complex and fashioned as a grotto with rocks and pools and wooden bridges over them. They arrived to find it was their curry night, and discovered that they both loved curry, of which there were at least six varieties.

'I make quite a good curry, although I say it myself, as shouldn't!' Verity smiled ruefully and sipped the wonderfully smooth, clean wine he'd chosen.

'So do I—what a coincidence. We could swap recipes.'

'So cooking is another of your skills?' she asked as she took a forkful of cucumber and cream. 'If that's so, you and my mother should swap recipes. She's a genius, and all I know I've learnt from her.'

'I don't like conventional cooking,' he replied, looking amused. 'I'm useless when it comes to boiling eggs. But there are times when it's tiresome to be a bachelor and totally dependent on other people's cooking.'

'What about things like breakfast, though? I mean, if you can't boil eggs?'

'I make a mean omelette—perhaps it's because I don't *like* boiled eggs that I have such difficulty with them.'

'Well, what kind of things do you like to cook?'

'Oh,' he sat back, 'filet mignon, spare ribs, pan-fried fresh barramundi, barbecued lobster tails, garlic prawns—I once did some trout I caught in New Zealand in Benedictine and tinned peaches...that was all there was, and it was delicious.'

Verity had to laugh. 'I might have known.'

He raised an eyebrow at her.

'That it would be exotic and...expensive.'

He looked injured. 'Is that a slur?'

'No. But, as you yourself remarked once, your imagination is so wide-ranging—or words to that effect. Not many people would think of using Benedictine and peaches even if there wasn't anything else to hand. How come there wasn't?'

'It was at the end of the trip and I was running out of resources—I know what you're going to say, my resources were pretty exotic, but in fact I was given the Benedictine.'

'Ah. That explains it all perfectly,' she murmured.

'What kind of a cook are you?' he queried.

'I'm very good at boiling eggs, mashing potatoes, making gravy—all those uninspired kind of things.'

'It seems to me we would complement each other perfectly, then,' he said idly. 'But then, it shouldn't come as a surprise, should it? We've been doing that for two years when you think about it.'

'You mean,' she said wryly, 'all the brilliance has been on your side and on mine there's been the down-to-earth plain common sense.'

'Don't knock it. I'd have been lost without it. But I seem to remember it was not I who came up with the touch that took, will take, hopefully, the Kneg ads out of the realm of the ordinary. A touch of genius.'

'A fluke. And not terribly original, don't forget.'

'There's another side of you that's—breathtakingly inspired, Verity,' he said quietly and, when she blushed, added, 'Don't clam up on me now, or lose your appetite.'

'Well,' she said with an effort, 'tell me how you got into writing school textbooks, then.'

'By accident. I ran into Sonia Mallory at a party and somehow or other got on to one of my hobby-horses—how kids can do geography at school, for example, for years these days and never know what the capitals of most of the world are, or where the Rocky Mountains are, et cetera. So she challenged me to do a set of basic handbooks and, God knows how, managed to sell them to the Department of Education as library material. They—caught on rather well, that's all.'

Verity pushed her plate away. 'It's always fascinated me, this rapport you have with kids.'

'I hope you're not going to accuse me of being a kid at heart myself,' he said wryly.

Verity looked across at him and their gazes caught and held. 'No,' she said after a moment with her skin prickling, and lowered her lashes.

He put a hand over hers as it lay loosely on the table. 'Dessert? Or coffee?'

But she couldn't answer because her heart was suddenly pounding and she felt weak with an onslaught of desire and something else, something new and even more frightening than the physical aspect of what he could do to her just by sitting across a table from her. A flood of tenderness for him and all the facets of his personality... No, she thought, oh, no...

'Verity?'

'I think—I think I'd like to get out of here if you don't mind,' she managed to say shakily.

He did it with extraordinary ease.

And he held her hand all the way across the water gardens, stopping once as she stumbled and steadying her, taking her key from her, as she didn't seem to be able to fit it into the lock, steadying her again once they were inside.

'What is it?' he said with a frown as she stood trembling, her hand still in his.

'Nothing,' she breathed. 'Nothing—I'll be fine in a moment.'

'You look as if you've seen a ghost,' he murmured and drew her into his arms.

She hid her face in his shoulder for a moment as she fought for composure. 'No. Brad—I don't want to do this.'

He didn't reply immediately and she looked up at last, to see not contempt, as she'd steeled herself for, but that reticence and reserve she'd noticed once before, an austere setting of the lines and angles of his face that was unreadable but riveting, and her lips parted involuntarily.

And he said in a voice she barely recognised, 'Tell me why.'

'I... can't,' she whispered.

'All right. Don't look like that, it's not the end of the world.' But he didn't smile, and he touched his lips briefly to her forehead then released her completely. 'Will you be all right?'

No, something inside her cried. I might never be all right again—am I being a fool, and a coward, to deny all hope?

She closed her eyes and her lips moved; then she lifted her lashes and said starkly, 'No, I don't think so; please... stay.'

'I can't. Not platonically——'

'I've changed my mind. Sorry, you must think I'm an awful fool——'

'Verity,' he said roughly, 'it has nothing to do with anything like that.'

She tried to smile. 'It feels like it to me, if not worse.'

He stared down at her, at the sheen of tears in her eyes and the way her arms had crept around her as if to protect herself, and for a moment it was as if he debated something silently. And she found herself holding her breath.

'There would be only one kind of foolishness to my mind,' he said at last. 'That would be to regret it if I do stay, and to hate yourself tomorrow.'

'I...' She licked her lips. 'I can't guarantee that I won't regret it,' she said huskily. 'But I promise you I won't hate myself.'

'What are you doing?' she said unsteadily some time later.

He lifted his head briefly. 'Tantalising myself almost unbearably. Don't you like it?'

'I...' She stopped and bit her lip and turned her head sideways, but that was a mistake because she was leaning against a wall next to the bed and she could see at an angle into the bathroom, and see reflected in the wide mirror, a silvery image—they'd turned all but one soft light off—of exactly what he was doing. He'd taken her blouse and bra off and he was standing with his legs wide apart so that he could kiss her breasts while she had her hands on his shoulders—silly question, she thought and averted her eyes and laid her head back against the wall.

'Go on; you were going to say?' he prompted.

She lifted her hands and touched his hair. 'You're tantalising me almost unbearably too.'

She felt him laugh against her skin. 'Is that a subtle hint—in other words, get on with it?'

'No.' She ran her fingers through the springy brown curls and shivered with pleasure as he bit one nipple gently. 'Well, I would like to be able to return the tantalisation, but you have me pinned here, semi-clothed, and——'

He stood up straight. 'I love the thought of that, but first I think I should unclothe you completely.'

And he undid the buckle of her belt and unzipped her trousers.

'I could do that,' she murmured, but made no move to. In fact, she put her arms around his neck as he slid his hands beneath her briefs and caressed her hips, and raised her mouth to be kissed.

It was quite some minutes later before he got rid of her last items of clothing and carried her to the bed that had been obligingly turned down for the night. She lay with her hand under her cheek and unashamedly watched him get rid of his clothes, then she rolled on to her back and stared upwards at the draperies, and had to smile.

'What,' he eased himself down beside her and propped his head on his hand, 'is amusing you?'

'I'm thinking that the Bali Suite has fulfilled all Len's expectations,' she said softly and moved luxuriously as he put his hand on her thigh. 'I'm thinking a lot of things; that I was a nervous wreck only a short time ago and now I'm... like this.' She turned on her side and played her fingers down his upper arm. 'I'm thinking that you have to take a lot of credit for defusing me tonight. Thank you.' Her hand moved rhythmically.

'Shall I tell you what I'm thinking? That I regret having any part in making you feel a nervous wreck, but one reason things have been defused is that we do this so well together. It... speaks for itself. There is another factor at work, only I can't quite put my finger on it except to say that you seem to have changed and not just because of this.' He took his hand away from her thigh.

She breathed unevenly. 'Perhaps it's because I decided to take your advice. About talking at times like these.'

She saw his eyes narrow and tried desperately to stay still because of course, while it hadn't been an untruth, it had only been a small part of it. The truth was that she'd decided not to abandon all hope, and it had come upon her, this decision, when he hadn't tried to persuade her to do anything against her will. It had come like a curling of optimism against all odds, but more—a feeling of courage and a feeling that to be any other way would be a denial of her innermost self, whatever the outcome. A feeling that she could no longer run away from this or absolve herself from any responsibility, or, for that matter, lie in his arms and love it, then cite Primrose Carpenter as her own sort of devil's advocate or, similarly, everything she'd suffered.

For better or worse, she thought, and trembled suddenly.

'On this occasion,' he said at last and barely audibly, 'I seem to be the one without words. Why is that, I wonder?'

'It's my turn, that's all,' she responded and didn't know where the words were coming from but was dimly grateful that some vocal part of her mind and soul was supporting her. 'You said earlier that I was seldom lost for words in other respects. I guess it had to come to the fore finally.'

He smiled faintly and cupped her cheek. 'I hesitate to think what might be unleashed—no, don't take offence, I love it. I'm all yours,' he added.

She lifted her hand and laid her palm on his cheek. 'There's only one problem—my next words are about to be rather banal. I would love to be held very close right now.'

'In a moment,' he murmured. 'I would love to just look at you—am I allowed requests?'

'Yes.' Her lips curved.

He did just that. 'They are all over you,' he murmured at last. 'A lovely bloom.'

'I feel like a grape. I used to hate them. They made me feel very plain.'

'Plain.' He grimaced. 'With a figure like this? After a child, too.'

'You're—put together quite well, you know.'

'Thank you,' he replied with mock solemnity and put his hand on her hip.

'I used to,' she made a wry little gesture, 'think that women felt maternal about you. I was probably about as wrong as one can be.'

His eyes were amused. 'Did you ever feel that way?'

'No... About this talking,' she said with an effort as he moved his hand over the curve of her waist and up beneath her arm to her armpit, 'how long does it have to go on for?'

'Oh, ages,' he said softly and with a wicked little grin. 'Besides, I wouldn't dream of proceeding to the next stage without your consent.'

'You're a—something of a tease, Mr Morris,' she accused. 'I can see I'll have to deal with you— severely.' But all she did was move into his arms with a little sigh of pleasure and a murmured, 'If that's not consent, I don't know what is.'

He said into her hair, 'I might have died if we'd talked any longer.' And wrapped her tightly to him as he began the act that united them in such rapture.

They slept for a while afterwards then made love again, but instead of feeling exhausted Verity got up and ran the bath.

'What are you doing?' he said from the doorway as she lay back in its triangular depths amid drifts of fragrant bubbles.

'Just felt like it.' She glinted a smile at him and watched him run his hand through his hair and finger his jaw. 'Why don't you join me? It's big enough for two and you look as if you could do with it.'

He grimaced. But a few minutes later, lying back against her with her legs and arms around him as she soaped his chest, he said, 'This wasn't such a bad idea, after all. Are you always this full of *joie de vivre* after sex—once you really let yourself go?'

Her hands stilled for a second, then she went on soaping. 'No.'

'That was badly put,' he said quietly. 'One of those stupid things you say without thinking——'

'It doesn't matter. I could have done the same. Shall I wash your hair?'

'I'm yours to command. Hell,' he said as she squeezed a flannel over his head. 'You sure you're not feeling maternal, Verity?'

'Far from it. Brad!' she protested as he flipped over and wrested the soap from her. 'I hadn't finished.'

'What's sauce for the goose is sauce for the gander,' he remarked, wiping rivulets of water from his eyes. 'Besides, I was afraid you were going to start on my ears.'

'I told you——'

'Whatever, it's my turn to wash you. Mmm,' he lathered her breasts, 'feels good. Like it?'

But she was laughing helplessly.

'You're not supposed to do that!'

'I love it!'

'No more than I.' And he stopped washing and gathered her in his arms and kissed her.

They got out finally and once again he took her wet, satiny body in his arms. 'All my fantasies come true,' he murmured, looking down at her wryly.

She kissed his shoulder. 'And mine,' she confessed, and the laughter and fun subsided as they stared into each other's eyes.

Until he said, 'It's my turn now.'

'What for?' she whispered.

'This.' He let her go, but only to wrap her in a towel. 'Dry yourself and I will do the same, then we can don these robes so thoughtfully provided by Club Tropical.' He handed her the white seersucker robe trimmed with pink and shrugged into an identical one, then picked her up and took her back to bed, pulling the pillows up behind her.

'Stay there. I'll be right back,' which he was after popping a cork, with two glasses of champagne from the bar fridge. 'Cheers.'

'Cheers,' she repeated. 'I'm only surprised it's not vodka and lime.'

'That's good as a pick-me-up. Champagne has other uses.'

'Intoxicating ones.'

'Not in small proportions. My father always used to maintain that a good, cleansing glass of champagne before bed worked wonders.'

'What for?' she queried.

He laughed. 'I'm not too sure, to be honest.'

'Perhaps he was a romantic?' she suggested. 'Sipping champagne together at two o'clock in the morning, in bed is—quite lovely,' she said wryly and raised her glass. 'Here's to your father!'

He echoed the toast solemnly but added, 'Doing anything with you in bed at two o'clock in the morning is rather lovely. Finished?'

She nodded and he removed the glasses. 'Sleepy?' he queried.

'Mmm... Are you?'

He didn't answer but arranged her with her back to him, an arm around her and one hand stroking her hair. And she fell asleep without knowing it or knowing that it took him quite a bit longer to do the same.

But something alerted her the next morning to a change in him—or perhaps it was the memory of the way he'd lulled her to sleep that made her wonder if she'd given away more than she'd intended in her lovemaking and the way she'd been afterwards. And then she'd also woken to find him awake and watching her.

'What are you thinking?' She reached across and traced the line of his eyebrows. It was early, about six o'clock, and the daylight was still pink-tinged.

He stirred and pushed his hair out of his eyes. 'That I'm liable to get caught leaving your room in compromising circumstances.'

'I thought only I worried about things like that.'

'I'm only worrying on your behalf.'

'Well, you don't need to; I've,' she hesitated, 'changed.'

He caught her hand and kissed the palm. 'So I see. Was it anything I did or said?'

She considered and wondered what to tell him. Should she plunge in and confess that last night, when she'd been so affected in the restaurant, she'd deeply suspected it had been a rush of love that had taken hold of her heart? And that it had felt like that because she couldn't recall experiencing anything like it, not even in the heyday of her attraction to Barry Wood? Not that sensation of being so powerfully moved by someone. Or should she tell him his actions had inspired her to hope because that was also part of it—or should she take things more slowly? And how to know why he was... different?

'It seemed,' she said at length, 'rather twisted, for want of a better word to—— Well, it *was* something you said, I suppose. About denigrating it to... carry on the way I was, and I couldn't help feeling I was tarnishing myself in the process, if that makes any sense to you. Which is not to say I don't foresee all sorts of problems ahead for us still, but...' She shrugged delicately then said huskily, 'There are no regrets, Brad.'

He closed his eyes briefly then kissed her lips. 'These problems—let's talk about them——'

'No, not now,' she said softly. 'Guess what?'

'What?'

'It's raining.'

'Hell!' He lifted his head. 'It started off fine—it's not only raining, it's pouring!'

She laughed. 'For once in my life, my working life, I can't seem to care.'

He pulled her into his arms. 'That's my girl.'

CHAPTER NINE

THEIR luck with the weather ran out that day.

It was still pouring at three o'clock in the afternoon and the weather report wasn't hopeful of any change overnight. And, apart from having Maddy on her mind more than usual because she'd never been away from her this long and it looked like getting longer, Verity couldn't help being quietly happy in the calm, peaceful hours they spent together, watching a video, listening to music and, for once, not plagued by interruptions. The rest of the crew, obviously grateful for some time on their own, too, stayed away. Even Len Pearson stayed away until late afternoon, causing Verity to wonder a little ruefully if it was a diplomatic omission on his part.

And, when both Len and Bob did surface via the phone to claim Brad's attention, she decided to go for a walk.

'You'll get wet,' Brad said.

'I've got a raincoat—I love walking in the rain.'

He studied her for a moment then kissed her forehead. 'All right.'

'Is—something wrong?' she said involuntarily. Because that change she'd detected in him at the crack of dawn had stayed with him all day. A different, quieter sort of mood than she'd ever seen him in, and, despite the fact that she'd loved every minute of their time together, it puzzled her.

'No. Very right. Why do you ask?' He put a finger on the frown line between her eyes.

She opened her mouth then shrugged and smiled. 'No reason. See you soon...'

She walked for nearly an hour then went into the newsagent on the way back and bought a paper, thinking to update herself on world affairs, which seemed to have passed her by lately.

What she did update herself on when she got back to the deserted Bali Suite was only world-shattering to herself, as it turned out. A little item on the third page headed 'Peer and model cancel nuptials'. She read on with widening eyes. There was not a lot to read, just that Primrose, looking strained and tired, had announced to the Press that she had broken off her engagement and would be returning to Australia immediately.

She put the paper down very slowly then picked it up again and refolded it neatly, page one up, and Brad knocked briefly and entered, before she had time to gather her thoughts, with Len and Bob on his heels. But they didn't stay long, and as soon as they'd left Brad walked up to her, took her in his arms and said, 'I'm starved!'

'It's only—five o'clock, but we could get a snack sent up.'

'I'm not starved of food,' he said gravely.

'Oh—you mean...?'

'Mmm. Precisely. Can you think of any better way to spend a rain-soaked dusk?'

'Well—no,' she conceded, but it struck her as ironic that he should be more like his old self now, while she was... how was she? she wondered. A bit shell-shocked seemed to be the only comparison she could make.

'But you're not absolutely dancing with joy at the prospect,' he murmured, his eyes actually dancing with wicked little glints.

'You took me by surprise, that's all.'

'Ah. I think I can remedy that.' And he picked her up and took her over to a settee, where he sat down with her in his lap.

A few minutes later she said a bit breathlessly, 'I see what you mean. Can I ask you something?'

He lifted his head and closed up the front of her blouse. 'Fire away. This sounds serious.'

She ran her hand through his hair. 'No. But something seems to have put you in a very good mood.'

'Something has,' he agreed.

'What?'

'Not that I was in a bad mood by any manner of means.' He shrugged.

'No, but—contemplative.'

'Not so much that either, but—a bit awestruck, I guess,' he said with not a flicker of a smile. 'By you.'

'You were not——'

'Verity, you do a lot of things to me, but one thing I must insist on is being allowed to retain some mastery over my thought processes. I was.'

'Very well. May I be allowed the same privilege?'

'Of course!'

'Then I have to tell you, Mr Morris, that, to my mind, you lie with a great deal of charm.'

He looked comically affronted.

'But if you don't want to tell me I shall not insist,' she continued. 'Although you could tell me what changed things.'

For a moment she thought she detected something serious and different in his eyes, but it was gone before she could be sure. 'Other than the prospect of this,' he said slowly and moved his hands on her waist, 'I have just had a spot of good news.'

Verity held her breath and felt her heart contract.

But he went on without seeming to notice, 'Len has given us the frozen-food account.'

The relief she felt was stunning—and inexplicable. *Did I really imagine he was going to tell me Primrose was coming home? I must have...*

'That seems to have come as a bit of a shock to you,' he said wryly. 'He told me he hasn't enjoyed himself as much since his wife died; he said he knew it sounded silly, but, whether the Knegs sold or not, he felt the money had been well spent because she would have loved the ads, although, of course, the frozen foods will have to pay their way, I'm sure—which reminds me, we're going to have to do a hell of a lot of consumer research on that one—— You still look stunned, Verity.'

She tried to compose her features. 'On the contrary, I never doubted you would get it. But congratulations!'

'Well, you deserve them as much as I do. What a team!' he marvelled.

'What a team,' she echoed. 'You did say, though, the frozen-food account was like manna from heaven because it's already a household name.'

He grinned. 'If I remember correctly, when I said that I was being particularly persuasive, or trying to be. But, unlike the Knegs—which are, of course, unique,' he said humourlessly, 'there's a lot of competition in the food business. And a lot of diversification. I mean, it's not only overworked housewives one can target but also teenagers, the elderly, et cetera, et cetera. And he is moving out of the traditional area of frozen peas and fish fingers into pizzas and that kind of thing.'

'I can see that the challenge has already started to get to you,' she remarked.

'As a matter of fact, it's not. The only challenge I have in mind at the moment is getting you back to the point of no return; well, I was almost there until you started asking questions.' And he opened her blouse again.

It was impossible not to respond to his lovemaking even while she had Primrose at the back of her mind, but during the dinner they had sent up she was quiet, and afterwards she roamed around the suite, unable to settle, beset by the sight of the paper every time she turned around, or so it seemed.

Until he said quietly, 'What is it?'

'Nothing. Well,' she made an effort, 'I've had Maddy on my mind a bit today.'

'You rang only an hour ago and she was fine,' he pointed out.

'I know, but I've never been away from her for so long before.'

'I hate to sound in any way callous, which I'm not, but I think you've done wonders for her: you've got your life going again, you've got a career that will help to provide for her—and I'm sure that the time you do spend with her is "quality time".' He grimaced. 'I hate catch-phrases like that, but there's probably something in it. And when you can't be with her you make good arrangements for her.'

Verity sat down and clasped her hands in her lap and said before she stopped to think, 'It's still hard to know what's best for her sometimes. Take the Woods, for example—I don't know what to do about them.'

'Go on,' he said.

'Well, it is a bit of a quandary. They are her grandparents and she can never know her father. *They've* lost their son and only child and—and I don't for one minute have any financial considerations in mind when I say any of this——'

'I believe you.'

'But I just can't help trying to look at it from Maddy's point of view, in a family sense, if you know what I mean. Because lately I've thought of her growing up and wondering why she should be so estranged from anything to do with her father. It would probably be only natural, don't you think?'

'Yes, I do,' he replied without hesitation. 'Were they really as—cold-blooded about it all?'

Verity stared abstractedly before her for a long time. 'I probably didn't help,' she said with a sigh eventually. 'After Barry died they—well, we all said and did things that might not have been quite fair. But then, later, they obviously had her on their minds and they made some approaches, but the way they *did* it made me all the more determined to...' She shrugged.

'Go it alone?'

'Yes,' she said bleakly. 'I could see them trying to sort of take her over.'

'Verity, you said to Sonia that when you desperately needed help they were unforthcoming—what kind of help?'

She grimaced. 'I thought they might be able to stop him drinking—I couldn't. But they virtually accused me of driving him to it. When I told them that he'd confessed to me he'd started drinking at school they told me I was lying.'

He picked up her hand. 'I don't know them well at all, but it sounds to me as if you need an intermediary. I would say that the hurts on both side are so deep still that it's impossible for you to communicate with each other. What about your mother?'

'She's offered,' Verity said quietly. 'I wouldn't let her. Up until recently I've been so angry...'

'But now that you've started thinking of Maddy growing up with only half a family?'

'Yes, although, wise as she can be, she can't really be impartial. She adores Maddy, and she's given me so much support that I... I don't know.'

'They might listen to me, then.'

'They might if you were——' She broke off and bit her lip.

'If we had an arrangement?' he supplied.

'Well,' she hesitated then said bluntly, 'yes. Not that I'm suggesting for one minute...' She gestured and moved on, again hastily and unwisely, as it proved, 'I'd have to think very carefully before I made any arrangements with anyone, on Maddy's account too.'

'Oh, you would,' he drawled. 'Can I ask you something, Verity? How do *you* see what's happened to us? Is it still a no-regrets situation but not much more?'

She looked down at her hands in her lap. All she had on was the Club Tropical robe, as did he. And she lifted her shoulders eventually in a helpless little shrug.

'Or is it that you're not going to allow it to become any more because of all those problems you mentioned last night? The way you are now seems to indicate that they've resurfaced. I think we should at least define what they are. Otherwise they're going to rattle away in the cupboard like skeletons,' he said drily.

A curl of anger licked through her. 'It's funny you should say that because that's rather what they are. All right, let's define them. Last night, for example, you couldn't help wondering if I was always so full of the *joie de vivre*——'

'Verity, I apologised for that and you said you could easily have done the same.'

'I could,' she replied very quietly. 'I could have asked you how I measured up to Primrose in bed—it flashed through my mind the night before, I have to confess. So that's a problem, it has to be.'

'And if I was to tell you that it's *over* and done with between me and Primrose?'

Verity stared at him, opened her mouth then closed it foolishly.

He came over to stand in front of her and went on, 'Do you honestly believe I would embark on something like this just to make me forget Primrose—is that the kind of man you think I am?'

'Brad...' She swallowed. 'No. Not consciously or coherently. But there *has* to be a gap in your life, if nothing else.'

'And what,' he said slowly, 'would I have to do to make you believe otherwise?'

'I don't think there's anything you can do,' she said and brushed away a ridiculous tear. 'As you yourself said, there can be... a lot of things between a man and a woman.'

'I wonder how many times you're going to cite me in your own defence,' he said with a cutting little edge, then swore beneath his breath, drew her to her feet and led her to the bed.

'Brad,' she protested.

'I'm only surprised you haven't reverted to "Mr Morris",' he said and picked her up, deposited her on the bed and lay down beside her. 'What exactly are you trying to tell me, Verity?'

'I...' Oh, God, she thought, how to tell him— should I be the one *to* tell him?

'It seems to me,' he said deliberately, 'that you're trying to tell me you'll sleep with me while I get over Primrose but that's all. I must tell you that, while I thank you for such a self-sacrificing gesture, there is no need for it.'

Her lips parted and she trembled as he opened the cotton gown she still wore and cupped one full breast, tracing the aureola and crushed velvet tip until it flowered, then sliding his hand down her body to the triangle of curls that was a slightly darker version of her hair.

'Don't you see *anything* incongruous about allowing me to do this while you have the gravest doubts about my integrity?' he added with soft mockery. 'You, of all people?'

She caught her breath and was flooded with a sense of angry confusion. 'What are *you* saying?'

'That you're using Primrose as a shield again, Verity.' She flinched, and he felt it and went on. 'I thought we'd gone past all that; the way you were last night and this morning seemed to suggest it——'

'Brad, we're not discussing me; it's *you* ..' She stopped abruptly and flinched.

'Oh, but we are,' he said with his eyes narrowing and a rapier-intent look in them. 'Discussing you, my dear. You and your intentions. You didn't seem to mind announcing to the world today that we were sleeping together, but tonight you're a nervous wreck again. I've noticed this blow-hot, blow-cold approach of yours before——'

'I'm not!' she cried. 'I said I couldn't regret sleeping with you and I meant it. That *doesn't* mean to say there's any future for us——'

'Why?'

She sat up furiously. 'I don't believe you can be this—dense,' she said intensely. 'I all but wrecked my life once, count one.' She ticked her finger. 'I have a child who means more to me than anything, count two, and I have to plan for her welfare—what *is* there ahead for us, Brad? An office affair? I'm sorry, but I couldn't do it, and if you imagine that's a ploy to force your hand in any way you're wrong!'

'I don't,' he said grimly. 'All the same, it's what I have in mind.'

'What?' she whispered incredulously. 'That we do try to work together and sleep together and become the object of tawdry gossip, further tawdry gossip?'

'No. That we start to plan our future more sensibly. Tell me something—what do you really feel for me?' he said almost casually.

'I...I...' She couldn't go on because her heart was pounding in the most extraordinary way.

He smiled but unamusedly. 'When you're not blaming Primrose for this state of affairs? Because I have to tell *you*, Verity, after having slept with you several times now, if you don't feel a hell of a lot—God help the man you do fall in love with——Don't,' he warned as her eyes flashed gold and she raised her hand. 'I have no faith in your spurious desire to hit me or throw things at me. It's generally only a cover-up for your lack of honesty.'

'How,' she said in a raging undertone, 'you can expect anyone to cherish the slightest feeling of warmth for you after saying things like that to them is beyond my comprehension!'

'Well, I can,' he said idly, 'because, while I understand why you suffer from such chaotic emotions, I object to being your whipping-boy on account of them, and it's often the only way to get through to you—by saying things like that. I am not,' he paused, 'objecting to the way you make love to me at all.'

'Oh!' She lay back and ground her teeth, but that was a mistake too because he rolled on to her before she had a chance to escape.

'Let's approach this differently,' he said quietly. 'We might not have realised it, but we've got to know each other pretty well, Verity. Haven't we?'

She stared up into the grey depths of his eyes but they were entirely enigmatic and he rested his head on his hand and ran the other one through her hair.

'Yes,' she said ungraciously. 'Well enough to know that you're impossible, anyway.'

'There are times when I have to return the compliment,' he murmured. 'But—are you trying to tell me you seriously believe I would want to make you the object of tawdry gossip or that I'd want to harm you or, through you, Maddy's future? From what you know of me?'

She closed her eyes.

'Verity?'

Her lips moved but no sound came because all of a sudden she was burdened with a new understanding and it came in the form of having to agree with what he said—she did know him well enough to know it. But that in itself had other consequences and she suddenly knew exactly why he had been different this morning: because she had given more away than she'd meant to—did she know him well enough to know he would take full responsibility for that? She thought she probably did, and it was something she couldn't allow to happen.

Her lashes lifted at last and they stared at each other for a long, wordless moment.

Then he said, 'What would you say if I asked you to marry me, Verity?'

She licked her lips. 'I *couldn't* accept...'

He smiled briefly. 'I know you couldn't, but why are you contemplating making the other mistake you admitted you made once before? Trying to walk away from it as if it doesn't exist, in other words? Why not give me a chance, at least, to prove myself? I might just surprise you rotten.'

She took a breath then sighed.

'There's a saying, you know,' he went on. 'Live and let live. I think that's what you should do. Put away your images of yourself as a confused teenager and everything that went with it. Admit to yourself that the effect we have on each other is not only electrifying but also deeply moving, and nothing that's gone before changes that—and it moves you to want me in your own magnificent way. And let us take things from there. You said yourself that any other way would be tarnishing it. And, if you could bring yourself to trust me a bit in the process, that might help too.'

'Brad,' her lips quivered and there were ridiculous tears in her eyes again, 'you could sell ice to the Eskimos. You're also a dangerous lover——'

'*Dangerous*?' He raised a quizzical eyebrow at her.

'Yes, dangerous,' she repeated firmly, 'in that you're so hard to resist——'

'Ah, well, I don't take exception to that——'

'I'm sure you don't,' she said with a tinge of tartness. Then she sighed and slid her hands round his neck. 'It's still not that simple...' She hesitated, and the phone rang.

He swore softly, then said, 'I don't *believe* this—ignore it!'

'No,' she said with an effort. 'Brad, please——'

'Well, I'll answer it!' He got up and strode over to it impatiently, but after a couple of terse interrogations he stilled, listened for a moment, then said, 'Yes, she's here, Mrs Chalmers. I—hope it's not serious?'

Verity flew up. 'What? Who?' she whispered.

'Don't panic,' he said quietly. 'It's not that serious.' And handed her the phone.

It was not, according to Lucy. Maddy had fallen off a stool about ten minutes after Verity had rung and broken her arm, a clean, simple fracture, Lucy said, that would heal with no complications; it had been X-rayed and treated, and she had a cast on and was a little bewildered by all the fuss, and, according to the doctor, broken bones weren't nearly as traumatic for little children as adults...

'I'm coming home, tonight if possible,' Verity said abruptly into the phone.

'Darling——'

'Look, Mum, I'll ring you back in a few minutes when I've made the bookings. Can I speak to her?'

She put the phone down a few minutes later with tears in her eyes. 'She's being so darned brave.'

'Braver than her mum,' Brad said softly, and traced one tear down her cheek.

Verity turned away. 'I must——'

'I'll do it. Sit down. And cry a bucket if you want to. Mums are allowed to.'

But the earliest booking he could get was on the first flight out of Cairns the next morning. And he rang Len and explained the situation and organised a ride into Cairns at the crack of dawn. He also said to Verity's intense look of frustration after she'd rung Lucy back, 'Don't feel guilty—if anyone should, I should. But, you know, it could have happened any time.'

'I know. But I should be there!'

'Well, you can't be unfortunately, and in the meantime you've got me.'

Verity stared up at him, her face pale, her eyes still anguished.

'For comfort and consolation,' he said very quietly, and kissed her gently.

'Thank you,' she said but distractedly.

'What does that mean?' he queried.

'I wouldn't feel right about—well...' She paused helplessly.

'Nor was I about to rush you to bed, but, when you've calmed down, if it made you feel better, if it made you feel less lonely and helpless, it has to help her,' he murmured. 'You're surely not contemplating the wages of sin or anything like that?'

He saw it in her eyes before she could formulate any words. 'Listen,' he said firmly and took her hand, 'that's ridiculous. Neither of us went into this lightly, nor for sex alone—we're two adults who came together because of a force between us that we found we couldn't deny. You're not *still* of the opinion that I'm toying with you, are you, Verity?' he said compellingly.

No, she answered him in her mind. But I still can't help wondering how you'll feel when you find out about Primrose, and how much, for you, that force was generated by her desertion—the same old question!

'No,' she said slowly.

'And are *you* only toying with me?'

She blinked and started to colour and opened her mouth to deny it strenuously, but the quizzical little glint in his eyes stopped her and made her blush more vividly. 'You're...' she started to protest, but he stopped it with a light kiss on her lips.

'I know,' he agreed. 'Tell you what, in order to take your mind off Maddy, not to mention my mind off you, should we spend a little time trying to organise how we're going to cope without you for the rest of this—three-ring circus?'

'Oh—yes!' she said gratefully.

They worked for an hour, then he stretched and said, 'Ready for bed? You've got an early start tomorrow.'

'Mmm.'

'On your own?'

She thought about it briefly and in a matter of moments started to feel cold and lonely. 'No,' she said huskily.

* * *

But he fell asleep before she did, and it was her turn to stay awake and staring into the darkness with three separate sets of thoughts doing a slow, revolving procession through her mind. Maddy, Primrose Carpenter and why she should have called off her engagement—and Brad himself and all he'd said. But of course all he'd said had been said from a wrong premise in a sense, if not two wrong premises: not knowing about Primrose, and not knowing that she could see the weight of his decision not to hurt her... And for a mad instant she felt like waking him up and telling him about Primrose because it seemed a bit sneaky to have kept it to herself.

But the moment passed and she finally fell asleep with nothing resolved.

He woke her, and in the rush to get to Cairns there wasn't much opportunity for in-depth conversation, even though he made the trip with her. But just before she boarded the flight he took her in his arms and said, 'Take as much time off as you need. I'll ring you this evening. And remember——'

'I'll remember,' she broke in. 'Live and let live.'

'I'll miss you.'

'I know you will,' she said with a laugh.

'Well, that way too, probably,' he confessed, 'but in a lot of other ways.'

'I'll... have the same problem,' she said a bit shakily.

CHAPTER TEN

VERITY lowered the newspaper and stared at her mother over it. 'What did you say?'

Lucy put down her knitting and took off her glasses. 'I said the papparazzi are having a field-day in Port Douglas, aren't they?'

'And after that?'

'You're not deaf, Verity. How is that article you're reading titled? "Is this the man Primrose deserted her earl for?" Something like that. I said,' she looked at her daughter sternly, 'what are you going to do about it?'

'You amaze me sometimes, Mum.' Verity threw away the paper and went to stand at the window. 'What on earth do you imagine I can do?'

It was three days since she'd returned from Port Douglas, and it was only a day since Primrose had flown into Brisbane and announced on her arrival when besieged by the Press that she'd made a terrible mistake, the man she loved was right here in Australia and she could only hope and pray he'd have her back. She'd refused to divulge his name, but in a week that had been remarkably devoid of news this had only added fuel to the flame. And Verity hadn't heard from Brad since yesterday morning.

'Anyway,' she swung round, '*why* should I do anything?'

'Because you're in love with the man yourself and——'

'How do you know that?'

Her mother merely looked at her.

Verity hugged herself and made an exasperated sound. Then she said, 'Assuming that is the case, he's now in the position of having two women in love with him. Lucky him! But, if you think for one minute that I'm joining a queue, think again.'

'My dear, I can understand that you feel confused and desperate, but there's no need to be cynical and bitter.'

'Yes, there is! I *told* him he was only on the rebound——'

'He might not have been. I have it on good authority that he was impossible when things weren't going well between you, and she hasn't spoken for *him*, only herself.'

'She might as well have—what do you mean?'

'Well, how *could* she speak for him? She'd only just set foot back in——'

'No, Mum,' Verity broke in angrily. 'Whose good authority?'

'Ah. Well, if you really want to know, it was your Mr Pearson.'

Verity stared at her incredulously. 'How?'

'He rang me while you were flying home. To find out how Maddy was and to ask if there was anything he could do. We had quite a chat—I must say, I thought he was absolutely charming. And naturally when he let slip that things had been resolved so happily between you and Brad I...pricked up my ears. I mean to say, it wasn't as if I was going to get any information from you, was it?'

Verity grimaced and sighed. 'Sorry.' She sat down again. 'It's not that easy to talk about. For me, that is,' she amended, and added bleakly, 'No one else has the same reservations, apparently.'

'What are you going to do?' her mother said gently after a time.

'I think there's only one thing I can do.' Verity hesitated.

'Tell me, my dear. I might be able to help.'

'Verity?'

'Hello, Brad,' she said into the phone only an hour later.

'Verity—how's Maddy?'

'She's fine. Coping with the cast really well.'

'Good—Verity, have you seen the newspapers?'

'Yes. Yes. And you don't have to explain, Brad. I understand.'

He swore. 'What do you understand?'

She paused then took the plunge. 'That you might have two women who think they're in love with you, Brad. Which is probably highly embarrassing but it needn't be. I'm... retiring from the lists. Primrose need never know about me, always assuming you can persuade just about *everyone* who knows us to refrain from mentioning it let alone making a field-day out of it. It's the only thing to do, and *please* don't try to get me to change my mind; I couldn't.'

'Did you say *think*?'

'Think?' she repeated bewilderedly.

'Verity,' he said roughly, 'don't play dumb with me. Primrose may be the one who *thinks* she's in love with me, but you're the one who is——'

Verity put the phone down.

'Didn't take it too well?' Lucy queried.

Verity, who was actually shaking with anger, said through her teeth, 'He's wrong. And anyone who falls in love with him needs her head read!'

'He's a man with a problem, don't forget.'

'I don't know why you always side with him!' Verity cried. 'He has never told *me* he's in love with me, yet he thinks he can tell me categorically that I'm in love with *him*.'

Lucy shook her head. 'Despite the fact he's right, I would object to that too.'

'Well, I'll tell you what I object to!' Verity put her hands on her hips and glared at her mother. 'I object—— This has all the makings of a comic farce! And anyone who dares raise the subject to me again can expect to——'

'Get her head bitten off. Why don't you take Maddy for a walk? It might help you to cool down.'

'I will,' Verity said tautly. 'But listen, Mum, don't you dare have any interesting little conversations with *anyone* while I'm gone.'

'I wouldn't dream of it,' Lucy said innocently.

'You did agree with me this was the way to go!'

'I agreed that until he sorts out Miss Carpenter he couldn't expect to simply take up where he left off with you. I agreed that you should tell him you all need a bit of breathing-space—which wasn't quite what you told him.'

Verity said something incomprehensible and turned abruptly on her heel. She didn't see her mother sigh and follow her retreating form with anxious eyes.

She went into the office the next morning because she knew she had to and the longer she delayed it the worse it would be, apart from the fact that she was desperately trying to avoid Brad. And sat in front of William Morris to tender her resignation.

For a man who could often look perplexed, he looked even more so. But he also made a surprising suggestion. 'Why not take a month's leave on full pay instead, Mrs Wood? And if, at the end of it, you're still of the same mind, well—fair enough.'

Verity stared at him. 'That's a... very generous offer... no, I couldn't accept, but thank you for making it.'

'It's not that generous,' he said ruefully. 'It occurred to me you might be able to take a holiday, I mean a real holiday, away from here while... things get sorted out.'

Verity flinched visibly. Then she said quietly and honestly, 'Whichever way things—get sorted out, I can't work for Brad any longer.'

William formed a steeple of his fingers and cleared his throat. 'That's what Brad said you would say. He—er—rang me last night and told me that on no account was I to allow you to resign. What he neglected to tell me was how to stop you. But he's actually due here shortly——'

Verity couldn't prevent herself from glancing over her shoulder.

'They finally managed to get the last Kneg ad made, in the rain,' he smiled briefly, 'so... Would you at least consider speaking to him yourself?'

'No. No...' she said, rising awkwardly. 'Please, I'll just collect my things.'

'If I know Brad, if there's any... that is to say... unfinished business between you, it won't matter where you are, Mrs Wood, he'll find you.'

'But at least on my home ground——' Verity stopped and bit her lip, then stiffened her spine, 'I'm going, Mr Morris. I'm sorry it has to be this way; I've really enjoyed working for the agency——'

'Is that why you're running away again, Verity?'

She swung round and William Morris rose. It was Brad, leaning against the door-frame, and it was not hard to tell from the lines of his face or the glint in his eye that he was in a dangerous mood. He also looked tired, as if he might have slept in his clothes, and he hadn't shaved.

William said, his uneasy tone contrasting oddly with his words, 'Great to see you, little brother! And, of course, marvellous news about the other Pearson account—I'll leave you two alone, make full use of my office! A cup of tea, a cup of coffee!' He gestured broadly. 'Please help yourself, Mrs Wood.' And left.

'So,' Brad said as Verity stirred, 'what's it to be, Mrs Wood—I'm moved to venture that famous remark—"coffee, tea or me?" Quite inappropriate, I'm sure, but it just sprang to mind—you haven't attempted to slap my face or throw anything at me,' he marvelled. 'You're slipping up, Verity.'

'Brad,' she swallowed and licked her lips, 'I——'

'Then again, you are wearing almost the same outfit you wore the day you all but allowed me to have my way with you on the floor, just next door, as a matter of fact. Does it have any significance, I wonder?' His eyes mocked her.

Verity looked down at her white jacket and black skirt, the same black skirt, it was true, and felt the heat rising to her face. 'No,' she said shortly, however. 'It only means that my wardrobe is not that extensive. But can I ask you something? Does it have absolutely *no* significance for you, Brad, that Primrose has declared to the world that she loves you?'

'Well, I do feel she might have consulted me before making sweeping statements of that nature and subjecting me to intense hounding by members of the media,' he drawled. 'But, so far as the accuracy of what she said goes, she got two things wrong. No amount of hoping and praying will influence me into taking her back, and I'm not the man she loves anyway.'

Verity blinked. 'There's someone else?' she whispered, feeling her heart starting to pound.

'No, I'm the man who could probably make her feel better about things—or could have, that's all. She just hasn't made that distinction yet.'

'Have you seen her?'

'Not yet. The first person I wanted to see was you.'

Verity turned away with an inward sigh.

'What does that mean?' he queried.

'It means,' she said after an age, 'that I still believe you have two women who think they're in love with you and, whatever you say, I will never be able to *know* whether you feel you have to take responsibility for the way I feel, or to know whether your pride won't allow you to take Primrose back, so...' She shrugged.

'So in typical Verity style you're determined to believe the worst?'

'Yes,' she retorted, stung, and swung round. 'I honestly don't believe you know your own mind on the subject, Brad. I never have, so this, what's happened, is hardly calculated to make me feel better, and that you should imagine it would makes it even worse——'

'I never for one minute imagined it would,' he countered coldly. 'I merely hoped it would not induce you to scuttle into the nearest hole to hide. It's over between me and Primrose, Verity,' he said deliberately. 'It was over before I kissed you for the very first time and you responded so—freely.'

'So you say!' she flashed at him. 'It didn't stop you from expounding quite bitterly on Primrose's shortcomings—why would you have given a damn whom she married if it was so *over*?'

'Because, although,' he said precisely, 'there was no more romantic attachment, I happen to be fond of Primrose; I've known her since she was a kid and I thought she was making a mistake—I was right.'

'Well, you were wrong about the romantic attachment from her point of view—you're not always right, in other words, Brad. You misjudged Primrose—it's quite possible you're misjudging me——'

'I doubt it, dear Verity,' he straightened and strolled into the centre of the room, 'because you are exhibiting all the classic symptoms of a deeply jealous female, for one thing——'

'Brad—I was the one who made the bookings for you and Primrose, I was the one who sent the flowers and the cockatoo, and the bicycle *made* for two! I was the one who said to my mother that in my estimation it was only a matter of time before you married her—and then this. No normal person could fail to have doubts and you may insult me all you like—which I find strange, to say the least—but I just can't help it!'

He stood right in front of her and stared down into her eyes. 'And what difference would it make if I was to tell you that what—flows between you and me makes anything I felt for Primrose pale in comparison? Yes, all right,' he said drily, 'there was a time when I thought I would marry her too, but I kept putting it off, we both kept putting it off. Why do you think she got seduced by visions of being a countess? Why do you think I let her go? Oh,' he grimaced, 'I actually did everything in my power to stop her, everything bar the *one* thing that might have done it. But I just couldn't take that last step.

'As for insulting you,' he continued quietly while she could only stare up at him, 'my insults are prompted by your failure to understand that not a damn thing stands between us, Verity, and your persistent belief that you know my mind better than I do.'

She drew a shaky breath but managed to say quite evenly, 'Do you honestly believe anyone else in my situation would not have reservations, Brad? I don't think you're being very fair——'

'I'll tell you what I think,' he said with sudden menacing softness, 'I think that, if there was no Primrose, you'd manufacture some other escape clause. Because you're still afraid to love and trust. And *I'm* suddenly afraid of such rigidity of mind because it indicates the kind of deep-seated stubbornness that takes pride in itself; it could even be called bigotry. Well,' he shoved his hands into his pockets and smiled faintly at her, 'I tried. I don't think anyone could say I didn't try. But that's the last overture I'll make, Verity. If you should ever change your mind, you'll have to come to me.'

She said through stiff lips, 'Don't hold your breath, Brad.'

He laughed, bent his head and kissed her lightly on the mouth, 'Remember me when you're lonely and sad.'

'Your Mr Pearson rang, Verity.'

'He's not my Mr Pearson, Mum.'

'All the same, he called and was most insistent that I should get you to call him back.'

Verity sighed. It was a week since she'd stormed out of the Morris Advertising Agency, a week during which she'd been unable to settle to anything—even the urgent matter of finding herself another job.

'Here.'

Verity turned to see her mother holding out the phone to her. 'There's nothing I want to say to him or that he could want to say to me,' she protested.

'There must be, otherwise he wouldn't be ringing you!'

'There's only one thing—he's probably going to try to get me to change my mind and go back to the agency. I'm not doing it!'

'Of course not. Here.'

Verity compressed her lips and took the phone. But when she put it down about ten minutes later she was looking somewhat dazed.

'He didn't try to persuade you to go back?' Lucy queried.

'No,' Verity said slowly. 'He agreed with me entirely, in fact. He said Brad must be off his mind to expect me to have anything to do with him while there were other women roaming around the country declaring they were madly in love with him.'

Lucy grimaced. 'He has a colourful way with words.'

'He also offered me a job. Which I accepted.' Verity sat down suddenly. 'In Port Douglas.'

'*Verity*...!' For once in her life, Lucy was astounded.

'Well, it is over a thousand miles from here. I'd prefer it to be at least two thousand, but that might take me overseas, so...' She shrugged, still looking dazed.

'What *kind* of a job?'

'To be in charge of his charter-boat operation. He said he thought I had unparalleled organisational skills as well as obvious experience in the promotional field... I said I lacked boating skills, and he told me he already had that but he needed someone to co-ordinate it all... Mum, will you come to Port Douglas with me for a while? It is a lovely little town.'

'What about—the memories?' Lucy said gently.

'There can be no better way to cope with memories than to confront them head-on, can there?'

'My dear,' Lucy walked over to her and put her arms around her, 'don't cry. Of course I'll come!'

It was about two weeks later on a Saturday, a week before they left, that Sonia Mallory arrived unannounced on the doorstep with Verity's parents-in-law.

'I've come,' she said to Verity's look of absolute shock, 'because ever since I met you with Brad it's been on my mind. But I've warned my aunt and uncle that I am doing this, as *you* should do it and so should *they*, with only one thought in mind: Maddy's well-being. The time for all else is past.'

It was Lucy who stepped forward and said resolutely to Sonia, 'We haven't met, but Verity has told me about you. I agree with you, so please come in, although I must make one stipulation: it's no good accepting Maddy without accepting Verity too.'

'I can't believe it,' Verity said much later. 'They were so... different.'

'So they should have been,' Lucy said trenchantly, then grimaced ruefully.

'Brad said...' Verity broke off and bit her lip. Then she decided to go on; it was part of her plan, after all, 'He said once that we needed an intermediary. He was right. They even accepted this move to Port Douglas with reasonable grace.'

'I'm sure they'll be beating a path to your door, though.'

'Mum—do you mind? I have no intention of allowing them to take Maddy over, but I was beginning to think——'

'So was I, darling. It's for the best. Although, if we're honest, we'll probably both mind from time to time——'

'And you were magnificent!'

Lucy drew herself up to her full five feet two. 'If you can't go in to bat for your own daughter, who can you go in to bat for? But I must say,' she subsided with a twinkle, then looked serious, 'I've got the feeling they'd changed their minds somewhat about you without my intervention.'

'I can't imagine why,' Verity said wryly. 'So, life goes on. And Port Douglas, here we come.'

'I must say, I'm getting quite excited about it,' Lucy remarked.

It was Verity's turn to do the hugging. 'I don't know how to say thanks.'

'Why should you? That's what mums are for.'

Verity pondered that remark later as she put Maddy to bed, and added a drawing of a flower to her cast. She also tried to discover her daughter's feelings about the remarkable events of the afternoon. Of course, Maddy was far too young to understand that she now had a doting set of paternal grandparents, but she didn't seem to be in any way disturbed.

She did, though, say suddenly, 'Mummy make faces on the wall like that man did? I liked him.'

It was like a knife-thrust in Verity's heart, and for one piercing moment she wondered if she hadn't made an awful mistake. But of course the crux of the matter was—well, there were two things, she realised as she tried to make shadow faces on the wall. What it would do to her if she fell deeper and deeper in love with Brad Morris, only to find he didn't feel the same, and what it would do, through her, to Maddy? And if that's bigotry, she told herself sadly, I just can't help it. I'm also a mum.

CHAPTER ELEVEN

'I AM impressed, Verity,' Len Pearson said to her four months later. They were seated in her small office behind the shop front in the Marina Mirage, and what Len was impressed about was her suggestion that they branch out into day cruises, small, leisurely, intimate cruises, to the Low Isles and similar destinations that were already served by other operators, mostly on much larger, faster boats.

'In fact, I'm impressed by everything you've done since you came to work for me! Business is up, we've established a reputation for efficiency and reliability—I think it's fair to say we've filled a spare corner of the market. Would I have been invited to participate in this tourist convention at the Sheraton Mirage otherwise? Which is why I'm here!' He beamed at her with unmistakable pride. 'You're invited to the dinner at the end of it, by the way.'

'Thank you,' she murmured. 'But Len, don't forget, we're going into the off-season now.'

'That's just why I think your suggestion is such a good one. Fewer people do come up here in the cyclone season and, although you may not realise it, it gets very hot!'

'I believe you.' She grimaced.

'Think you'll handle it?'

'Oh, I will. I'm tough. I'm a bit worried about my mother, though. It's not so easy to adapt to this kind of climate at her stage of life.'

'Oh.' He looked worried.

'But that's not your problem, Len. You've already been so good to us, finding us that house on the hill et cetera.' She moved some papers on the desk. 'I'm greatly in your debt,' she added quietly.

'I haven't done anything for you I wouldn't have done for any other employee who is worth her weight in salt, Verity,' he replied equally quietly.

'Perhaps not, but you gave me this opportunity when I really needed it.'

Len sat back. 'He didn't marry her, you know.'

She smiled briefly. 'That's not to say he won't or that he won't marry someone else.'

'Have you heard from him at all?'

'Not a word.' She smiled briefly. 'How...' she hesitated but couldn't help herself '...is the frozen-food campaign going?'

Len rolled his eyes. 'It's about to hit—I think it's *brilliant*, but an awful lot of blood, sweat and tears went into it.'

'That sounds like par for the course,' she murmured. 'So he hasn't changed much.'

'No. Some things about him won't ever change either. But, while he can be one of the most difficult, temperamental characters you're ever likely to meet, he has a caring streak in him that's quite unique. For example, he persuaded me to give you this job—he even created it.'

Verity's mouth fell open.

'Mmm,' Len agreed. 'He got hold of me and told me what I needed up here was someone like you in charge. Of course,' he said modestly, 'once I'd got around to thinking about it, I would have made the decision myself, but—there you go.'

'I don't believe it—why?' she whispered.

He shrugged. 'He didn't confide that far in me. But something else he did, incidentally—and I only know about it because I happened to be in his office at the time—was to take up the cudgels on your behalf with your parents-in-law.'

'*How?*'

'Well, he was on the phone to someone called Sonia and he was telling her they all ought to be shot for the way they'd treated you. He also said she was the one who could attempt to bring you all together but would she please refrain from mentioning to you that he'd got in touch with her. Oh, dear, I've spilt the beans, haven't I?' Len Pearson said without the slightest tinge of regret.

Verity swallowed several times, then managed to say, 'Why are you telling me all this? You've never mentioned his name—until now.'

Len looked at her piercingly for a moment. 'He's here, that's why.'

'*Where?*'

'At the Mirage——'

'He can't be——'

'He is, Verity. He's here for this tourist convention; he's getting a travel writer's award. By the way, he's likely to get an award for the Kneg ads, you know. Were they ever successful! Did you see them?'

Verity closed her eyes. 'How long is he here for? Don't tell me he's using *you* as an intermediary!'

'No, he's not. He never responds to anything I say about you. *I* just thought it would be kinder to mention it to you in case you bump into him on the street.'

'But he must know you were liable to.'

Len Pearson rose. 'I really don't know what he knows, so it would be safe to say that, from here on in, you two are on your own, Verity.'

'But,' she rose too and stared at him with agitation, frustration and apprehension warring in her eyes, 'I'd just got myself over it all!'

Len's eyes travelled down her figure in a kindly, fatherly way. 'It took some getting over by the look of it. Well, perhaps he's over it too. In which case, there's no problem, is there?'

That night, after Lucy went to bed, Verity sat on the veranda in the fragrant darkness and found her thoughts turning inexorably to Club Tropical and the Bali Suite, which were just down the road. And she had to ask herself how much she'd really got over Brad Morris, and confess that the thought of his being in Port Douglas filled her with a trembling kind of sadness as well as all sorts of unanswerable questions. Would he get in touch? Why had he come—apart from the obvious reason? What would she do if she did bump into him?

She closed her eyes and her mind drifted back over the last lonely, aching months, in which the only solution to her misery had been to batten it down, work as hard as she could, and try to make Lucy and Maddy happy. She thought she'd succeeded there, although Len had certainly helped with Lucy by introducing her to friends and befriending her himself when he was in town. In fact, Verity had thought on more than one occasion that when Brad had remarked that Len should meet her mother he might have been more right than he knew, and it had struck her as exceptionally ironic.

She went to bed finally with nothing resolved.

Two days passed and Brad neither came, nor did she bump into him—and it was the evening of the closing dinner for the convention to which Len had invited her to accompany him.

To go or not to go? she was still asking herself as she closed up and walked home through the park in the gathering dusk.

'I think you should go,' Lucy said.

'I knew you'd say that.'

'Well, if nothing else, you now tell me it was Brad who got you this job and Brad who was instrumental in getting the Woods to bury the hatchet——'

'I'm only "now telling you",' Verity said exasperatedly, 'because I've only now been made aware of it!'

'Don't split hairs, darling,' her mother said kindly. 'And do go. You'll upset the numbers otherwise, anyway.'

'He might not even be there. He might have left. I haven't seen Len today.'

'All the more reason *to* go!'

Verity made a curious sound and took herself into her bedroom, where she closed the door firmly.

She went.

In an above-the-knee dress with short sleeves and a scoop neck, in a pale vanilla silk taffeta. She also wore white gloves, shimmering pale stockings and gold shoes. And stood in the wonderful green marble and glass foyer of the Mirage feeling as if her knees were knocking. But Len was waiting for her and he came across with an outstretched hand. 'Verity—you look stunning!'

'Thank you. I haven't dressed up for ages, so it feels a little strange. Is——?' She broke off and bit her lip.

'Well, he was a moment ago—ah, there you are, Brad! I don't think I need to introduce you, do I?' he said over Verity's shoulder.

Verity turned slowly and experienced the unusual sensation of all the blood going to her head then draining to her feet. Indeed, although she felt like fainting but didn't, she then felt as if she'd been frozen into immobility, unable to think of a thing to say, let alone do. For one thing, she thought dazedly, he looked so tall and distinguished in a black dinner suit with a snowy white shirt-front, despite the fact that his brown hair was still long and a bit wild. For another, after months of trying to block it from her mind, she was suddenly plagued by the clearest image of lying in his arms and allowing him to play her body like a master musician, and she started to tremble inwardly with a mixture of desire and terror because nothing had changed, she hadn't got over Brad Morris, and she thought that it was possible she never would.

He broke the spell. 'Verity,' he murmured with a faint smile, 'how are you?'

'F-fine. Fine, thanks,' she tried to say brightly and commanded herself to take hold and stop making an awful fool of herself.

'And Maddy? And your mother?'

'They're both really well. Maddy is at a play group now——'

'She's as bright as a button, that kid,' Len said jovially and took Verity's arm. 'I believe we're due in the restaurant!'

At times during the evening Verity thought it was the longest, worst night of her life, and she couldn't believe that she'd been prepared to put herself through this torture.

Brad wasn't at their table but only one table away and clearly visible, which was at one and the same time a cause for relief and torment. Relief in case she'd been dumbstruck again, torment because it was being inexorably borne in upon her that she'd subjected herself to this for one reason alone: hope, to put it quite simply, the glimmer of hope that he was here because of her. Why? she wondered wildly. If that had been the reason he would have sought you out. If that *was* the reason, why would he be sitting only feet away being charming and amusing, as only he could, to other people?

And through it all she tried to be charming and amusing herself. She even danced with Len when the band struck up after dinner, but then, suddenly, it all became too much for her and she made her excuses quietly but quite firmly to him, and he let her slip away with a frown in his eyes but no comment.

She breathed deeply and wiped her brow with the back of her hand as she stepped out into the moonlit concourse, paused as she tried to remember where she'd parked her car—and Brad said her name from right behind her.

She froze, then turned slowly, and they just stared at each other for an age.

'Would you like to walk for a while?' he said eventually. 'The gardens are lovely—even at night.'

But perhaps he realised she was incapable of saying anything, because he took her hand and added lightly, 'We could wend our way down to the beach. Have you ever seen Four Mile Beach in the moonlight? I suppose you have.' His hand tightened about hers as he began to walk, and she stumbled, then managed to put one foot in front of the other beside him. 'Now that you're a paid-up resident of Port Douglas, the beach is probably old hat.' And he guided her down a pathway and out of the limelight.

'It took me a while to find my way around here,' he went on, then stopped and turned to look at her. 'All right now?'

'Yes,' she whispered. 'Thanks... Brad, you don't have to do this.'

He started walking again. 'I'm not doing it because I have to. But I'd like to ask you a question. Why did you come tonight, Verity?'

They were walking beside a smooth lawn that smelt damp, and there was a breeze sighing through the casuarinas. The hotel pool that lapped right up to the rooms was romantically lit, but they veered away from it towards the beach. 'I... There are two things I have to thank you for,' Verity said huskily. 'Taking up the cudgels on my behalf with the Woods, and getting me this job.'

He grimaced. 'Len, no doubt. I thought I swore him to secrecy. But how are you getting on with the Woods?'

'So far, so good. They came up here for a holiday about two months ago. Maddy now has the most expensive jungle-gym in Port Douglas, but apart from a tendency to shower her with gifts they've been pretty good.'

'How are they treating you?'

Verity considered. 'With caution at this stage.' She smiled faintly and added honestly, 'I think it will probably take years for us to lose our inward animosity towards each other, but we are all trying. One of their biggest frustrations has to be being so far away now—well, there are two. Maddy just doesn't understand yet who they are. I live in daily expectation of hearing that they're moving up here themselves. But Barry's father did say just before they left that I'd done a good job with her—"I'll give you that, Verity!"'' she mimicked. 'But, I have to confess,' she went on, 'it made me feel surprisingly good.'

'And the job—— Would you like to take your shoes off?' he queried as they came to the beach path. 'There's a beach when we get there.'

Verity hesitated. 'No. I'll be fine. The job is great,' she said briefly, and stopped speaking as she concentrated on the path.

They came out to the beach and it was a breathtaking sight in the moonlight, but it crossed Verity's mind to wonder what she was doing as he led her to the bench.

'So everything in the garden is lovely,' he said barely audibly as they sat down.

'No. Not quite,' she heard herself say and felt herself start to tremble within again as they sat side by side but not touching. 'I...' she licked her lips '...well, I'm worried about my mother. She's finding the heat hard to take, and in any case, although she won't hear of any other arrangement, I feel that she should be able to live her own life. Still, I'll work that one out too.' She gestured then folded her hands in her lap.

The silence was broken only by the lapping of the moon-silvered water along the shore. Until he said, 'Then it wasn't an—overture of any kind that brought you here tonight?'

'Brad...' Her voice caught in her throat.

'I've often cursed myself for making that stipulation, by the way, but then again it also seemed to me that, unless I put the ball in your court, I wouldn't be able to make any headway at all. So that's what I did. It had crossed my mind that I should labour for you—how long was it that biblical bloke had to? But I'm afraid when this convention came up my willpower sort of broke up. Yet I still decided—although I was quite sure Len would let you know I was here—to wait and see.'

'I was... Oh,' she said on a breath and wove her fingers tightly together.

'Can I tell you more?' he queried and went on without waiting for a reply, 'You seemed to be so convinced I was on the rebound from Primrose that it hit me that I had to—take it into account. And after a period of sober reflection I perceived that, from your point of view, what happened had to have a flavour of,' he paused, 'off with the old and on with the new. And that, as you were someone who had real cause to be wary of these things anyway, *I* had, perhaps, been a little unfair to you. Unfortunately, at the time it all hit me with such force that I wasn't able then to take such a rational view, but *since* then—well, since then,' he said and put his hand over her clenched ones, although he didn't turn his head, 'I've been able to see that circumstances might have made it all look a little odd.'

Verity discovered she was holding her breath and at the same time was intensely aware of the feel of his hand over hers. She forced herself to breathe.

'So I then set about trying to rectify matters,' he continued quietly and evenly. 'I went to see Primrose and we had it all out. I have to tell you that, while I'll always be fond of her and care what happens to her, I was not the slightest bit affected by her in the way we'd once affected each other, or the way you affect me, but in my new and more logical mood I thought, Perhaps that means I'm a rather shallow person, not to mention a cad. But, funnily enough, once Primrose...calmed down and told me her own tale of woe, it seemed to hit her that we were destined to be friends rather than anything else. Now this all might seem rather facile and a matter of mere words to you, but she's also recently fallen in love again. This time with a millionaire grazier with his own Lear jet, and, although he's one of those strong, silent types, I've got the feeling he adores her and she'll be able to wind him round her little finger. Is any of this making any sense to you, Verity?'

Oh, God, she thought, what to say? 'Why...why did you persuade Len to give me this job? When he told me, I thought it might be so you could send me...a thousand miles away from you.'

He moved his hand on hers. 'No,' he said sombrely. 'It was so that I could keep tabs on you. I knew Len would need no encouragement to fill me in on your progress; I knew I'd be seeing an awful lot of him,' he said wryly. 'I knew he had enough respect and, indeed, affection for you to make it a worthwhile position.'

'And...' Her voice had a tendency to stick in her throat. 'And the Woods?'

He was silent for a time. Then, 'I might have been wrong but I couldn't help feeling a lot of our problems were caused by a lack of self-esteem for you that they'd added to directly.'

'No, you weren't wrong,' she conceded barely audibly. 'I told you just now how I felt after a little bit of praise from them.'

'Then can you see any more problems that I should attempt to address before I tell you that for these past months I've lived a kind of hellish half-life filled with thoughts of you—and us?'

Verity blinked several times and tried to speak, licked her lips, then managed to say, 'Yes, there is one more problem. You saw the effect you had on me. I nearly fainted, I could barely walk——'

'If you think I mind having that effect on you, I don't——'

'But it could be an awful trial——'

'Not if you were my wife. That should help to take the element of surprise out of it—and be a wonderful way to channel the rest of it where it belongs. Because, and I hope you don't intend to argue with me, Verity, there is no doubt in my mind now that I love you; I can't, even though I railed against it, help but respect and admire the strength you showed, I *need* you—and how I managed to wait this long for you is a miracle, but it seemed to me to be the *only* thing I could do to establish my credibility.'

'Oh, Brad,' she whispered, and then was lost for words.

He looked down at her. 'Do you think you could at least give me some hope that I'm on the right track?'

She tried to smile. 'If you are so sure——'

'I've never been surer of anything in my life, Verity.'

'Don't forget there are sides to me that might be hard to live with. I am stubborn, I'm——'

'Do you honestly think I'm just looking for a pretty face?' he queried. 'Yes, you're stubborn and you're a fighter and you're a thinker—and it all adds up to a total that fascinates me like no other. You're also,' his voice deepened and his eyes were very grey and steady in the moonlight, 'the only woman in the world I want to make love to.'

'Well, then,' she said shakily, 'I have to tell you you were right about one thing: I do love you, and, if your life's been hell, mine has been...' She shook her head and silent tears streamed down her face.

'Don't.' He took her in his arms at last. 'I think we should promise ourselves something now: all the turmoil and sorrow is over, and we should just concentrate on the joy. Promise me?' He tilted her chin and stared into her eyes.

'I'm only sorry it isn't Club Tropical,' he said as he undressed her slowly in his room. 'But we could have our honeymoon there, or part of it.'

'If you only knew how Club Tropical tormented the life out of me,' she said softly.

'Well, I have to confess, that was another reason I persuaded Len to give you this job. I thought it couldn't but help to keep me in the forefront of your mind.'

'That's diabolical!'

'Mmm,' he agreed. 'But then I was in a pretty diabolical frame of mind at times. Unfortunately, when I'm without you I tend to be that way, and don't forget I not only had to work in the same office we used to share but I also had to cope with someone else doing your job.'

She had to smile. 'It's a wonder you all survived.'

He removed her bra, stared down at her breasts, then looked up with something wryly amused in his eyes. 'One thing kept me sane—do you know what I used to dream about? Your freckles. I even got to the stage where I'd start to try and count them—I only tell you this because I'm now moved to kiss each and every one of them. But,' he sobered, 'you've lost weight, my love. I'm *sorry*,' he said intensely.

'Brad, I think I might be more to blame than you, but anyway, you made me promise something just now,' she reminded him. 'That's behind us—and I can gain weight. Just you watch me!'

'With pleasure.' But his eyes were still serious.

'What now?' she whispered and touched the lines beside his mouth with her fingertips.

'I'm a little apprehensive, that's all.'

'Of...me?'

'Of what I feel for you. Having you in my arms like this, at last, makes me feel I might never be able to let you go.'

Her lips quivered. 'Then I'll just have to be strong for both of us, won't I?'

'Are you telling me you have plans to go somewhere at this moment?'

'Not at the moment, no,' she said gravely. 'But when the time comes...'

A flicker of amusement lit his eyes at last. 'I wouldn't let you go far,' he warned.

'Well,' she pretended to consider, 'you could come with me. My mother, who has remained a fan of yours through thick and thin for reasons best known to herself, will be delighted to see you. So,' she said with a soft sigh, 'will Maddy. I'm still trying to make shadow faces on the wall that live up to yours. Brad—we should talk about that.' Her eyes were suddenly anxious.

'About Maddy?' he queried.

'Well, it can't be easy to take on... another man's child.'

'Verity, it won't be a problem, if for no other reason than that she's *your* child. And I solemnly swear that I will never treat her differently to any of our children. Don't forget, you're also talking to someone who has an innate respect for children.'

'Oh, is that how you do it?'

He grimaced. 'I suppose so.'

'I love you,' she whispered. 'I hope it doesn't bore you—the number of times I seem to want to say that.'

'I've never been less bored in my life. I hope it won't be a problem for you, the number of times I'm liable to want to do this.' He moved his hands to cup her breasts.

'I doubt it, but I seem to remember being in this position once before.'

'This position?' He moved her away from him.

'Yes,' she agreed. 'Semi-clothed and——'

'Do you really mind?'

'Not really, but——'

'Good, because I have years and years of semi-clothed, not to mention totally unclothed plans for you, my darling Verity. So I think it would be a good idea if we got married, preferably tomorrow. What do you think?'

She told him.

But it took a few more days to organise and it turned into a surprisingly large wedding. Brad's mother came, as well as William and Gloria. So did the Woods, and gave Verity to understand she'd gone up another step in their estimation, and Len flew the original Kneg crew up for one thing as well as offering them the *Jessica* for a honeymoon cruise to Cooktown and insisting they drive back through the Daintree in one of his four-wheel-drives because he said he felt sure they hadn't been able to appreciate its wonders the last time they were there. And it was certainly his doing that Verity and Brad walked down the aisle of St Mary's-by-the-Sea as man and wife with Maddy beside them and Lucy looking on radiantly—to the strains of bagpipe music.

They looked at each other.

'Not *Hamish*,' Brad said.

It was, in full regalia, standing at the bottom of the steps in the sunlit park.

'I don't know why, but now I really feel married,' Verity said softly.

Brad turned to her and kissed her deeply. 'So do I.'

MILLS & BOON

Relive the romance with

By Request

Bestselling themed romances brought back to you by popular demand

Each month By Request brings you three full-length novels in one beautiful volume featuring the best of the best.

So if you missed a favourite Romance the first time around, here is your chance to relive the magic from some of our most popular authors.

Look out for
***Having His Baby!* in March 1998
featuring Charlotte Lamb,
Lynne Graham and Emma Goldrick**

***Available from WH Smith, John Menzies,
Martins and Tesco***

Karen Young

SUGAR BABY

She would do anything to protect her child

Little Danny Woodson's life is threatened when he witnesses a murder—and only his estranged uncle can protect him.

"Karen Young is a spellbinding storyteller."
—Publishers Weekly

MIRA

1-55166-366-X
AVAILABLE NOW IN PAPERBACK

JOANN ROSS

NO REGRETS

Three sisters torn apart by tragedy each choose a different path—until fate and one man reunites them. Only when tragedy strikes again can the surviving sisters allow themselves to choose happiness—
if they dare pay the price.

"A steamy, fast-paced read."
—Publishers Weekly

1-55166-282-5
AVAILABLE FROM FEBRUARY 1998

HEATHER GRAHAM POZZESSERE

If Looks Could Kill

Madison wasn't there when her mother was murdered, but she *saw* it happen. Years later, a killer is stalking women in Miami and Madison's nightmare visions have returned. Can FBI agent Kyle Montgomery catch the serial killer before Madison becomes his next victim?

"...an incredible storyteller!" —LA Daily News

MIRA®

1-55166-285-X
AVAILABLE FROM FEBRUARY 1998

SANDRA BROWN

THE THRILL OF VICTORY

Stevie Corbett's life is on the line, but her fate rides on keeping the truth a secret. Judd Mackie's job is to uncover secrets. After dogging Stevie for years, Judd now has the story of the year. All he has to do is betray her trust.

"One of fiction's brightest stars!"
—Dallas Morning News

MIRA

1-55166-025-3
AVAILABLE FROM FEBRUARY 1998

DALLAS SCHULZE

Home to EDEN

Some temptations can't be denied

Kate Moran's perfect life threatens to disintegrate when she falls in love with her fiancé's brother.

"a love story that is both heart-warming and steamy...with an unexpected twist that will keep fans going well into the night." —Publishers Weekly

MIRA

1-55166-290-6
AVAILABLE NOW IN PAPERBACK

JANICE KAISER

FAIR GAME

Dana Kirk is a rich and successful woman, but someone wants to kill her and her teenage daughter. Who hates her enough to terrorise this single mother? Detective Mitchell Cross knows she needs help—his help—to stay alive.

"...enough plot twists and turns to delight armchair sleuths" —Publishers Weekly

MIRA®

1-55166-065-2
AVAILABLE FROM MARCH 1998

Catherine Coulter

✦

Afterglow

Chalk-and-cheese lovers Chelsea Lattimer and David Winter finally find happiness after a series of disastrous relationships—thanks to their match-making friends.

Afterglow is a wonderful romantic comedy from *New York Times* bestselling author Catherine Coulter.

MIRA®

1-55166-472-0
AVAILABLE FROM MARCH 1998

JAYNE ANN KRENTZ

Lady's Choice

Travis Sawyer has a plan for revenge. Juliana Grant has a plan too—she has picked Travis as Mr Right. When Travis takes over the resort in which Juliana has invested her money, Juliana takes matters into her own hands.

"Jayne Ann Krentz is one of the hottest writers in romance today."—USA Today

1-55166-270-1
AVAILABLE FROM MARCH 1998